A TRAITOR SISTER

REMNANTS OF THE FALLEN KINGDOM
BOOK 2

A TRAITOR SISTER

DAY LEITAO

SPARKLY WAVE, MONTREAL 2025

ISBN: 978-1-990790-17-1

THE CRYSTAL COURT

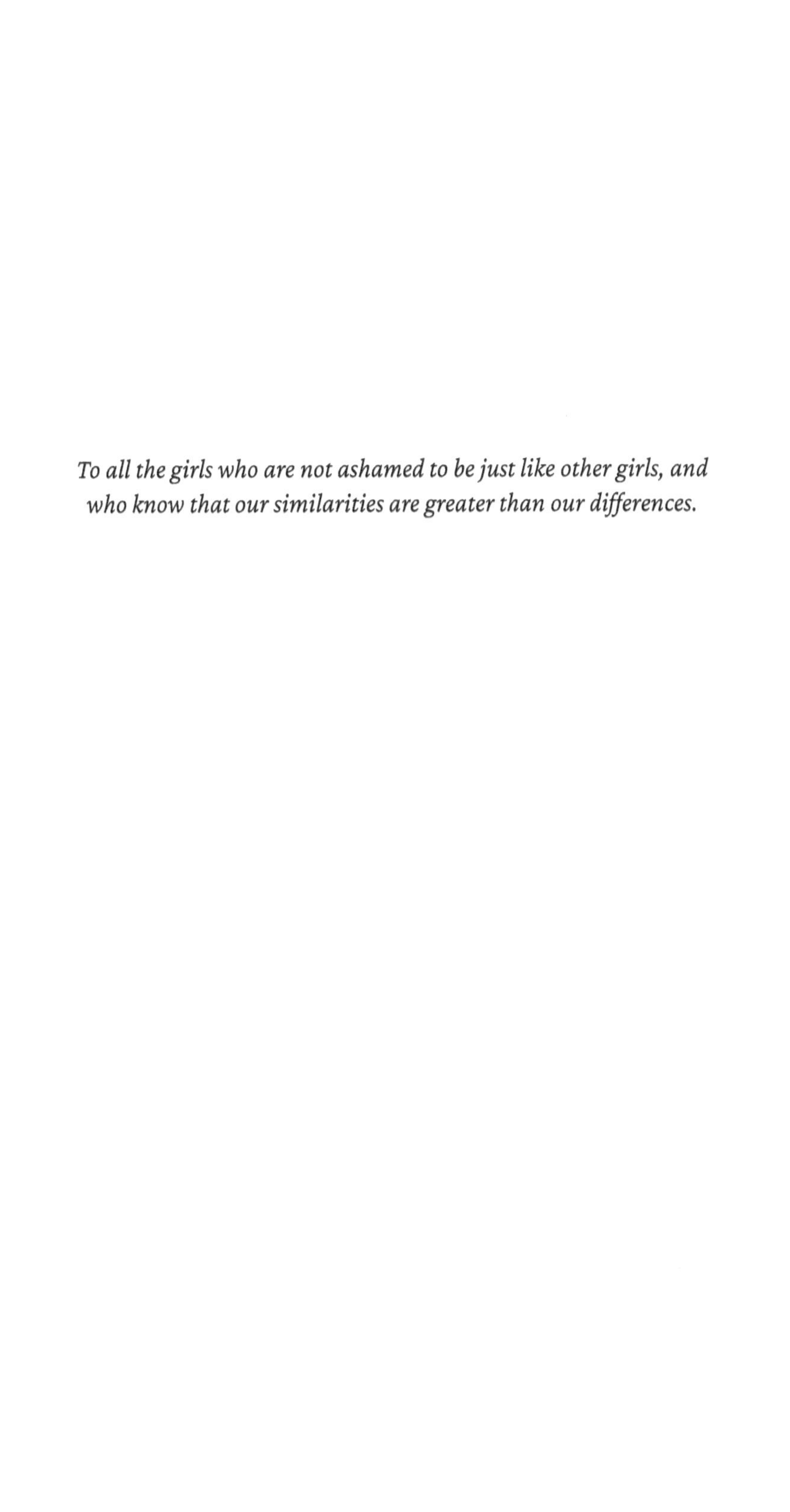

To all the girls who are not ashamed to be just like other girls, and who know that our similarities are greater than our differences.

MARLAK

It takes all my strength to keep my breath steady and my expression calm as I follow my brother up the stairs, the red light of the sanctuary stones fading behind me. Everything fading behind me.

I failed. For years, I evaded my brother. And yet now, when it mattered the most, I failed.

Worst of all, I failed Astra.

Her last look at me, so full of hurt, will be scarred in my mind forever.

Will she ever forgive my desperate attempt to protect her?

Now is not the time to consume my thoughts with worry or regret, but to come up with a strategy, a plan. With my magic disabled and dark metal cuffs weighing me down, how can I overcome Azur and four pixies?

A failed escape attempt will only put me—and her—in even more danger. Plus, there's a glimmer of hope in my chest, a hope that perhaps I'll be taken to the very place I seek—and yet even that hope is poisoned with worry about Astra.

Outside, the stone guarding the entrance has been shattered to pieces. Disrespect and destruction—so typical of my brother.

Brother.

What a strange word to describe what we are and what we're not. What we'll never be.

A round flying carriage lies amidst several broken trees, surrounded by pixies who'll strain their wings to carry us. Neither Renel nor his lackey cares one bit about them. How convenient, when they benefit from their mistreatment.

As we approach the carriage, my brother opens its door then turns to me, his forehead creased in thought.

"How does it feel? To be overpowered?" His voice carries only mild curiosity, as if he were wondering what we were having for dinner.

I chuckle and raise an eyebrow. "You tell me. Aren't you the expert?"

He looks away as if avoiding the question. "Indeed. I guess you're getting a small taste of my reality." He then turns to Azur. "The Desert Keep. Can you take us there?"

No. No. I was hoping they'd take me to a tower. *The tower.*

At least I catch myself before I show any reaction.

Azur blinks. "I thought—"

"The Desert Keep," Renel repeats. Lack of magic or not, he's quite comfortable wielding authority.

The blond fae glances at us both. "Sure." His blue eyes then settle on me. "Don't you dare try anything."

My brother is entering the carriage when I smirk at his personal guard, bootlicker, and likely cocksucker. "Scared?"

"No." The smirk he returns is ominous. "But *you* should be."

Scared? Nah. Of course not. I'm terrified, that's what I am.

They have Astra without any deal to keep her safe, without any promise that she won't be harmed. They have all the cards while I'm here, hoping for a blast of luck.

My chuckle comes out wrong, but I doubt they'll notice it. "Ooooh. I'm shaking."

"In." Azur gestures to the carriage.

I take one last look at the forest around us, one look at the pixies. Could I find a way out? I could slit Azur's throat, punch Renel, and then… Then face four enchanted pixies. My chances are minimal.

That's when I feel Azur's hot breath in my ear. "Try anything and I'll slice your wife into pieces."

His words hit me harder than a kick to my gut. Still, I roll my eyes and keep my voice monotone. "Why do you think I care?"

"Why do you think it's all about you? Maybe I'll enjoy making her scream."

An ember awakens inside me, but I smother my anguish under a mask of defiance. "Poor you. Is that the only way you can get a woman to react?"

He exhales, his eyes glinting with malice, his lips curled in a smug smile. "You tell me. Aren't you the one who had to force a girl to marry you?"

For once I'm grateful for the heavy cuffs. Without them, I would have punched his pompous face.

"Enough," Renel's voice comes from inside. "Let's go."

I enter the carriage in silence, resigned to my fate. If Azur's goal was to keep me docile, his threat accomplished it.

Renel sits across from me, the Shadow Ring glinting on his finger—and blocking my magic. Could I snatch the artifact off his hand? Nonsense. I gave the ring away, and to take it now would be theft—and pointless.

The ring would never serve me. I wonder what deal my brother made with the human king, how the artifact found its way into his possession. Useless wondering. As if tracing back where things went wrong could somehow fix them.

Two pixies enter the carriage and sit on either side of me, I guess as an extra precaution to keep me from fighting.

Only two pixies remain outside, and right as I wonder how they'll lift us all, the energy in the carriage shifts. It's subtle, but I feel it—a strangely familiar current of magic, but with an intensity I've never experienced before.

Next to Renel, Azur has his eyes closed. Is he doing what I think he's doing?

My magic is gone, but I still feel as if icicles were forming around me. This can't be possible. And yet, Renel told him to take us to the Desert Keep.

I couldn't have guessed he meant it so literally.

Few fae can transcend the in-between through faerie circles. I'm lucky that both Nelsin and Ferer can. Transcending from any place is a much rarer ability. Even then, almost none of those fae can carry someone else with them. I've only seen Crisine do it. Crisine, a queen's daughter from the second most powerful court, with all the extra magic her royal blood gives her.

To transcend a carriage with four people in it—that's something out of legend.

Unless I'm wrong. I hope I'm wrong, and Azur isn't that powerful. Why does hope have to be so unrealistic?

Outside, the forest is fading along with my hope, replaced by darkness. Across from me, my brother has a placid expression. Does he realize the magnitude of the magic he's witnessing?

Every muscle in my body stiffens, as if unable to grasp this reality, as if wanting to shrink away and escape it. And there's no escape as darkness sets in and a strange hum reverberates throughout the carriage.

I only breathe again when light comes through the window once more. Across from me, Azur still has his eyes closed, while Renel's expression hasn't changed. I guess witnessing unreal feats of magic is just part of a normal day for him.

Renel's eyes meet mine, and I suppose my expression gives me away, because he chuckles then asks in a mocking tone, "Never transcended, Marlak?"

"A few times. This one was a lot bumpier, though." I won't give him the pleasure of verbally acknowledging his knight's feat. I point at the blond fae with my chin. "Tell your servant he needs to work on his magic."

Azur opens his eyes and glares at me, while my brother laughs. I'm not sure why he's so amused. Can't he see how vulnerable his lack of magic makes him? Of course, they likely have some kind of deal.

Deals, deals, deals. That's the currency of the fae. Keeping some of us safe, some of us shackled. And yet deals can be broken. Not only that, now I can call upon the Sundering Dagger to cut them—when the time is right.

For years, I searched for the right opus stones to activate the artifact, when in fact all I needed was a powerful Tiurian—Astra. She activated the dagger without even knowing what she was doing. Astra. Her name is a dagger in my heart.

A pixie opens the door and hot, dry air greets me. I step out onto stiff, arid ground. Sparse bushy vegetation is all I see, other than a humongous stone wall with a copper gate. So this is the Desert Keep. And we're in the Shadow Lands.

This is no longer Crystal Court territory—or even fae territory, for that matter. This is the dangerous, uncivilized north, where monsters roam free. I've traveled here before, looking for the tower, but never risked staying past sunset. I never even knew our court had a prison here, and it has to be a prison, if this is where they're bringing me.

The metal gate screeches when it opens, as if in agonizing pain.

No.

The pain is all mine, entering a fortress from which I don't know how to escape, while the people I love are so far away.

Inside the walls, small buildings surround a courtyard. When I look back at the gate, I'm stunned. A giant is pulling the chains. A giant. Of course I'm aware that there are giants in the Shadow Lands, but it's still impressive to see one of them, let alone one working for the Crystal Court.

I notice then his glassy eyes. An enchanted giant, likely bound to my brother's service. Why would the giants allow one of their own to be enslaved like this, in a land where they have more power than the fae? I don't even know what to think anymore—not that I'm capable of much thinking right now. Anguish and rationality don't mix, which only means I need to push my worry away.

I'll need my head more than ever if I want a chance to escape.

Run. Run now. Before they lock you up.

Great. Now I'm getting stupid ideas. I can only try to do something once my brother—and his dreadful ring—are far away. And I can only do something once I'm sure Astra is safe and far from his reach. Quite a pickle, when I'm isolated here. Perhaps I don't have an answer, but I'm sure that trying to escape right now isn't it. Now, if only my mind would shut up and stop coming up with ludicrous suggestions, that would help.

My brother walks to a large metal door and opens it. Inside, a fae man with purple skin and empty eyes stands abruptly, then bows. Behind him, there's a hallway with a row of cells with metal bars, all empty. My new lovely abode, by the looks of it.

"You'll have a new prisoner." Renel's voice is dry as he addresses the fae. "He'll take the fireproof cell."

Fireproof? Is this some kind of attempt at dark humor?

We follow the fae to the end of the corridor, where he touches a copper handle and a door opens. A magical signature lock. Now, if this fae is enchanted, and if I still have the sundering dagger, I could try to set him free. Perhaps there is a way out.

I step inside the cell before someone pushes or orders me to move. The bed is a copper sandbox, the table and chairs are made of packed earth, and there's a hole in the ground with an iron grate covering it. Nothing flammable indeed.

I turn to my brother. "What a dreary decoration."

A corner of his mouth lifts. "I hope you enjoy your time here." He turns to Azur. "Unshackle him."

The blond fae hesitates for a moment, staring at me. His lips part, as if he's about to say something, but then he approaches me quickly and releases the lock keeping the armbands together. The dark metal cuffs still weigh me down, though, and I think they'll be my companions for the time being.

Azur then steps out of the cell, and it feels so slow. Such long seconds when I could push him and try to run. A short eternity when foolish ideas take hold, when I forget the giant out there. A short eternity of ignoring Azur's extraordinary magic.

When the door clicks shut again, I exhale in relief. Now I can try to come up with a real escape plan instead of entertaining such illogical nonsense.

Renel stares at me from between bars, his eyes holding a new darkness. Maybe they always had it—I just couldn't see it.

"Leave us," he says.

The guard walks away, leaving Azur facing me defiantly, while my brother looks pensive.

Renel turns to his knight. "You too," he mutters.

Azur glares at me. Me. What do I have to do with it?

"Not a good idea," he says.

My brother runs his hand through his long, black hair. "I'm not asking for advice. Leave us."

Now Azur's glare is murderous. Just to mess with him, I flip him off.

Oh. Provoking my brother's overpowered knight might not be the most brilliant idea. A gust of wind fills the room, then some of the sand from the box moves up and hits my face before falling on the floor.

Azur approaches the bars. "Remember what we have in our possession."

I roll my eyes. He turns and retreats in slow steps, as if reluctant to leave or hoping to hear some of my brother's words.

The sound of the door closing is muffled and distant, perhaps because of the stone walls, and yet I still notice Azur slammed it shut. Quite a temperamental knight. A super powerful, temperamental knight. Just great.

My brother runs his hands over his tunic, as if to straighten it, and stares at me. A curious, detached stare, as if he were watching our sister and I practicing magic. But this time, satisfaction, not yearning, gleams in his eyes. I can tell he's delighted to have me as his prisoner and plotting all the ways in which he'll torment me.

And I realize then, that it's just us. After so many years, we're alone again.

Twelve years, and the rotten taste of betrayal still hasn't left my mouth.

Twelve years, and somewhere inside me, the little boy who trusted his brother hasn't stopped crying.

What tainted deal will he offer me this time?

TARLIA

We're still in fae lands, our carriage moving slowly towards the River of Tears. I had never thought I'd see this side of the continent; this magical, lush land of colorful plants and unique forests. I had never imagined that I would witness a fae coronation, that I would drink strange drinks and eat strange foods at a party where guests undress, kiss, and make love with no shame or fear. Being here is like a vivid, colorful dream.

A dream about to end.

Ziven looks out the window, his arms crossed, his face resting on the palm of his delicate hand. By now I have memorized the map formed by his bluish, thin veins, memorized the shape of his short, square nails, memorized the way his fingers move through his light brown hair. So many trivial details that I want to commit to my memory, engrave in my consciousness, keep with me forever.

This was also something I never expected: to spend so much

time with Ziven. Ziven, the drunken prince who never noticed me before we planned to come here.

We've been traveling together for three days, practically alone. Our retinue consists of only two guards, doubling as coachmen, and sitting outside. It means that for three days I've been in a tiny, enclosed space with Prince Ziven, sitting so close to him that I can see the texture of his skin, and sometimes even the streaks of gold and green in his light brown eyes.

But those amazing eyes are focused elsewhere now. Far away, as if not truly looking out the window.

His index finger touches his lips. Those lips. I wish I were that finger.

I've tried to deny my feelings, lie to myself, but while I might be able to control my thoughts, I can't control my body. Such a ravenous body.

All I have are my wishes, my own desires, while he looks outside, ignoring me. All I can do is look at him as if I was staring at the moon. Unattainable. He's a prince. I'm practically a slave.

Perhaps he would take me to his bed if I asked. And perhaps he'd laugh at me, tell me I'm pathetic.

Even if he said yes, it would be a dangerous game, as it wouldn't be my body, but my heart at stake. Foolish heart, beating like a maniac, obsessed with a prince who'll never see me as his equal.

And yet I can't help it. I see his finger parting his lips and imagine it parting something else, something warm and wet and hungry. The obsession has taken over me, but at least admitting it means I don't need to spare any effort in fighting it. Why fight feelings I can't control?

The truth is that I want my nipples against his lips, his fingers inside me. I want to taste his skin, feel his weight against mine, feel his hair tickling my breasts. I can't calm the intense heat in my lower belly. Even his soft voice makes me wet. And yet.

He doesn't see me that way.

And then, despite everything, I thought we had something, some kind of friendship, at least. We planned this trip together, spent such pleasant moments in the castle. We talked, joked, had fun, but now…

"You're silent," I blurt.

Still staring at the window, he drawls, "What a brilliant observation."

"I guess I'm stupid now."

At least he finally turns to me. "Is that what you gleaned? Perhaps your wit is indeed leaving you."

"Don't be obtuse. Since the coronation, you've been…" Strange? Distant? Cold? "Moody."

He leans back in the seat and closes his eyes. "All that dancing, you know?"

At least he's talking to me, and I don't want him to stop, so I try to lighten the mood and laugh. "Dancing on their table, dropping all their drinks, then destroying a chair. You caused quite a scene."

His chuckle should be warm, but it sounds like nails on ice. "I have a reputation to uphold, after all."

I snort. "I thought they would banish or punish us. Nope. They love you."

"Love." An odd chuckle. "Do you always misuse that word?"

"No." What's he getting at? "I just mean that you could be…" If I suggest he could have any power, he'll deny it. Sometimes it's as if he thinks even the air has ears, ready to label him a traitor. "A good emissary. Loyal to your king, of course. Someone who could help Krastel have good relations with the fae. They're loose and playful. You'd fit right in."

"Who knows?" He shrugs, then turns back to the window.

I can't stand his attitude. "You've been avoiding me," I finally say. "Since last night."

"Impossible to avoid you when we have to travel together."

"Is it an ordeal? To travel with me?"

His eyes finally settle on me. "No. But we need to be alert.

Have you wondered why King Leonius agreed to our trip so quickly?"

I almost mention that it's because Master Otavio suggested it, but it wasn't quite like that. That means...

My breath stills. "You think this is a trap?"

Technically, Ziven's the true heir to the Krastel throne, so it would make sense for King Leonius to get rid of him.

Ziven swallows. "Every time I travel, I wonder if it's when they'll finally kill me, then blame it on some robbers or my own foolishness. This is no different." He lowers his voice. "I'll always be a threat to my uncle and cousins. Every day, I wonder if it's my last."

"You should live like it's your last day, then." I almost want to make a bold suggestion involving some skin-to-skin contact, but his coldness keeps the crazy idea from forming into words.

"Don't I?"

His laughter seems fake. Who can truly laugh at their own possible demise?

I try to think. "They wouldn't do it in fae territory. Too risky, to commit a crime in foreign lands."

"True. I guess I'll spare my worry until we cross the river." His voice is still dry, almost as if he's angry, and it's not the possibility of an assassination attempt that's bothering him.

I decide to be more direct. "You're upset. I know we came all the way here to help Astra." The knot in my stomach tightens, still convinced of Ziven's infatuation with her. "Now, it seems she's happy with her husband and doesn't need help, and I know you were hoping—"

"Tarlia." He raises a hand, showing me his palm. "Please. I used to think you were the most brilliant person I know—but I'm changing my mind. I've already told you I'm not interested in Astra."

My chest feels an odd warmth. *The most brilliant?* I ignore my mind telling me I misheard him and try to get back to the point. "So why did you come—"

"The same reason as you. Because she's our friend. I thought you cared about her."

"I do."

He tsks. "You don't. If you cared about her, you wouldn't assume I had an ulterior motive to come here. You'd just think it was normal to want to check that your friend is well. And that's not what you're thinking."

"Oh. What am I thinking?"

He leans on his hand again, his fingers now touching his chin. "That I'm in love with Astra. I'm not. Have never been."

"That's not an ulterior motive! It would mean you care about her. Just like I care."

"Do you?" His hazel eyes look like glass, and he frowns in a way I've never seen him do before. "Or did you come here in the hopes of attracting *a certain fae king*? Is that all you care about? Power?"

He's going to blame me for a conversation he shouldn't have heard? I was talking to Astra, sure we were alone, telling her I thought Otavio would ask me to seduce King Renel. Maybe I was playful about it. Maybe I said it as if it was something exciting. Regardless, it was for Astra's ears only.

"Don't you dare judge me." A lump forms in my throat. "You have no idea what it's like to be an orphan forced into this disgusting job, having to pretend to be someone else, having to be ready to marry someone if they tell me to. It's not like I can walk away and survive, Ziven."

"Oh, yes." His eye roll feels like a punch. "Such torment. You sounded absolutely devastated that you might have to marry a king."

"It's my job!"

"But you want it. You *want* to marry him."

"How does someone like me get out of that tower? It's either getting married or serving Otavio forever. Being killed. Who knows? Getting married would be my escape."

"You're in fae territory. Do you think they'll come after you if you run?"

"Run where? It's not that simple. Why don't *you* run, instead of fearing murder every day of your life?"

"I considered escaping, I did." His chuckle sounds sad. "It sounded very romantic. I'd start a new life in a fae court. They like allies, deals, royal blood, so I thought maybe…"

"Why didn't you escape?"

"My plan wasn't to escape alone." Obviously. He was hoping he'd rescue Astra, just like I thought. He sighs. "For now, I just want to get you safely to Krastel."

"Had you escaped, I would be making this journey on my own. Not sure why you're worried now."

He stares at me, his eyes narrowed as if they had a meaning I should comprehend.

"What?" I ask.

"Forget what I just said." He throws his hands up in the air. "Everything. And you're the stupidest person I know."

"Wow. You don't know a lot of people. Do I always have to get a prize? Can't I be the *second* most stupid? The *third* most brilliant?"

He shakes his head. "No."

"I'm flattered. What about the prettiest? I'm sure I'm the tenth, twentieth, or one hundredth. Or ugliest?"

"First place for both."

"Shouldn't you think the girl you wanted to escape with was the prettiest?"

He blinks. "Don't I?"

If I mull over his words or try to glimpse any meaning, I'll go insane. "Isn't it Astra? You thought you'd save her, and—"

"Why would I want to escape with a married woman?"

"Because we thought she was forced into that marriage. You know that. And now you're not making any sense."

He turns to the window. "Obviously not. I'm a fickle drunk, Tarlia."

"You know you aren't."

"Do I?"

"Ziven, tell me what's wrong. Yell at me if you're upset.

Don't leave me here…" Why is the lump in my throat becoming liquid and threatening tears? "We were friends. I thought so, at least. We planned this together. I thought…" What do I even want to say? "We were getting along."

I'm not stupid enough to think he could ever fall in love with me, and there's an odd kind of pain in being close and apart, and yet his coldness is ripping my heart in two.

He stares at me again, or rather, glares, for some reason. "We were. You're right. See, growing up in the castle, it's hard. My only living family wants me dead. Everyone else is only looking out for their own interests. They see me as a means to an end, a way to gain some advantage. Perhaps it's why I decided not to care."

His golden eyes settle on mine, a rare raw pain there. "Then, I started talking to Sayanne. You know the story. It was all false. All lies. She likely wanted something from me." He chuckles. "They all want something from me—when they don't want me dead. I started to think everyone was like that: false, ambitious, incapable of caring for others. It was like they were all stones in a wall. But between stones, flowers grow. Life grows, defying everything."

He raises an eyebrow and lowers his head. "At least it's what I thought. You were worried about your friend. That was it. No pretense, no ulterior motive."

"I *was* worried about Astra. She's like a sister to me."

"That may be true, sure. What is also true is that I found something beautiful in your sincere friendship. I thought you were caring, selfless. I thought you were different from everyone in the castle, I thought…" His stare is odd. "Maybe you and I could run away together."

What? How? Those are impossible words dropping me into a precipice.

His chuckle is cold and wrong and strange. "What a silly thought. You want a king." With that, he turns to the window again.

My mind is spinning, trying to make sense of his words,

trying to undo them, trying to find the part where I misunderstood everything.

But if I didn't...

A metallic, bitter taste stains my tongue, constricts my throat. The air in the carriage crushes me with its heaviness. No.

I'm the one crushing myself with my foolishness.

ASTRA

The bath water is tepid when I step out of it, enjoying my last precious minutes before facing Otavio, my last precious minutes in solitude.

I can still feel Marlak's skin against mine, can still feel him inside me. Just this morning, just a mere hour or so ago, we were together. My entire body feels like a stubborn ember refusing to quench, carrying the heat of a long-gone fire. I'll hold on to this feeling, this phantom touch that for once is not an echo of a dream, but the remnant of a wondrous reality. A reality I'll do anything to materialize once more.

As I put on the dress my master chose for me, I consider the mask I must wear. Obedient pupil? Isn't that what I've always been? But our dynamic has shifted now. Secrets have been revealed. Will he believe I'm still the same?

There's so much I want to learn, so much I want him to tell me. At the same time, I need to find a way to save my foolish husband—without letting anyone know my intentions.

A coldness settles in my chest as I wonder what's happening to Marlak. His brother might be torturing him at this very moment, and here I am, powerless.

But then, a lot of it is Marlak's fault, and for that, I'm still furious. He didn't have to stick a knife in my heart and twist it like that, didn't have to keep me ignorant, feeling betrayed. His words were cruel, sharp, and meant to wound. He knew I'd leave him if he hurt me.

But wondering if he's safe hurts even more. I take a deep breath, the air coming in with difficulty through my knotted throat.

My foolish husband. A bitter chuckle escapes my lips. As if I had been so much wiser.

Pointless thoughts. Dwelling on what cannot be changed will only keep me stuck in the past, and I need to look forward and find an answer, a solution, rather than looking back to figure out why we were such blundering idiots. It's why I need a plan for Otavio, a plan for Renel.

With my master, I can still be curious. Curious and excited, ready to help him with his convoluted, bizarre plans, pretending to be unaware that he doesn't see me as a person, but as a means to an end. What end?

A shiver runs through my back. What *are* his plans?

Everything is so new and confusing that I can't even come up with a theory. Is it true that he doesn't know my family? My heart jumps at the thought of learning who they were, learning where I come from.

Perhaps learning who killed them.

A dark cloud settles over me, and my hands tremble. Thoughts like that should be buried or they'll sneak into my face and ruin my mask.

I have to play the silly, oblivious girl Otavio thinks he knows. What's extraordinary is how long I've played this part and couldn't see how ridiculous it was.

With a deep breath, I focus. Oblivious, curious, helpful. I open the door and step out of the bathing chamber.

Sitting by the vanity table, Otavio turns to face me, his smile turning into his signature disapproving frown. "Why did you wash your hair?"

For so much of my life, I've dreaded that frown. Just a frown, and the prospect of seeing it terrified me. I need to pretend I'm still that person.

I stop walking and bring a trembling hand to my head. "Why? I thought…" My voice is quivering, weak. Could have convinced me.

"Come." He clicks his tongue and shakes his head. "I'll comb it and put cream on it. You know the soap will damage it. Not good, right?"

"I'm sorry. That bath…"

"Was tempting, I'm sure." He gives me a broad smile that makes his eyes sparkle. Odd. "Just be more careful next time."

He must be in an excellent mood to let it slide like that.

I sit in front of him and stare at the largest vanity mirror I've ever seen, framed in delicate wood engraved with flowers, birds, and dragonflies. Behind me, my master takes a golden comb and runs it through the tips of my hair, while applying a thick cream with his other hand. It smells like orange, and while the citrusy smell is not the same as Marlak's, it's a painful reminder of his absence, his imprisonment.

But this smell also reminds me of my childhood, when I delighted so much in the feel of my hair being pulled softly, in the pleasant smell of Otavio's creams and concoctions, in the belief that someone cared for me. Mistaken belief, of course, and I can't let this scent hypnotize me into thinking otherwise.

He's inspecting me, and at least nods in approval. "You kept your color well. But your hair is a little dull. It needs to shine, Astra. Your skin needs to glow. We'll take care of that. You're not looking dreary, but it's clear you didn't take care of your skin. You're brown!"

It's just a tan, and I don't think it looks bad, but this is not the time to show any defiance. "I spent some time outside." My voice is mild. Apologetic, even.

He shakes his head. "Be thankful I'm here to take care of you, or your skin would peel like a snake's." His movements then get slower. "Where were you?"

I went over this question in my mind, the question I knew I'd have to answer, so I have a lie ready to go. "It was like a little fortress, surrounded by walls, with a hut inside it."

"So it had a roof. You could have avoided the sun."

That's what's worrying him? Some obsession with my skin.

"We walked to the Court of Bees," I explain. More like we flew over the clouds, something I'll obviously never mention.

"Hmmm. Try to recall your trajectory as much as you can. I bet King Renel would like to find his brother's hideout."

Would he? "He already has Marlak. What's the point?" It was just curiosity, but I guess it came out as defiance, which wasn't my intention.

Otavio doesn't seem bothered, though. Yes, his mood is excellent.

He parts my hair, then raises his eyes to me. "Information. The disgraced prince must have allies, and the Crystal Court King will want to find them. Have you seen anyone?"

"I was kept in the fortress. Alone. Saw very little."

"And despite your mistreatment, it seems you two grew close."

I look into the reflection of his eyes. "Wasn't that my job?"

He combs my hair in quick, harsh strokes. "I was very clear that it wasn't. Oh, Astra. You were never supposed to be used like that, to be given to that brute. You know that. Did it hurt?"

"What?"

"To pleasure him?"

Oh, gross. Will he want the details? I keep the disgust from my face and try to sound resigned and obedient. "I relaxed, master. Like Andrezza told me to do."

"Good, good. Good to hear." It doesn't sound like he cares one way or another. "You're safe now, and that's what matters. And you'll need to be absolutely enchanting. We can't make any mistakes."

"We won't." I smile as if I felt proud to be important, proud to be included.

It's not hard to pull that feeling from my memories. Not

even memories; wishes. I spent my childhood wanting to matter, wanting to be important, while being cast aside in favor of my sisters.

I understand now that *they* were the distraction, something horrific in its own right. And still, understanding that it was all part of a greater plan doesn't ease the pain of feeling like I was never enough. I can't linger on those feelings, but I can still tap into that old yearning to be appreciated.

He keeps combing my hair, even though it's already untangled, keeps combing as if he was doing it because he liked it, and gives me a smile so broad that I can see the front row of his perfect white teeth. "I know."

I should be jubilant with that demonstration of trust, so I try to bring that feeling to my face as I look at the reflection of his eyes. For a second, I see fatherly love there. But it's not love, is it? It's joy in reacquiring his tool for his oh-so-important plan. A plan he'll never fully share with me.

Still, I need to take advantage of his mood and try to pry some answers from him. There are thousands of questions I want to ask about my kind, my magic, my family. I know he said my records were burned, but it could have been another lie to protect me. But it's better to start with something easier— and more pressing.

"Will you teach me about my magic?"

"You're human, Astra. Don't be silly." He chuckles but narrows his eyes, as if in a warning. I guess he's afraid we could be overheard, which means I won't learn anything from him while here.

Fine. Let's play silly, if that's what he wants. I manage a laugh that sounds playful and relaxed. "What? You mean being in a fae castle won't grant me any magic?"

He shakes his head. "This castle moves, and probably listens." There's a not-so-subtle emphasis on the last part. "But alas, doesn't gift any magic."

"Has it moved? Since you came here?" I keep my voice curious and excited, even though I wish we could talk about my magic and my origins. That said, I can't deny that this castle is quite intriguing, so the curiosity is genuine.

He's still combing my perfectly disentangled hair as if his fingers were enchanted. "It seems to do that only once or twice a year. I've been visiting for a few weeks and haven't had the pleasure to witness it moving."

Visiting. So he's been going back and forth to Krastel. I need to take note of even unimportant details that could shed light on his plans and perhaps tell me more about Renel—and Marlak.

A pool of pain stirs in my chest, but I wave it away and hide it behind a smile. "Moving or not, it's an incredible castle."

Behind me, Otavio nods in agreement. "The most majestic, no doubt."

No. There is another castle, more impressive and magical than this one. A place I've only seen in dreams.

Funny how I just realized that it wasn't only Marlak that plagued my dreams. There was a castle too. "What about the Amethyst Palace? Do you know—"

I was going to say *anything about it*, but Otavio's trembling hand and the sound of the comb hitting the floor stops me.

He chuckles but the corners of his lips are tight. "Where did you hear about it?"

"I..." I never planned any false story for this and could never have guessed that the mention of a palace would disturb my master this much. "A book, I think?"

He crouches to pick up the comb, then stares at me, all the joy in his face gone. "What book?"

I ignore his accusing tone and pretend to think. "Marlak brought some books to distract me. Stories, legends. Some history. I think one of them mentioned it. I'm not sure."

"You need to remember, Astra. Isn't your job to pay attention to details?"

"Of course. Let me recall." I frown, as if in thought. In reality, I'm obviously thinking. He'll want the name of the book—and I need to tell him something or he'll realize I'm hiding things from him. "It was a history book, about Tiurians. *Tiuris, the Fallen Kingdom.*" I'm not sure if that book mentions the palace, but this is my best bet. "I didn't read it much, didn't trust it, since it's written by the fae." I read nothing of it, in fact, and now I want to bury myself in regret.

Otavio's lips form a line, while his eyes are no longer focused on me. "They're probably mixing in some legend, then. That's what it is." He shrugs, his face calm again, even if the smile is completely gone. "Why did you ask about it?"

I look up as if trying to recall something. "I think the story mentioned that it was lost or something." Indeed, in my dreams, it seemed abandoned. "I was wondering if a castle could get lost. Since we're in a moving castle and all…" His stare prickles my insides, but I ignore the discomfort and chuckle. "Nonsense, of course."

He places the comb on the dressing table with a loud thud and gives me a clearly fake smile. "We won't get lost, Astra, so don't worry about it. Worry about being beautiful, compelling, enchanting. That's what you need to do."

At least I can pretend better than him, as the mirror tells me my smile looks genuine. "I know. You can trust me."

He nods, but it's a rigid, odd nod. There's a feeling there that I've never seen before. Fear? That makes no sense. Worry? Distrust? I'm not sure.

What I do know is that Otavio *has* heard of the Amethyst Palace, and it rattled him enough to make him drop his comb.

I used to think that castle was part of my dreams, a concoction of my mind. But Marlak exists. Why wouldn't the Amethyst Palace exist as well?

But why did it discompose Otavio?

He's fiddling with a cosmetics bag now, while I'm fiddling with my thoughts. One thing has become clear; I can't trust him to give me the answers I need. Perhaps it's for the best, and means I'll have to find my own, free of his manipulation.

Free. I swallow the bitter chuckle coming to my lips. Will I ever be free?

And how will I find these answers?

Will I ever learn anything about the Amethyst Palace? My origins?

But there's a bigger question taking hold of all the air in my lungs: how will I save Marlak?

My heart is a boiling cauldron ready to explode.

MARLAK

It feels strange to face my brother from behind bars.

Maybe we've always had something standing between us—except that I didn't see it when it mattered the most. At least this time, there's no deceit.

He's not the same teenager who betrayed me. Taller and with harsher features, he can pass for a king. A sham king.

A liar and a fraudster—who has Astra. This humongous little detail is a clamp around my throat, its weight heavier than the dark manacles on my wrists.

He stares at me, his eyes cold and distant. "You still hate me."

What an incredible discovery.

"Hate? Why would I? You're so kind to me." I point to the sandbox. "Give me such comfortable quarters."

He rubs his hands and stares at them. "You aren't naïve enough to assume that this is the most uncomfortable you can get, are you?" He raises his eyes to me. The threat is clear, even if his voice is soft.

I sigh. "Are you going to tell me what you want? Or are you going to keep stating platitudes?"

"Platitudes." He huffs. "Tell me, do you care for the girl? Your wife?" He asks it as if it was only mild curiosity, not a punch to the gut.

At least I was fully prepared for that question, so prepared that I don't even flinch. Instead, I frown. "Wife? Since when does the Crystal Court recognize human weddings?"

"You're going to tell me you abide by our court rules, Marlak?"

"I'm just saying I'm not married."

"And you don't care for her."

I shrug. "She was useful."

"What relic did she activate? What did she do?" His question means he was listening to our conversation, as I suspected.

"What difference does it make?"

"Did she succeed? Does she have Tiurian magic?"

I was not expecting *this* question, and I can't imagine what he plans to do with this information. But then, if he has plans for her, at least it means he won't kill her. "How can I know? I'm here. Never had time to test anything."

His chest moves up and down slowly. "I can grant you freedom."

Right. Here comes the tainted deal. "In exchange for what?"

"You'll crown me king and leave this continent, never to return. You'll cross the ocean and go to the Nowhere Lands, where you can grow old and happy, with nobody after you."

For a fraction of a second, the idea tempts me. I could see myself away from the Crystal Court, away from this struggle, away from these painful memories. But then, I wouldn't want to leave on my own, and if I ask him to bring anyone with me, he'll know my weaknesses.

I smirk. "I have a better proposal. Hear me out because this is good. You free me and don't stop me from taking the throne. In return, you get to keep your head. Don't you like your head?"

He runs a hand through his hair. "You can't harm me, Marlak. Or take the throne. Our deal is clear. Why do you delude yourself otherwise?"

"Deals can be broken." I approach the bars and raise my fist. "And I'm sure these manacles count as harm."

"So ungrateful. Unlike me, there's a line of fae who want you dead. You should be glad I found you first."

I roll my eyes. "I'm delighted."

"Think about my proposal. You don't need to live your life on the run like a criminal. It's your chance to start over."

Start over. Things can't restart, can they? The echo of our mistakes follows us like a shadow.

I smile. "Think about mine. It's your chance to stay alive."

Renel snorts. "Delusional."

"I'm not the one pretending to be king."

"I've heard otherwise, Marlak." He stares me up and down, then pauses, as if debating what to say next, and exhales. "Enjoy your stay. I hope you're more reasonable when we meet again."

He turns and walks away.

Twelve years. I've dreaded and yet secretly hoped to meet my brother many times, and now, when it happened, all I saw was a stranger clad in a wall of quips and insults. But then, my brother, the one who played and read with me, that's a creature from my imagination, a fantasy.

No mention of what happened. No mention of his betrayal. No mention of our sister.

Our sister.

Not a day goes by when I don't think about Mirella, and yet I have to bury all my thoughts, all my pain. Bury it all and plan.

I sit on the packed earth chair and take a deep breath. I need to escape, but first I need to get Astra out of Renel's grasp. Astra, who must hate me now. Well, I hate myself for what happened, for the cruel words I said in my desperation to hide my love for her.

Perhaps there's a chance we can still bond in hatred—if there's even any chance for us. The manacles feel heavier than ever, weighing me down.

Still, I refuse to waste time doubting whether I can save anyone. My time is better spent coming up with a way to do it.

Something shifts in the air.

No.

Inside me. A spark of magic.

My senses, which had been blunted, are awakening, perceiving the surrounding environment. I feel connected to the air in the cell. So much air around me. And so little water.

But I have magic again. That's a start.

TARLIA

Am I hallucinating? I can't hear anything other than the pounding of my heart echoing in my head. A buzz numbs my senses.

"Did you…" I swallow and gather all my courage. How can a question be so scary? "Consider escaping? With me?"

He turns to me, and his fake smile becomes a concerned frown. I must look scary—or pathetic. Pathetic, most likely.

"Forget what I said, Tarlia. It doesn't matter." His voice is gentle, at least.

"Is it true?" Speaking through the lump in my throat is hard and my voice comes out high-pitched—and desperate.

"Forget it." I think he shakes his head, but I'm not sure. My vision is too blurry.

"You're asking me to do the impossible." I feel tears on my cheeks, tears on my face. Stupid tears. "You can't casually say that you once thought about running away with me and ask me to forget it. You never mentioned it! Never discussed it!"

"I wasn't sure if you'd want to escape. After hearing that you want to marry the fae king, I know you have better plans for your future."

"If I knew running away with you was a possibility, you think I wouldn't choose it?"

He takes a deep breath and rolls his shoulders as if trying to push something away. "You say it now." His voice is low, careful. "It was just a foolish thought, likely impossible, highly nonsensical. I should never have mentioned it. Forget it."

What can I even reply? Can I bare my heart for him? My

chest is hot and cold, empty and full. "I can't. There's not a single day that I don't think about you, don't dream about kissing you. But I thought it was impossible."

He raises a finger. "A wise thought."

"So it was a lie? You were playing with me? Do you hate me that much, to humiliate me, mock my feelings?"

"I wanted to get to know you better. Understand who you are." He shrugs. "I did. So forget it. Perhaps for a crazy moment, I became interested in the person I *thought* you were. But that person doesn't exist."

"I *am* that person. I care about my friends."

He stares at me and takes a deep breath. "I'm sorry. I shouldn't have mentioned my past intentions, my fleeting thoughts. I didn't mean to hurt you."

"You won't forgive me for something I said in private, when you weren't supposed to be listening?"

I think he's eying me with pity. "There's nothing to forgive. You're just not the person I thought. I can't change how I feel."

"I *am* that person, and I can prove it to you."

"My feelings changed."

I snap my fingers. "Like that?"

"They weren't profound. It was just a maybe, a possibility. And perhaps it's for the best. Who knows if we'd ever find any belonging in fae lands."

Amidst the buzzing in my head and the beating of my heart, I decide I have nothing left to lose and say the scariest words I've ever told anyone. "I love you."

He closes his eyes and shakes his head. "Yes, I can see how beautifully that would work out once you married your fae king."

I swallow, but it tastes more bitter than dandelion leaves. "But then I wouldn't..." My words are jumbled. "If I knew..."

"Wait." He raises a hand and looks out the window. "We stopped."

It's true. Plus, there are too many trees around us, and it doesn't look like we're on the road anymore.

Ziven opens the door. "I'll go check. Stay here."

"No." I slide to his side of the seat and jump out of the carriage before he has time to stop me.

He flashes me a glare, then walks to the front—where our two guards are gone. My stomach feels hollow and airy.

"It's a trap," I mutter. Then I hear something zinging in our direction, and yell, "Get down!"

I try to push Ziven, but we bump into each other instead—and the arrow hits his arm, embedding itself. Another zap, but from out of nowhere, a thin ice wall shields us. And I hear steps approaching us.

Ziven breaks the arrow but keeps the tip in, which is smart to avoid losing blood.

The ice wall crashes, and I see our guards accompanied by two more men. Traitors, probably trying to kill Ziven. I pull out a dagger, even though we're outnumbered.

Ice shards fly towards our attackers. Ice.

It's Ziven doing this magic, as if he were the most accomplished water wielder ever. The shards melt. Of course. Leo, one of our guards, also has an opus stone.

Ziven isn't the only one with water magic here. I hate to lose a weapon, but I throw one of my daggers at the traitorous guard and it hits his chest. When he stops to look at the wound, an ice dagger slashes his throat, and he falls. Still, two attackers advance toward us, dodging ice shards, while the third one aims an arrow. A large ice shard hits his bow and breaks it.

Behind me, I hear more steps and turn. To my surprise, I see Fachin and another guard.

Fachin. I don't know if I should be happy or relieved. He was furious when I asked him to stop coming to my room, but we used to get along before that. I meet his eyes—and find only disdain there.

He pulls a sword and smirks at me. "Step aside. Killing you is not part of our plans." Dreadful plans, I'm sure. My chest feels cold.

Ziven is valiantly keeping the other men at bay, but I don't think we have a chance against five.

"We'll pay you!" I yell. "Pay more." More than the king? Than Krastel's princes? I don't let my doubts get to my voice. "You can lie that you killed Prince Ziven and get extra."

Fachin points at Ziven. "The biggest prize is for his head. We need to bring it. Step aside, or you'll also get hurt."

Ziven turns and throws shards at Fachin and the other man, but they protect their faces with their hands, and the shards aren't sharp enough to hurt them. I notice then that Ziven's sleeve is soaked with blood from the arrow wound. His arm is bleeding badly, and that might be impacting his magic.

We are surrounded, and at this point, I think they're toying with us.

Still, I look at Fachin, trying to appeal to the person who once was my companion. "Please. Let us go. I know you're not evil."

Fachin shrugs. "This has nothing to do with good or evil."

Beside me, Ziven mutters, "Forget it."

"They'll kill you," I whisper.

"I'll die fighting."

Die is a problematic word. I'm ready to fight, not to die. But I don't think any fighting will be enough.

3

TARLIA

I should stay calm and use my mind to find an escape, but the possibility of seeing Ziven dead overwhelms me with terror.

Fachin and his companion are standing, looking at us.

Here we are. Outnumbered. Surrounded. All I have is one tiny dagger, while Ziven's magic weakens by the second.

I feel his hand grab mine, then he says, "Let's run."

There's a thin opening between Fachin and our guards, and we dash in that direction, jumping over bushes and dodging trees. I'm not sure if this will work, but I don't have any better idea.

When you can't fight, run.

I can still hear some of Otavio's bootlickers telling us this precious piece of wisdom, ignoring the fact that when you are at a disadvantage in a fight, running won't help much either, unless you know for sure you're faster than your adversaries. I don't know if we're faster.

The forest is dense, making it hard to gain speed. Shrubs scratch and cut my legs, while we dodge trees and jump over roots. My heart feels heavy like lead and thin like glass, about to shatter into a million pieces, and yet it's working at its full capacity, pumping blood in my veins, pushing me into running faster and faster, even if there are no guarantees that running will save us.

"Run," Ziven says. "They want me, not you."

I turn to look back at him, and my breath falters. He stopped running, and his eyes are unfocused. Fachin and two guards approach him, and my entire body trembles in fear.

Ziven gestures for me to keep going. "Go. I'll hold them off." He turns his back to me as if to convince me to ignore him.

I should hold them off, if it's Ziven they want—but I don't think he can run anymore. Or fight. And I can't protect him from five men.

My legs make the decision before my mind, and I find myself running away from Ziven, from Fachin, from Krastel, running away from everything.

Coward legs. Or perhaps not coward, but rational.

The faces of those guards flash through my mind, and mix with the Krastel princes, with Otavio, feeding my thirst for revenge. Now it's not only my family I have to avenge, but Ziven. I want to scream, to lie down and cry, but if I want those men to pay for what they are doing, I have to remain strong. I have survived so much for so long, survived and waited for the right moment. I can do it some more.

They'll pay for this. Oh, they'll pay. It doesn't matter that I have no idea how. Rage fuels my heart, gives strength to my legs, even if they feel brittle and weak, even if all I want is to allow myself to shatter like ice, then melt and disappear, so that this pain stops. So that I escape this emptiness.

Tears blur my eyes and I don't know how I keep moving forward.

Coward.

Maybe all these thoughts of revenge are just an excuse. But no, the easiest choice would be to return to Krastel, then go back to my flimsy position as a substitute, while biding my time. Instead, I'm running into nothingness, with nowhere to go and absolutely no plan. Alone and lost in fae lands.

And burning with guilt.

"Stop!" a voice behind me shouts.

I guess my conscience's voice is not my own, after all.

"Stop!" I hear it again, muffled by the rustling of leaves and the buzzing in my head, muffled by all the pain in my chest. "Stop, princess! You're safe."

I decide to pause and turn. Far behind me, a blue-skinned fae beckons me. Perhaps this is a dream. Perhaps I fell and hit my head, and now I'm imagining some heroic rescuers. Either way, I don't think she means any harm, and I approach her.

Blue skin, blue hair, pointy ears. It's a gorgeous fae girl staring at me with worry in her eyes. "Are you all right?"

"No," I grunt. My throat is so dry that no decent sound comes out. "Ziven's dead."

Dead. Dead. I can't believe I voiced it. Can't believe it happened. Can't believe any of this is true.

"The prince?" Her voice sounds oddly cheerful. "He's fine."

I stare at her, digesting her words, trying to find a trick. But she's fae.

She's fae. And she's saying Ziven's alive!

My crumpled heart gains new strength, and I run back the way I came, my eyes still blurry, except that now they're shedding tears of relief.

From a distance, I see Ziven lying on the ground and two blue fae standing beside him. I approach him, kneel, take his hand, and check his pulse.

His heart's beating.

No new wounds.

I can breathe again. His eyes are closed, though, and he seems unconscious.

"Ziven…" I mutter. I'll do anything to hear his voice again, even if it's uttering harsh words condemning my choices.

"Overused his magic and lost blood," a fae beside me says. "He'll need rest."

It's the same blue-skinned fae who called me. It's when I dare look around me and see all our attackers fallen.

"What about the men?" I ask.

"Dead. We had to be fast, and we aren't breaching the treaty. They aren't allowed to commit crimes on this side of the river."

Dead. All dead. I'm relieved, perhaps even glad that they got what they deserved, and yet a part of me mourns Fachin. I can still recall those nights when his presence, his body erased all my agony. He was my friend once, my relief, my escape—before he decided to trade everything for some pointless reward. He got his reward now.

And then it hits me. We were saved. I don't know why these fae did it, or what they'll ask in return, but right now, I don't care. My heart's bursting with gratitude and joy. The tears in my eyes wash away my horror, my fear. I turn to the fae near me. "Thank you. Thank you."

"Dangerous words." The fae raises an eyebrow.

Never thank a fae. I know. And yet *thank you* doesn't even come close to expressing what I feel. "You got rid of some dangerous men. I think I'll take a chance with my words." And I'll need even more help from them. "Do you know where I can take the prince? To rest?"

The fae look at each other, then one of them says, "Promise you'll never tell anyone who rescued you, and never disclose the location where we're taking you."

"Yes. Of course."

Those simple words go against all the training I had on how to deal with the fae. I should ask for some guarantees that they won't harm me or Ziven, but right now, I just want to save him, and to be fair, I don't think they have any ill intentions.

If they did, they would probably find a breech in my words anyway.

Two blue girls crouch and lift Ziven's unconscious body. The other fae approaches me. For a few seconds, I feel dizzy.

Then there's nothing.

RENEL

Victory is volatile.

So I vanquished my brother. Captured him. Something I never thought I'd be capable of. And yet as I leave the cells in the Desert Keep, the feeling in my chest is not satisfaction, but dread. How long until he escapes? What if he's killed? Would it count as my fault? A cold chill creeps up my back despite the suffocating desert heat.

The thing with victory is that once there, your only way is down. Down, down, down, where I've always been told I'd end. Yet I'm still hanging, driven by a steadfast will to survive.

It's not a survival instinct. Oh no, none of that. I have no love for my life. And yet once I realized my own family wanted me dead, I had no choice. Spite made me want to survive.

Here I am. Alive. Leaving my brother in one of the safest prisons of the Crystal Court, and yet wondering how long it will hold him. Wondering if he'll even consider my proposal.

Azur walks beside me, his breath huffed, the way he always does when he's displeased. Sometimes I wonder if he does it on purpose, as a way to scold me, or if he's just that transparent. While I usually don't like to upset him, I had to send him away, as the conversation was between my brother and I.

Great conversation, when no words came out. What was I supposed to say? Can a bottomless emptiness form words?

And yet he truly wants me dead. Well, I'm alive—and therefore winning by default.

As we pass the gate, I look back at the giant closing it behind us, an eerie feeling in my stomach. I don't like to have giants serving us, but I wasn't going to contradict the Council about such a small matter.

I'm glad when I step back into the flying carriage, eager to leave this intolerable heat behind. Azur sits across from me, his eyes distant, while the pixies stay outside.

I wonder if their fragile wings will survive this heat. "Are they going to fly?"

Azur huffs. "They'll hold the harnesses and transcend with us." His voice is sharp like a sword.

I pretend not to notice his tone and mutter, "I see."

He glares at me one last time before closing his eyes. The brightness of the desert transforms into darkness, and in a few seconds we're back in the forest bordering the Shadow Lands, where I found my brother and the Tiurian girl.

Azur opens the door. "Back to the castle," he tells the pixies. He then closes the door and smirks. "Let's hope it's where we left it."

I swallow but it feels like my throat is full of tar. Five more moves. Five more. And one of them could be happening just now, as our carriage lifts into the skies.

Azur tilts his head and narrows his eyes. "You think it will be gone?"

"I left the castle. You know what happens when—"

"Two hours, Renel." He waves a hand. "I know you love your drama, but let's not exaggerate."

"Oh, no. I'll just sit quietly and watch the Crystal Castle make its way into a pit of fire."

Azur looks down and bites his lip, hopefully not biting a laugh. I don't think he fully believes me, and I'm not sure if it's any relief that he doesn't dare contradict me openly.

He looks me in the eye. "You found your solution. Soon you'll acquire magic, and the castle won't bother you anymore."

His tone... Something about it feels odd. "And the idea upsets you?"

He shakes his head quickly. Too quickly. "You know it's not that." He stares outside, even though there's nothing but endless sky around us.

"You wanted to overhear me and my brother." It's not a question.

"Not overhear… I…" He snorts. "I'm sworn to protect you. Why would you send me away when facing your greatest enemy?"

Greatest enemy. I don't know if it's a gross exaggeration or a hilarious insight, and don't want to consider it.

"He was behind bars." I raise my hand with the Shadow Ring. "His magic subdued. You really think I'm that much of an incompetent?"

"Of course not. I wanted to protect you, that's all."

I shrug. "There wasn't much to overhear, but I thought he would be more…" Brotherly? Friendly? Loving? What crazy ideas are going through my head? "*Malleable,* if it was just me."

"Was he?"

"No." The word comes out with an odd laugh.

He stares at me. "You need to threaten his wife."

"He says he doesn't care about her."

Azur raises an eyebrow. "Do you believe him?"

"It doesn't matter. Unlike my brother, I wasn't born with the ability to lie. How can I threaten someone I don't mean to hurt?"

He leans back in his seat and puts his hands behind his head. "Just be creative. Tell him if he doesn't collaborate, you'll send him pieces of her. You don't need to mention that you're going to send her hair."

"I have more pressing issues." I stare at Azur. "Now, don't tell anyone we found him."

He chuckles. "You think I was going to announce it to the council or something?"

I don't like his playful tone. "Give me your word, Azur. You won't tell anyone where he is, won't tell anyone you've seen him, won't tell anyone I've captured him."

His face hardens at once. "You don't trust me."

"Your word," I insist.

He stares at me and leans forward. "I give you my word that I won't tell anyone you've captured your brother, where he is, or that I've seen him this morning, and I accept your command, Your Highness."

I guess he's back to his dramatics. I pretend not to notice it. "Good."

"Any other *command*?" He stresses this last word.

"No." I sigh. I should ignore his tone, but Azur is not only my sworn protector; he's my best friend. "Azur." I look into his eyes. "You're the person I trust the most in this world."

"A little more than zero is still a little. You trust nobody. I don't blame you, but—"

"If I didn't trust you, you wouldn't be here with me."

His jaw relaxes and he chuckles. "And who would have taken you to the Shadow Desert?" It's a joke but a slight provocation at the same time.

"Someone else. Might have taken longer, but it's not like I went to the Blue Tower. And the promise is for your own good. Imagine if someone captures or corners you, forces you to answer them. You can rely on the word you gave me, and nobody will fault you."

He stares at me for some time. "Is that how you feel? About your deal with Marlak? That you're glad your promise keeps you from killing him?"

"I'd gain nothing from causing his death. A curse, maybe. Nothing else."

"Unless you got him to crown you first," Azur suggests.

"He wouldn't do it without some life guarantee and who knows what else."

"His wife's safety."

I roll my eyes. "He doesn't care about her. I, on the other hand, need her."

"You could also capture the dark unicorn. He was spotted—"

"Near the Court of Bees." I make an effort to keep my voice steady, to prevent any unwanted emotion from overwhelming me. "Yes, I got the reports. Spotted by fae high on sprinkled wine and starry powder."

"Spotted by more than one fae. The beast is around. Alive. If you capture it—"

"If. That's such a gigantic word. Why should I go on a futile chase, when I have the Tiurian girl?"

"I was just saying you have options." He takes a deep breath. "But if she has Tiurian magic—"

"She does. That's why my brother abducted her. She absolutely has Tiurian magic. I'm sure of that."

He raises one shoulder. "Then the rest is easy. She'll give you your magic."

Easy is a strange, foreign word. Can it be that easy? Can I truly avert disaster? Five more moves.

TARLIA

Water drips somewhere, drips and echoes like it never does in the constrained walls of the Elite Tower. My eyes snap open and I reach for my dagger —but find my pocket empty. I sit up quickly and realize I'm in a cave with rough stone walls, sunlight coming from a slit in the ceiling. A blond fae man crouches by a straw bed where Ziven lies down. Ziven.

The memory of what happened comes to my mind at once, and yet the lingering image is me—running like a coward. Leaving Ziven behind.

The fae turns to me and smiles. "I see you woke up."

His face is handsome and friendly, untying the knot I had in my chest.

I approach him and crouch by Ziven. His chest is moving slowly, and I exhale with so much relief, so much joy. His pulse is normal and he has a bandage on his arm, but he's asleep—or unconscious. "How's he?"

"Lost some blood, almost severed his magic connection, but all he needs is some rest."

"Severed what?"

The fae points at the bandage around Ziven's arm. "His opus stone arm was hit, so it affected his magic. It's like piercing a pipe that transports water. But it's healing. And he'll be fine."

Fine. Unbelievable, after being outnumbered like that. "You saved us."

"Not us," he says. "Some fae from the Lost Court. They claim they owed Astra a favor, and that the favor was paid now."

"What favor?"

He shrugs. "I didn't ask."

"But how—"

"They think Astra will be happy that they saved your life."

"I suppose. And who are you?"

"Astra's friends."

I take another look at him and realize that he has cat ears on top of his head, among his messy hair. Fae are weird.

"We might need your help." Another man's voice comes from the other side of the cave, from a handsome fae with dark skin and puffy hair.

"For what?"

He approaches us slowly, his movements graceful. "Astra's in the Crystal Castle. There's also a man from Krastel, a noble, scholar, something like that. Do you think she was captured—"

The blond fae cuts him off, "*Of course* she was captured."

Astra in the Crystal Castle? With a man... Otavio? Is she the one he'll use to seduce the Crystal Court King? But they would know she's not the princess. Was everything meant for her?

The dark-skinned fae sighs. "I'm asking the questions here." He turns to me. "Did she ever intend to leave Marlak?"

"We didn't discuss her plans." I recall then the look she exchanged with her husband. "But she was in love with the prince. And vice versa. Of that, I'm sure."

"We know that," the dark-haired fae says. "But—"

I sit on the edge of the straw bed and straighten my back. "We're going to do this right. Like people. Fae are people, right? I'm Tarlia. A princess substitute." There goes our kingdom's secret, but at this point, I couldn't care less about that horrible place. "And you?"

"Nelsin." The cat-eared fae points at himself, then points to his companion. "That's Ferer, your grumpiness expert."

Ferer rolls his eyes, then stares at me. "So you're a guard, like Astra."

"Yes." But not the same, obviously, if Otavio is taking her to the Crystal Castle.

He points at Ziven. "Is he a guard, too?"

"A prince. Not one of the important ones, but their cousin. I mean, technically, he's the most important prince, being the former king's son, but there's a complicated story around it. Complicated enough that they wanted him dead."

Ferer shakes his head. "You were lucky that your assassins were so completely foolish as to try to murder him on this side of the river."

I snort. "*Lucky* and *almost killed* make an odd pair, but I'll take it. We were also lucky that there were fae following us, eager to get rid of a debt." I sigh. "I can't believe Ziven's alive."

Ferer points to him. "When he awakes, we can escort you back to your kingdom."

"Are you nuts?" Nelsin asks. "Return them to their killers?" He realized the lunacy of the suggestion even faster than I did.

Ferer glares at his friend. "I appreciate how much you think I'm stupid."

"I don't think that." Nelsin frowns. "Idiotic ideas also visit brilliant minds. Sometimes."

Ferer turns to me. "I assume you have somewhere to go, right?"

Right, right? Wrong, wrong. I point at Ziven. "He's a prince. Raised in the Krastel castle—where people want to kill him." The futility of my words hits me. It's not like these fae are going to provide us shelter. The idea of running away and finding belonging in these lands feels childish now. I exhale. "I guess we could hide somewhere."

"We'll find a solution," Ferer says. "But help us understand what's going on with Astra."

"I know less than you do. Last time I saw her was at the coronation. She stepped away, then... Wait. There was this fae woman, a princess from the Spider Court, I was told. She took Astra to a corner, and they disappeared. About an hour later, the Court of Bees princess herself came to me and told me Astra was safe, but she had to leave. Was she lying?"

"Astra has been taken to the castle this morning," Ferer said. "Meanwhile, Prince Marlak disappeared."

"Like..." I snap my fingers. "That?"

Ferer nods slowly. "None of our sources knows where he is."

I try to think. "You mentioned a man from Krastel. Do you know what he looks like?"

"Long brown hair, not very young, not too old."

"That might be Otavio, her master." I recall more details then. "He's my master too, and before I came to the fae lands, he asked me to tell Astra that he hadn't forgotten her, that her torment would end soon. So I can see that he was planning to rescue her. But why would she..." I remember then Astra's obedience, almost devotion to Otavio. "I mean, she could have followed Otavio out of her own will, yes."

The two fae stare at me, and I feel I need to explain it a little better. "Not will, but lack of choice, let's say, or maybe lack of belief that she can trace her own path. But I'm also sure she loves her prince." Another detail pops into my head. "She also told me she thinks Renel is cruel, so she wouldn't go there willingly. But she was raised by Otavio and respects him. So... I don't know."

Ferer glances at his companion, then looks back at me. "You think she wouldn't say *no* to this man, this Otavio, if he asked her to do something?"

"I think she would have trouble saying *no*. But then..." A

chill fills my stomach. "If something happened to her husband, maybe she had no choice." I can't imagine her pain if her prince was killed.

Ferer bites his lip and nods. His worry is noticeable like a dark cloud over him.

Nelsin shakes his head with those odd cat ears. "Marlak's alive. Has to be."

Ferer keeps staring at the rough ground. "We hope so."

"You know how I know it?" Nelsin lifts a finger. "They said Astra is unharmed. She wouldn't just stand there and let them kill him."

His certainty cheers me up, even if I barely know Prince Marlak.

Ferer turns to his friend, looking unconvinced. "And *he* would do whatever it took to prevent her from putting herself in danger. *Whatever it took.* You know him."

Nelsin grimaces, then sighs.

At least Astra's alive. Obviously. Otavio wouldn't go through the trouble of raising her—and us—just to kill her. It was always her. I've known it for a while and yet ignored what it could mean.

Now my life has been changed forever. Even if I decided to return to Krastel and pretend I never saw anyone attacking Ziven, is there anything there for me?

Whatever plan Otavio had, it was for Astra, and now she's exactly where he wants. This could be my chance to run away, to find a new life, but all I see is emptiness. And selfishness, thinking about my own problems when Astra might have lost her husband.

I ask, "What can I do to help?"

"I have an idea." A young woman's voice comes from the entrance of the cave.

I turn and see a pretty, dark-skinned fae girl, wearing a fuchsia dress and flowers in her hair, her brown eyes bright with determination.

Ferer frowns. "What are you doing here?"

"Helping. And I have a plan."

MARLAK

The Sundering Dagger is still in my pocket, my rings still on my hands. All dulled by the dark bracelets. I'm still surprised my brother didn't search me, didn't try to pry the relics from me. Perhaps he knew it would be useless, or maybe didn't want to risk getting too close.

Would the dagger still work? I could break one of the guards' enchantments, then get them to open my cell. It would exhaust the dagger's magic, though. And if Renel is keeping an eye on this keep, he could find me. Maybe there's something else out there ready to catch me if I escape. Would it count as his fault if I was killed in the desert?

The hot, dry air from the cell feels like sand in my lungs. There's also Astra. What will they do to her if I escape? If only I could contact her, get her far from Renel. As if she would even listen to me.

At least she's safe.

It doesn't matter how many times I tell myself that, it never feels true. She's hurt and angry. Angry at me. Hurt because of me. And in the hands of my enemy. I have no way to contact her, no way to warn her. No way to apologize, beg for forgiveness, tell her it was all a lie.

An escape attempt would be foolish now. My brother could decide to take out his frustration on Astra, or use her to lure me back, and I can't risk it. I need to wait, make sure she's safe first, even if every second here is an agony.

Perhaps my brother had a point in picking a fireproof cell. I fear I'm about to combust.

4

RENEL

The castle hasn't moved.

Yet.

It's still by the hills of the Western Domain, still at the same place it's been for three months now. We might have a few more months here.

As we approach the Royal Terrace, I remove the Shadow Ring and extend it to Azur.

His eyes widen. "You want me to have it?"

"We can't *have* it. It's borrowed, and eventually will be returned to the human king."

"I'm sure *when* was never specified."

"Before I die, for sure." Why do I have the feeling it might be soon? I place the ring on Azur's palm. "Now take it and put it in the smallest drawer in the onyx cabinet in the Royal Chambers. Don't tell anyone you've seen it or that I have it."

He nods. I want more than a nod.

"Your word, Azur."

His eyes harden. "I *won't* tell anyone."

"Then what's wrong in promising?"

"People order their servants, not their friends." He extends a hand as if to stop me from replying. "But you don't need to justify yourself. I know what I am, Renel."

"The promise protects you. Again, it's not that I don't trust you." As I say it, I feel the soft thud of the carriage landing.

"I can't disobey you." His voice is quiet. "Isn't that more than enough?"

He shakes his head and leaves the carriage, giving me no chance to reply. What could I say anyway? Tell him that he has a lot of freedom, that I trust him? Insist that clear orders are for his protection? He never sounds as if he resents being bound to my service, just that he doesn't appreciate being reminded of that. In truth, he *is* my friend, and I believe I treat him as such—except when my life's on the line.

I sigh. He'll soon forgive me.

I barely step out of the carriage when a guard comes to greet me.

"Your Highness." He bows. "Lord Zorwal summons you."

That was faster than I expected. A familiar chill creeps up my neck, an odd chill that never goes away. At least I had the presence of mind to give Azur the Shadow Ring, or Zorwal would sense it even if I hid it in a pocket. I'd rather not have to dodge his questions about the artifact.

My stomach moves more than my feet as I follow the guard. After so many years, I should no longer feel intimidated by the leader of the council, but on an occasion like this, with so many secrets to conceal, I can't help the tinge of panic running through my blood.

Panic.

There was a time when Zorwal was someone I trusted. Of course I still trust him to a certain extent, except that the size of this extent has been dwindling and dwindling each year. Perhaps it's just that I've learned to trust myself more and gained the strength to step away from his protective shadow.

Instead of leading me to his office, the huge room that once belonged to my stepfather, the guard takes me to the chamber where the council meets and where the fate of the kingdom is decided.

Zorwal is sitting in the highest chair, as if waiting for the council to assemble, dressed in an embroidered light green tunic contrasting with his long black hair.

I put a hand on my chest and bow my head. "You requested to see me?"

The door closes behind me, and I know I'm alone with him. I think about wildflowers in a meadow, a soft, warm wind blowing them, blowing my face, the smell calming me.

My master gets up from his chair and approaches me. "Of course. You never warned your guards that you left. I wondered about your safety."

"An oversight. Apologies, Your Grace."

"Hmmm. And where did you go in such a hurry?"

"The dark unicorn has been spotted." The deceptive and yet true words come out of my mouth without any effort. "We flew over that area."

He frowns. "Just you and Azur? Did you hope to capture it?"

"Hope is a persistent itch. Of course I'd like to acquire magic. But we also had pixies with us."

He laughs. "You think the pixies would help you capture a legendary beast?"

"They flew the carriage."

He clicks his tongue and shakes his head. "Still the same silly boy. Why this insistence? Do you think having magic will make a difference?"

Suggesting it would *not* make any difference is insanity. "It would help secure my position—"

"*I* secure your position. As long as I remain the leader of the council, you have nothing to fear. There's no need to go on pointless quests."

I bow my head slightly. "I appreciate your support."

"Hmm. And did you see it? The dark unicorn?"

"No."

He huffs. "There. See? That's why I tell you not to risk

making a fool of yourself. If anyone catches you trying to find the unicorn, you know what they'll think?"

"That I want his horn. It doesn't necessarily mean—" I was going to say *that I want his magic,* but a sting of pain makes me stop. I touch my cheek and feel blood coming out of a gash. I mutter, "I'm sorry."

"Don't say you're sorry. I'm tired of it."

I feel another slash on the back of my hand and wonder if he'll let the cuts become scars this time, like he always threatens to do.

He continues, "If you ever want to capture the dark unicorn, what do you think you should do?"

"I thought I wasn't supposed to—"

He slashes the other cheek. It should be just a cut, but there's something in the way he does it that makes it sting in a pain that's blinding.

"Answer me. Before I slash your throat. If you want to capture the dark unicorn, what do you need to do?"

Fair. I know what answer he wants. "I must tell Your Grace. Then ask for your advice."

"Very well. Do you want scars this time?"

"It's not up to me to decide."

"Funny. For a moment I thought you made the decisions here."

"That's certainly not the case." The words came more cutting than I expected. "I appreciate your support and advice."

"Is that so? Tell me then, why do we have another human visitor in the castle?"

Of course he would know about the girl already. I'll need to change all the servants in that area if they're reporting information so quickly. "I'm hoping she'll entertain me."

"Humans are a dangerous thing to have as visitors, Renel. One wrong step and you could be breaching the treaty."

"She's here out of her own free will, as a guest. And can leave when she wants. Would you like me to send her away?" My heart pauses, dreading his answer.

He stares at me and licks his lips. "Bring her to me. And I'll make a decision."

"Now?" It takes all my effort to keep my voice from cracking.

"No. Later. I'll summon her." He waves a hand. "I have more pressing matters than lowly humans. Have your fun for now, just don't ever try to make any deals or bargains with her, and never compel or force her to do anything."

He truly thinks I'm stupid. "I won't."

"You can kill her, however, and I suggest you do that if you grow too attached. A human consort kept in secret is fine, but not in public, not for the Crystal Court King."

"Wise words, your grace."

"Go now. I have other matters to oversee."

I'm still bleeding, still hurt. One day I might walk away like that, but not today.

"My cuts, your grace. Might not befit a king and create gossip."

He smirks. "You need to ask for the head of whoever creates this gossip, then." He takes a golden sphere from his pocket and holds it. "You know what happens when you don't have a tight grip on an object?"

He opens his hand and the ball rolls to the tip of his fingers, but then he grips it again, before it falls.

"You may lose it, Your Grace."

Raising his hand with the ball, he stares at me. "Just like the kingdom."

Yes, and what does that have to do with my face? I would look like a fool leaving this room with such obvious cuts. Of course, I can't say any of that.

Instead, I say, "The kingdom has a strong council, with an incredible leader. It makes the job easy for me."

He laughs. "It makes the job for you."

At least I finally feel the cuts healing and the pain subduing. "And I appreciate it."

"I know you do. Now go taste your human. It might cheer you up."

"Thank you." I bow and leave the chamber in slow, heavy steps. Always too heavy, as I swallow down all the replies I'll never dare utter. I always remind myself that I should be grateful. Without Zorwal, I'd probably have been dead a long time ago, and not only me. His methods might be ruthless, but he has my well-being at heart.

Even then, I don't trust him, not with all my secrets. It's why I can't let him know I captured my brother, and why he must never, under any circumstance, realize that there's a Tiurian in this castle.

TARLIA

It feels odd to be here, in a strange land, among people I don't know, especially when they're about to argue.

Ferer puts his hands on his hips. "Lidiane, you shouldn't be here."

She smiles. "I disagree. And I bet you were preparing to rescue Marlak without getting Astra out of the Crystal Castle first."

"How do you know all that? And how did you find us?"

"I *also* live near a river." Lidiane rolls her eyes as if it was an obvious explanation. "And am I wrong about your plan?"

"Unfortunately, yes." Nelsin steps toward her. "We have no idea where Marlak is, and so far, no plan to rescue him. Even if we knew his location, our oath is to rescue Astra first."

The girl's enthusiasm evaporates like water on hot, dry ground. "Oh." She pauses, then smiles again. "But I have a plan to rescue her. An amazing plan, in fact."

"This is not your job," Ferer says. "You need to be safe, away from all of this."

"No." There's an impressive strength in her soft voice. "I won't sit quietly waiting for the day some high fae convicts me of a crime and then enchants me to serve them. I won't. I'd rather die trying than die of old age, hiding while my kingdom crumbles."

Ferer approaches her and takes her hands. "I'm fighting for you. *We're* fighting for you."

I realize how much they look alike and assume they're siblings.

She shakes her head. "I *will* act. It's up to you if you want to be informed about it or not."

Nelsin places a hand on her shoulder. "I'm sure your plan won't put anyone in danger. But before that," he points at me, "have you met Tarlia?"

I was enjoying watching their conversation and pretending I didn't exist, but I wave. "Hello."

Lidiane approaches me. "I'm so sorry! I'm Lidiane, former dressmaker, current troublemaker."

I laugh. "That's a good job."

She scrunches her nose. "The pay is crap." Then she sees Ziven lying down. "Is he all right?"

"Overused his opus magic," Ferer says. "He's Ziven, one of Krastel's princes."

She eyes the cave. "Why are you *here*? I mean, that bed looks awful."

"Someone tried to kill them," Nelsin says. "Fortunately, they were rescued and brought to this cave by some fae who don't want anyone to know how nice they are. As much as we'd love to take them somewhere more comfortable, it will be much easier once the human prince awakes, and it should be soon."

"Makes sense."

I wonder where they plan to take us. It's clear they'd rather be rescuing Astra than standing here watching us as if we were lost children, waiting for Ziven to wake up to finally dump us across the River of Tears and wish us good luck.

It turns out freedom is not that exciting when you have nowhere to go.

"What's your plan?" I ask Lidiane. I guess I'm wondering if there's any way to delay our return to Krastel, at least until... I don't even know.

Her brown eyes brighten with contagious excitement. "It's something I've been working on, and I think it's ready."

Ferer glares at her. "You *think*?"

"By *think,* I mean I'm sure." She points to a large bag she's carrying. "This will change everything. I've always been good with glamours and enjoyed creating clothes. I combined my talents." She opens the bag and pulls out some black fabric. "These capes will make people ignore you. You won't be invisible or glamoured, just *unworthy of notice.*"

Nelsin raises an eyebrow. "Who's not going to notice someone wearing a *cape*?"

She chuckles. "I mean that people won't see you, even though you'll be perfectly visible."

Her brother narrows his eyes. "That could be great in a crowd, but how—"

"The Crystal Castle is guarded by enchanted lower fae," she explains. "They obey precise commands and need to vet all visitors. But hey, they only need to stop the visitors *they notice.*"

Her brother watches her intently. "And you think we should wear your capes and walk right into the castle?"

She puts the capes back in her bag. "Not exactly."

Nelsin makes a circle with his hands. "Oooh. Mysterious plan. Got us all curious."

Ferer glares at Nelsin, then turns to his sister. "What *is* your plan, then?"

She raises a finger. "First, be glad I'm telling you about this. I just thought you'd be running after Marlak right now, when it's not the right time. Second, if you want to come in and out unnoticed, it's easier if you aren't a strong fae knight."

Ferer rolls his eyes. "I can wear a servant's clothes. That's not an issue."

Lidiane shakes her head. "This is a mission for women."

Her brother's entire body turns rigid at once. "No. No."

She giggles. "I didn't even say I was going."

His shoulders sag. "Who, then?"

Lidiane is still laughing. "Me, obviously, but you were all stressed even before I said it."

"No."

She sighs. "It needs to be me, to keep the magic of the capes active. I can't just hand them to someone else. I'll go in, find Astra, give her the other cape, then walk out. Nobody will see me. Nobody will stop me. If they do, I'll pretend I work there. It's my wish and my will. I'm almost twenty, and you have no right to stop me."

"I can give you advice," he says.

Lidiane lowers her head. "Advice taken. I will not go back to my city. Yes, I love to make clothes. Yes, I used to want to be the most renowned dressmaker in all fae lands. But I can't do that if I fear a high fae could walk in at any minute and trap me into their service. And I won't simply sit quietly and hide or work in the Owl Inn's kitchen. Life is fire, Ferer. It burns anyway. It's nothing but a short moment, soon gone. I want to feel like I'm living. If it all goes wrong, I'll look back and tell myself that at least I tried. I'll know that I wasn't just a walking corpse counting the minutes until death."

There's something inspiring and contagious about her resolve, even if it sounds reckless.

Ferer snorts. "Oh, don't exaggerate. You could leave the Crystal Court."

"Right. And spend my life in fear of being sent back?"

Ferer and Nelsin stare at her in silence, while I wonder about life in the Crystal Court for a lower fae and ask, "What do you mean, sent back?"

She grimaces. "The Crystal Court can search for lower fae outside its borders without a conviction. Then they say that running away is a crime. It's an excuse to hunt us down to enchant us."

"That's awful. And how do they decide who's a lower fae?" I

ask. "I mean, I know lower fae have animal characteristics, but you don't look—"

She huffs. "I guess you said it. *They* decide it. Some of it depends on our appearance, sure, but it can be hidden. Glamours are tricky, but some fae replace parts of their skin, color their hair, some even cut off their horns or extra ears. And then it can depend on your family, your upbringing, your connections. At the end of the day, it doesn't matter that much, as long as the rich fae from the Jewel City can exploit and enslave some of us, the way they did with humans not long ago. And the funny thing is that high fae have a lot of human blood, or they wouldn't look like that. Fae used to live for hundreds and hundreds of years, but they rarely had children. Now? We live for a hundred years or so, but have children easily. It's all the human blood. A fair trade-off, perhaps, except that some fae now use the way we look as an excuse to divide us. And things have only gotten worse in the last few years."

"Because of Renel?" I ask.

She nods, then turns to Ferer. "I'm going, brother, whether you like it or not."

Ferer takes a deep breath, while Nelsin places a hand on his friend's shoulder and turns to Lidiane. "We can take you to the castle's perimeter and stick around. Just in case. We'll support you."

Ferer slaps away Nelsin's hand and crosses his arms. "How are you going to find her?"

Lidiane's eyes sparkle with glee. "I know in which room they're keeping her, and I've seen a map of the castle."

"How?" Her brother raises an eyebrow.

"That's my secret, if you don't mind."

"Of course I mind!"

Lidiane shrugs and gives no answer.

I wonder if they're just going to abandon Ziven and I here, which is a silly, selfish thought. I *am* glad they're about to rescue Astra.

Astra!

A crazy idea hits me. Too crazy, but it might be true that life is just a short moment, and I don't want to sit here, in an abandoned cave, wondering about my lack of prospects.

"You have two capes?" I ask.

"Yes, for me and Astra."

"I can come with you. I could color my hair black and stay a little longer in the castle, pretending I'm Astra, so it gives you two time to escape. Later, I can climb down the walls or something. I trained to find escape routes. I can do it."

Her eyes sparkle. "Yes, until Marlak is safe. That would be ideal. Meanwhile, I could glamour you." She approaches my face. "You and her, you look alike, you know?"

I snort. "Story of my life."

She smiles. "Your idea is perfect."

Ferer doesn't look thrilled. "You forget that she can't make any deal with us or work for us."

"What do you mean?" I ask.

Lidiane eyes him and exhales. "The river treaty."

I'm not sure I quite follow. "I thought it only forbade humans from being enslaved."

She nods. "Yes, but they could be tricked into enslavement, so the treaty forbids any deal on this side of the river and forbids employment. Even if a human wants to, they can't work for a fae in exchange for any compensation."

It's odd that I studied that treaty and didn't know the specifics. "Astra was here."

"Humans can come to Fae lands as guests," Ferer says. "Work or servitude is forbidden. Powerful magic will prevent it from happening."

"I'm going to the castle because I want to," I say. "It's not employment or servitude."

"And it will never be," Lidiane adds. "The treaty won't let it. Also, it's better for us to go later, when the sun is almost down, so we need to wait. I think I'll split one of the capes, so we'll have three." She turns to Ferer and Nelsin. "I'm being careful, see? And once Astra is out of the castle, you can find Marlak."

Nelsin's strange cat ears perk up. "I bet Astra can help us find him. I think... they're somehow connected. Their minds. He came to her rescue when we were... That day."

Still addressing his sister, Ferer points at me. "Tarlia could go instead of you. Just lend her the cape."

Great. Now they're volunteering me to walk into a fae castle on my own.

"I have to go!" she says. "I'll be careful."

I point to Ziven. "What about him? While we all go to the castle..."

Nelsin crouches by him. "When he wakes, we decide what to do."

Lidiane nods. "Meanwhile, we plan."

My heart speeds up, but strangely, it's not fear, but eagerness. After coming all the way here, I suppose in the end I *will* rescue Astra.

And then my heart speeds up for a different reason.

Ziven will wake up soon—and realize I ran and left him to fend off the attackers on his own.

He might also remember the foolish words I let him hear: *I love you.*

RENEL

The castle's heart is a room at the highest level, almost under the crystal on the roof, with a semicircular window from floor to ceiling, protected by a handrail. At its center, stands a pillar with a dark sphere floating above it.

My lack of magic and my inability to command the castle should make me hate this place, but it doesn't. It's where I feel most at ease. Maybe I like to look at the scenery outside, maybe I like to imagine the sphere one day obeying my command. I don't know.

What I do know is that my palms are sweaty. Fae shouldn't

sweat, and yet here I am. Had I been a water wielder, I would be able to use my magic even in a desert. Alas, I have no magic—just embarrassingly sweaty palms—and a heart that often feels like it wants to punch a hole and escape this unlucky body.

I take deep breaths as I watch the green hills by the castle, realizing that the beautiful view isn't bringing me any peace today, when I hear the door opening.

Azur comes in, staring at me with worry in his blue eyes. "Did he give you a hard time?"

"No. Just the usual."

I've never told him what *the usual* entails. I guess once I told him in part, and a glimpse at his horrified expression made me stop. The worst was his look of pity, and I don't want anyone's pity, not even my best friend's.

Still, Azur has such a concerned frown that for a second, I wonder if this time Zorwal left any marks.

"What did he want?" he asks.

"To know where we went."

His frown deepens. "What did you tell him?"

I lean on the rail in front of the window and can't help but smirk. "That we flew by the area where the dark unicorn was last seen."

His eyebrows shoot up. "Did he believe you?"

"He did. And he thinks I'm quite foolish, hoping to acquire magic." A chuckle escapes my throat. "Right? Magic. What a silly, useless thing."

Azur tilts his head. "Is that all he said?"

"He might also think I'm too incompetent to catch the unicorn."

"*Nobody* has caught it. Being unable to apprehend the beast doesn't mean you're deficient in any way."

"Maybe. Or maybe he wants to watch my steps. Sometimes I wonder if he prefers me like this." I almost say *vulnerable*, but stop myself, unsure if I can open up *that* much. "With no magic."

He bites his lip, as if hesitating, then asks, "Do you want my opinion?"

"Why wouldn't I?"

He rolls his eyes then narrows them.

I'm not sure what he thinks the gesture means, and don't want to guess, so I ask, "What?"

"You've been making decisions on your own lately."

Oh. That. "You're going to hold a grudge for life now?"

"It's been only a couple of hours. But I understand. I do. Marlak's your brother, and you wanted to talk to him alone. But it's just..." He takes a deep breath. "Perhaps I'm silly, that's all."

"It's not silly. Nobody likes to be excluded." These words salt a wound much deeper than any cut. "And of course I want your opinion, Azur. I always do."

His breath is slow and deep, while a shadow crosses his eyes. "Zorwal might not want you to acquire magic. If you do, it could undermine his hold on you."

"The thought has crossed my mind." Quite often, in fact, but some words are too bold to leave their confine.

He nods, eyes lost in thought. I wonder if forbidden, traitorous thoughts cross his mind, or if, like me, he's come to the conclusion that there isn't much to be done. Zorwal is my main supporter and protector. While I sometimes hate him, it's not as if I could get rid of him—if that was even possible. He has some impressive magic, and I'm not even sure of its extent.

Azur stares at his fingers, then back at me. "Does he know about your human guest?"

I rest my forehead on my hand as if it alleviated the impact of the thought. "Yes. He even heard about the girl, who barely arrived here. He doesn't know what she is, though, and it must remain a secret."

"What did you say? How did you explain her presence here?"

I shrug. "Amusement. He didn't seem to mind it. Not too much, at least. I mean, he told me not to breach the treaty and not to fall in love. Sometimes I think he actually takes me for a fool."

Azur laughs. "Our council leader is short-sighted, that's for sure."

"I wish." Something else comes to mind. "He almost caught me. Did you hide the ring?"

He nods. "Where you told me to hide it. Quick thinking, Renel. If you hadn't given it to me..."

"Perhaps I knew what was coming."

"Speaking of knowing..." He glances at the sphere at the center of the room. "I know you asked him once, but did you ever consider asking him again about the trajectory of the castle? Discuss possible solutions?"

"He didn't want to hear anything about it, and I don't plan to contradict his wishes." My entire skin still recalls the sharp pain it felt when I dared mention my theories to Zorwal. I never told Azur how strongly the council leader reacted, and I don't plan to tell him.

Azur looks at the sphere. "It's just... Again, it's not that I don't believe you."

I laugh. "But you don't believe my predictions will come true."

"No. Hear me out. Zorwal *lives* in this castle. I'm pretty sure he doesn't want to see all his belongings getting swallowed up by a volcano, not to mention himself. If he doesn't see any danger—"

"It's because he doesn't trust me, Azur. Doesn't trust my calculations. For three years now, I never missed. Not once did I fail to predict where the castle would end up. You know that. I calculated its trajectory. I know where it's going, and it's spelled out in all the books that if the castle goes to the Fiery Gorge, it will destroy our land. Why would they write that? Why don't they tell us not to put the castle in the sea or a lake? Why warn against something that sounds completely absurd? Because it's bound to happen."

Azur eyes me with that odd sympathy again. "Your calculations might be right, but there must be something you're missing. Self-preservation is the first law of magic."

I shake my head. "I thought about it, and I disagree with that principle. Self-destruction has a strange allure. Everything ends. Everything dies. Sometimes we spiral downward, from where we can't escape. Why should magic be different? Perhaps when we see our demise looming on the horizon, we want to speed it up rather than live under its shadow."

"You predicted it a couple of years ago. I don't think anything's speeding."

"For a millennia-old castle, a few years is but a blink of an eye. The castle is heading to the Fiery Gorge. I know it."

"But no magic scholar has predicted it."

"Nobody else *knows* where the castle is going. Nobody took the time to look at it. And why would they? It's not like this castle is supposed to go rogue and trace its own trajectory. The castle master controls it. And that's me. They don't know I'm not controlling it."

"Zorwal knows. And he's not worried."

"Maybe he wants to bathe in lava. What do I know?"

Azur chuckles. "You know what? None of it will matter. You have the Tiurian girl, and she can give you your magic. Wasn't that what you researched?"

I chuckle too, even though deep down I want to scream. "I hope so."

"You need to be more optimistic."

"I…"

"You're not sure about her magic?"

"Of that, I'm sure."

"Then what's bothering you?"

"To gift someone magic… It's not like activating a stone. It needs to be willingly, needs to have feeling behind it."

He waves a hand. "Oh, no. It's easy. Get her to fall in love, that's all. Why wouldn't she fall for you? You're the Crystal

Court acting king, who also happens to be good-looking. She was with your brother, and he's hideous."

"What if she likes the rugged, scarred type?"

He shakes his head. "You're looking at it all wrong. It's hard to make someone fall in love with you when you care. When you don't care, it's easy."

Does he think his words are encouraging? "I'm doomed, then. I happen to care."

"About the magic. Not about her. It's loving, confusing feelings that make people stupid. Manipulating people is easy. Making people love you is easy. You just have to find out what they crave—and feed them. But just enough. Make them want more and more."

A bitter feeling covers my throat. If only I could believe it was that easy to be loved.

As much as I'm feeling foolish and weak, I need to be honest. "Can you help me?"

He opens his arms. "I'm always helping you. It's not different now. When are you going to see her?"

"Soon. Fifteen minutes, to be precise."

"Why?"

His question is bizarre. "Why not? You think I can make her want to give me magic from a distance?"

Azur chuckles and shakes his head. "You can't see her yet. You're the king, too important for a mere human visitor. You need to make her feel special when you do see her, feel like your attention is a prize."

He might have a point, but if I have to wait even another hour, my heart will explode. "I need to see her, Azur, look at her and figure out if this plan has a chance. Then I can spend time away from her, but not too much. Soon the castle will move again."

"You said you had two years until—"

"Five moves. It could take five days."

Azur shakes his head. "Renel, no. You can't be desperate.

Desperation is like a stench you can't smell, but you sense it's there. You need to feel powerful, cool, and collected. Feel that you have all the time in the world. In reality, the castle will take at least a year to move five times. That's an eternity."

"You live in this castle too, you know? Perhaps *you* want to bathe in lava."

His chuckle is light and relaxed. "I want the best for the kingdom, Renel. You know that."

"I also know that a year passes by in a flash."

He nods. "True. And what after? After she gives you your magic? Are you going to torture her and force your brother to crown you?"

"I'm not thinking that far. Either way, I doubt that prison will hold him."

His joyous mood evaporates in a second. "Then why? Why not take him to the Blue Tower?"

"I don't think it would hold him either—unless it killed him, and I don't want that."

Azur bites his lips. "You need to find a way to keep him locked up. His magic is not that impressive, Renel. And he goes around defying you, weakening your claim. You're going to let him escape?"

"Well, I can't kill him." I don't know what to do other than shrug. "What am I going to do?"

"Let him roam freely, calling himself *king*?" He spits the last word.

I point to the sphere. "I have bigger problems."

Azur rolls his eyes. "That's the issue with your obsession. It could cost you your kingdom. Or your head."

"Oh, what a silly obsession. I'm glad to hear what you really think about it."

Tired of this conversation, tired of never being believed, I leave the room. When I close the door, I hear him yell, "I never said you're wrong! You're missing something, that's all."

I wish his opinion didn't matter; wish I didn't care. Averting disaster is hard enough on its own. Having no support, no trust, makes it even worse.

I stop and take a deep breath.

There will be no disaster. I'll acquire magic, take control of this castle, and prevent it from reaching the Fiery Gorge—or at least that's what I hope.

ASTRA

Otavio left me alone in this bedroom, right when I wanted to pester him and ask a thousand questions about who I am. Sure, he doesn't want to discuss these details here, but I could ask some general questions that wouldn't look suspicious.

Does he know who my family was? And what does he think about darksouls' evil nature? Is our magic truly doomed to be evil? I try to swallow these questions, but they taste so bitter...

Perhaps he left me on purpose, to avoid any questions.

But what's strangling my heart is Marlak. Is he safe? Alive? He needs to be alive. How else am I going to yell at him?

I open my window and look down at the surface of the castle. It's not like our tower and seems much smoother. From here, I can't see an outer wall or guards down below, but then, who knows what kind of magic keeps this castle safe? And where am I even going to go if I escape?

A river.

The thought comes to me suddenly. The nymphs have helped me before. If they help me find Nelsin and Ferer, we'll have a chance of freeing Marlak. All I need to do is figure out a way to escape.

My stomach feels hollow and heavy at the same time. If I escape this castle, I might throw away my only chance of learning who I am, where I come from. I might squander my only chance to understand Otavio's plan.

Stupid thought. It's not like he's telling me anything now. I spent my entire life being raised by Otavio, and what have I learned?

To be gullible, it seems.

No, I have to escape and figure out another way to get my answers—once Marlak is safe. Just thinking about him chills my tangled, knotted heart, bathing it in anger and fear.

Why did he have to be such an idiot? Idiot, idiot, idiot, and it all started by giving away his Shadow Ring. Of course a powerful artifact like that would fall into nefarious hands. What was he thinking? Now here I am, wanting to strangle and hold him and kiss him, desperate to find him—while confined in this castle.

The door opens and Otavio walks in, that strange, satisfied smile back on his face.

"It's time, Astra."

"To learn about my past?" I pretend to be hopeful and foolish, wondering if this version of me could crack his armor.

He shakes his head. "Even better. The king has granted you an audience. You'll have lunch with him." He approaches me, his steps slow, and places his hands on my shoulders. "Keep in mind all that you learned."

I'm starting to think that the only gullible person here is Otavio, so sure that I'll do anything he asks. I could just nod and smile, but if I do too much of that, he'll eventually think Marlak addled my brain.

"Why?" I ask. As expected, his smile fades. My goal is not to challenge him, though, so I add, "I want to understand why I need to—"

His hands squeeze my shoulder in a gesture that's more

threatening than friendly. "Being powerless is the worst thing in the world." He eyes the door. "The Crystal Court is the seat of power in these lands, and its king, the key for it." He frowns. "Would you rather be a fugitive? Would you rather be persecuted and killed for what you are?"

I confess I'm puzzled. "Is this... meant to protect me?"

"Not only you," he whispers.

"My kind," I whisper back.

For a second, I think I understand him. If I become the Crystal Court queen, I could perhaps grant other Tiurians safe haven here. I could maybe change their view of us. I almost tell him that we could do that with Marlak, who's the true king, that there's no need of all of this pretense. For a second, I almost ask Otavio to help me escape and find my husband.

And then I recall a lifetime of secrets.

There's no need to go even that far. I recall our recent conversation when he refused to discuss the Amethyst Palace. I can't trust Otavio—which is a pity. If his goal is to protect Tiurians, I'd love to help him—but I don't know if he's telling the truth.

Still, I cling to that moment of understanding, that moment when I thought I could trust him, and let that feeling take over my face as I nod. "We'll secure the Crystal Court."

His arms then wrap around me, and to my surprise, he pulls me in for a hug, the hug I had been craving for years.

"I knew I could trust you," he says, his voice cracking with emotion. "From the moment I saw you, I knew you were our hope."

I have a thousand questions about the day he found me, but his tone shifts in a second and he steps away, his usual formality back in place. "Let's go. You don't want to keep the fae king waiting."

Technically, being too obliging is not a great seduction strategy, but there's no point arguing, especially when I have absolutely no intention of seducing my husband's treacherous brother. If everything goes well, I'll be far from this castle by nightfall, and then none of this will matter.

Outside the room, a guard gestures for me to follow him down the corridor. It looks like a human palace, except that the walls are white, instead of having visible stones like in the castle I grew up. I glance beside me, hoping to see Otavio, and realize he stayed back, staring at me with that odd hope in his eyes.

They can't be the eyes of someone evil, can they? But then, people don't need to be evil to do great harm, and don't even need to do any harm to be someone who doesn't belong in our lives.

I guess a part of me is hurting, the part used to a lifetime of having him as a father figure. Now that same part is trying to vilify him, so as not to feel guilty for escaping, for defying him. But I need to do what I need to do. Right now, it means finding out where Marlak is. At least I'm about to meet the person who can give me that information. The issue is how to get it.

The guard leads me to a room with large windows and a long, rectangular table where Renel is already sitting. He stands up when he sees me, and the door closes behind me, leaving us alone. It's odd to see a member of royalty unattended like that, unprotected. By instinct, I reach for my daggers, then realize that this dress has no pockets. Would I dare murder Renel? I would need to plan this properly and make sure I can escape after the deed.

I approach him slowly, taking in his appearance. He does look like Marlak—same eyes—except that his frame is slenderer, his face narrower, and his hair longer. He also has pointy ears—and no scars.

No scars at all.

Highly suspicious, considering he was present when his sister, mother, and stepfather were killed, and when his brother had half his body burned.

What happened that day?

This is not the time to figure it out, though. I take in more of his appearance. The way a person dresses can tell so much about themselves.

His wavy black hair is partly pulled back with a delicate silver comb on one side. Is he trying to look like his brother, who doesn't have hair on that side of his head? Weird.

On his ears, he has hoops near the tip of his left, pointy ear, and star earrings adorning his lobes. His black shirt has only two buttons, so that the neckline is rather a chest line in a deep v down until his belly, showing many thin necklaces, which remind me of the queen of the Misty Court. At least in this case, there are no nipples in sight, not that male nipples would be that much of an issue, but I'd still rather not face my brother-in-law's tits right in our first encounter.

On his wrists, he has several thin bracelets, but no rings on his fingers, not even the Shadow Ring. Fae can be so flamboyant that I have no idea if he's trying to impress me or if this is how he gets dressed in the morning. I have no idea why he wanted to meet me so soon. He got the Shadow Ring and imprisoned his brother. That should be it, right? But then he knows I'm Tiurian, so he must want something from me.

But what?

He gets up from his chair. "Welcome, Astra." His voice is different from what I heard in the sanctuary, with none of that arrogance. If anything, he sounds scared. Odd.

"I'm glad to be here." It's so good to be human—or Tiurian—and be able to spew blatant lies. I pass by the table and approach the window. We're on the other side of the castle, and I want to see what's below. "The view is so beautiful," I say. There are no hills on this side, just treetops and what looks like a small village. No rivers either, at least none that I can see. That's a problem.

Renel approaches the window and stands beside me. I hope he doesn't realize I'm trying to check our surroundings, so I try to look excited and add, "I never thought I'd ever visit fae territories, let alone step into this legendary castle."

His chuckle sounds strange. "Legendary. Yes."

"How do you decide where the castle goes? Can you use it to travel?"

Renel rubs his hands and chuckles. "As you saw, we have carriages for travel. Much more practical."

"But the castle still moves, right? So you can take your whole court to another city when you want."

He leans a finger on his face, and his posture shifts. "There's more to the trajectory of the castle than my selfish wishes." His voice is confident, I'm assuming because he's so used to answering the same silly questions about the castle that he has this sentence memorized. That said, his words answer nothing.

Still, I smile. "It's incredible."

His lips tremble and he extends his hand. That's not a fae gesture. Is he thinking we'll shake hands? Hoping to kiss my hand? I have no desire to touch him, but I don't want to be rude, so I decide to go for a handshake.

I expected to feel disgust at his touch, obviously.

Instead, my entire arm hurts as if it were immersed in ice, even though there is no change in temperature.

Then there's fire—and screams. Screams and more screams, while flames consume this room. Outside, no sunlight, only fire. And so much horror.

And then I'm back in this dining room, on a quiet morning —or lunchtime. I gasp, horrified, pull my hand, and step back. What in all the kingdoms was that? The screams still echo in my ear, and I can't shake the horror I felt.

He stares at me, his brows furrowed. "Are you all right?"

Of course I'm not fine. I'm horrified, puzzled, and yet I have to come up with a reply. "Uh. Tired." I manage a smile even though I can feel my lips trembling.

What was that fire? It can't have been a memory, like Marlak's, if I saw this room, if I saw everything burning.

He puts his hands behind his back. "Yes. Yes. I... ordered a human meal for you." He snaps a finger, and two servants come in carrying trays from the same door from where I entered.

Of course he isn't unattended, if they can come in so quickly.

I need to figure out what I saw. And see if I could kill him.

Renel walks to the table and gestures to a chair. "Come. Sit."

True. I was standing here like an idiot, lost in my own thoughts, still stunned by that vision. I shake off those images and take a seat.

A servant uncovers the tray in front of me, revealing a roasted chicken. He gives Renel a tray with some vegetables and grains, then fills our cups with water. At least I hope it's just water.

When I take my cup for a sip, no liquid reaches my lips.

The water has frozen.

And this is when I realize that somehow I have a trace of Marlak's magic—in all its hectic, uncontrollable glory. I can still feel him with me, feel his warmth. Perhaps blood isn't the only way I can acquire some of his magic, and it was only this morning that we...

I can't even think about us together, as the thought hurts so much.

I place my cup behind the tray cover and keep my hand around it, hoping it will thaw the water.

Renel is staring at me. "Do you like it?"

For a moment, I don't even know what he's asking, when I realize he means the food. At least it's what I think. I need to act normal. Now.

"I... haven't tried it yet."

The servants are gone, and I look around for a plate, but there's none. "Is there a plate? A knife to cut the chicken?"

Renel blinks and points to the tray. "That's a plate, isn't it?"

Right. A tray with an entire chicken on it. "I'm not going to eat it all, so I need to cut it."

He frowns but snaps his fingers again. A servant comes in, and Renel whispers something.

The servant takes the tray away, and now I place both hands around my cup.

Renel stares at his food, then at me. "I thought... humans ate more. Not that you're... You know." He puts a finger over his lips, his bracelets jingling with the gesture.

"Not a whole chicken at once." I smile. Then I feel that the water in the cup is no longer cold. It feels warm, but it must be an impression, and I remove my hands from around it.

He smiles. "I have much to learn."

Indeed. He should learn not to capture his own brother. Still, I return the smile. "Don't we all?"

He leans forward and rests his elbow on the table and his chin on his hand. "What would you like to learn, Astra?"

I sure hope he isn't trying to be seductive, or else I'll want to puke. I shake away those thoughts and try to sound enthusiastic. "Everything. Anything. About your kingdom, your magic, this castle. It's amazing to be here."

Renel's eyes widen. "Amazing, yes. Amazing."

He's definitely weird, or maybe it's just that he's incapable of making any conversation.

The servant then walks in with the tray again. That was fast. There's a tiny chicken leg and some leaves from a vegetable I don't recognize on the tray. Just one leg? One tiny leg? Perhaps I should have clarified that even though I don't eat a whole chicken at once, I can eat half of it.

Renel points to the tray. "I hope the meal is to your taste."

"I'm sure it is."

I take a piece of the chicken and some leaves. Ugh. It's the blandest food I've ever had.

Renel stares at me with an odd smile. "I asked them to cook it in human style; just salt."

What an idiot.

Our food is not that bland—but I don't want to make him feel like a fool, not when I still need to get information from him, so I decide not to mention it.

I chew fast, then say, "I wouldn't mind tasting some fae specialties. And your seasoning. I'm sure the food in your castle is amazing."

I don't even know him and yet I can see the disappointment spelled on his face. "I can ask them to—"

"It's fine. I mean next time."

He nods. "You'll have your fae meal."

At least he starts eating, which gives me time to think. As if I could think. This lunch reminds me of my time in the island house, reminds me of all my moments with Marlak, when we sat together in that kitchen. I don't know if I'll ever have those moments again, and the fear tears me apart.

Why is the memory of those moments so sweet, if we weren't even a real couple then? Why do I think I was happy, if I hadn't even kissed my husband?

The answer shocks me: because I *was* happy.

I was happy—and madly in love—before I ever dared to admit my feelings. I was happy before I ever dared to kiss him. I was happy—before we ever felt each other's touch.

All the more reason to try to do something now. I need to think.

If I really have some of Marlak's magic, I can use it. Perhaps I could kill Renel, then jump out of the window and use air weaving to escape.

Ugh. The memory of us falling from the Misty Palace hits me like the ground almost did that day.

Too dangerous.

And I need to learn where Marlak is.

Wait. I can do it.

I remember my husband telling me that he needed to touch someone with the intention of seeing a thought. Can I try it? Well, I saw that weird fiery vision, whatever it was, when I touched Renel's hand. But I need to bring up the thought.

"I appreciate being here." I smile. "And being rescued."

Renel nods. "No trouble."

"And Marlak's imprisoned, right?"

His hand clutches his fork tight. "Yes."

"Is it safe where he is?"

Renel frowns as if puzzled. "He won't be killed or harmed there, no."

Weird answer. "I mean if he can escape," I clarify.

He tilts his head and bites his lip, and I reach out and touch his hand. Yes, it's weird, but what am I going to do?

Several images invade my mind at once. A dark tower, a raven, a bridge, a gate, a lake with an island in it, a plaque with the drawing of a heart, an eye, and a teardrop.

"Are you afraid of him?" Renel asks.

He's staring at my hand, his eyes wide, and I pull it back.

"Just curious," I reply.

I'm shaking and need time to think about what I just saw, figure out what it can be, make sure to commit these images to my memory.

I get up. "Can I take my leave? I'm feeling indisposed."

He gets up too. "Of course, Astra." He sounds relieved, if anything. "You have a guard at your disposal. Let him know if you need anything."

"Appreciated." I bow, then turn around and walk out of the room.

I know where Marlak is!

Technically, I have no idea what I just saw. But I saw it, I saw where he is.

And now I need to concoct a plan to rescue him.

ZIVEN

Being alive again, after graciously accepting my death, is a strange experience. I still recall those last moments when I was surrounded, wounded, outnumbered, still recall the relief of seeing Tarlia running to her freedom while I welcomed death.

My only pain was in missing the chance to avenge the people who wronged me, who killed my father, but I told myself that perhaps it was not up to me to bring them justice.

I embraced the end.

And now, I feel reborn. I'm lying on a small double bed in a room with a wooden, slanted ceiling and a round window, in a house that belongs to a strange fae with cat ears. He and his companion claim they're Astra's friends, but I'm more likely to bet that they serve her husband. Apparently, they carried me like a sack of potatoes after I took too long to wake up. I'm grateful to them, even if I'll never utter the words *thanks*. And then Tarlia's here too, alive and well, and there aren't enough words to express my relief in knowing that.

This would be the perfect opportunity to enact the foolish idea that had been plaguing my mind: to escape with her and disappear in these fae lands. Of course, in reality, things are a lot more complicated than in my mind. If we can't even work for the fae or make deals on this side of the river, how can I find any belonging here?

And how can I return to Krastel? I can't.

I hear two soft knocks on the door and know who it is before asking. I'm not even sure why anyone gave me a room, when I'm the intruder here.

"Come in."

Tarlia walks in, her hair colored black, wearing a simple dark blue dress, her stunning beauty standing out like a jewel on a velvet cushion.

Her words never left my mind.

I love you—said just like she would have declared that the day is hot. *I love you*, as if she was asking me to pass her the salt. But does love need any ceremony?

And then I recall her eagerness to marry the fae king. Maybe all she wants is power. Or maybe this is my own excuse, my own explanation as to why I cannot utter the same words she did. Maybe all I had was a strange, feverish dream with no substance, and all it took was a little reality to wake me up. The truth is that I don't understand my own feelings.

She approaches the bed. "How are you?"

"Well rested, I'd say."

I chuckle, but there's something in her look that makes me pause. I get the feeling that she's about to say goodbye, and an odd sensation that I'll never see her again, even if in theory she's supposed to be back tomorrow. Still, her plan to go to the Crystal Castle strikes me as dangerous and foolish. Regardless of what I feel for her, I don't want to see her getting hurt.

"Don't go," I blurt. "I'm sorry for what I said, for being angry. Don't go."

I can see thousands of thoughts stirring behind those big brown eyes, but then she says, "We'll be in and out. I trained for this."

"You never trained to counter fae magic, Tarlia. While I

support rescuing Astra, obviously, the fae girl can do it on her own."

She looks down, sits at the edge of the bed, then looks at me. "Fae can't make deals with us. I know. But they can and will repay favors. I'd rather be useful to them than sit here like a useless burden."

"Like me, you mean?"

She shakes her head, her hair flowing with the movement. "You're hurt. I'm not."

Tarlia's so pretty that I almost lose track of my thoughts, then I recall she's about to step into an enemy castle as an impostor, and insist, "It's an unnecessary risk."

"It's for Astra. And for me, for you. Like I said, I'll feel safer knowing I can be useful to them. You'll be safer too."

"I can take care of myself."

"True." She bites her lip, then says, "Once you're better, you could go to a human kingdom. They'd harbor you."

Me. On my own. She's clearly thinking our ways are about to part. "This idea has crossed my mind—then left quickly." I chuckle. "They would do it for a price."

"At least you're worth something." Her laugh is jagged and cutting, and then she stares at me, unspoken words suspended in her eyes.

"My head is also worth something, and therein lies the problem."

"I know." She still stares at me, as if a question hung between us.

I can't evade the topic anymore and decide to be direct. "What you said in the carriage. Did you mean it?"

Her tone shifts. "I said lots of things. You'll have to be specific."

Of course she knows exactly what I'm talking about. And I need to know her answer. Could I love her? Could she make me happy?

Maybe I'm still dazed, drowsy, and dizzy from the pain and

the potions, and then maybe feeling like I was born again grants me an odd boldness.

Tarlia's sitting so close. I lean over—and brush my lips on hers. She trembles at first, then wraps her arms around me, returning the kiss with sweet, inviting eagerness.

I'm kissing Tarlia, kissing those lovely, luscious lips. My hands trail down her body, caressing her shoulders, her arms, then moving to her legs. I want to feel more of her skin, touch her entire body, so I move a hand up her stomach and finally cup her firm, lovely breast. I'm rewarded with a delicious moan and her small, delicate hands moving to my chest.

I kiss and caress her as our bodies intertwine, kiss her as I push her down onto the mattress and feel her body under mine.

A grunt of pleasure escapes my throat as her hand reaches down my trousers. Amazing hand, sending ripples of pleasure through my entire body, her grip just right. Perfect grip. Gorgeous, sexy Tarlia.

I want her now, on a borrowed bed. I've wanted her for a long time.

As I lean back to remove my shirt, our eyes meet.

What I see in hers stuns and terrifies me; those are adoring, loving eyes. Tarlia's giving me a look that I can't correspond. I can't. And then I realize it: I'm consumed with lust. Pure, plain lust. I cannot look at her in the same way she looks at me, cannot tell her the three words she told me. I like her as a friend, sure. I'd love to fuck her, no doubt—but that's where it ends.

And if she's my friend, I can't deceive her.

Carefully, I push her hand. My cock wants to murder me.

Keeping my voice as gentle as possible, I say, "Maybe we shouldn't."

Tarlia looks confused for a moment but then glares at me, her eyes like arrows ready to be nocked. "You started it."

"I know. And this is amazing. You're gorgeous." I sit up and point at her incredible body. "It's a dream, any man's dream to have you."

"But?" She raises her eyebrows and sits as well.

"I..." A nervous chuckle escapes me, and now I see murder in her eyes. I take a deep breath. "I want it to mean something when it happens. And your words in the carriage..."

I love you. If I wanted an answer, I found it. I don't feel the same, and it's not even that I'm jealous of *a certain fae king*. I'm not in love with her, and I don't know if I'll ever be.

"I might have exaggerated," she says quickly. "I was taken by the moment. Didn't mean it."

"Fair, but then... Why? What were we doing?"

Tarlia crosses her arms and tilts her head. "Oh, poor little baby. I guess nobody explained it to you." Her voice is mocking and high and ridiculous. "When people are attracted to each other, they kiss, then do more than kiss..."

"But that's the problem, Tarlia. I wouldn't make love to you. Not now, at least."

"Oh. Did I ask you to marry me?" Her eyes are narrowed and her voice is shrill.

"No." I sit at the edge of the bed. "But I don't want to hurt your feelings."

She chuckles and rolls her eyes. "You're not the only one who almost died. You think I don't deserve to live in the moment?"

"You do. There's nothing wrong with that. But if it means more to you than to me... It's wrong."

"Incredible excuse." She snorts.

I stare at her. "Tarlia, I want you to know that I like you. You're kind, smart, funny." I'm not sure what I'm trying to say. "You're so much more than just your body."

"Do you think I can walk around as a disembodied entity?" She points at herself. "This is me. Who I am. And this part of me has wants and needs too, just like you. I'm not trying to make you love me, Ziven. I just wanted a pleasant moment."

"Did you really want us to use each other for a quick release?"

She gets up. "You don't know what it's like. What it's like to live with the man who murdered your family. To wonder when they'll kill you."

That doesn't make sense. "You're literally describing my life."

"Fair." She crosses her arms. "But at least nobody's training you to one day warm a stranger's bed. Not even my body belongs to me. Why would you blame me for using it while I can? Using it before it's given to some creepy old king?"

Now I have to laugh. "Oh, yes. I heard exactly how much you dreaded the possibility."

"The possibility of marrying a handsome, young king. Yes, I cherished that, since they prepared me for much worse. The chance of maybe acquiring some tiny bit of power, to enact my revenge. Every day of my life, I considered the ways I could murder Otavio. Hoped for the day I could do it. Every day. But maybe I was a coward because I didn't want to jeopardize my safety."

I know how much she despises her master, and feel bad for her. "I'm sorry."

"I don't want your pity. I just wanted your body, but I don't even want that anymore."

"You deserve more, Tarlia. You deserve someone who loves you."

"Love is stupid."

"You deserve it. And you'll find it."

She walks to the door. "Maybe I should try to snag that fae king after all."

I get up and approach her. Suddenly I understand why she agreed with such a dangerous plan. I was a dimwit not to have realized it. "Is that what you're doing? Why you're going to the castle? To seduce the fae king?"

"What if I am? Do you have a problem with that?"

I don't know if she's serious or trying to irk me. "I hope you're not delusional. The fae king would never fall for you."

Anger flashes in her eyes. "Right. I'm unlovable and worthless."

"Your worth is your worth. If people fail to see it, it's their problem."

"*You* fail to see it. And you're wrong, Ziven."

Before I can reply, she opens the door and dashes down the steepest and narrowest wooden stairs I've ever seen. I want to follow her, but my legs wobble and I step back, my vision suddenly blurry. I'm still tired, that's all. *Overused my magic*, they said. Useless magic, if it fails on the very day I need it.

Everything is so pointless. I like Tarlia. If I didn't like her, I'd gladly take what she was offering—but I think she deserves more. Why did my words come out so wrong? Now she probably hates me.

And then, I still have that eerie feeling that I'll never see her again. And we parted like that. But I'm too dizzy and tired to follow her, and she's now going on a dangerous mission to a strange castle, where her life will be in danger.

I wish I could love her so much that I would be able to stop her, wish I could love her so much that we'd be too busy making love and she wouldn't want to leave this room.

I wish I could love someone, wish I could feel something, wish I knew where my life's taking me.

For now, back to bed, before I fall on the floor.

TARLIA

Tears are trying to burst through, but I swallow them. Now they're solidifying into a stone blocking my throat as I descend the stairs. What's the sadness for? I knew Ziven and I would never be anything. I've always known I had no chance with him. And yet I can still taste my momentary illusion that the world was upside down.

Or was I trying to catch lightning and make the most of a moment I knew wouldn't last?

Why did he start it? Did he want to break my heart? Tease me then leave me hanging? Prove a point?

Of course he wants nothing with me. And yet perhaps I thought... we could spend some moments together, but no. Oh, no. He doesn't want me.

Not only that, he thinks nobody will ever love me. What an idiot. A truthful idiot. What a jagged dagger truth is.

Downstairs, Lidiane, Nelsin, and Ferer sit around the table. This is Nelsin's house, a cute, warm cottage in a fae village. I have no idea what the village looks like, or even what it sounds like, since the windows and walls are enchanted with acoustic blocking to give us privacy.

I wish I could walk down these fae streets, but a human here would attract too much attention, and that's the last thing we want.

We came straight into this kitchen, traveling through a magic circle, Ferer and Nelsin carrying Ziven, who took forever to wake up. After that, Ferer picked up some of Astra's belongings, and I was able to dye my hair black. It's odd to look at myself in the mirror and see my hair any color other than the burgundy I'm used to, but at least this means less glamour for Lidiane, which will make things easier when we head to the castle.

We'll leave right before sunset.

I take a deep breath. I'm going to a fae castle!

I want to pinch myself. Perhaps if I do it hard enough, I'll smarten up, gain some sense of self-preservation, and quit this stupid plan. But then, what would I preserve myself for? I'm not a piece of meat—and have no future ahead of me.

They turn to me as I approach the table, and worry replaces the sparkle in Lidiane's eyes. "Something wrong?"

Is my almost-crying face that obvious? I shrug. "Goodbyes are hard."

Ferer frowns. "Hang on. How long are you planning on staying in that castle?" The question is directed at his sister.

"One, two days. Who knows?" She lifts a shoulder. "Until Marlak and Astra are safe."

He rubs his eyebrows and asks, "What if it takes longer?"

"We'll be careful," she says. "And we'll leave the castle when it's safe."

"Leave with Astra," Ferer suggests.

Lidiane shakes her head. "They might notice she's missing and raise the alarm. Then the *three* of us will be in danger."

This is probably the third or fourth time she's explaining her rationale, and I admire her patience, even if I also understand her brother's caution.

He crosses his arms. "And when you leave the castle, they'll notice Astra's missing."

"Yes, and they'll look for Astra, not Tarlia, not me." Her voice is soothing, as if her tone, in itself, could appease her brother.

I doubt he'll stop worrying, and I can't blame him. We are about to step into an enemy castle. Strangely, the idea of facing possible dangers doesn't discourage me. On the contrary, I feel a thrill of excitement, anticipation. I want to deceive the king, want to rescue Astra, want to use some of those stupid skills I honed all my life.

And then, I want to leave this cottage, Ziven, and what happened upstairs behind.

I even wish I could seduce the fae king, just to prove that I can. I know I can, if I set my mind to it. Unfortunately, I doubt I can seduce anyone in just one night.

Ferer shakes his head. "I don't like it."

The tension in the kitchen feels like a thick, heavy mist.

Lidiane taps her fingers on the table, then takes a sheet of paper out of her bag. "I'll show you something that... should be a secret."

She's looking at Ferer and Nelsin, but glances at me quickly. She then focuses on her brother and pulls back the paper. "I can tell you how I know where Astra is, but you need to promise you won't stop me from going to the castle, and won't interfere, no matter what happens."

Ferer observes the paper in her hand, his eyes wide. "*No matter what* is too broad. If they take you hostage, am I supposed to wait here twiddling my fingers?"

She sighs. "Don't interfere unless…" She looks at Nelsin. "*He* agrees it's necessary."

Nelsin's cat ears perk up, and he points at himself, clearly rattled. "Me?"

"Yes, you," Lidiane says. "Because you won't treat me like a baby sister—I hope."

Nelsin, whose skin is already fair, gets even paler, and turns to Ferer. "I care about her safety. You know that."

Ferer exhales and his body relaxes. "I'll trust you." He glances at his sister. "Trust you both." Finally, he seems to notice me. "You all." He turns to Lidiane again. "Show us what you have."

"I told you I worked at the Owl Inn's kitchen, right? Well…" She bites her lower lip, mischief in her eyes. "I wasn't exactly cooking. They needed someone good at undoing glamours, someone who could swear to keep things secret." She shows the paper. "This is a transcending note. Somebody writes on one end, and we read it here. This is from the Crystal Castle. There's an informant there."

Nelsin and Ferer stare at her with their jaws dropped, and Nelsin asks, "Do you know who it is?"

"Nobody knows. And the information…" She pauses. "Is not always the most useful."

"How come it's in your hands now?"

She giggles. "I borrowed it." The two fae don't look impressed, and she adds, "Look, I have reason to believe that the fae reading it were connected to the *Nether Court*."

Something in her tone and the reaction of the two fae suggest this is a fearsome, dangerous court.

"What's the Nether Court?" I ask.

"It's not a real court in the sense we know," Lidiane

explains. "It's one of the smaller courts, but I think their line ended or something, not without vowing to destroy the Crystal Court. Now, it's the name used for some scattered groups fighting for us, lower fae."

I'm confused. "Isn't fighting for the lower fae a good thing?"

"Destroying the Crystal Court, for them, means destroying its *entire family*."

Her emphasis on these last words should mean something, but I don't quite get it. But then... Oh. "That includes Prince Marlak? They'd like to see him dead?"

Lidiane nods. "Exactly. So, just to be safe, I decided to keep the note with me, and replaced it with a replica. I still pass them information. Most of the time it's useless, and hasn't yet threatened Marlak."

I swallow. "So both King Renel and his enemies want Marlak dead?"

"Renel can't kill Marlak or cause his death," Lidiane says. "But everyone else can."

A horrible thought occurs to me. "I bet they'd love to get their hands on Astra. And if Renel can't kill Marlak, but if he has his wife, he could..." Horrific images of torture flood my mind.

Nelsin waves his hands. "And that's why we need to rescue her."

Lidiane raises the paper. "The note says she's unharmed and that Renel might have some interest in her."

"It could be a trap." Ferer raises an eyebrow. "An anonymous informant?"

"It could be, of course," Lidiane says. "But I'm more inclined to think it's someone trying to do what they can."

Nelsin stares at the note. "Did it say anything about Marlak?"

Lidiane purses her lips and shakes her head. "Nothing at all. But I'm not surprised. The information they send is... mundane. Ins and outs. Maps. It must be someone who works in the castle, but doesn't have any access to Renel or the Council, you know? It's as if they are reporting the little they see, but from a very restricted vantage point. They're trying to do as much as they can." There's a note of admiration in her tone.

"But they knew about Astra," Nelsin says.

"I'm not sure how much. They said it was a human guest, so they probably don't know who she is. It's part of their strategy of mentioning bits and pieces, as if they don't know what can be useful."

Ferer glares at her. "Were you planning to keep this transcending note a secret from us?"

"Well, you think I can't help, think you're the only one who can be the glorious knight. Of course I wasn't going to share *my* findings." She takes a deep breath. "But maybe we can all work together. I'll leave this with you as a token of my trust. You need to touch the paper to reveal the writing, but I'm sure you can do it."

Ferer takes it. "How do I know when there's a message?"

"The paper gets a little darker," she says.

Ferer lifts the paper and stares at it. "So if they capture a fae intruder and a human impostor, I suppose I'll read about it."

She gives him a cheeky grin. "You have to hope they'll deem it either important or mundane enough to inform you."

He glares at her. "Is that how you mean to comfort me?"

"I'll be all right," she says. "Trust me."

Trust me. Her words uncover a well of feelings.

I've never had anyone protecting me, let alone *overprotecting* me, so I can't exactly imagine how she feels, and yet, in my eyes, her plea is clear: *consider me your equal.*

Ferer walks around the table and wraps his arms around his sister. "I'll trust you, even if I wish you would never get involved in any of this." He then breaks the hug and faces her. "No more secrets, all right? No need to go around stealing transcending notes behind my back, you little traitor. Next time, let me help you."

There's so much relief in her warm chuckle. "I will." Then she adds, "Also, I never told you about the note before because it never mentioned Marlak. And I am telling you about Astra."

Nelsin then looks around. "It's almost sunset. You'd better leave soon."

Ferer turns to him. "Perhaps you could take them. Your transcending is better than mine."

The cat-eared fae widens his eyes but then nods. "Fair." He looks at me and Lidiane. "Ready?"

Like, now? Now? We aren't even wearing the capes. True that the first step is just to get close to the castle.

Now.

I feel as if a thousand little ants are walking on my back.

"I'm ready, yes," I say, all my remaining confidence going into my smile.

Lidiane grabs her purse with the capes, and Nelsin gestures for us to go to the corner of the kitchen.

We're about to transcend again, and I hope this time I don't feel like puking.

I'm about to take Lidiane's hand, when I hear a voice.

"Wait." Ziven is at the bottom of the stairs, holding onto the wall. He's still pale, and his hair is a messy bird's nest, and yet my heart almost flips seeing him so vulnerable.

That said, he was strong enough to humiliate me a few minutes ago.

His eyes are focused on me now and tell me a different story. He breaches the distance between us and holds my hands. I wish I had the strength to push him away, but I'm too stunned to move. In reality, I feel above the clouds. Any crumb of his affection is enough to make my mind spin tales of eternal love and happy endings.

He's still staring at me, as if my tales were all true. "We'll talk, Tarlia. When you come back." He squeezes my hand. "We'll..." His chest moves up and down slowly. "Talk," he repeats, but this time the word is an entire story about to be solved, a book to be finished. "Come back. And don't do anything foolish."

I'm still bitter about his rejection, so I pull my hands, even if

I smile at him. "No foolish plans. And of course I'm coming back."

He kisses my cheek, quickly, as if he just decided to do that, as if it was a strong demonstration of... something. "Come back, Tarlia. Come back to... this house."

Lidiane steps between me and Ziven. "That's the plan." Her tone is stiff, as if annoyed. "And you should rest now."

He gives her a lazy, playful smile. A drunk Ziven smile. "That's my plan. I'll be resting." He looks at me. "And waiting."

She waves her hand as if scaring away a fly. "Yes. Go to bed." That's an incredibly rude way to treat a prince, but then, he's not her prince.

Ziven puts a hand on his chest. "I love beds."

Lidiane holds my hand and Nelsin's, then says, "Let's go."

I feel Nelsin's hand wrapping around mine, and then the world swirls while my organs twist inside me. Everything dark, except for the image in my mind; Ziven, staring at me.

When that odd darkness stops, we're at the margin of a brook, in the middle of a forest.

Her reaction puzzled me, so I ask, "You don't like Ziven?"

"I don't know him, but I do know all about men saying *maybe*. Come back and we'll *maybe*. Giving you just enough hope so you might still be an option for him."

The truth of her words stirs my stomach some more, but I try to ask something else. "Do fae do that too?"

"Sometimes."

Nelsin glares at her. "I don't see the issue with *maybe*. Sometimes people need to think."

Lidiane huffs. "I don't mean my brother. He loves you."

"Really?" His cat ears perk up so much that he almost looks like a rabbit. "You think that?"

She rolls her eyes. "It's obvious. Meanwhile, the human prince pretty face is just trying to make sure she doesn't forget him."

I don't have a response to that.

I'm glad when Nelsin says, "Which is fair, if he's still considering her."

"Nah." Lidiane turns to me. "Are you two together?"

Her question makes me queasy, but I say the truth, "We're just friends."

"People don't look at friends like you look at him. Meanwhile, he's all…" She places a finger on her cheek. "*Let me think.* He promised you *nothing*. Absolutely *nothing*."

It's true. But it's not like she's revealing some ancient secret. "I know. I know these things. I'm not stupid. I don't think I'll come back and he'll…" A lump constricts my throat. "Declare his love."

"I know you know." Her tone is still ferocious. "But I'm still annoyed on your behalf."

Does she care? Are we friends? I don't know how to ask any of that, so I just nod. "Right."

Nelsin eyes her attentively. "Hmmm. It all sounds like it reached close to your heart, didn't it? Recalling past experiences?"

She scrunches her face. "I'm not going to discuss my love life with my brother's beloved."

"We broke up!" His cat years move down, hiding in his hair.

"He's just upset," Lidiane says. "And he'll forgive you."

I should remain silent, but they're too nosy for me to repay them with nonchalance. "I love how you two talk as if I wasn't here."

"True!" Strangely, she sounds delighted. "You don't know the story! We still have to walk for some time. We can tell you."

"For now," Nelsin says. "We'll soon need to be quiet."

"Obviously," she says. "You can still tell her your story—unless you want me to do that for you."

He narrows his eyes. "Oh, you know all about it?"

"Yes, my brother told me. You broke his heart, Nelsin."

"*I* broke his heart?" He snorts. "You have to be kidding me."

Her eyes are mischievous. "I'm assuming your version will

be different from his. Go on. I'm curious. And enlighten our friend Tarlia."

Our friend. Why does my heart warm hearing these words? I laugh. "Yes, don't leave me here trying to piece stories based on random bits of conversation."

"I'll tell you as much as I can." He then turns to Lidiane. "And you'll tell us about the mysterious flaky fae who broke *your* heart."

She laughs. "Nah, didn't break it. Just strengthened it." Then she adds in a lower voice, "But don't tell my brother."

Nelsin has a mischievous grin. "Who was it?"

"You go first."

He raises his arms. "What's there to tell? Ferer is my soulmate. I know it."

"How do you know it?" I ask.

His face has a dreamy expression. "The moment I saw him. Each person sees it differently. If you're wondering if you'll recognize your soulmate, you'll know it when you know it."

Could Ziven be it? Oh, wow, delusional Tarlia. And Nelsin's answer is anything but helpful. "What if I never know it?"

He shrugs. "Then there's no soulmate for you."

"That's depressing." Why do I have the feeling that's going to be my fate?

Lidiane clicks her tongue. "It's not bad. You can still find love, and you can do other things, focus on yourself. Eventually, you'll meet your person in some other life."

"Exactly, it's not bad," Nelsin says. "I suppose. Meeting your soulmate can be painful in its own right. Anyway, I've been with Ferer for two years now, and I volunteered to help Marlak when he did, so we would still be together. Then, one day, I was trying to be helpful and traveled with Astra, but we were attacked." His shoulders shrink. "Ferer thinks what I did was dishonorable and shameful and doesn't want to talk to me."

That doesn't sound right. "He spoke to you just now."

"Only the necessary." He turns to Lidiane. "What did *he* say?"

"I suppose your stories match, Nelsin, but he also mentioned that you and Astra almost died, she got unconscious for two days, and your *traveling* with her was an act of treason."

Nelsin shrugs. "Sometimes rules don't make sense, you know?"

"Honor is very important for my brother. He needs to trust you again, but letting you guide us is already a sign of trust, so be patient."

"Really?" Nelsin's grin is the type of silly, happy grin that can wash away any worry.

Lidiane chuckles. "Really, Nelsin. It will all turn out fine in the end."

"What about *your* story?" I ask her.

She sighs. "Larjax claims he's the leader of the Nether Court."

"Larjax? I didn't know he was a royal." Nelsin stares at her wide-eyed, while I'm here wondering what kind of evil parents gave that name to a kid.

"He isn't, but who's going to complain when the court is gone? He still leads a small group trying to bring down the Crystal Court."

"You were involved with him?" Nelsin asks in disbelief.

She narrows her eyes. "You're not helping, you know? Anyway, yes, I was."

Nelsin chuckles. "Ferer would have a seizure or something."

"And why he will never, ever learn about this," she says. "It sounded exciting, romantic, adventurous. I know Larjax doesn't like Marlak, but I thought he meant well."

"He doesn't mean well?" Nelsin asks.

"No. He's self-serving. It's not that he thinks Marlak would be bad for the Crystal Court, but that he would like to take the power for himself."

"That's dangerous," I say.

"No." She waves a hand. "He's pathetic, actually. He boasts more than he does—concerning *everything*. And he has a bunch of lovers."

I can feel the hurt buried beneath her casual tone. "I'm sorry."

"No need to be sorry. He was a sign, I think. What I saw in him was passion, courage, a commitment to making the world better—and I fell in love with that. Love, I know. Stupid. He's none of what I saw in him, and yet I realized that if I really love those qualities, I could embody them—and love myself, not that I didn't love before, but I had never thought about being in a romantic relationship with myself, and then suddenly I did, and now I'm in love with someone who won't let me down."

"That makes sense." Nelsin looks up, thoughtful. "And the sex tends to be great. Good call, little sister."

"Right?" She smiles.

Are they really talking about *self-love* that nonchalantly? But I disagree with her. "I don't think you truly have sex with yourself." They give me pitiful looks, and I feel I have to clarify what I mean. "There's someone else in your thoughts. It might not be one specific person, it can be like a formless idea, but there's someone else. At least for me."

"Sexy formless blob?" Lidiane says. "I suppose. Still my own blob. No, wait, I'm certain that Larjax only has sex with himself, and thinking about himself. All the time, even when he has someone else on his bed."

Nelsin grimaces. "What a dreadful lover."

Lidiane nods. "I must confess it took me a while to notice how bad he was. It's embarrassing. But I think I had this idea in my head... Well, if I'm going to sleep with my own imagination, why not Formless Blob?"

Nelsin and I laugh. Obviously. We all have our blobs. No. Lately Ziven's the one who's been in my mind, as pathetic as it may seem. I bet Nelsin thinks about Ferer.

Lidiane snorts. "But Larjax is not dangerous, no. His group has few fae and they're disorganized. The only thing he did was promise a prize for whoever brings him Renel's head."

Those words catch my attention. "What prize?"

She laughs. "Two thousand swans. Ridiculous, right?"

Her words make me tremble. Two thousand golden swans. I could run away and live happily until the end of my days.

"Can he pay that?" I try to keep my voice casual.

Lidiane shrugs. "I suppose. His family owns some taverns, and he promised it. Fae can't break their word."

My head is turning, thinking. No. It can't be that easy. "How come nobody has killed Renel yet? For the prize?"

She has a light chuckle as if the idea was ridiculous. "Killing the acting king is a little hard, you know? Many fae have sworn oaths to him, and we can't break oaths. The castle protects him, and he's usually surrounded by tons of guards—or his powerful knight."

"Would you kill him?" I ask.

"I can't. I have strong reasons to believe that he has a deal with Marlak; if one of them kills or causes the other's death, he'll also die. If I kill Renel, considering I know Marlak, that could count as his fault. And I don't want that stupid prize."

But I do.

And I barely know Marlak, so killing Renel wouldn't cause his death.

If Lidiane got that enchanted paper at the Owl Inn, this rebel leader must live in the area, or have contacts there. I can find an inn. My heart is accelerating in my chest. Murder is bad, sure, but if Renel is evil, and if I can earn enough to guarantee my freedom...

Can I do it? Will I have an opportunity to kill him?

I decide to focus on one thing at a time. Rescuing Astra and pretending to be her will be quite dangerous on its own, even without trying to kill anyone.

And then, if the opportunity arises... I'll guarantee my future.

7

ASTRA

Salt. The priestess said it could protect against evil spirits. I'm thinking—or hoping—it can also block magic.

I couldn't believe that Otavio left me alone and could believe even less when one of my guards brought me some salt. Now I'm rinsing my hair with salt water. I think my master would go berserk if he saw it, but if everything goes according to plan, he'll never see it.

In fact, I hope he never sees my hair again.

Why does my heart feel like a paper I'm crumpling? A paper like all the pages in the many books I read. A page in the life I lived, in all the useless knowledge I gained. Crumpled. Left behind.

I take a deep breath, the light smell of salt strangely assaulting my nose. It's like leaving a part of me behind.

Onward to a new page. I don't want to be a tool anymore.

And that is why I can't risk Otavio using my hair coloring to locate me. How did he even do that? Was it Tiurian magic? Some kind of dark magic? Or just some odd property of whatever ingredient he put in the lotion?

No, there's no ingredient that will let anyone locate you

from so far away. How much magic does he have? How much magic has he never told me about? I wish he could tell me everything he can about my power, my people, and yet wishes won't make any of that true.

I have to leave. And save Marlak.

The hill in front of my window has a castle-shaped, triangular shadow on it, as the sun lowers on the other side. Soon we'll reach that in-between moment when it's not day or night, when the eyes haven't gotten used to the dark, when things aren't yet silent. That moment when shadows are longer and stark.

This is something I learned in the Elite Tower, under Otavio's instructions. At night, sounds spread further and guards are more alert, not to mention the overbearing silence, so it's the worst time to try to sneak in and out of anywhere. Sunset and sunrise, on the other hand, are the ripe time for thieves, intruders, and fugitives. Otavio would know that's when I'd try to escape, but I doubt the thought would even crosses his mind. Still, just to be sure, I want to be far away when the sun kisses the horizon. Far away, before Otavio realizes I'm no longer his puppet.

No time for regrets, not even time to think much.

I checked the walls of the castle. While they might be smoother than Krastel's, they still have gaps that will let me climb down.

Once on the ground, I'll find a river.

As far as plans go, this is bold and dubious, but I don't want to spend even a night here, not when I saw where Marlak is being held, when I can do something to rescue him.

The first step is to find Nelsin and Ferer. They'll know what to do.

Nelsin's playful face comes to mind, as well as Ferer's focused, thoughtful demeanor. Do they know I'm here? Would they try to rescue me? I don't want them doing anything foolish, and that's another reason why I need to leave.

I take one last glance inside, at this fancy room that doesn't belong to me. I'm wearing the leggings, blouse, and shoes made for me by Irene—comfortable clothes that will let me move freely, or at least as freely as I can.

My only other possession here is the sword that's too far from my reach. I won't get sentimental about it. A sword can be replaced, even a legendary sword.

With no regrets, I sit on the windowsill and find a place to put my foot. A cold chill raises the hairs on my skin. The gap is not deep. With a deep breath, I hold on to the ledge and let my other foot search for another opening. A sigh of relief escapes my lungs. This one is deeper and comfortable enough for a safe descent. My hand then searches for a place to hold below the window—a thin fissure, not enough to hold my weight, but enough to give support to the other limbs.

Slowly, I descend, making sure I always have at least one foot and one hand secured to the wall. Hanging precariously like this, I feel as if this is an interminable precipice, a wondrous, horrific height. No. With a steadying breath, I calm down.

Regardless of the height I have to climb or descend, all my focus should be on where to put my hands and feet next. That's it.

And that's what I do. Still, for some horrifying seconds, I fear there's nowhere to grab, and during other seconds all I want is to return to the castle and concoct a better plan, but there's so much wall between me and my window that going back would mean more dangerous climbing, just in another direction. At this point, down is my only option.

All of Marlak's magic within me is gone. I can no longer sense even a spark of his magnificent power, even a sliver of it, and I regret not having tried to escape earlier. Well, earlier I was being watched by Otavio.

I'm searching for a gap with my left foot, still too high above the ground for my heart to beat normally, when I sense something shaking. Shit. Was that an impression? Another tremor, and I press my body against the wall. This is either an earthquake—or the castle's about to move.

Right. Moving castle, Astra. What kind of dingbat tries to scale the walls of a moving castle?

This is the time to call for the Almighty Mother and her light, even if I don't know what it can do. Perhaps it's time to ask for forgiveness for being such an imbecile.

But I don't have time to do that. Another tremor hits, and it's accompanied by such a strong gust of wind that my poorly placed feet lose their hold on the stone. I try to put them back, but I'm only hanging by my arms when another windblast throws me off balance, and I find myself sliding down the wall, trying desperately to slow my descent and find a gap for my feet or hands.

That's when another gust hits me like a huge hand slapping me, pushing me away from the wall.

In free fall.

The sky is dark above me while I feel my body accelerating towards the ground.

I think about light. Love. Magic.

Magic. I reach for the tiniest trace of Marlak's magic, trying to control the air below me, trying to slow me down.

But I can't feel it. Can't feel anything other than regret.

And yet I haven't yet reached the ground. All that wind is not letting me fall, at least not as fast. So much wind—and then I stop.

Did I... did I connect with Marlak's magic?

I feel my body moving up. This is too precise, too controlled. It isn't me.

While I'm grateful, so grateful that I'm not going to kiss the ground, I don't know who's pulling me, what they want, or what price they'll ask for saving me.

Air moves fast below me, tickling my back, and I relax, wondering if it makes a difference like it does in the water. I relax as I feel myself pulled through an open window, relax as my body enters a bedroom, and then I finally fall on hardwood floor.

I'm alive. Alive. My heart accelerates, not in fear, but in celebration, as I take in my surroundings. It's a small bedroom with plain walls and a single bed with a simple wooden frame. I'm wondering who pulled me in, when a man steps out of a shadow.

He has long, blond hair and wears a black hat with a wide brim and an embroidered green waistcoat. I can see just a glimpse of the tip of a fae ear on his right side. Only when he approaches me, do I recognize him.

Azur. Azur, but his countenance is so different. At the coronation, he looked like a human courtier, despite his pointy ears. My stomach recoils as I recall the disgusting words he told Marlak, telling him he wanted a taste of his wife. A thousand times yuck.

In the sanctuary... I was so stressed that I don't even remember much of what he looked like, but he seemed cruel—needlessly cruel and gloating.

Now, he looks calm and mildly curious.

Regardless, this is Renel's number one man—and I'm in trouble.

MARLAK

P atience. I always thought it was one of my noblest qualities, allowing me to remain steadfast in my darkest hours, and yet now that I'm locked here, the wish to break these bars and destroy this prison is stronger than ever.

Renel has Astra. *Azur* has Astra. A great reason to escape and get her out of that castle. Also a great reason to wait and only make a move once I know she's safe.

I sit on the packed earth table and rest my face on my

hand. There are other fears gnawing at me. These are the Shadow Lands, where monsters roam free. Giants are the mildest of them. Ghouls, ghosts, and sand sprites roam these plains. Soulsuckers can feed on fear and drive a person insane.

Maybe the walls of this prison keep them out, maybe there's enough magic to repel the horrors of the Shadow Lands. And then again, maybe not.

Would Renel risk his own life imprisoning me in a place where I could be killed? Or does he think that it won't count if it's something else that kills me? Is he expecting me to escape and die in the desert? *That* would be my own fault—and would cause him no harm.

Can my subdued magic even break these walls? There's so much air around me, and my connection with it, while weak, is still there. I think I could damage the walls, yes, then run.

Right. In the desert of the Shadow Lands, to face monsters when all I have is one tenth of my magic.

While Renel has Astra. An ember of fury burns in my chest.

The wall cracks.

Horror seizes my heart. Is my magic getting out of control again? Even with the dark metal cuffs?

When the wall breaks, I don't know if I'm relieved or troubled. I'm not the one who broke it. Actually, I'm definitely troubled.

Something's here. Something's about to catch me.

ASTRA

Azur stares at me, all his cruelty hidden under a mask of mild curiosity.

Did he save me? Or did he push me and blow me off the wall so he could bring me inside? His air magic is deadly and incredibly powerful, if he could pull me as if I were a leaf.

Waiting for him to break the silence is getting on my nerves, so I wave. "Hey. Fancy seeing you here."

He raises an eyebrow and glances at the window and back at me. "Fancy seeing you falling. What exactly were you trying to achieve?"

"Now? Or before? Now, it was obviously holding onto the wall. Before, well, the view is pretty."

He tilts his head as if seeing me from a different angle will make my explanation make sense. "So you had to go *outside*?"

I almost lie that I was just by the window and slipped, but it won't be convincing, considering I climbed down so much.

I shrug and smile. "I like the wind on my face, the air from the outdoors." This is absolutely ridiculous as far as explanations go, but at least it's something. I won't elaborate because long explanations tend to sound suspicious.

"Were you trying to escape?" His tone is neutral, oddly neutral, with no anger or accusation in it.

I feign shock and confusion, as if the question was absurd. "Why would I? I'm not even a prisoner."

His fingers brush his chin. "So you decided to climb the walls of a moving castle for fun?"

"I was just outside my window. Not sure what happened."

With two steps, he breaches the distance between us, then leans down so that his nose is only a palm away from mine. "I saved your life, Astra. This is what happened."

That would mean an incredible debt. "I was doing fine, actually."

He steps away, thankfully, then snorts as if amused. "Don't worry. The treaty doesn't allow humans to owe us anything. So there's no need to repay the favor. Or even thank me. Not that you were going to do that, of course."

"I was fine. Fresh air and all."

His chuckle is amused and surprisingly not as chilly as I expected. Then he stares at me, a smirk on his face. "I don't know what you were doing, but if *I* wanted to escape, I'd take the servants' exit. The main rotation is right after sunset. We watch carefully who comes in, but not who goes out, so if you're dressed like them, nobody will notice you."

I blink, unsure what his goal is, and if it's some trap. "And you think I'm going to follow your instructions?"

He spreads his arms and grimaces. "Didn't you just say you don't want to escape? Why would I think you'd do that? I'm making conversation."

"Oh, yes, it's so normal to tell people how to do something they don't plan on doing."

"It makes more sense than climbing down the castle walls." He stares at me with a raised eyebrow. "How did you hold on for so long?"

"I was fine until the tremors started. What was that?"

There's a mocking edge to his smirk. "Perhaps you were tickling the castle."

"Wait. Is it going to move?"

"Perhaps." He fiddles with a blond strand of his hair, as if uninterested. "It's prone to do that, which is one more reason you should appreciate the view while *inside*."

"Yes. Great advice." I smile at him and walk to the door, but then he steps in front of me.

"Nah-ah. Not so fast. I'll escort you back to your room."

"Like a prisoner?"

"Like a clueless visitor who might get herself killed."

"Charming." I can't help but hate him, and there are several reasons why. His behavior at the coronation is the biggest one, and I blurt, "I heard you. Talking to Marlak. About me."

He chuckles. "Don't fret. I was just testing your husband."

"What was the result of your test?"

He pauses, blinks, then says, "My conclusions are my own."

That's quite a fae answer. While a human could say they found out nothing, for example, Azur can't lie.

I shrug. "Well, escort me to my room, then."

He raises a finger. "Careful there. I only take orders from *one* fae."

Renel, he means. I don't know how he can say that with his

chest full of pride. Also, it wasn't an order, but I don't care to contradict him. "Oh, no." I mock pretend that I'm disappointed, then smile. "I guess I'll have to walk by myself."

With that, I leave the room, sure that he'll follow me, but he stays back. Is he trying to prove a point? The idea to escort me was *his*.

I stare at the long hallway with its interminable doors. Is this the same floor as my room? I don't know. Otavio told me not to wander around the castle on my own. Is that advice for my protection? His? Perhaps I could explore and learn something but all I want to do is leave this place and find Marlak.

I still want to yell at my husband, obviously. He made such a mess of things. And hurt me, on top of that.

But I also want to kiss him, want to tell him how much he means to me, want to tell him that I love our house, that I enjoyed all our time together, that I appreciate his attentiveness, his kindness.

They might be hurting him right now.

"You're crying?" Azur's abrasive voice reaches my ears.

The answer's yes, as I feel a tear on my cheek, but I ignore all my nostalgic thoughts and smile. "This is such a beautiful castle. And I'm here."

He squints and looks in both directions. "It's... a hallway. With doors. What do the hallways look like in the human castle?"

"Similar, I'd say, just not as long. But the walls there aren't white." I can bring up the memory of being there—and strangely, it's the perfect explanation for my tears. "I spent all my life in that castle. Sometimes, I wondered if I'd ever see anything else. Well, I'm here now."

He nods. "Indeed. Would you like me to escort you to your room?"

I should tell him that I can go on my own, but the truth is that I can't. And I need to spend time planning my next move, not being lost, so I swallow my pride. "If it's not too much work."

"The hard work was pulling you through the window." He gestures with his head, pointing sideways. "Follow me."

I do as he says, and we reach a heavy wooden door. He opens it, revealing a staircase.

He turns to me. "If you go all the way down to the red door, you'll find the servants' exit."

I snort. "You truly think I want to escape."

"I'm just showing you around. Come. Your room is this way."

We climb two flights of stairs and come up at another wooden door leading to a similar but wider hallway. This is where my room is, and I see two creepy-eyed fae passing us by.

I'm curious, so I ask, "Do they even know what's happening? Or are they in a kind of trance?"

His steps stop. "Imagine being a prisoner in your own body, except that it moves."

"How do you know what it's like?"

He lifts a shoulder, then keeps going. "Heard accounts."

"Isn't it…" I was going to say *problematic*, but I don't want to antagonize my hosts, as temporary as they might be. "Is it right?" The question came out worse.

"It's the way things are." His voice is strangely void of emotion, almost eerie.

"You mean the way Renel wants things to be."

"Fae ways predate him." He looks at me. "Are you interested in learning about our laws?"

"Yes." I mean, I'd rather learn about it with Ferer and Nelsin, but I can't say that, can I? "It sounds fascinating."

He snorts. "*Fascinating*. Like a rare, exotic insect?"

"I'm not really into insects. Or arachnids." The Spider Princess comes to mind, and I want to shake that memory away.

We stop in front of a door.

"Here's your room. I might not be around to catch you if you fall, so I suggest you look at the scenery from inside. Ah, and wandering on your own is not advised either."

"I appreciate the advice."

He narrows his eyes. "You don't, do you? Liars are fascinating."

"*Fascinating.* Like a rare bird?"

Azur smirks. "One without wings."

I chuckle and enter the room.

If he weren't Renel's minion, perhaps I could tolerate him and take advantage of his goodwill to learn more about the fae. As it is, I hope he perishes with his master.

Do I, though? He might have saved my life—but might have blown me off the wall before that. His air magic is dangerous, and to make everything worse, he knows I'm trying to escape. Is he hoping I'll use the servants' exit and then catch me? Kill me? Is that red door a trap?

I don't know. But I'll need to find another way out.

TARLIA

We're silent now, walking down a hill covered by a thick forest, from where I can spot the top of the fae castle from among the canopy above us. It looks impressive, with no towers, a triangular shape, and a crystal on its very top. The walls are made from some gray, smooth stone, so that the castle itself reminds me of a crystal. It's also quite high and perched on a tall, black rock.

The building is imposing and magnificent—even for me, who grew up in the Elite Tower.

For a moment, I wonder why the castle would be built so near a forested hill, from where enemies could approach undetected, until I remember: the castle moves. But then, it means the king chose to place it here, which strikes me as odd. And then again, there's no talk of war in the fae kingdoms, so I suppose he can stick his castle wherever he wants. I think I would place it by the ocean if I could, from where I could see the foaming waves I've only ever read about.

The Crystal Court King has likely been to the sea many times, and perhaps even had this castle on a wide, sandy beach. What a neat way to travel.

"This is it," Lidiane whispers.

"What?" I ask. Not that I haven't memorized the plan, but I'm not sure which *it* she means.

Her chest moves up and down slowly, with a slight tremor —the first time I realize she's not as fearless as she looks. I wonder if *I* look fearless, not that it matters, of course.

She pulls the capes from her bag and gives me mine. "Put it on."

All my remaining worries fade the moment I put the garment on my back, comforted by the thought that I'll remain unnoticed. There's always the possibility that she overestimated her magic, but believing in it at least calms me.

My hair is tied back in a low ponytail that covers the tips of my ears. In theory, it shouldn't matter. The magic of the cape will keep anyone from noticing me, let alone checking my ears, but it doesn't hurt to be extra cautious.

Lidiane faces Nelsin. "You know what to do."

He nods. I'm not sure exactly what his part of the plan comprises, but I think he'll approach the castle shortly after us. My fault for going to Ziven's room for whatever nonsense we did.

"Good luck," I tell Nelsin.

He gives us a wide grin. "You too."

I wave goodbye and continue the descent with Lidiane, our steps careful and quiet.

Soon we're near the base of the castle.

I looked at diagrams of it a few times. The base is pure rock, except for a large atrium and a staircase in the front, and another stairwell on the back, from where servants climb up to the castle. Most of the fae nobility come from the top, using their air magic or flying carriages that land on the Royal

Terrace, a flat open area near the top of the castle. I can't see it from here and assume it's on the other side.

The more we approach the rock at the base of the castle, the larger it looks, as if it could squash me like an insect. There are no guards around it, no fence, no walls. Bizarre, but then it's possible that there's some magic protecting the castle. Will these capes work against magic? I guess we're about to find out.

The sky is getting pink above us when we reach the other side of the castle, and I finally see the entrance to the stairs we're supposed to climb. My heart jumps. It's a tiny door. Tiny. With two fae guards standing by it, wearing intricate golden armor and helmets. I assume they're high fae, not enchanted servants, but I can't be sure.

Near this area of the castle, there's a pebbled road, and further below, a village with wooden houses and some canvas tents. Lidiane told me that villages like these are built around the castle, mostly for suppliers and merchants.

Two fae leave through the door, and that's it. Nobody else coming in or out. When I agreed to come, I was imagining a large gate, like at the castle in Krastel, and that we would sneak in among some twenty, thirty people. I didn't imagine we'd be the only ones coming in or that the door would be just like a regular bedroom door.

Lidiane's steps are firm, though, and nothing in her demeanor suggests she's surprised or reconsidering her plan. I look up, wondering if climbing the walls would be safer, but the rock at the base of the castle looks quite smooth and dangerous.

On we go. I keep my steps steady but can't manage to do the same with my heart as we walk right between the two guards. Soon we're on a winding staircase, illuminated by holes in the rock and some glowstones. We're in the fae castle, or at least almost inside it.

Oh, that's a lot of stairs. I hate to think that anything Otavio ever did was right, but I don't know how long it would take me to climb this if it weren't for all that stupid physical training. Lidiane, ahead of me, isn't even panting.

Do fae ever get tired? It's a miracle they didn't squash the humans in the war, considering they have more magic than we do, they're stronger, and they don't tire as much. Even with some magic from opus stones, our strength doesn't even come close to the fae, and yet we got the River of Tears Treaty and lasting peace. That is an interesting question—for some other time. Right now, I need to focus on finding Astra and not getting caught.

We come to a red door with no guards around it. Lidiane pulls it open while I brace myself for some kind of magical intruder alert, but there's nothing. Nothing. We reach another staircase. This one is not winding, but square, wide, and beautiful, and connects the main floors of the castle.

Astra should be on the fourth floor from here, and Lidiane memorized the position of her room.

And then this could also be a trap. I feel my daggers in my pockets, just to be sure. Yay, daggers against magic. Is there any doubt which of them wins?

We leave the stairs and come upon a wide, white hallway, too refined, too polished, too empty. Sterile, eerie. A fae comes in our direction. I guess this is another test for the capes. When she approaches us, I realize her eyes are unfocused, lost. I suppose we could be jumping up and down and she wouldn't notice us.

If my memory of the map of the castle serves me right, Astra's room should be three doors down. We'll have to hope she's there—and that Otavio isn't around.

"Hold there!" a man shouts behind us.

We're in deep shit. I mean, not yet. I can pretend I'm Astra, walking around. If she's not a prisoner, it should be fine. If she's a prisoner, I suppose I'll be thrown in a cell and then they'll realize there are two of us.

I turn and see a fae with long blond hair, wearing a wide-brimmed black hat, his face so perfect that it doesn't look real. Unreal fae beauty, I suppose.

He's staring at Lidiane, who's doing the whole empty-headed expression. A bit too much, perhaps. She's practically cross-eyed.

He walks towards her in slow strides, approaching her carefully, then frowns. "You're not enchanted."

We just got caught—and I'm pretty sure Lidiane's cape's defective. The blond fae staring at her most definitely noticed her.

Lidiane's shoulders sag. "No. But I'm doing my work here."

"Not enchanted." His eyes widen. "How?" The crack in his voice sounds like desperation, but it must be anger.

I'm about to tell him to leave her, but then I see her hand by her hips, palm facing me, as if telling me not to intervene. But she can't lie. What's she going to answer?

Lidiane swallows. "I can pretend." She makes that ridiculous face again. "Nobody has noticed."

He stares at her as if she had five heads, each of them more fascinating than the other. With his mouth hanging open like that, he'll drool at any moment. Instead, he scowls.

"And where are you going?"

Lidiane lowers her head, like in a bow, and looks down. She's quite good at looking humble. "Taking a garment to the human visitor, my lord."

He blinks. "No lord. No. After you do that, come to my room."

This time, she trembles. It's subtle but not imperceptible. "I have tasks to do."

The fae man stares at her, then chuckles. "Don't we all? Finish the *task* you're doing and come right away. If I'm not in my room, wait for me."

Room. Shit. I hate this.

He leans toward her, so his face is close to hers. "Do we have a deal?"

"Yes." The smile she gives him barely disguises a snarl.

This is a problem, and our plans are already getting ruined when we just barely walked into the castle.

We turn around, but I still sense his eyes following us as we walk down the hallway. I glance back. To my relief, he finally turns and walks away, perhaps to torment a servant or to care for his pretty hair.

"Do you *have* to go?" I whisper once I'm sure we're out of earshot.

"It will be fine." Her voice carries a fake levity, almost as if she is trying to convince herself of those words.

I understand. Once she agreed with his deal, she can't back out. Being fae has many advantages, but being bound by words like that must be dreadful.

I mull over what she agreed with. "Don't finish your task."

"It will be finished once she leaves. And I can deal with him." This time, I hear a hint of her spunk and confidence. I still don't like any of this.

"Over there," she whispers.

There. Where a guard wearing golden armor stands by a door. Astra's door. We knew this was a possibility, but the sight still chills my bones. In theory, any guard wouldn't mind or notice us, but now that I know Lidiane's cape is not working, I'm not so sure.

"You could stay back," I whisper.

"We stick to the plan."

The plan. She can't be serious. It has already flopped. That said, this hallway is hardly the place to argue, and maybe there's some kind of fae magic binding her to what we agreed. I hope not. If things keep going wrong, we'll need to adapt and improvise.

We approach the door in silence. The guard doesn't even glance at us, staring straight ahead like a statue. Odd. And guards in the fae castle are not enchanted. Perhaps he just ignores servants.

As quietly as I can, I do mine and Astra's secret signal. One knock, pause, two knocks, pause, one last knock. *Please be alone.* We could use some luck.

The door opens—and Otavio stands there.

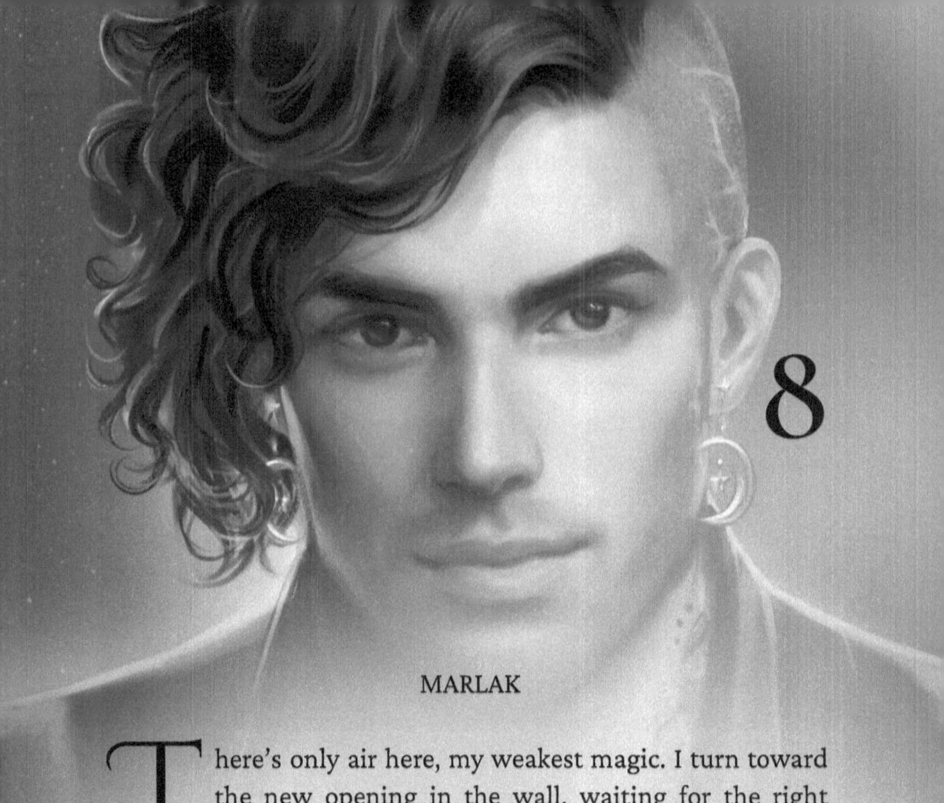

MARLAK

There's only air here, my weakest magic. I turn toward the new opening in the wall, waiting for the right opportunity to attack, and see an arm—a humongous arm.

The giants are here, or at least one of them.

I don't see why they would want to kill me, so it must be something else. "What do you want?"

The arm moves away, and a big head stares at me through the opening. "Free you."

Giants are smart, even if snobbish high fae don't think so, except that they severely lack communication skills, so I need to ask simple questions.

"In exchange for what?"

The giant frowns as if confused, and I rephrase my question. "Why? What do you want?"

"Monsters will come." He brings that enormous hand again and points at me. "Protect us."

That's a huge request—and vague. What does he mean by *monsters*? And quite strange. I mean, me, protecting giants? As much as I have strong magic, they're up to five times my size and said to have their own spells. I need to understand their request.

"What monsters?"

"Monsters. Many monsters." His voice is raspy and loud, and yet I can sense the fear in it.

His answer doesn't help much. The Shadow Lands are brimming with monsters. And then, to be honest, I wasn't even planning on escaping. But refusing a giant's favor will get me into even more problems.

"You're stronger than me," I say. "Why do you need my help?"

"New monsters. Future."

I hear a scream outside and realize this giant isn't alone, and that the longer I remain, the longer they'll have to fight. It means possible fae deaths. And now it's too late to stay in a broken cell.

I decide to make a proposal. "When monsters come, call me. If I can help, I'll help."

"We need promise."

I'm not sure if he doesn't like the conditions I imposed, or if he wants to make sure he has my oath. "It's a promise. I'll do what I can. I can't do what I can't."

"Come." The giant extends a hand, palm facing up, and I realize he wants me to climb on it.

At this point, I don't think I can explain that I had no intention of escaping, so I have no choice but to do what he asks.

The humongous hand takes me out of the cell, then out of the prison, where I can see the purple, darkening sky above us. I almost avert my eyes to avoid any carnage, but to my relief, I see no bodies. It doesn't mean no fae was killed, and doesn't mean it wasn't my fault, at least in part. I should have been more careful. I should have done so many things to avoid getting caught—but there's no point regretting.

As the giant lifts me high above the ground, I survey the area and see four more giants around the keep, two of them holding fae guards as if they were toy sticks. Neither the gate nor the outer wall were broken, and I realize that the giant who was manning it perhaps wasn't as enchanted as he seemed. A very easy victory for the giants. A chill takes over my chest as I wonder what would happen if they decided to defy the fae. We have superior magic and more weapons, but still…

At least there's strong magic keeping them north of the Shadow Hills and the Charmed River. And yet these giants fear monsters? And think I can help? Upside down world. Either they're delusional or… But giants don't have foresight as one of their powers, do they?

"Where are you taking me?" I ask.

"Near Cursed River."

His voice is still raspy, but lower now, careful. I'm not surprised he doesn't find the river keeping them north that charming, but I'm still mulling why they would ask for help from a being so much smaller than them.

"Why do you fear monsters?"

He moves his hand up and down, and I wrap my arms around his middle finger, afraid of falling.

"Earth moves," he says. "Stir things."

I don't know if he's being curt because he can't talk well or if he wants to end the subject, but I have to ask more.

"What things?" I insist.

"Old things."

For some reason, his words send a jolt of terror down my body. And again, what can giants fear?

"And you think I can defeat an ancient terror that threatens your kind?"

He pauses and brings me up so that I'm right in front of his face. "Help is help."

"Is there a way to prevent it?"

"Pushes up." He makes a gesture with his other hand. "Evil, old magic. We feel it. Only fire kill old creatures." He points at me. "Fire prince."

Fire.

A cold chill embraces my body.

I could tell him I don't wield fire, and yet I don't want him sending me back to the end of the Shadow Lands or even crushing my body. And I never promised to do anything I couldn't. Even though I'm trembling, I nod.

Above me, the sky is getting darker and darker while he runs and runs without stopping. Nights here are dangerous, and I hope to cross the Charmed River before it descends upon us, along with all the evils it conceals.

The giant stops, puts me down, then points straight ahead. "River. Near river."

I don't see anything other than bushes and small hills, but it's true that it's just a rivulet, barely with any water, and unfortunately with no nymphs, so perhaps it's not surprising I don't see it.

Still, I'd rather sound like a whiny coward than risk this place. "Can you take me closer?"

He picks me up again, walks ten steps, then puts me down. "River magic. Can't go. You can."

"I appreciate your help."

"We wait for yours." He points a finger at me, then turns around.

It feels like an accusatory finger. If they can't cross the river, how will they ask for my help? And that was the condition I imposed. Did he not understand what I said?

But then, the giants might be taken with some overzealous fear or some old superstition. Old. Like *old things*. A shiver runs down my spine.

Anyway, I'd better run before not-so-old things catch me here.

Unconcerned with what it may look like, I bolt in the direction the giant showed me, my legs moving faster and faster. While running can attract unwanted attention, it also gets me faster to my destination.

A tug of energy pulls me. Cherry Cake. I want him as far from here as possible and push him away, tell him not to come. And I run. And still see no river. I'm wondering about the giants' definition of *near*. That said, if the magic doesn't let them come closer, there was nothing he could do.

The dark cuffs still weigh me down, like heavy bags of rocks in each hand. My head hurts and I feel weak from not eating or drinking for so many hours.

And then, ahead of me, I see a wall of fire. I should be able to control it or quench it. And yet all I see is Astra, screaming for help. My sister screaming. My mother screaming. My ears are ringing and I don't know where I am anymore.

I'm falling into that horrifying pit of panic and pain.

I can't—I have to reach the river.

But

I'm

falling.

TARLIA

Otavio. My breath pauses. What a disgrace.

I look down quickly, unsure if it will make a difference.

Whenever I see him, my instinct is to tremble, part in fear, part in anger, but then I stiffen to hide that reaction, except that trembling is the least of my issues when I'm looking like Astra.

Where's my luck now? I mean, I knew there was a high possibility I'd come across him, but I wasn't expecting it to be so soon.

In a second, I know what to do. I can beg him to take me in, pretend I'm here to be Astra's substitute, claim I have nowhere else to go. I'm not sure he'll believe me, but it's the only idea that crosses my mind.

He steps aside, though, and doesn't address me.

Doesn't see me.

In disbelief, I catch a relief exhale and swallow it before it gives me away. He didn't notice me.

With a new appreciation for Lidiane's phenomenal magic, I step into the room, and she follows. Otavio doesn't ask her anything either, probably because he assumes we work in the castle. Her cape might be defective, but her disguise is working.

Then I see Astra, sitting at a dressing table, lost in thought, a green paste covering her face. I step behind her, but she doesn't notice me.

Between me and Lidiane, I'm the one who can lie, so this is my task. I make sure to make my voice sound different, and say, "Excuse me, we'd like to measure you."

I'm looking down, but sense Otavio turning to us. "Can it wait an hour?"

"I'm afraid not," I say as I stare at the ground, hoping he won't see my face. Then I add, "But it won't damage her beautiful green painting."

I know it's some kind of beauty treatment, but it's fun to pretend I'm a clueless fae who thinks it's attractive.

"It's fine," Astra says.

Otavio huffs, but steps out and closes the door.

Astra gets up and turns to face us, not a single sign of recognition on her face.

"Astra," I whisper.

She blinks, looks at me, at Lidiane, then finally her eyes widen.

"You're here!" She wraps an arm around me and another around Lidiane, bringing us all in for a hug. She then steps back, her expression full of worry, as she whispers, "Isn't it dangerous?"

"Everything is," I whisper back.

She turns to Lidiane. "Any news of Marlak?"

The fae shakes her head. "Ferer and Nelsin wanted to rescue you first. They'll tell you everything once you're away from here." No mention that they have no idea where he is.

Astra's shoulders sag, disappointment spelled on her face. "What's your plan?"

Lidiane gives her one of her capes. "This will make sure you're not noticed."

I recall then that her cape is malfunctioning, so I remove my own and hand it to Astra. "Take this instead. I'm sure this one works."

Astra takes it, and Lidiane continues, "I'll walk you down to the servants' exit."

"No." She shakes her head. "Azur knows I'm trying to escape and that's exactly what he suggested I should do. It must be a trap."

Lidiane emits a sound similar to a growl. "Azur. His magic is strange. I'll take care of him. But he barely saw Tarlia when she was wearing this cape, so it will protect you."

"You mean that blond fae?" I ask.

Lidiane nods. "Yes. But I'll deal with him."

Astra's eyes are wide. "Let's just leave and forget him."

"We're staying," I say. "So they won't notice you left."

Lidiane adds, "And I have *things* to do." She gives me a significant look, as if to warn me against telling Astra about her promise to Azur.

Well, worrying Astra would only further complicate our plans, so of course I won't say a word, even if I'm anguished for Lidiane.

Astra stares at me as if finally understanding, finally realizing I'm glamoured to look like her, but then steps back. "Otavio's here. He'll know you're not me."

"You forget I just saw him," I reply. "And walked right past him. He *thinks* he knows everything. I can trick him." In fact, I can't wait to deceive that horrible worm.

Astra's thoughtful. "And your plan is to stay here until Marlak's free?"

"Or longer." I glance at Lidiane. "I could find a way to defeat Renel."

In reality, I want an opportunity to kill him, but I don't want to confess that. The only problem is that I'll need Lidiane's glamour, and I don't think she wants to stick around.

To my surprise, the fae grins. "I knew you'd agree with that. Let's take down this false king."

We share a smile, while Astra stares at us with an open mouth. "Fair. Good. Dangerous, though, so be careful. Renel, I think he wants something, I'm not sure what. Maybe he just wants to spite his brother. I don't know. Otavio…" She pauses. "I told him I didn't see anyone, that I was kept in a hut in a small fort, and that we walked to the coronation. And…" She stares at us and bites her bottom lip. "I'm Tiurian."

A darksoul? Like the ones they claimed would steal us from our beds when we were kids? The creatures who threatened our kind for so long? But then, this is what Andrezza told me, that horrible hag. How much of it was true?

I think Astra noticed my reaction, as a flicker of disappointment crosses her eyes. Well, I'm surprised!

She continues, "Otavio knows it. He's Tiurian too. I don't know what he wants. I don't know anything. My natural hair is purple. He's been coloring it since I was a child, telling me he's the person keeping me safe."

It makes so much sense, explains so much. I always found her obedience and devotion to Otavio exaggerated, but I can see now that he trapped her because he knew her secret. I can't believe I despise him more than I already did.

She continues, "He found me because of my black hair coloring, so be careful. I don't know what he wants, only that he expects me to seduce Renel. Also, he thinks I have no magic."

That's intriguing. "Do you?"

"I'm not sure. Don't let him see your natural hair color. Your glamour…" She takes a deep breath. "Might fool Renel, but…"

"I can deal with Otavio," I insist.

"Let's go," Lidiane says. "Before he suspects anything."

Astra nods, then says, "Please leave, escape if you suspect any danger. Can you promise me that?"

Lidiane shrugs. "*Suspect any danger* is too vague of a condition for a promise, but I assure you that our self-preservation instincts are intact."

"We trained," I say. "You know that." And now I'll turn my training against the madman who trained me. The irony is delicious.

Astra looks at us. "I know you're both amazing. Let's do it, then."

We exchange our clothes quickly while Lidiane fills her in on Nelsin and his location, then Astra removes the paste from her face and applies it to mine. We need to add some water since it was already drying, but I think it looks fine.

"I'll walk her down," Lidiane says. "You stay here."

"I thought you were going to distract Azur."

She smirks. "By getting his attention while Astra's beside me. It's perfect, actually, and better than if both of us were unnoticeable. My task is to get her out, so I have no choice."

Meaning that Lidiane has to see him *after* she leads Astra out of the castle. I still hate the idea and want to punch his face or maybe remove his appendage, but I also have to trust that Lidiane's capable of taking care of herself.

Astra smiles at me. "We'll see each other soon."

I nod. "Bye."

When they're almost at the door, I reach for Astra again and pull her in for another hug. "I love you. To me, you're my sister."

"Same. Please be careful."

I laugh, even if the paste on my face is drying and I feel it cracking. "Careful is boring. I'll be reckless and wild."

She laughs too. "And smart. I know you'll do great. And I love your wildness."

I pat her shoulder. "See you soon."

Then I sit back on the chair in front of the mirror, actually eager to trick Otavio, eager to take down a king, eager to be at the center of the most important kingdom in our land. I can dethrone a king. Not only that, I can kill him and get a reward.

A strange chuckle comes out of my throat. I don't know if the idea is laughable or if I'm thrilled with the power I'm about to wield.

I can change the fate of a kingdom. And I sure will.

LIDIANE

Walking out should be easier than walking in, and at least I'm sure that Astra's cape is working. It has to be, as we cross her master who does not pay us any mind. At least we've overcome one hurdle. And then I see another hurdle—Azur, standing in the hallway, watching me. Me only, which given the circumstances, I suppose is a good thing, but it doesn't change the fact that his stare feels like a spear crossing my body, pinning me to a wall.

Astra walks beside me, her steps firm, but not too tense, her body relaxed. Even without the cape, nobody glancing at her would guess she's escaping the castle, and that's quite helpful.

We enter the staircase, and an inaudible sigh of relief escapes me when we're no longer under Azur's gaze.

We descend the stairs in silence, these strange stairs in the castle and in the rock. They say that the core of the magic moving this castle is in the rock supporting it, but oddly, I don't sense anything, don't sense any current of power like I do in most enchanted places. Either the magic here is something my senses can't recognize or maybe it's on the crystal on top of the castle.

My goal was just to lead Astra to the exit, but now that she suspects this could be a trap, I walk outside with her and then meet Nelsin by a tree. My farewell is in silence, a silence concealing so many words I'd like him to tell my brother. He and Astra look at me one last time as I keep a defiant, confident smile. I don't want them to worry more than they're already worrying.

I watch as they walk away, disappearing in the increasing darkness.

I barely know Astra, and as much as I like her, I didn't do

this for her. I'm here for my people. I'm here to defeat Renel—and his guardian.

And now it's time to return. This time, if someone stops me, I have a legitimate reason to enter the castle: to see Azur.

My insides are shaking, shaking, shaking, no matter what I tell myself. When I told Tarlia I could deal with him, what I meant is that I trust myself not to reveal any secret. In my heart, that's what matters. I could die today, and maybe, just maybe, I'll regret thinking that I'd rather die trying than live until old age and do nothing. I'd really rather live *and* make a difference.

And there's so much difference I can make with my enchanted garments. I could make more of them, try different properties. So many possibilities. There's so much I want to do, to see.

But now I have to see Azur—and face the consequences of my actions. Why so soon? The worst part is imagining my brother's face when he learns something happened to me. And worse than worst is proving him right, that coming here was too dangerous for me.

My steps feel heavy like my heart, the unpleasant anticipation stiffening my body. I just need to make sure it doesn't cloud my mind.

It's incredible how many servants walk past me and pay me no notice. How nobody notices me. Except the blond scum, of course. He's often referred to as Renel's dog, but Marlak thinks that's very demeaning and quite unfair towards canines. It's why he calls him Renel's pig.

Azur's hovering near Astra's door, a beast waiting for his prey. Well, here I am.

I approach him and bow. "I finished my tasks."

He raises an eyebrow, his face so imperious and punchable. "Was it here that I asked you to meet me?"

"No."

"Well, then." He extends a hand. "Go."

"I don't know where your room is."

He cocks his head and laughs. "Of course you don't."

Of course... Ugh. A wave of terror moves through my body. Real castle servants would know the location of all rooms. I just confirmed I'm an intruder.

"Come. Follow me," he says, his tone strangely pleasant.

I have no option but to follow that black-hatted pile of feces, even if I was hoping we'd have a conversation here. Dread takes over my thoughts to the point I need to focus to hide the webbing in my hands. Is he thrilled to have a new victim? Who knows? Unless his interest is for a different reason. My entire body feels cold.

He leads me to the stairs, and we descend. Great. I'm going to a prison or to some torture chambers. It feels unreal, like watching myself in a strange story, unreal because if I grasp the reality of what's about to befall me, I'll collapse.

Instead of descending to some dark dungeons, he leads me two floors below, where we walk down the hallway, then he opens a door and gestures for me to walk in.

No torture instruments. No cells. Just a simple wooden bed and a wardrobe. A bedroom, but it's too modest. This can't be where Renel's number one man sleeps.

Maybe Azur's goals are less nefarious than I thought, which only makes them *more* nefarious. Quickly, I glamour my face to look unremarkable, even ugly, and I also undo the glamour in my hands. This snobbish wretch won't want to touch a lower fae. Of course, that means I have no way of using my charms to try to wiggle my way out of this, but I had no intention of doing that.

The door clicks closed behind me, and I feel a wind whirl of panic inside me. Caught. At the mercy of one of the most powerful fae in the Crystal Court. At least I'll face my fate head on, with dignity.

MARLAK

Fire, so much fire.

Fire around me. Fire inside me. There's an inferno within me, ready to destruct everything. And screams, so many screams.

Screams are the sound I hear when everything is quiet. Silence is never silence but a memory.

There's a light. And fire. And something wet on my face. Wet—and comforting.

I open my eyes and see darkening sky above me, and a familiar face: Cherry Cake. Cherry Cake, who should never have come to this place, and yet he's here, licking me. All I want to do is protect him, even if the dark unicorn might be much more powerful than I am.

But there's no threat around us, no threat other than inside my own mind. No, I see it, slithering away like a snake, but too fat to be one. It's a soulsucker. That was the cause of my fear. For a moment, I consider killing it with ice, but I gather all my strength to climb on Cherry Cake. Too high. The cuffs are too heavy.

I see then a small rope ladder leading to the saddle and climb it. This is a magic saddle, created by Cherry Cake, and can adapt, change, and even disappear. Now it's helping me climb onto his back.

"Take me to a river," I tell him. "A river with Nymphs, not this one. And let's go."

I run my hand through his rough coat, so thankful for his help. My gratitude is the size of the world, and yet I fear I'll never be able to repay it or make it right for him. Being the last of its kind must be lonely.

So lonely. And for so long, I felt that me and Cherry Cake, we were the same. Strange looking—and lonely.

Now I have to find my friends—and my wife.

TARLIA

I watch as the door closes, as Astra leaves me to face my fate. Not mine, actually. Hers. At least in theory. Who's to decide which fate is whose anyway?

My heart presses down on my stomach in worry for Lidiane. I wish I could accompany her and murder Azur, but I bet there are two problems with it.

First, he must be hard to kill. Second, being as important as he is, there's probably some wacky magical rule that will make hair grow on my hands or something if I kill him. Third, I'm supposed to stay here and wait.

All that remains from Astra is a fresh herbal scent where she stood.

Shit. I'm. So. Screwed.

Astra was smelling all fresh and flowery, while I'm all armpit sweat from walking here then climbing those ridiculous stairs. Otavio will notice there's something wrong.

I pull one of the blankets from the bed, wet it with some water from the pitcher, then take a fragrant soap that's lying on the table and wipe out some of the sweat. Just in time. A few knocks sound on the door as I'm putting the blanket back on the bed.

There he comes. Will he believe I'm Astra?

9

LIDIANE

Azur stands in front of me and looks me up and down. "Why the glamour?"

Isn't that just great? He can see through glamours! I want to smother him with his hat.

I don't think I can skirt around his question, so I tell him part of the truth. "Trying to appear unremarkable." I omit that I'm also trying to look ugly.

He squints and stares at me, then shrugs. "Huh. It isn't working."

I nod and hold his stare so that he knows he can't intimidate me. I also keep the glamour on, since he made no request about it.

And then he stares. Is he trying to pierce my skull with his eyes?

The silence and expectation exasperate me, but I don't dare break it.

Finally, he crosses his arms. "Are you here to kill, poison, incapacitate, or wound Renel?"

"No." My voice conveys how absurd I think his question is.

Not that I would mind killing the sham king, but I wouldn't

dare put Marlak's life at risk. Not only that, trying to kill Renel in this castle would be idiotic suicide, and I'm not *that* reckless.

He pauses. "Are you here to kill or hurt his female human guest?"

"No." Again, I think my tone of voice conveys what I think of the question.

"Fair, then. When did you infiltrate the castle?"

A few words cross my mind, like *recently*, *not long ago*, but I think he's looking for a specific reply, and I'd rather not delay my inevitable fate. "Today."

He strokes his chin and stares at me. "I don't want to know what you're doing here. If you want to survive in this castle, you'll need a role. Who's supervising you?"

Here comes the enslavement.

I knew it. I'll be enchanted and become a servant here. My throat feels dry and bitter.

No matter. I'll have to hope that Marlak, my brother, or perhaps even the rebels will find victory and bring me freedom. Perhaps even Tarlia will be able to do something. I'm not afraid.

His voice then breaks me out of my stupor. "I asked you a question. Who's supervising you?"

"Nobody."

He snorts. "You won't last a day here. If anyone asks, tell them you work for me."

I swallow what feels like sand and nod.

"I want your word," he says.

"If anyone asks, I'll tell them I work for you."

"Good, and you won't tell anyone your true intentions here."

Hmmm... What? I don't know what game he's playing, and I certainly don't want to guess it. It's not like I was eager to talk about my plans with the guards here, so I agree. "I won't tell anyone about my true intentions."

He smiles. "See? Much better, isn't it?"

I'm so completely creeped out I think I'm about to faint. "Better than what?"

Oh, no. Blurting a stupid question is definitely worse than fainting.

"You tell me." He raises an eyebrow. "Or rather, don't tell me. No, tell me something. Were you leaving the castle, or do you plan on staying?"

This is the tricky question, of course.

"Staying," I mumble through gritted teeth, hating that he's not even giving me any opening to dodge his questions.

"And you want to pretend to work here."

When he puts it like that, it sounds stupid. I shrug. "Yes."

"Doing what?"

"I don't know. Anything."

"What do you want to do?"

"Nothing."

His laugh is relaxed. "Don't we all?" He gets serious again. "You need a task. What would you like to do?"

I wriggle my hands. This could backfire tremendously, but it's worth a try. "I've always loved to make clothes, to help women be beautiful. If I could accompany a female fae... Or a guest..."

He crosses his arms again and strokes his chin. "A guest? You mean the human visitor?"

"She's... female, right?"

His eyes narrow. "Promise not to threaten her life."

"Of course I won't threaten her!"

"Go, then. You can be her lady-in-waiting."

I don't know if I smile or cringe. What is he planning? Perhaps it's better to ask than to dread for every foreseeable second.

"Are you going to punish me?"

He raises an eyebrow. "Would you like me to?" His voice is soft, measured, careful. Seductive?

I think I'm about to puke. "No!"

"You make that face, but I'm sure you know there's a taste for everything in this world. Now go! Before I ask you more than I should."

"Go... be the human visitor's lady-in-waiting?"

He taps his earlobe, where a small earring glints. "Got a problem in your ear?"

"No." I turn to walk to the door, but I feel as if there are worms in my stomach. I turn back to him. "Is this a trap?"

"Trap for what?"

"You realized I'm not really a servant, and I'm here pretending to be one. You didn't even ask for an explanation."

He closes his eyes and takes a long, deep breath. "I mean no harm either. If anything, I'm saving *you* from harm."

"You didn't even ask my name."

"Perhaps I don't want to know. See, I'm a very busy fae, sworn as a guardian to the acting king. My survival is tied to his life, my will tied to his wishes. This is who I am: Renel's weapon. You're right to be afraid. But even the mightiest sword sometimes rests. I'm not his weapon right now, and you should embrace your luck. I don't want to hear your reasons or your explanations."

I bow and retreat to the door without turning, facing him in disbelief. When I feel the door behind me, I open it and leave. All the muscles in my body tell me to bolt and run. Instead, I take a deep breath. I'm on my way to Tarlia's room. This is good, right? We'll plan and plot together. I'll support her, help her find Renel's secrets, and defeat him.

But at what cost? Why is Azur letting it happen? What's his goal? I don't know, and this not knowing is a cold void sucking up my joy.

And then again, I survived. I can keep fighting.

TARLIA

I tell my heart to quiet down, as if it were a scared bird I had to soothe, when Otavio walks in.

"Sit." He points to the chair.

I do as he says, realizing I'm more nervous than I expected. This is going to be the hardest part.

Otavio wipes a wet cloth on my face. The touch surprises me. Maybe it's an impression, but I could swear it's softer, more careful. Maybe it *is* an impression.

He's removing the paste from my face, and I'm waiting for him to notice that something's wrong.

I don't hope to fool him completely. That would be impossible. He knows the texture of my skin, the thickness of my hair, even the shape of my face and body. Still, I'm counting on his skewed perception—and using his teachings against him.

People only perceive what they deem to belong in the realm of possibility. They'll adjust their perception and ignore any divergence, rather than challenge their beliefs.

Otavio thinks I'm Astra, and has no reason to believe that his adored pupil would have run away. He has no reason to think I've taken her place. From this vantage point, he'll overlook some details, since they don't fit his expectations. The issue is that there's a limit to how much he'll be willing to ignore, and I'm not quite sure where that limit is.

He rubs a finger on my cheek and frowns. "Your skin is so dry!"

I almost want to roll my eyes. White flower extract tends to remove oil from the skin, and the mask had a lot of it. But then, Astra's skin is oilier than mine, so here's the first test.

"I think…" I try to sound like Astra; sweet, apologetic, obedient. "The soap I used while in captivity…"

Otavio shakes his head. "Had some curse. That's the only explanation." He huffs and takes something from his cosmetics bag. "We'll have to start over."

He's angry at himself, not at me, probably puzzled that he

gave me the wrong facial treatment. I want to snigger but hold a placid expression instead.

As he's preparing some kind of cream, someone knocks on the door.

Otavio shakes his head. "I was told we would be undisturbed. Fae's vague promises are nothing but worthless."

Undisturbed. A wave of nausea comes to me. Why does he want to be alone with Astra?

When he opens the door, Lidiane walks in. All at once, my entire body uncoils and releases my worry about her.

She hesitates, then says. "I'm the human girl's lady-in-waiting, sir."

I wonder how she got rid of Azur, and if she did.

Otavio narrows his eyes and stares at her up and down. "Then you can wait outside."

"Of course. I'll be in the hallway." She bows and leaves.

Otavio shuts the door.

"You know, I wouldn't mind some company." I try to sound sweet instead of assertive.

"She's probably here to spy on us, and we already had more than enough interruptions."

"Weren't you going to treat my skin? She can see it."

He clicks his tongue. "And then tell Renel, and he'll suspect I'm changing the way you look. That won't do. He'll want someone naturally beautiful."

"I'm naturally hideous, of course." Ugh. Too snappy.

He steps behind me and puts a hand under my chin, so that he looks at my reflection in the mirror. "You will be the queen of all the fae kingdoms."

So he has some grandiose, devious plans. Of course. Nobody spends nineteen years on something insignificant. I pretend to be puzzled. "Wasn't it just the Crystal Court?"

There's something sinister in his laugh. "One step at a time. Look too far ahead and you'll trip."

What's his plan? He won't tell me, of course, even if he

hasn't realized I'm not Astra. But there's a part of it I need to know.

"What about Tarlia and Sayanne?"

He laughs again. "You need to forget them. They're inconsequential. Nothing. They were just pebbles so that I could hide the diamond."

Pebbles. Nothing. That's what my life is worth to him. That's why he killed my family: for nothing. Every nerve in my body tenses while heat rises to my head. I could strangle him right now.

I control myself and say something Astra would say, "The Almighty Mother says every life matters."

His fingers squeeze my shoulder. "Will you stop reciting that dreadful religion? It's all lies. All fake. While it was cute to pretend to be pious in the Krastel castle, idiotic beliefs will only drag you down."

I agree with him, but Astra would be hurt. This is my excuse to stop holding back my tears. So much anger in each drop.

I'm not a pebble. Oh, no. I'm a boulder. A boulder who'll stand in his way.

The only reason I don't kill Otavio right now is because it would be too easy. I want to see him suffer, see him watch his precious plan fall apart, see him despised and rejected by the girl he molded from infancy to serve his whims. That will be more satisfying. It's the reason I wake up, the reason I breathe. I'll watch Otavio being humiliated.

"Great. Just great." His voice prickles my skin. "Now your eyes will be red and swollen."

"Maybe Renel will console me."

"You don't want pity. You want adoration. Devotion."

"And your creams will help me with that?" I deserve a prize for managing to ask that without a trace of sarcasm.

He smirks. "That, and all your training."

His strong concoctions must have damaged his brain.

· · ·

When Otavio finally leaves, I take a deep breath. I can't believe he didn't realize I wasn't Astra. He probably noticed some odd little things here and there, but they were not odd enough to make him question his assumptions.

I can't say I'm relieved. There's that old anguish creeping up on me, marring my thoughts, clouding my sight. That old anguish, my longest companion. In Krastel, in nights like this, my solace was Fachin, and before him, another guard, and another. Not hard to invite one of them to my bed, and then fuck away all my anger, my fear, my worry. But I'm not in Krastel.

I'm also worried about Lidiane, and instead of letting that worry eat me alive, I open the door. There is a guard there, sitting on a stool. Cute, with dark brown hair and pointy fae ears. I wonder what it would be like to bite those ears.

I smile at him. "Are you here to make sure I don't escape, or to protect me?"

He doesn't even get up, but returns the smile. "I can escort you if you want to go somewhere. And I can't let anyone in."

Except that he let me and Lidiane in, but that was likely the power of my cape. Old Tarlia would most definitely find a way to bring him to her bed. I wish I could. That would make me forget Ziven, at least for a few minutes. But I'm impersonating Astra, who wouldn't do that, and I'll have to at least pretend to try to seduce the fae king, and I'm not sure if screwing one of his guards is advisable. And yet I wish I could push my anguish away.

"If I have a request, can you help me?"

"It depends."

"A lady-in-waiting was assigned to me, and I'm wondering where she is."

He gets up, looks at both sides of the hall, then back at me. "When someone passes by, I'll ask them about her."

I'm not sure if that's enough. "Can we look for her?"

"I'm here." Lidiane walks in brisk steps toward me, carrying a bundle under one of her arms. When she approaches us, she addresses the guard. "I was told to remain in the room with her. Azur's orders."

The guard shrugs and sits down again. "Sure."

I decide to ask the guard an important question. "Can you hear us from here?"

"No. Rest assured, you have your privacy."

"Can anyone else hear us?"

He raises an eyebrow. "Not that I know of." His eyes then travel to me and Lidiane, and he smirks. "Have fun."

"You too."

Lidiane and I walk in and shut the door behind us.

"How did it go?" I ask.

She throws the bundle on the bed, and I realize they're some blankets and a pillow. "Very strangely."

"How?"

"Azur assigned me to be your lady-in-waiting."

"He did?"

"Yes." She presses her lips together.

"Why?"

"I don't know, and I hate not knowing. He questioned me, and found out I got here only today, so he knows I'm not a castle worker. I'm glad nothing happened, but at the same time…" She raises her shoulders and shivers. Then she points at the beddings. "I was given this, so I can sleep in the room with you. That will make it easier for me to keep your glamour. So it's good." Her tone contradicts her last words.

I try to think. "Maybe… Do you owe him a debt?"

"No."

Only one explanation comes to my mind. "Then he must want what all men want."

She huffs. "Oh, I bet he has more than enough of that."

"There are things you can't get enough of."

"He's one of the most beautiful fae in the kingdom. And one

of the most powerful. Most women would be delighted to visit his bed."

"But not you."

Lidiane rolls her eyes. "He's a disgusting high fae, working for Renel, making sure we are exploited. I *would* go to his bed if it meant a chance to kill him. And either way, he didn't seem interested in that, thankfully." Her tone then changes. "To be very honest, I *was* afraid he'd coerce me." Her chest moves down as she exhales.

That's one thing in common between human and fae women; that fear in the back of our minds of what can happen when alone with a man. I feared for her too, but I want her to forget what must have been some stressful moments.

For some reason, I sense my body trembling from head to toe. Not my body—the floor.

A low-pitched rumble comes from the walls and everything trembles then shakes. I hold on to the pillar of the bed. Lidiane does the same, her eyes wide. It's when I notice that all the furniture is bolted to the floor. Still, the room is trembling so much I fear the ceiling will collapse on us.

Curiosity gets the best of me and I decide to go to the window and see what's happening outside. A sudden jerk drops me to the floor, but I get up and make it. There's nothing. Just darkness outside, and it's not the darkness of a moonless, cloudy night or a windowless room. It's something else. Eerie, strange, fascinating—terrifying.

And then slowly, stars appear in the sky. Endless sky, with no mountains blocking the way. The trembling and rumble stop, replaced by a soft, continuous whooshing.

Lidiane joins me at the window. "We're near the sea, I think." There's some apprehension in her tone.

"The castle moved." I don't know why I need to voice the obvious, and still, only when I voice the words I accept that this really happened, that I just experienced one of the most spellbinding magical phenomena in our lands.

It moved. I experienced the castle moving. And we're close to the ocean.

I'm overcome with happy laughter.

For a moment, all that matters is that I'm here, experiencing something magnificent, seeing the world outside Krastel, experiencing fae magic.

Wondrous, amazing fae magic, in these lush fae lands.

ASTRA

The soup in front of me is hot, well seasoned, and delicious, but everything inside me is cold, numb.

After I got to Nelsin's house, I told him and Ferer what I saw in Renel's mind, without going into details on how I saw it. I was expecting that they would know immediately what my vision meant.

Perhaps it was silly hope, but I swear, when I saw those images, it was as if a lock clicked open, as if the vision had been a key, even if it didn't make sense to me at the time.

And yet they didn't know what the symbol meant. The vision also had a lake, and they had some suggestions of where it could be located, but nothing precise.

Now I'm anxious, wondering how we'll find Marlak, considering even returning to the Crystal Castle to try to pry more information from his vicious brother. But if it's useless information, what's the point?

And then, to make matters worse, I felt as if Marlak was in some horrific pain, horrific torment, a grisly feeling crawling under my skin. And here I am, eating, as if this was a normal evening.

Ziven just came downstairs and is also eating, in an unusually deep, thoughtful silence.

I was horrified to learn what happened to him and Tarlia.

Attacked.

Almost killed.

All for coming here to see me. And now they can't even return to their lives. Was there any life for Tarlia in Krastel?

At least I'm glad Ferer and Nelsin helped them, and I'm incredibly thankful that they took in Ziven.

Still, my stomach knots and knots with too much worry, too much annoyance at my incompetence.

Ferer stares at me, always so perceptive. "It will be fine. Finish eating for now, then we'll go over your vision in more detail and try to decipher it."

I nod. Even breathing is hard.

Nelsin is by the stove and turns to us. "I can bring some books and we'll figure out that symbol."

Ziven is staring at his soup as if it was a deep pool with fascinating fish in the bottom, then turns to me. "Are you sure that what you saw was where your husband is?"

My shoulders sag. Of course I'm not sure of anything. "I was thinking about Marlak and his location when I touched Renel, looking for that answer. I could be wrong, of course. But the vision was *so* specific."

Nelsin steps behind me and places a calming hand on my shoulder. "Eat, Astra. We'll find him. And we have other ways to locate Marlak."

We will. In the future.

I was expecting that we would be rushing to save my husband right now. Of course it was a stupid idea. Even if we discovered his location, it's likely a highly protected prison, so we'd need to plan carefully. Still, if we knew it, we would have a direction, a starting point.

"For how long do Tarlia and Lidiane plan to remain in the castle?" Ferer's voice is deceptively casual.

A nervous laugh almost escapes me, but I rein it in. There's no point hiding, and I tell him the truth. "Until they defeat Renel."

Ferer covers his face with his hands.

Ziven snorts and rolls his eyes. "How not surprising."

There's anger in his tone? Odd. I feel that I need to explain Tarlia and Lidiane's motivation, even though it should be obvious. "They want to learn something to help us defeat Renel, and they are in the perfect position to do that. But I can return to the castle and do that myself—once we rescue Marlak."

Ferer shakes his head. "Don't say nonsense."

"But it's smart," I protest. "Take him down from the inside. It's a wonderful opportunity. Why squander it?"

Nelsin, who was standing, sits. "They're both capable and should be fine."

At least one person is trying to be helpful.

I recall something they told me, and say, "They claimed their sense of self preservation was intact, meaning that they won't risk their lives."

Ferer looks up at me. "I guess we'll have to trust them."

Why are they making me feel guilty? Sure, I could have insisted that they leave the castle, but I know Tarlia, and I understand her stakes. With nowhere to go, she likely felt the need to do something useful.

Be useful or be expendable.

Why do I hear it in Otavio's voice?

And Lidiane likely wants to fight for her people, and I respect that too. Frankly, I would do the same. In fact, if needed, I won't hesitate to return to the Crystal Castle to try to topple Renel.

But understanding doesn't stop me from feeling guilty. "It wasn't my idea, but I'm sorry... for being out here while they're there. I just wanted to find Marlak."

Ferer traces a finger over the wooden table. "Threads of destiny will be woven, and resisting them will only trap us." He raises his eyes and faces me. "Lidiane's an adult, and asked me to respect her choices, so I guess that's what I'll do."

He doesn't sound the least happy about it, which makes sense.

Silence falls over the table like a thick, prickly blanket, broken only by my spoon tapping the side of the bowl.

For so long, I'd been dreaming of hot soup.

I don't want hot soup. I want my husband.

As I'm swallowing the hot broth, someone knocks on the door. I sit still, and so do Ziven and Nelsin.

Ferer, for his turn, exhales in clear relief and rushes to the door. I'm not sure if I should hide or remain where I am. When the door opens, I can't believe my eyes.

Dark blue shirt like this morning, but wet. Messy, curly black hair, and rings. That's Marlak.

Marlak.

My heart is about to explode with surprise and joy and relief. And then there's all that anger still stirring in my chest, asking for a turn in my wheel of emotions.

"They took her," he says, his voice shaky, desperate. He sounds out of breath, as if he had run here.

Ferer steps back and points at the table—and at me.

In one moment I'm standing, looking at him, in the next I feel his arms around me, his lips on mine. I'm not sure how he breached the space between us so fast, I'm not sure how he got here, all I know is that this is the kiss we never had before, swallowing all the anguish of the last few hours, burying the pain of his absence.

Our lips meet like it's the first and last time, like it's an eternity—and I want to melt in his embrace.

But I also want to yell at him.

I push him away, but he doesn't budge, since his arms are still around me. At least our lips are not joined anymore.

His dark eyes are focused on me with so much love, so much emotion, and yet I hope he sees all the rage in mine.

"I'm furious. Furious, Marlak."

ASTRA

Marlak closes his eyes and takes a deep breath, then leans down and rests his forehead on my shoulder. "I never meant to hurt you."

I try to push him again, but he remains still, and keeps his arms tightly wrapped around me. "Oh. What exactly did you mean to do?"

From a distance, I hear Nelsin. "We'll be back in the morning."

I nod, but my focus is on Marlak, waiting for his reply.

It takes a while, but he moves his head and stares at me, a pool of sadness in those eyes. "I just wanted to keep you safe. I told you I'd do anything—"

"No." I manage to free an arm and wave a finger in front of his face. "No. What you did was *despicable*. You didn't trust me. You made a decision and left me out, as if I wasn't capable of making a choice with you."

"There was no time. When I noticed Renel was near, he was probably already hearing us. I had to think fast. Maybe it was stupid."

"Not maybe. It was. You hurt me. You could have winked,

could have whispered in my ear to pretend to hate you. You could have done so many things differently, but no. You chose to stick a knife in my heart and twist it and twist it and twist it. And then you claim you didn't want to hurt me. What did you think you were doing?"

He stares at me in silence, then says, "I feared..."

"I wouldn't agree with you? I'd try to fight them on my own?"

He closes his eyes and nods.

"I'm not stupid, Marlak. I'm not stupid to take on a fight I can't win."

A small voice inside me wants to remind me that I jumped down a cliff thinking I'd face four foes to protect Marlak, but I tell it to shut up. I continue, "And you can't simply take away my choice."

"To protect you."

"Protect me from harm by harming me?"

His arms still grip me tight, even if I wiggle, trying to break free.

"I..." His throat bobs and he inhales. "As long as you're alive, there's a way."

I try to step away again, but it feels as if there's an iron chain around me. "A way? What if I thought you had really fooled me? I would probably be having revenge sex with your brother right now. How would we come back from that?"

"I'd get you back."

His grip on me is annoying. "Let me go."

"Never."

"You plan on spending your entire life holding me?"

"Until you forgive me."

"How is holding me against my will going to help?"

"Better than letting you go."

"I just want some space. Space to think, talk, pace around the kitchen. You used to be nice. I bet old Marlak would never keep me in his arms against my will. *He* was respectful."

There's a hint of a smile on his lips. "So you liked me then?"

"Ugh." I give up on stepping away and stop fighting and fidgeting. "Words, once said, can't come back, can't be erased. Can't be forgotten. All the moments we had together in that sanctuary, you ruined them. I'll always wonder if you thought it was boring."

He rests his forehead in the crook of my neck again and embraces me even tighter. "No. Never. I didn't have time to think, so I was just saying the opposite of everything. Want to know how I feel? Just turn my words upside down."

"It doesn't work like that." To my horror, my voice sounds softer, almost whinier. I don't want him to think I'm forgiving him. "I'm still angry."

"But you're here."

"Yes."

He looks at me again. "And how did you realize I was pretending, back in the sanctuary?"

"I... thought it was unlike you, didn't make sense. Then I remembered the coronation, when you said your brother couldn't know that you cared about me."

"Does it count for anything that it was unlike me to act like that?"

I shake my head. "What you said was hurtful, and a lot of it unnecessary."

He sighs. "Before we ever met, I had been dreaming about you for about a year. You had the same experience, right?"

"Yes. But it doesn't—"

"Listen. Please. Just listen. And what did we do during most of those dreams?"

"We lied down together."

He nods. "For me, those dreams were exhilarating, wonderful, magical. Just lying by your side, feeling you close, running my hands through your hair... It was everything. If cuddling you is so wonderful, how can anything else we do be boring? It's impossible, Astra."

His words soothe some of the soreness in my chest, alleviate some of the pain, but they barely touch the deep wound, stil open, underneath it all.

"You still didn't have to say all that, didn't have to humiliate me the way you did."

"I can't change the past. But I'm here." His chest moves up and down. "What can I do for you to forgive me?"

Forgive him. Of course I want to forgive him, wipe away those horrible moments, get rid of this anger running through my veins like poison. "It takes time. But... don't do this again. Don't try to protect me as if I were a pet, without consulting me."

"There was no time."

"Like I said, it could be something as simple as a wink. Let me know what you're up to. We can pretend together. Don't shut me out."

"Would you have let my brother capture me? Would you have followed your master?"

"Yes. It would have been the wisest decision, considering we were outnumbered. I could try to rescue you later, under different circumstances. There was no need to... do what you did."

"I'll never do this again. I'll never hurt your feelings to push you away. But please, please Astra, tell me that you'll place your safety above heroics, that you'll... be cautious."

I shake my head. "You take me for a fool."

"No. I think you're brave and capable, and you have incredible magic. Just... sometimes we need to lose a battle to win the war. Sometimes it's time to retreat."

"Again, you think I'm foolish."

"I'm sorry. I'll trust your judgment, trust your wisdom. You're right that I made a mistake. If it helps, I feared losing you, feared you'd hate me forever. The thought consumed me with anguish, with terror, for hours. Please consider my anguish enough punishment."

"What about me? I didn't realize you were pretending right away. My heart was being ripped as I wondered how I could have been such an idiot for so long, how I could have let someone deceive me... It was horrific."

"I'll never do anything like that again. Ever. It's a promise, wife."

For some reason, I chuckle. "Wife. Now I'm going to think you're jesting."

He squeezes me tight. "Never."

"I can barely breathe. Can you let me go? I forgive you."

Instead of breaking his hug, he kisses my neck. "Do you still love me?"

"Do *you*, Marlak?"

"Loving you is like breathing. I've always done it. I'm always doing it, even when I don't think about it, even when my mind is elsewhere. It's part of who I am. It's what keeps me alive."

"You can't have always loved me."

"Soulmates do. Their love is eternal. Unbreakable. Throughout their many lives, they'll be connected. And you know that's what we are."

"I do. So imagine the pain I felt when you uttered those horrible words."

"I had to live with the fear of losing your love, and it was awful too, even if I can't know what your pain felt like." He kisses my temple, then my cheek. "But I'll make up for that."

He's kissing my neck now, his lips spreading shivers through my body. Silly, easily impressed body, with no sense of pride. It has completely forgiven him a long time ago.

"Marlak, you're tired. Eat."

He's still kissing my neck, and mumbles against it. "Can I choose what I eat?"

"There's soup."

His palms press against my lower back while he kisses my collarbone. "I want *you*."

A happy laughter escapes me. Isn't that what I was just thinking? "I'm here."

"Do you still love me?" he asks again.

This time, he manages to sound so vulnerable that I almost

feel bad for him. Almost. Still, I say, "I love you. Even furious, I still loved you."

"Is the fury gone?"

"Most of it."

His arms loosen around me, finally, and he brings his hands to my face. "You're here."

The smile he gives me is fire, melting away all my remaining resentment, all my remaining anger. It's light and life.

And love.

And then those lovely lips cover mine. Perhaps there is some remaining fury in the desperation of that kiss. A different type of fury, bringing us close instead of apart.

His hands move to my waist, gripping my skin tight. There's nothing soft, nothing sweet about the way he kisses me, nothing gentle about the way he holds me. His fingers dig into my skin as if to make sure I'm solid, as if to make sure I'm his.

Marlak's eyes bore into mine, his gaze intense as he lifts me onto the table. I wrap my legs around him and feel his hardness pushing against me, even with all the clothes between us.

He awakens an ember in my core as he stares at me with those dark eyes, now even darker than usual, his lovely lips parted, his breath ragged. That look would be terrifying in anyone else, a dark, dangerous look with the intensity of a smelting fire.

Our eyes meet, and the corner of his lips lifts in a wicked grin. One of his hands pulls up my dress while the other digs into my inner thigh, his rings grazing my delicate skin, his fingers caressing me in gentle yet firm strokes, my breath hitching with each touch.

He pushes up my breastband and removes it, freeing my breasts, devouring them with his eyes. My nipples feel hard like iron spikes, one of them soon covered with his warm, soft tongue igniting an intense fire throughout me.

I can see his collarbone and part of his chest in the opening of his shirt, but it's not enough skin, not enough of him. He's wearing too many clothes. I place my hand under the fabric and touch his rugged, scarred chest that I love so much, then push up his shirt. He finishes taking it off, then tosses it.

It's the first time I let myself admire his body from up close like this, when there's enough light to see him fully. His scars and tattoos form a fascinating pattern on his skin, covering a muscular chest and corded arms. On his taut abdomen, the v-shaped muscles and a trail of hair point downward, a stunning sight that turns my core into an incandescent inferno.

Marlak is perfection, absolute perfection, staring at me with a determined, focused expression, a sheer intensity in his eyes.

He's not in a gentle mood—and neither am I. No time for nonsense. No time for talking. No time for joking.

He lifts my legs and removes my underwear as if he were removing an annoying boulder in his way.

I watch as he unlaces his trousers, his ringed fingers quick, frenetic, watch as he frees his rock-hard member, a pearlescent bead on its tip, bluish veins marking its length. I want it inside me. I want everything.

His fingers find the sensitive spot between my legs, then caress my entrance. I adore his fingers, adore the feel of his rings grazing my skin, and yet I want more.

Our gazes are locked, our souls connected. *I want more*, I let my eyes say.

His hand slides down my thigh, replaced by his hips, comfortably nested between my legs, the tip of his member almost where it belongs. He gives me a searching, questioning look.

We're eye-to-eye level, and I move my head slightly, just enough to convey a nod, and yet not enough to break the spell between us, not enough to break the bond between us.

And then I feel it—inside me, in one swift stroke. The sound coming out of my throat is a moan, a grunt, a groan. I don't even know. My senses are overwhelmed with a hint of pain and an overload of pleasure as I feel myself stretching around him, opening up for him to dig in even deeper, filling me so completely. I love the sensation of his throbbing member inside me, caressing deep within me, as his hands claim my body.

He moves his member back, leaving just the tip inside me—and then slams in again. And again.

My moans become yells, become screams. I don't care if anyone hears me, don't care about anything. I want to be held tight like that, to be fucked hard as if it was the last and only time. Hard as if we were burying all our fear and anguish.

All this time, I'm looking into the ocean of darkness in his eyes, getting lost in it. Lost in space and time. Nothing but us.

RENEL

Keeping my eyes open is a struggle after a sleepless night.

Four more moves. Four more. Time's running out, and I'm feeling like an idiot. I should have seen Astra again. Should have... I don't know what.

I stare out the window of my private dining room. We're near the plains by the Golden Sea—exactly where I predicted we'd be.

Sometimes, strangely, when the castle moves, I hope it will end up in a completely unexpected location, just to prove me wrong, just so I can question whether we're really heading to the Fiery Gorge. It hasn't happened yet. The upside is that at least the castle always lands on a rather empty area, without any risk of crushing houses with everyone inside, since I made sure to evacuate the locations in the trajectory of the castle. Many more areas than needed are evacuated, of course, just so people don't realize where the castle is going.

A servant brings a tray with three large bowls in it, one with a fruit salad, and two with oatmeal and almonds.

Azur walks in after the servant, takes his usual place, and

serves himself as if nothing was happening. He's dressed like usual, wearing a leather vest and a black hat.

My stomach is turning, but I sit by him.

"It moved," I blurt, my words unable to convey even a fraction of my horror, my agony.

Azur swallows, then says, "It was bound to do that."

"Four more moves, Azur. Four. It's nothing."

He sets the spoon and stares at me, as if finally grasping the gravity of the situation. "Weren't you sure you had found a solution?"

"*Finding* a solution is not the same as using it. The girl is... I don't know. Distant." I felt as if there was an insurmountable wall of ice between us.

He puts some more almonds on his plate. "The castle won't move again tomorrow. Have some patience."

Patience when anguish is corroding my blood?

I decide to take a plate and eat. It's not as if a hunger strike will stop the castle.

"Also," he says between two bites, "I placed a lady-in-waiting with the human girl."

"Why?" I never took Azur for the type who watches the castle maintenance closely, and this decision puzzles me.

"You asked me to help you. The human girl probably feels uncomfortable with enchanted servants, and an unbound fae will make her more at ease, keep her company."

I'm still not sure I follow his logic. "Astra should seek *my* company. It's bad enough that I have to keep that oaf who calls himself her master here."

Azur raises his spoon. "Renel, a Tiurian needs *love* to grant someone magic. Love, not desperation due to loneliness."

"Are magical rules that picky?"

"You want the girl to feel happy, at home, right? Details like that matter."

He might have a point. Still, something about the idea still bothers me. "Is this fae trustworthy?"

"I trust no one. But I'm assuming you're not going to tell her your secrets."

I huff. "I'm thinking about Astra. If word goes anywhere that we have a Tiurian here…"

Azur pushes a strand of hair behind his ear. "Astra's trained. Wasn't she what they call *an elite guard* in her kingdom? It means she's disciplined and won't give away a secret like that —or she would have been unmasked a long time ago. Humans have no love for Tiurians."

"Fair."

Azur smiles. "You need to trust me, Renel."

"As if I didn't." The food is all tasting ashy and weird and I'm not sure I should be eating, and then I feel awkward by having to ask something so personal. "Any tips? I'm going to see her today. And don't tell me to wait. I'll die if I have to wait right after seeing the castle move."

Azur stares at his spoon, his bowl, then back at me. "Well, I read that you should make her laugh."

"That can't be right. Who wants someone ridiculous?"

"Not ridiculous. Fun, relaxing, entertaining."

"I have no doubt that I can entertain her. The issue is getting to the point where she'll let me."

"Yes. A long journey. Anyway, one tip is to make her laugh."

That makes no sense. "If that were true, comedic bards would have women falling—" I stop myself even before I finish the dumb sentence. Of course they find a lot of women. "Fair. I mean, unfair. Can't they like gloomy and grumpy? Anxious and apprehensive? It's no wonder nobody has ever fallen for me."

Azur points at me with his spoon. "Princess Crisine seemed pretty smitten."

"Yes, fascinated with the crown she doesn't know I don't own."

"You should ask your dear brother."

I'm not sure if he's brilliant or demented. "How to seduce Astra?"

"Ask him for the crown."

"As if he'd give it to me. And I don't need the crown. I need magic to stop the castle. To do that, I need to make Astra fall in love with me. Can we focus?"

"Right. So... If you want to make her laugh, you could tell her jokes."

"I don't know a single one."

"Learn some. There are books with lists and—"

A bell sounds in the corner of the room. It's the sign that Zorwal is approaching. I had to order the fae in the hallway to ring that, so that I know he's coming. Azur sits straight and removes his hat.

I stop eating, now deeply regretting consuming the fruit that wants to escape my stomach.

A few long seconds go by until the council leader steps in, unannounced, as always. He glances at Azur, then bows to me.

"Your majesty. An emergency meeting has been called. You need to present yourself to the council chamber in five minutes."

Five. The council members probably had a lot more time to get here, but Zorwal likes to warn me at the last moment. Still, I get up at once. "I'll be there."

Zorwal leaves, and I remain here wondering what exactly is happening. Emergency meetings are rare, and this one is giving me a queasy feeling.

I turn to Azur. "I'll talk to you later."

He gets up. "Do you want any help?"

"No. I'm fine."

I rush to my dressing room and pull back my hair with two silver side combs, then put on a more ceremonial attire, with a silk shirt and leather trousers. In moments like this, I always like to look like a king, but never like someone who's making an effort to appear kingly, and finding the balance is tricky.

It's just a meeting, like many others before. Just a meeting because an emergency happened. What emergency? I suppose I'll find out.

I arrive at the council room and find that five of the nine

councilors are already in their places. Zorwal glances at me from his usual seat, while I take the biggest and highest chair.

A knight of the Royal Army stands in the middle of the room.

"You can proceed," Zorwal says. "The other councilors couldn't make it."

The knight turns to me and kneels, his posture too rigid, too tense. He's nervous. "Your majesty. There was a breach at the Desert Keep."

His words would make me tremble if I didn't have so much self control. I don't even flinch. Hiding my fear is something I'm an expert at. "Explain."

The knight hesitates while I stand here wondering if Marlak's hurt, and if they'll find out I took a prisoner without authorization.

So many things about to go wrong. Did something happen to my brother?

ASTRA

The soft, shallow rhythm of his breathing tells me he's awake.

I feel a feather touch on my forehead—and open my eyes, to find Marlak, so close, staring at me with the tenderness of a thousand embraces, running a finger over my face. I'm lying on his chest, just like I've done so many times before, except that it's real now. I can't believe it; it's real.

A bubble of joy fills my chest and spreads to my entire body, so much joy that I feel I could fly.

I trace a finger over his star, never breaking that precious eye contact, those threads of destiny pulling us closer, as morning sunlight bathes the room in a golden hue. What a wondrous reality. Fantastic, amazing reality.

He's still caressing my face, and says, "I didn't want to wake you."

"Why not? This is worth waking up for."

He kisses my cheekbone. "I've dreamed of mornings like this with you." He chuckles, then frowns. "Quite... literally."

I chuckle too. "I can't wait to go back home."

He pulls my hand and kisses the back of it. "It's just a hideout."

"It's home." And then I think about the Amethyst Palace, that castle calling me to it, that castle I know I need to find. And I have a million questions to ask my husband. "How did you escape?"

"Funny. I'm wondering the same thing here."

"I asked first."

Still caressing my hair, he tells me about a royal prison in the desert in the Shadow Lands. His description stuns me, as it's nothing like the place I saw in Renel's mind. The way he escaped is surprising too.

I'm glad he's here, and still curious about all these alliances he's made throughout the years. "So the giants also support you?"

He looks down and rolls a strand of hair on his finger. "No, but—" His hesitation is significant, I know it.

"What?"

He takes a deep breath. "They're afraid of something, I'm not even sure what. Giants are not great communicators. I promised to help them *if I could*, which is an easy enough promise. And I said that one of them should come and find me when they need help. They can't cross the river."

"So you tricked them."

"No." He frowns, visibly offended. "I just agreed with what they asked. To be very honest, I wanted to stay in the Desert Keep until I knew you were free and safe. It wasn't *my* idea to escape, but once they broke the wall, what was I going to do? The Shadow Lands are dangerous, even for me." He raises a fist.

"And I had dark metal cuffs dulling my magic. The Nymphs removed it."

"I'm glad you had no choice, then."

"And you? Did Ferer or Nelsin actually—"

"Kind of. It was Lidiane and Tarlia who infiltrated the castle. Lidiane had these capes, and when you wear them, you're not noticed. So I left." Odd how it sounds so simple when I explain it.

"Magical capes?" He blinks, thoughtful. "That sounds quite useful. And where are they?"

"I have mine, but the magic is gone. They kept—"

"I mean Lidiane and your friend. They weren't here last night."

"They're in the castle. Tarlia's pretending to be me, and Lidiane's working her glamours on her."

The sparkle in his eyes dims at once, replaced by a shadow of something dangerous. "In the Crystal Castle? And you aren't worried?"

I sit up. "It's a great opportunity to take down Renel."

He sits as well. "No, no. Wait a minute. You mean they are going to *stay* there? With my enemy?"

"To bring him down."

"So let me get this straight. The moment Renel decides to threaten me, what am I going to do? Imagine if he says, *crown me king, or I'll cut her tongue.* Or worse. Should I just laugh and say, *Hey, she's not my wife, she's my wife's sister!* How's that going to help me? And Lidiane? Of all people? She's Ferer's little sister. What am I supposed to do if he threatens her?"

"I don't think those are your brother's plans. I think... he wanted something from me."

"Right. From you. And what do you think will happen the moment he realizes she's not you? Or the moment Lidiane is caught? She's a lower fae, Astra!"

I huff, annoyed that he's thinking I'm callous or something. "First, it wasn't my idea—or my orders. Second, I don't under-stand why you're worried about them. Didn't you break my heart, stick a dagger in it, and twist and twist it? All so your brother would think you don't care about me? Well then, great! You don't care about them, so they'll be safe, right? Isn't that the whole point? Or did you hurt my feelings for fun?"

He rolls his eyes and shakes his head. "It was a last resort attempt to save you, and I wasn't even sure if it would work."

"Marlak, if you truly think your stupid lies wouldn't save me, then there was no point in what you did to hurt me."

"Astra, I already apologized! I know I was wrong. At the moment, all I thought was that the pretense would keep you alive—for some time. I wasn't sure for how long."

"Consider then that you barely know Tarlia, and there's no reason for them to think you know Lidiane. And if you think their being there is that much of an issue, no problem! I can return and replace them." He glares at me, but I continue, "It's a once-in-a-lifetime chance. Didn't you say you wanted to defeat your brother? Lidiane wants to defeat Renel. Nelsin, Ferer, we all want a better kingdom. You have no right to complain that Lidiane and Tarlia are trying."

He fiddles with his rings, then stares at me and huffs. "What does Tarlia want? Why should she care?"

"She was attacked on the way back. Someone was trying to kill Ziven. He's the true Krastel heir, you know? So now, with Otavio in the Crystal Castle, Ziven here, what is she going to do? I know what it's like, Marlak, to wait for that moment, that opportunity when you can..." I sigh. "*Achieve* something. Prove your worth."

"You have nothing to prove!"

"I know. But I understand wanting to matter, wanting to *do* something. She can't hope to go back and do anything for Krastel. What's she going to return to? Here, she can make a difference. Why wouldn't she seize the opportunity?"

Marlak rubs a hand on his face. "You're assuming she thinks like you."

"We had the same upbringing. Of course she thinks like me."

He stares at me, some deep pain in his eyes. "I don't like it, Astra. I don't like Lidiane there. Or your sister. Renel obviously doesn't seem evil. I bet he was really nice. That's the whole point. It's what he does; he gets you to trust him, then stabs you."

I realize he's no longer talking about Tarlia or Lidiane, but about himself. "Are you ever going to be able to tell me what happened?"

"Slowly, yes."

He looks up and up until his eyes go white. The only reason I don't worry is that he's being casual about it. He reaches out his hand, and a ball that looks like a dark storm cloud appears on his palm. It vanishes suddenly, leaving in its place the dagger he showed me in the sanctuary. I realize this is how he accesses the relics.

He points to the object that just appeared in his hand. "With this, I can break some of my promises, some of my deals with my brother. But I'll need all the help I can get, so I'll want to tell Ferer too. It's easier to tell you both at once." He raises the dagger. "And not overuse it."

The fact that he'll need help for whatever plans he has doesn't put me at ease. "There's something worrying you."

He pulls me close and kisses my forehead. "Always. But at least *you* are safe. No words can convey how much it matters to me."

I'm anxious to hear what he has to say, but at the same time, I don't want him complaining that Tarlia and Lidiane are in the castle. "I'm safe. I'm here. I trust Tarlia, she's... my sister. Let her do her job. Let her find honor in defeating a tyrant."

"It's not like I can rescue them, wife. I'm just... Maybe you're right, and it will be fine."

"Lidiane is great with glamours. They can escape easily with her capes. I trust them."

"All I can do is let the threads of destiny do their work, and hope they won't lead them to their doom."

"Ferer mentioned something similar. I didn't know fae believed in threads of destiny."

He smirks. "I didn't know *humans* did. Well, it's the same land after all, and we were not always apart." He runs a finger through my hair. "Let's get dressed. Nelsin should be back soon, and it's his house, after all. Unless you have any more secrets you want to tell me."

His words remind me of what I saw in Renel's mind. "Not a secret, but... I had lunch with your brother, and he shook my hand. At that moment, I saw something horrific; fire consuming the room where I was, swallowing the entire castle. But it didn't seem to be a memory."

Marlak raises his eyebrows. "What did you think it was?"

I'm not even sure. "A... fear? An intention?" The thought chills me. "A vision? Or else... a distorted memory."

"Most likely some kind of memory. I'm shocked that he would even care."

Of course Renel would care at least a little. He saw his mother dying in a fire. Even then—that vision... I can still recall the horror I felt, but this is not the time to poke Marlak's painful memories.

"There's more," I add. "Something... odd. I'm not even sure if it's important. I had some residue of your magic when I met your brother."

"My magic..." His forehead crinkles.

"Yes. I didn't know it at first, but then I froze a glass of water —after seeing that horrible vision. I have used some of your magic before, that day after we ran away from the Misty Court, on that island, after tasting your blood."

He blinks. "Is that what you did?"

"Didn't you notice I licked your palm?"

"Yes, but I thought you were sorry you had cut me. And if you wanted to lick me, I wasn't going to complain, you know? I even held myself back, didn't ask you to keep going."

I punch his shoulder lightly. "Crass. You're so crass."

"Really? You've seen nothing."

"I've seen enough. In case you're wondering, I do want to lick you in more *interesting places*. With no blood." His lips relax in an adorable smile. "But I was telling you something that might be important, might not."

"I'm just trying to understand. You're saying that if you taste someone's blood, you get their magic?"

My body tenses, somehow finding it strange to hear it out loud like that, said so matter-of-factly. "Yes, but I had never tried it. Never even knew I could do it, until that day, when... I was angry, out of control. I don't know what happened. Where did you think my magic came from?"

He contracts his shoulders. "At the time, I didn't know. Didn't really understand it. I thought perhaps you were part fae —or fully fae, like me. I mean, you're an orphan, right? It could be. I knew you were afraid of your magic. That much I understood, but I didn't consider what it could be." He bites his lip, then stares at me. "That's an incredible skill."

"Well, I don't know how to use it, and I'm not going to go around drinking people's blood. But yesterday morning, I still had a trace of your magic. I guess not from blood, but... your seed. It turns out that it doesn't need to be taken orally."

He reaches out and strokes my hair. "Maybe you should try both methods and compare."

"I will. Later. Just don't call it *that other milk* because it's the most asinine description I've ever heard. And I want to finish telling you what I was trying to."

His eyes darken. "Do you have any idea how crazy that dream drove me? You were so beautiful with your lips around my cock. Do you mind if I call it cock? You're all into..." He waves a hand in the air. "Polite words."

"I was under the table, you couldn't possibly have seen—"

A gust of air reaches me and lifts me from the bed for a second.

He raises an eyebrow. "Couldn't I? I recall removing that silly, pesky table. And you didn't answer my question."

"I don't have any problem with words. I'll suck your cock

until you fill my throat with come. Is that what you want to hear? But I'm trying to tell you something."

He grimaces. "And you expect me to pay attention?"

I roll my eyes. "Whatever. Anyway. You told me that you could extract a thought if you touched someone with that intention, and that's what I did. I put a hand on Renel's arm, trying to find out where he was keeping you, and I had a series of clear visions, except that they were obviously wrong, since I didn't see any desert or desert keep. I saw a strange place; an island with a tower, then a raven, a symbol..."

He straightens and his tone shifts immediately. "Tower? What exactly did you see?"

Tower... Right. Perhaps like the one he was searching in his dreams.

The images of the vision are still ingrained in my mind. "A tower, a raven, a bridge, a gate, a lake with an island in it, ice, a plaque with the drawing of a heart, an eye, and a teardrop. But it was wrong."

"Astra." His voice is shaky, his eyes wide, and he reaches a hand to me. "Can you let me see it?"

"Sure."

As soon as his hand wraps around my wrist, those images flash through my mind in succession, even clearer than in my memory. A dark tower stands on an island, with lush, green vegetation, in the middle of a lake with steamy water. A covered bridge leads to it, with a gate and a plaque with a drawing of a heart, an eye, and a teardrop

His eyes are even wider when he pulls his hand and stares at me. "You... Found it."

ASTRA

Marlak is stupefied in front of me, but before I ask him what exactly I found, the door downstairs opens, and Nelsin's voice reaches us.

"Hello, lovebirds, we don't want to disturb your sleep—or other activities."

Marlak holds my shoulders and kisses my cheek. "I love you, you know? And... Do you mind if I tell you and Ferer at the same time? It has to do with the secrets Renel made me keep."

"Tell Nelsin too. And Ziven." Marlak has a slight frown, and I add, "You said you'd need help. More people to help you."

He pauses, then nods. "You're right. Let's go."

"Go first. I'm half undressed." I look around the room, trying to remember where I left my leggings, when I catch Marlak's intense stare directed at me. "What?"

He chuckles. "Let me enjoy this moment. And I'll wait for you."

My leggings are lying in a corner of the room, and I put them on quickly.

Marlak extends a hand to me, and I take it. He pulls it to his lips and kisses it. I descend the stairs behind him, his hand reaching back to keep holding mine.

Ziven sits at the kitchen table, drinking water, or at least something I hope is water, while the two fae stand apart from each other.

Nelsin glances at our interlocked hands and smiles. I realize this is the first time anyone sees us together. The first time we *are* together. Marlak pulls back a chair for me with his free hand, where I sit, and then he sits beside me, across from Ziven.

The Krastel prince looks at me and gives me a lazy smile. "Have you ever had fae wine?"

"Just a little."

He scrunches his face. "The hangover is the same."

Marlak scowls. "I don't recall anyone asking."

Ziven raises his glass of water. "I'll gladly impart my wisdom freely and voluntarily. I'm that generous."

I notice then that Ziven is wearing a choker necklace made of leather, with a familiar blue stone at its center. I point at it. "Is that your opus stone?"

He nods. "Ferer's ingenuity. Now, if my connection to my magic is cut, I'll have bigger problems. Or no problems, considering I'll be dead."

Ferer sits beside him. "We're trying to see if it works."

Ziven turns his glass upside down and holds it above the table. "It does." The water is frozen inside it, but then the block of ice falls from the glass, ice shards going everywhere. "Oops." Ziven moves his hand over the table, palm down. "I can evaporate it." Indeed the ice turns to water, and then slowly evaporates.

Impressive magic. And he can heat water, unlike Marlak.

Nelsin takes his glass and refills it. "You're supposed to *drink* the water, not play with it."

"I'm testing the opus stone! It seems to be working great, maybe even better than at my wrist." He places the glass on the table and points at Nelsin and Ferer. "Two brilliant fae."

Beside me, Marlak rolls his eyes, and Ziven points at him. "I'm sure you're brilliant too."

Marlak turns to me. "Do you trust him?" His tone is playful, but I know that the question is true.

Ziven has no loyalties right now—which means someone could potentially bribe him. But I don't think he wants money or even that he wants his birthright throne by any means. What I see in him is a survivor, someone striving to keep going despite all odds, and I admire that. And then, there's a gut feeling telling me he's trustworthy.

I smile. "I wouldn't trust him with a bottle of wine, but other than that, he's mostly decent."

Ziven waves a hand in the air. "Decent with my friends, indecent with my lovers."

"Nobody asked you." Marlak's voice cracks with annoyance. "Are you still drunk? Go lie down and recover. I have serious issues to discuss."

"I'm not drunk." Ziven stops with the silly act. "Just trying to diffuse the situation." He points at Ferer and Nelsin. "Did you know these two won't talk to each other?"

Ferer glares at him. "That is *none* of your business, and if you bring it up one more time, I'll be the first to test what happens when your magic flow is cut."

Ziven shrinks his shoulders, but doesn't utter another peep.

Marlak gestures to Nelsin. "Sit. I have something important to discuss with you."

The cat-eared fae takes a place at the head of the table.

Raising his dagger in the air, Marlak continues, "And I can finally reveal a secret I've been keeping for a long time."

Nelsin's top ears perk up and he rests his chin on his hand. "Oooh. I love secrets."

Marlak glares at him. "Perhaps you and the human prince might want to go on a stroll. This is no joke."

"No joke." Nelsin shows the palms of his hands. "I'll be silent."

Marlak glances at me, a question in his eyes. I think he's

second-guessing his decision to trust Nelsin and Ziven, but I trust them, even if they're playful. I give him an encouragement nod, or perhaps a nudging nod. He squeezes my hand, then turns to the others.

"I made deals with my brother, deals I regret now, deals keeping me silent." He waves his dagger. "This artifact will help me break the deals for a short period of time, enough to talk about things he's forbidden me to mention."

He makes two slashing motions with the dagger in the air, forming an x as if cutting a hole in a thick fabric, then glances at everybody, and finally sets his eyes on me.

"My sister survived the accident."

Gasps sound in the kitchen, and indeed I feel air whooshing out of my lungs. I'm surprised, but when I think back, it makes so much sense.

Marlak nods. "She's been kept in a royal prison; the blue tower. If I make any move against my brother, he'll kill her. I can't even mention that I'm the true king or that I have the crown and could put it on my head if I wanted. For years, I've been searching for her prison and searching for a way to get rid of my deals with Renel."

So that's what he'd been searching for; his sister, a girl imprisoned when she was barely a child.

Waving the dagger, he gives me a warm look. "Thanks to Astra, the sundering dagger has been activated, so that's one step. I can't even kill Renel, and he can't kill me, or we'll both die. If I've been cautious, that's one reason. Now, back to Mirella."

He glances at me again. "Mirella Isabel—most people don't know her full first name—I need to find her and free her." His eyes dim with sadness. "I wanted to trust Renel, trust that he was trying to do the right thing, but only a monster imprisons his own sister."

Closing his eyes, Marlak takes a deep breath, then continues, "Astra saw what I'm certain is her location, and I'll need to go there as soon as possible. I don't want Renel to do anything against Lidiane or Astra's sister. And oh, never doubt what he's capable of."

For the first time I feel I understand him, understand what he spent so long searching for, even understand why he attacked my carriage. He was looking for his sister. Shame prickles my skin and constricts my chest when I remember thinking he was a villain trying to take the Crystal Court throne for selfish reasons. It was never that. And even if he wants the throne, it's fair. Still, there's one thing I still need to understand.

"Marlak, I know it pains you, but now that you can speak, can you let us know who killed your family? We don't need details."

He swallows and stares at the tabletop. "It was *my* fire. I walked in on Renel strangling Mirella in the treasure room. Strangling her, and she was slightly younger than him, mind you. Thirteen. What kind of teenager strangles a child? I was so angry. So angry. I regret it. I don't know what happened. There was fire. Screams. Our parents came to see what was happening... And I think the fire got out of control."

Tears pool in his eyes. "Fire magic can do that. It's my primary magic. Was, I guess. And there was a curse, a curse that the murderer of the king would be marked." He points at his scars and takes a deep breath. "As you can see..."

His breathing is labored and shallow, and when I'm almost telling him that there's no need to say anything else, he continues, "Then I remember being in my room, a healer applying some balm on my skin, and Renel walks in, saying he wouldn't tell anyone what happened, asking me to agree to keep that secret. I thought he was trying to protect me, despite everything. I was in pain, I was delirious, and I'm not even sure about how much time had passed. Next thing I know, a servant is telling me to run, that I'm a king killer and likely to be executed if I stay in the castle. I didn't understand. And then I see Renel again, offering to help me escape, claiming that everything was complicated. I took his offer, and he showed me a secret passage out of the castle. On the way out, he told me my sister survived. I was ecstatic, thrilled, relieved —until he said she was being kept in a high-security prison, and that I should never interfere with the dealings of the kingdom, or she would pay for that. I reached out and touched him, just a brief second, but long enough to get the name of the prison: the blue tower. Then I ran. Ran without direction, and then I started finding the royal treasure. It followed me. It's when I realized that I was the true king despite having killed my stepfather. You can't become king if you kill the previous king; there's old magic preventing it from happening, but I think it considers whether the murder is intentional or not, and it was never my intention. Still, guilt weighs on me. It was *my* fire. I vowed never to use it again—and haven't used it since."

I had guessed some bits and pieces of what happened, but could never have imagined that it had indeed been his own fire that killed his family. I didn't even know he could wield fire, and then, the truth is that he no longer can.

Everyone is somber and astonished at the table. Even Ziven and Nelsin are downcast.

Marlak grimaces. "So I *am* the king of the Crystal Court. My stepfather had named me as his heir, and the fact that I can summon the relics proves it. But what matters now is rescuing Mirella. I know where she is, but I'll need to plan this carefully. It's why I'm telling you this. And so you know."

He squeezes my hand again and turns to me. "You also need to understand why I traveled so much, why I... did things the way I did."

I nod. I can see that this is also an apology, an explanation.

He turns back to everyone. "Astra saw a series of visions. On their own, they might be incomprehensible, and I understand you wouldn't have thought much of them, but for me, they mean something. The raven is the old symbol of the Crystal Court. A heart, an eye, and a teardrop means that it has a spell not to be seen. And the location, it's a hot lake, and it has to be in the Southern Hot Pools. I have been there before, many years ago, but didn't find the prison—obviously. It was enchanted. But now, in Astra's vision, I saw where it was. I can find it."

Solemn silence hovers over the table, and we all stare at Marlak, until Nelsin scratches his fae ears. "So your plan is to travel south and rescue your sister? Not alone, I suppose."

"It will be safer if I go on my own." Marlak strokes his chin.

I hate that he has to leave, hate that we've been together for such a short period and have to be torn apart, but it's true that I understand him. And I don't suggest going with him because my magic is not strong enough, and when I use it, I get attacked, which is definitely not something I want.

I still need to understand where he's going. "Aren't the Southern Hot Pools outside the Crystal Court territory?"

He nods. "It's a royal prison, from the time when courts didn't have physical boundaries like they do now, and that's why you'll find Crystal Court buildings all over the land. And to be fair, the Crystal Court is an amalgamation of smaller courts, so that's another reason."

Ferer contracts his brows. "Isn't that by the Spider Court Territory?"

"A little south from there, yes," Marlak says. "In the unclaimed Icy Lands."

I recall my dream, the dream about the pit of death, and the fear we both felt in that moment. "Is it dangerous? Beyond a pit?"

Marlak shakes his head. "No. I've been in that area. I think your visions and dreams, they're not always literal. That palace you dream about, for example, doesn't exist."

I suck in a gust of cold air, and mutter, "I'm not sure of that. But if you're saying the Blue Tower is not dangerous and you've been in that area before, I suppose you're right."

"In your vision, there was a bridge to it, across a hot lake. The bridge gate has a heart, an eye, and a teardrop." Marlak really remembers minute details from my vision.

Ziven perks up, even more interested in the conversation for some reason.

I recall the lake from my vision. "You could freeze the water or glide above it, right?"

Marlak presses his lips together. "There could be some magic preventing freezing the water or crossing above it using air magic. I might have to take the bridge."

Ziven raises a hand, as if he were in a class. "Am I allowed to ask a question?"

"Ask away," Marlak says. "I've already told you what I couldn't tell you, and now, even when the magic of the dagger fades, we can still discuss how to reach that tower."

"Right." Ziven leans forward on the table. "This is all based on what Astra saw in Renel's mind, right? How can you be sure that's where the princess is? He could be thinking about something else, like reminiscing about a cool tavern or something. Fine, a tavern would not be hidden like that. Anyway, Astra was trying to find where Renel was keeping you. What makes you so sure that's where your sister is?"

Marlak bites his lip. "I just feel it. When you reach out for information in someone's mind, sometimes it gives you something else, but it has a meaning. My sister's location has been on my mind since the day I ran away from the castle. Why wouldn't Astra find that when thinking about me? It makes sense."

"You need to trust the way magic works," Ferer adds. "It's not always clear cut and straightforward."

"Fair." Ziven nods. "Now, that symbol you mentioned, the heart with an eye and a drop, I know what it means. It's not a teardrop, but a drop of blood. Human kingdoms also use it. When you have that symbol, only someone with a king's blood can do something. If it's a lock or a door, for example, only a king or queen or their descendants can open it or pass through. As far as I know, any monarch's blood will do. I know it because one of the old servants told me that, told me that this would be one of the reasons King Leonius would keep me alive; if he ever needed something opened, or needed to activate some magical object or whatever, I would be able to do it, not him. So it was one reason not to kill me."

Marlak half smirks. "That makes things easier, then, since I'm the true king."

One thing doesn't make sense. "But how did Renel get there?"

"He was with Mirella," Marlak says. "She's the king's daughter."

Ziven waves a finger in the air. "Back to my point. As far as I know, it doesn't work like that. A nominated king can't open that kind of lock. It's old magic, either fae or Tiurian."

"Tiurians had no royalty," I say.

"Maybe." Ziven shrugs. "But the whole point is to protect a monarch's family. Let's say someone coerces the king to nominate them. The magic still wouldn't work."

Marlak rolls his eyes. "Then what happens to kingdoms where kings die and are replaced, or new kingdoms? The magic will never work?"

"It will. For their children, if their father is not a usurper, like my uncle. You're the true king, right? Your children will be able to open whatever king's blood magical lock they need, even though you can't."

Marlak narrows his eyes. "I think you're making that up."

Ziven raises his hands, showing his palms. "I'm not. But hey, maybe someone made that up and told me that, so I would be a little more optimistic about my survival chances. As you can see, eventually King Leonius decided he'll never need me to open anything."

"I think Ziven has a point," Ferer says. "It makes sense that old magic would protect families. But we could research and double check."

Marlak taps his fingers on the table. "There's no time to research. I'll leave right away to get Mirella, and then if Renel threatens Lidiane or Tarlia, I can confront him." He looks at us all. "Meanwhile, find a way to tell them to escape. Once I have my sister, and once the girls are out of the castle, the way is clear for me. But I need to plan this trip and go there soon, before Renel realizes I've found my sister's location."

I want to tell him that if he's waited years for this, he could wait one more day, but if I knew where my family was, and if I had the means to rescue them, I wouldn't want to wait even an hour.

"We'll do our part." Ferer is thoughtful. "You could take a boat south, from Krastel."

Marlak shakes his head. "I'll go to the Queen's River, then fly over the ocean until the shores of the Spider Court, then walk south."

Ziven raises an eyebrow. "You can fly?"

"Yes," Marlak says between gritted teeth.

Ferer nods. "Too cold to fly closer, and no boats will get that far south. But the Spider Court keeps track of intruders, and then there are ice golems in the Icy Lands."

"They target fae magic," Marlak says, "and for some reason, can't sense me."

"Ha! They look for pointy ears!" Nelsin says.

"Something like that." Marlak runs a finger over his own round ears.

I'm trying to recap all that was said. "So that's it? The danger is *getting* there? Once there, you'll just rescue your sister?"

"There could be traps and other obstacles, but I think I can deal with them." He looks at the others. "What I need is help in preparing a place for my sister when she comes."

That sounds strange. "Can't it be our house?" I don't say *the island house* because I'm still not sure how much he wants Ziven to know, even though at this point he told him half his life story.

Marlak swallows. "Mirella... was raised differently. She would want something more... refined."

His words hurt for some reason, as if he's implying our house isn't good enough for his sister, even if it's good enough for me. The only reason I don't let go of his hand is that I don't want him to think I'm making a big deal about it.

Ziven snorts. "She's coming from a prison! Please tell me you're kidding. You can't seriously suggest your sister deserves a better dwelling than your freaking wife."

Wow, he said the words I couldn't say.

Marlak has murder in his eyes. "I don't mean *better*. I mean refined. I have a fancier hideout. And when I brought Astra, I wasn't worried about pleasing her."

"Yes, you were," Nelsin smirks. "You wanted servants and a luxurious decoration, and were terrified that she'd hate that house, but we told you that what mattered was that it was clean, comfortable, and safe. Eventually you agreed because you thought it was the safest place for her. Doesn't your sister need to be safe?"

"She has strong magic."

I let go of his hand. Asshole. As if I didn't have magic.

Marlak turns to me and pulls my hand. "Astra, you aren't jealous of my sister, are you?"

"No!" The thought is disgusting and ridiculous. Then I smirk. "It's just that I can see that she's your priority."

He kisses my hand. "*You*'re my priority. You're everything to me." His eyes are soft, beseeching. "But my sister is *also* important. She was raised by a king, unlike me and my brother. My mother was a tavern maid. My father was the king's guardian. I wasn't raised as a prince, not until much later, when my mother married my stepfather. I'm different. You weren't raised as a princess either. I just want to make sure Mirella feels at ease, that's all. It's not about being better. What's better than being among nature and mountains and a river? What's better than freedom? I *love* our house. But I don't know if Mirella would love it."

I sigh, and he kisses my cheek, then says, "I love you, Astra, have always loved you." He pulls me against his chest and I close my eyes.

Young love is so silly, so fragile. And yet it's true that our love is young like a sprout just coming out of the soil, when a heavy gust of wind can uproot it.

Nelsin's voice interrupts us. "Would you like us to leave, so you can make love on the table?"

Marlak huffs. "Don't be crass."

Nelsin points at himself. "Me? Since when is love crass?"

Ziven clicks his tongue. "Leave him. He owes Astra an explanation because it did sound as if his sister was more important than her."

Marlak glares at him. "Do you value your life?"

"A lot, actually." Ziven smiles. "I tend to hold on to it with utter stubbornness and tenacity, or I would have been gone a long time ago."

"Then why would you exasperate me?" Marlak's voice is thunderous. "You know you're no match for my magic, human."

"Hey, I'm just saying what everyone's thinking." Ziven raises his hands. "You should be thankful, if anything."

"You're saying what *you're* thinking."

Ziven points at me. "Ask her."

Marlak turns to me, his expression suddenly changed into concern. I smile. "He's just trying to help."

Ferer takes a deep breath. "So, can you bring Mirella to your temporary hideout?"

Marlak stares at him for a moment. "I guess so. For now."

"When do you plan to leave?" Nelsin asks.

"Right away." He turns to me. "I'm so sorry. But I'll be back. I promise."

This time I'm the one who squeezes his hand. "I understand. If it was me, I'd also rush to rescue my sister."

He narrows his eyes. "I'm not sure I agree."

Oh, he means Tarlia. "It's different. Tarlia's still safe."

"Until how long?"

"We'll try to get them out," Nelsin says.

Marlak nods. "Please. One less thing for me to worry about."

He runs a finger over my face. "We'll find a way to hide your magic, Astra." It's as if he can understand my thoughts. "And I want you to develop it, study it, while I'm gone. The stronger you are, the better protected you'll be." He smiles. "I've always told you that."

I smile back.

Ziven is resting his face on the back of his hand. "You're forgetting to ask something."

Marlak turns to him and frowns. "I think it's all clear. I was thinking I'd have a lot more trouble deciphering the visions, but they're quite straightforward."

"Yes." Ziven dips his chin and smirks. "And you need to ask me something."

"I think you still need to rest. Drained magic, right? It's what happens when you use trinkets."

"Ooooh." Ziven touches his ringless fingers. "Look who has no trinkets whatsoever."

Marlak raises a fist. "These are different. I still have my own magic."

The smirk hasn't faded from Ziven's lips. "Doesn't change the fact that you still need to ask me something."

"You know what? You're right. What are you still doing here?"

"Wroooong." Ziven's singsong voice echoes through the kitchen.

"Marlak," Ferer says. "The human is annoying but he brings up a valid point."

"What valid point?" Marlak sounds absolutely exasperated.

"The blood magic. You don't have a king's blood." Ferer pauses, glances at Ziven, then says, "He does."

"And?"

Shit. They're right. Ziven needs to go with Marlak. The Krastel prince seems to be willing to do that, if he's the one suggesting Marlak should ask him something.

I run a hand over Marlak's arm, trying to calm him down, and say, "I think Ziven's offering to go with you."

Marlak blinks.

Ziven leans back. "I want him to *ask me* to go with him."

I narrow my eyes for a brief moment, then smile at Ziven, hoping he gets the hint. "Just tell him you're eager to help."

Ziven shrugs. "If he asks, I might."

Great. Now he managed to annoy even me. "Why are you being an asshole?"

"Me?" Ziven laughs. "Right. I'm the asshole."

Marlak shakes his head. "He'll be a liability with his weak magic."

I guess I have to smooth things out. "But if only humans can step into the Icy Lands and not be targeted by golems, he's the only one who can go with you. And if he's right that the magic lock or whatever will only open to someone whose king's blood has been inherited, if you don't bring him with you, your journey will be for nothing."

Marlak doesn't look convinced. "Two ifs. Makes it iffy."

"Just ask," I whisper.

My husband takes the deepest breath I've ever seen him taking, then gets up and stands by Ziven. "Oh, mighty human prince, the true Krastel heir, will you give me the honor to accompany me on my journey to rescue my sister from the Blue Tower?"

Ziven gets up, all traces of mockery gone from his face, and extends a hand. "It will be my honor, fae king."

Marlak nods and shakes his hand.

I'm glad he's not going to travel alone, and I'm starting to think they won't strangle each other on the way, but I'm still feeling a lot of unease. The memories from the dream about the pit of death haven't left me, and with them, a bitter taste in my mouth and a hollow feeling in my stomach. I don't know if I can bear losing my husband. And yet I understand he has to go, and I need to trust his magic.

Marlak turns to me, regret and sorrow marring his eyes. I get up, stand by him, and say, "I can't wait to meet Mirella. I'm sure she's lovely."

He pulls me in for a hug. "I'll be back soon. You'll be with Nelsin and Ferer. Work on your magic."

"I will. Even if I hate it when you leave. I hated it last time you left."

"You did?" He has a soft chuckle. "I thought you didn't like me yet."

"I thought the same thing." I laugh. "I was wrong, of course."

Ferer gets up. "What are the supplies you need? Portable food, I suppose. Weapons. Anything else? Are you taking your suitcase?"

Marlak shakes his head. "Too risky. I'll need duffel bags. See what Ziven needs. I just need some time with Astra."

"Private time?" Nelsin raises an eyebrow.

"Not *that* private," Marlak says. "Ten minutes."

Nelsin shrugs. "That *can* be enough."

Marlak scoffs, then pulls me upstairs to the room where we slept and stands in front of me, holding my face. "Do you believe me when I say I hate to leave you?"

"Of course I do."

"And that Mirella is not more important than you?"

"Love has no hierarchy, Marlak. I like that you love your family. And your friends."

"You *are* my family. And... do you want to have children one day? I know we should have discussed it earlier, but—"

I don't know why he's bringing up these big questions, but they cause a chill to run down my spine. "You're scaring me."

He blinks. "You're afraid of having kids?"

I sigh. "You're talking as if you fear not coming back, as if you won't have time to ask these questions."

"How can I be thinking I won't have time, if I'm asking you about kids? We haven't made one yet. You're taking something, aren't you? To prevent—"

"Yes. And yes, we'll have a family, but focus on your journey now. And I swear, I'll spend all my time working on my magic.

I'll also read the books you left me. And when you come back, we'll plan what's next."

He pulls me in and kisses me. It's a slow, soft, kiss. It's a long kiss, swallowing up an eternity. It's a promise, a vow, but most of all, a goodbye. A painful goodbye.

The look he gives me when we part is so soft. "You made a promise this morning, and I can't wait to see it fulfilled."

I'm not sure what he means. "What promise?"

He runs his thumb over my lower lips. "It involved this." He presses his finger, then points downwards. "And this."

"Crass. Asshole."

He hugs me tight and kisses my cheek. "I'm starting to think it's an endearment."

"Maybe it is."

I laugh even if part of me wants to desperately cry in anguish.

12

RENEL

My face is calm, placid, the face of a perfect king. Inside, my stomach turns and turns, dancing to the rhythm of my berserk heart. I sense the eyes of the counselors watching me rather than the knight. They're always watching, searching for the fissure through which they'll break me.

The knight gets up and says, "A wall in the keep was destroyed, and a cell opened. The enchanted giant is gone."

I swallow, waiting for him to mention my brother. My hands feel cold even if they're getting humid, but I can't wipe them here.

He continues, "All signs point to a giant attack."

"Signs? Were there any survivors? Were they questioned?" My tone is haughty and annoyed, as the occasion demands.

"All the guards survived. But they were enchanted and don't remember anything. We would like to know how to proceed."

"Where are the guards?"

The knight lowers his head. "Restrained and brought back. They're in the Jewel Prison."

I was going to pretend to think there were no prisoners in

the desert keep, but then realize there was no reason for me to know that information, so I ask, "Who's watching the prisoners in the keep?"

"It was empty, your highness. That prison hadn't been in use for years."

"I see. You're dismissed for now."

Empty. It means nobody was found—or killed. My breath leaves my chest in a whoosh. I think I'd be dead by now if they had killed my brother, considering it would be my fault, considering my deal with Marlak.

The giants either freed or captured him. Freed, most likely, or they would have sent us a message or something. Great. Now he's conniving with giants. My only solace is that they can't cross the Charmed River.

The knight leaves the room, and I look at the members of the Council, waiting for their reaction.

I always wait, let them speak, let them voice their obvious conclusions, let them come up with suggestions, most of them moronic. All I do is stir the direction of these suggestions— when I care. Sometimes I just let them decide whatever they want, or else argue with each other until their throats are sore.

This was the first thing Zorwal told me when I assumed the throne. *Keep the counselors happy, and you'll keep your position.* This line of thought likely explains how he rose from mere healer guild representative to leader of the council.

Sometimes I feel useless here, but more often than not I feel that at least I'm keeping the kingdom from tearing itself apart, and keeping the most bloodthirsty members of the council from wrecking havoc in the Crystal Court.

The council has nine members, all from old, affluent, powerful families. When I first came to power, my instinct was to dissolute or reform the council, but Zorwal told me that this was just theater meant to keep those families happy, to make them think they have a say in the dealings of the kingdom. As long as they believe they're getting their way, they'll support me. If they feel their power threatened, they could try to assassinate me, question my claim, or even worse, turn their forces against the kingdom. Of course I don't want any of that, so here I am, trying to make sure all these snakes walk out of here satisfied with whatever decision is made.

I'm also hoping they won't realize there was a prisoner in the keep.

Zorwal doesn't give any indication he suspects me of wrongdoing and addresses the five members of the council. "What do you say?"

"I always said we couldn't trust the giants," Tuela says. She's an older fae with a round face. Her family has a lot of influence in the Jewel City, and for some reason, she's always afraid of everything. Her suggestions for safety always involve some kind of violence against the lower fae.

That said, this time I agree with her. Making a deal with the giants was madness, and wasn't something I supported, but I can't say *I told you so* to the council. Well, here we are.

Claus taps on the table. He's from a family of merchants originally from the south and always finds a very logical justification for violence. "Perhaps they changed their mind about their deal, and now wanted to rescue their kin."

He means the enchanted giant, who perhaps wasn't enchanted at all, but I don't want to bring that up.

"That's possible," Silvan says. He's ambitious and dangerous, and always says whatever will get him the most support. "But backing on a deal is an affront."

"Destroying the prison is an affront!" Tuela says. "It's an attack on the Crystal Court. Next, they'll be marching upon us."

Kilmar, a young counselor who never seems to care about anything, stifles a snort. "They still can't cross the river. Let's not be hasty."

"What if they can?" Tuela bangs a fist on the table. "This is a declaration of war! We need to get to them first."

"We could," Claus agrees. "Before they have time to make a bolder move." He turns to me. "Let's assemble our army, march to the Shadow Lands, and destroy the giants."

Unhinged. They're always unhinged—and yet I nod as if he'd given a very sensible suggestion.

Silvan, the bootlicker, straightens on his chair, likely sensing an opportunity to come up as a leader. "We could expand the kingdom to the Shadow Lands."

Exactly. Insane. I wait for one of them to mention the obvious fact that we have no chances against the giants in their own land, and minimal survival chances north of the Charmed River.

Instead, Tuela nods. "Yes, and get rid of their threat."

I'm positive she thinks that even her shadow is a threat.

Claus smiles. "If we take control of the Shadow Lands, we'll be on both sides of the Fae Territories. We could... It would be good."

The implied suggestion is to take over the fae territories standing between us and the Shadow Lands. They're absolutely deranged today.

Tuela places a strand of hair behind her ear. "Fighting the giants is dangerous. We'd face many losses."

Finally someone utters something mildly rational.

"We can send an army of lower fae," Claus suggests.

"Where would we gather that many of them?" Nora asks. She's one of the youngest members of the council, with long brown hair framing a thin face. Mild-mannered and quiet, she has flirted with me quite a few times. She claims to love the lower fae and that she wants to take care of them, but the truth is that her family is the one with the most enchanted servants in the entire kingdom, most of them coming straight from her "charitable" orphanage.

"Oh, there are lower fae everywhere," Tuela says. "They're hanging around, threatening us. This would be a great chance to conscript them, get rid of their menace."

The discussion is getting out of hand, and I have to intervene.

"Each of you has made wonderful points, and came up with

great suggestions." I didn't say when. "The giants can be a threat, no doubt, but if they think they can trick us into attacking them in their territory, where they're strongest, they're wrong." My voice has the confidence and command of a king. "If they want to threaten us, they'll pay for that. But not on *their* terms. On ours. If they do cross the river and march south, they'll first reach the other fae courts." I smirk. "Let them reach them. We'll be forewarned and will secure our borders. For now, what we can do is set some watch up north. Let's watch the giants, see what they'll do next. They won't take us by surprise again."

Tuela stares at me with wide eyes. I think she's even trembling. "What if they're in league with some fae courts?"

I refrain from rolling my eyes, but then again, if giants can rescue Marlak, what else can they do? "We'll surely notice if giants cross the river."

She shakes her head. "We need to prepare an army. Let's gather all the free lower fae."

"That's horrible!" Nora yells.

Claus grimaces. "We can't simply gather all the lower fae at once. They'll revolt."

"There's no threat of war yet." Zorwal's voice rises in the room with all the authority even I fail to have. Sometimes, I almost think he uses some strange form of compulsion that works on the higher fae.

He continues, "And no reason to believe the giants can or will cross the river. Our king is wise. Let's double our watch and wait."

Tuela raises her hands in the air. "Waiting, waiting. We're always waiting to be attacked."

I can sense the uneasiness in the council. They want action, blood, revenge, as if they had to do something to mend their wounded pride. Most of them would love an opportunity to attack the lower fae.

Zorwal then says, "We need to consider what to do with the Desert Keep guards."

Claus shifts in his seat. "Interrogate them until they tell us what happened."

At this point, only blood will appease them, and I think I know what to do.

"They *have* told us what happened," I say. "And yet the truth is that they failed. Our guards should protect our kingdom with their lives, and they clearly did not do that. My suggestion is to sentence them to death."

Claus nods. "A public execution would set a good example."

Nobody protests, and I sense that they all like the idea. Well, I hate it.

I keep my voice level. "Public executions are spectacular and exemplary indeed, but they can also incense the lower fae, and worst of all, create martyrs. We wouldn't want that. Our guards are the ones who need to learn a lesson. Whispers and secrets have a way to spread further and make a bigger impression than announcements. Let them know how we deal with traitors. We can order the guards from the desert keep to be executed tonight, in the dungeons of the Jewel Prison. Let only our army know about it. They're the ones who need to learn from the example."

Nora shakes her head. "I disagree. My family could take these lower fae—"

"As if you needed more enchanted servants!" Claus says.

"To protect them!" Nora yells.

"Your heart is in the right place, Nora." Meaning in the middle of her chest. I guess I *can* be manipulative, because I know exactly how to look at her to get her to acquiesce. "But setting an example is important. It's the honor of the Crystal Court at stake."

She nods.

I stare at everyone. "Is anyone against this decision?"

Tuela huffs. "We still need to prepare an army."

I pretend to consider her words. "We can discuss this later, for sure. And keep watch."

My thoughts spin as they call back the knight and Zorwal

relays him the orders. I'm surprised that none of the counselors wondered what the giants wanted to do in the keep, that none of them wondered if there was some secret prisoner there. Zorwal might have noticed, though, and I have to keep myself from trembling when considering our debriefing in a few minutes.

Those debriefings terrorize my sleep. Zorwal always finds something wrong, something I could have done differently. I learned to ignore his tauntings, ignore his criticism. If I can cool down the council and quash their maniacal suggestions, I feel that I succeeded, no matter how much pain Zorwal makes me endure afterward. This time, of course he'll notice I didn't mention the biggest issue, didn't pry on the reason the giants attacked the keep. As long as he doesn't suspect me, I can deal with physical pain.

And then I wonder what exactly the giants wanted with my brother. Some kind of deal? Would they rally behind him? But why? It doesn't make sense. And then there are the poor keep guards. Really, how could anyone expect them to face giants, of all creatures?

When the meeting ends, I rush upstairs to the training grounds by the Royal Terrace, where Azur tends to spend his mornings. No sign of him. Zorwal will expect me in ten minutes, so I have to be fast. I rush down to the lower tier area, which houses the fae taking care of the servants, and where Azur has his secondary bedroom, other than the one beside mine.

The reason he chose a room down here puzzled me for a long time, until I realized that it's probably so that he has some privacy for his dalliances, which is fair. It must be nice to have privacy, unlike me. In my case, everyone knows exactly who sleeps in my bed—or how empty it's been lately.

I knock on his door, hoping he's here—and alone.

In a few seconds, the latch clicks, and then the door opens just wide enough for me to see Azur's face, looking startled for some reason.

"The meeting's over?"

"Yes. I need a few seconds."

He hesitates, then steps aside and opens the door. "Come in."

I never understood why he keeps this room looking so drab and simple. At least this time he has some books on his table. A quick glance surprises me. *Soulmates & Soulbonds, Love Scents, The Manual of Seduction, Spells for Attraction.* This is so unlike him.

"What's with the reading?"

He flicks his hair back. "Didn't you ask me to help you?"

"Oh." I'm actually touched that he's going out of his way to help me with Astra. "Let me know what you find out—other than making her laugh."

He smirks and nods. "Of course. And what was the meeting about?"

His question is surprising. Usually Azur is on top of things, collecting information even before it reaches me or Zorwal. I clear my throat. "The giants attacked the Desert keep."

He raises his eyebrows, visibly surprised. "And?"

"The guards are enchanted not to remember what goes on in there, so nobody knows we've been there, for now at least. No mention of any prisoner—dead or alive. It means Marlak's gone."

Azur shakes his head. "You need to listen to me when it matters. I knew that prison wouldn't keep him."

I shrug. "How was I supposed to guess the giants would betray us?"

"You think they freed him?"

"It's the only option that makes sense."

"He's accumulating ally after ally." He snorts. "The giants... Unbelievable."

"Yes, but they can't cross the Charmed River, and that's not why I'm here. I only have a few minutes before my debriefing, and I need your help. It's urgent."

The corners of his eyes tense. "What is it?"

"The guards in the keep, they survived, and were brought to the Jewel Prison."

The color drains from Azur's already pale face as he stares at me.

I continue, "They were sentenced to death. I need you to free them."

Azur blinks "Uh. What?"

"They'll be executed tonight."

"And you want me to..." He swallows. "Who ordered the execution?"

I exhale. "I did, but I had no choice."

"Let me guess." He raises a finger in the air. "The councilors would have given you really nasty looks if you didn't order this execution."

"Something like that. Anyway. I want you to rescue them."

He stares at me, eyes wide. "From the Jewel Prison? And then where am I supposed to hide them? In my pockets? Oh, I know. In the royal coffers!"

"Just free them."

"Renel, they'll be dead men the moment they step out of that prison. They won't have any respite. No shelter will keep them safe." Azur has a point, of course. He gives me a sideways look. "And since when do you care for the lower fae?"

"Since always, and you know it. Regardless. This is about what's right. These men did nothing wrong. They probably never even chose to be guards in that prison."

"Obviously. But how do you expect me to—"

"Buy them passages to the Nowhere Lands. I know that the ships in the port smuggle people and have been doing it since forever. And don't tell me these guards have family, friends, or whatever here and would hate to leave the Crystal Court. I know it. But it's the best I can do."

Azur bites his lip and stares at me. "That's all? Free five prisoners from a high-security prison in less than eight hours?"

"Wasn't I supposed to trust you? There. I trust your magic. If anyone can do something like that, it's you. That said, don't risk your life. Can you agree to do your best to free them and not let any guards know it was you? Or that I ordered it?"

His eyes soften and the corner of his lips lifts. "I can try my best, of course."

I nod, glad to be rid of at least one of the worries dragging me down. Of course Azur can't deny any of my requests, but that doesn't mean I'm going to start ordering him around like a dog. And I don't want him to risk his life either. At the same time, he *has* more magic than any fae I know, and deep down, I'm sure he cares for the lower fae and wouldn't waste a chance to save five of them.

"I'm going now, before Zorwal…" I don't even know how to finish the sentence. Tortures me? There's no question he will.

Azur smirks. "Glares at you, I'm sure."

I narrow my eyes. "He'll glare really hard this time."

Azur chuckles and so do I, even though I have a feeling that Zorwal is going to flay me.

MARLAK

Of course I won't bring the annoying human prince with me. The only reason I agreed to it was to appease Astra. I should be offended that she thinks I'll need help from a weakling like him, but I understand she's just worried.

My plan is to ditch him in a safe hideout further south, and then find the Blue Tower on my own, with no hurdle slowing me down.

Ferer and Nelsin helped me pack clothes and supplies, and now it's time to leave. We all stand in Nelsin's tight kitchen, Nelsin and Ferer ready and alert, the human prince looking drunk and dazzled, as always, and Astra… I glance at her and my heart splits in two, wanting to stay, wanting to spend more time with her, wanting to solidify our newfound bond. She looks at me with a subtle, encouraging smile, but there's worry in her pretty eyes.

I walk to her and cup her face.

"I'll be back soon, and you shouldn't worry. You know why?"

She gives me an enchanting smile. "Why?"

"I'm going to the Icy Lands, a place with lots of water, and that's my strongest magic. I'll be invincible."

"I trust your magic."

I run a finger over her cheek and lean my forehead on hers. "I trust yours too, and I'm certain you're powerful beyond what you can imagine. There's so much you'll do, and I'm humbled to be by your side."

Astra laughs. "Don't exaggerate."

"No exaggeration." I caress her cheek with my nose. "I don't plan on leaving you behind, isolated."

"It's just now. I know." She places her hands on my shoulders. "Go rescue your sister. I understand why I can't come with you, and I know it's not because you think less of me."

I nod, and she runs a hand over my hair and kisses my cheek. "I'm looking forward to meeting Mirella, and I'm happy you found where she is."

"*You* found it."

"I guess. There's only one thing I need to ask you."

"There's nothing I wouldn't do for you."

She glances behind me. "Ziven is also good with water magic."

I frown, so taken aback by this random mention. "And?"

"I understand that you like to do things on your own, and you don't trust people, but let him help you."

Why is she asking that? As if she guessed my plans and wanted to ruin them.

I pretend to be surprised. "I already agreed he'd come with me."

"So let him help you. Don't be stubborn."

"I don't know why you think I'm being stubborn. That said, bringing someone with weak magic *could* be a burden."

"You said there would be no danger."

"There might be traps in the tower."

Her beautiful brown eyes are kind, but there's a tenacity to them. "So let him help you."

I don't think there's any point trying to argue, so I kiss her cheek. "You worry too much."

"No, I—"

I pull her in for a kiss. It's not that I wanted to silence her, but that I wanted to kiss her and taste her lips one last time, kiss her and drown in her arms, engrave in my memory the feel of her skin, her smell.

Why does it feel like I'll be gone forever? It will be two, three days at most. And then I realize that it's been only two days since I kissed her for the first time, two days with an eternity between them. Two days since I kissed her and she's become my wife in earnest.

Of course going away for that long feels like a lifetime. I want to kiss her forever, make love to her until our bodies pass out from exhaustion, then bring her thousands of breakfasts. And I'll do that—once my sister is safe.

I break the kiss, a new determination coursing through my veins. There's a time for everything. I can't wait to see Mirella, to talk to her. Can't imagine how awful these years must have been for her.

Astra tiptoes and gives me a peck on the lips, then smiles. "See you soon. And let Ziven help you."

I pull her hand and kiss it. "I will. Stay safe, Azalee."

It's hard to turn around, but I do it. I pull down my hood and walk out with Ferer. He'll accompany me to the closest river, from where I'll go to the Endless Mountains, since the Nymps can't take me further south. Meanwhile, Ziven is transcending with Nelsin, carrying our bags. The knights insisted that we should leave at the same time, for luck, and I didn't want to upset them by refusing their suggestion.

We cross the border of the village, then some sparse woods, until we reach a small river, barely big enough for any nymph presence. There's nobody around us, so I jump into the water and let the current take me until I'm caught in a swirl.

This is it. I'll rescue my sister, after all these years. I just hope I won't face too much trouble on my way.

I can't ditch the useless human prince anymore, not now that Astra asked me to trust him, so I'll have to drag that burden on top of everything.

When the swirl stops, I come out of the water and find that I'm by the Queen's River, but far from the island hideout. I can't wait to return home—to have a home with Astra. For me, this was just a place to hide while evading all kinds of enemies. And now it's *home*. Any place will be home if Astra's there. My heart can finally settle and rest, find belonging, contentment.

Nelsin is not around here, and I'm wondering if he got to the wrong spot, as he and the useless prince should have arrived before me. Maybe they won't show up. I suppose I can tell Astra it wasn't my fault, that Ziven gave up or something. Oh, what a tragedy.

I sense Cherry Cake's bond. Somehow, he always knows when I need to travel, and has been helping me for a few years now. I'm sure one day he'll fly away and disappear, and sometimes I hope he does—before an enemy finds him. For now, he wants to help, and I still need him. And maybe he knows I'm about to go on a journey alone, and that's why he knows it's safe to help. He's here, somewhere.

I walk inland, into the thick vegetation bordering this part of the river, then, in a clearing, I find Cherry Cake—with the human prince, who's petting his head as if he were a common horse.

"What are you doing?" I ask.

The prince grins. "What does it look like?"

"This is a legendary unicorn. Perhaps the last of its kind."

"And he's sweet, too." He turns to Cherry Cake and leans on his muzzle. "Right?"

"He's not yours. And not a pet."

"So? I like him."

I approach Cherry Cake and pat his flank.

"Wait a minute." The prince raises an eyebrow. "Is this *your* unicorn?"

"He's nobody's. Like I said, not a property, not a pet." I caress his mane. "He's his own creature."

"Are you jealous of the unicorn that's not yours?"

He's deranged. "Why would I be *jealous*?"

He shrugs. "I've seen you acting like this before. With Astra."

"Not only are you useless and weak, you're completely insane. Astra's my wife; I trust her. Why would I be jealous of her? Of you, of all people? Cherry Cake, on the other hand, is *not* my wife, as any person with a minimum brain would know."

Ziven frowns. "Cherry Cake? That's the legendary unicorn's name? Totally not a pet, no. I see."

"He doesn't mind the name." I sigh. "This is not going to work."

He smirks. "Marrying Cherry Cake? I'm sure not."

"I should encase you in ice again and leave you here. Or perhaps make you pass out."

The prince steps away from Cherry Cake. "I meant no offense. And I didn't know you'd be upset that I petted him. I still want to help you, Marlak."

Even his use of my name like that, as if we were the greatest pals, annoys me, and I need a deep breath. "Why do you even care?"

His expression becomes serious, earnest. "Perhaps I'm looking forward to being useful once in my life. Listen, I know you don't like me. I don't like you either, so I think we're good. But I can help, and I want to."

"You still didn't explain why."

"Fine. Humiliate me. I have nowhere to go. What am I going to do? Sit and depend on the charity and goodwill of strangers? If I can be useful, I can find a place for myself, have some hope.

So yes, I'm the beggar here. Make fun of me as much as you want."

"There's a chance you're wrong, and I won't need you to access that tower."

"I know. But there's a chance I'm right. And I can help you on the way."

"Then don't annoy me."

He shrugs. "What did I even do?"

I roll my eyes but decide to leave it. I touch Cherry Cake again, telling him where I'm going, and asking if he can help. The answer I get from him is better than I expected.

I turn to the prince. "Cherry Cake will take us to the shore of the Icy Lands. He'll fly over the ocean, to avoid the Spider Court. We could reach the Blue Tower by nightfall. You don't mind flying, do you?"

The prince smiles. "It's not like I have a choice."

"Why do you always look like you're joking?"

"I can't help it. My survival depended on not being taken seriously."

"You do an amazing job of that. I'm just not sure if it helps with your survival, considering it makes me want to ditch you on a desert island somewhere."

The prince laughs. "Different effects for different people, I suppose."

I nod, unwilling to push this discussion any further. If I'm lucky, there will be a lot of wind and I won't hear the prince's voice anymore.

I point at Cherry Cake. "Let me saddle him."

Closing my eyes, I focus on the saddle from the royal treasure. My magic is strong enough that there's no need for Cherry Cake to create his own. When I open my eyes, the double saddle is resting on the unicorn's back, with a little rope ladder for the prince to climb.

"The front's for you," I say.

He gives me a huge smile. "What an honor." I don't know if he's being sarcastic, but I decide I don't care.

What matters is my sister. I mount on Cherry Cake, and then my one-horned friend takes to the skies. We're soon above clouds, moving faster than the fastest boat can move, faster than most birds—on my way to the Blue Tower.

After all these years, I can finally rescue my sister. I think I would have felt something if she died, so I expect to find her alive. I just hope she didn't suffer too much.

Of course she did. The thought squeezes my chest.

And then I have to hope there won't be too many traps. I have to survive and go home. Astra's waiting for me.

13

I don't know how Tarlia can stand that creepy old man trying to fix the way she looks. He came here after she ate, and now he's applying something on her skin. At least this time he let me stay, but the procedure is boring. I feel like changing the tone of her skin or giving her dark circles just to mess with him, but then he would spend even more time treating her.

This is a reminder that my glamours can change the way someone looks, but can't change what they are. The texture of their skin and hair will still be the same. At least I'm sure my glamour is incredible, if her master has been looking at her from so close and has not yet realized she's not Astra, even though her skin is drier.

Tarlia thinks he can't see it because it's not something he expects, therefore not among the possibilities he would consider. Still, I'm pretty sure he's more than capable of differentiating the two of them, and I don't think he would have been duped without my glamour. Sometimes, when I see my magic working like that, I get a thrill of excitement, a wave of anticipation just wondering about the possibilities, wondering how much I could do. Well, I'm here now, closer to Renel than Marlak has ever gotten in the last years—and I hope we find a way to bring down this false king.

When Otavio leaves, Tarlia takes a deep breath, sits on her bed, then lies down, as if exhausted.

I sit by her. "Was your life like that?"

"With Otavio testing beauty procedures on me? A little. We also trained." She frowns. "I do miss that."

"I mean not complaining. You're going to spend a few hours in this room with nothing to do, and you didn't say anything."

She sits and whispers, "I think Astra wouldn't complain. I think it was her way of coping; believing in him, trusting that he'd lead her to some greater good, greater goal, trusting that her sacrifices would one day be worthwhile. So she obeyed him without complaining."

Her description is odd. "Astra didn't strike me as a pushover."

"I didn't mean that. I just think she would avoid direct confrontation, which is smart, by the way. I was always the most... difficult, he claimed. So I'm trying not to make him suspicious."

Someone knocks on the door, and we look at each other. I get up. "I think it's my job to open it."

Tarlia gets up too. "I don't want you doing any job." She then rushes to the door and opens it. I can't see who's there, but I notice her posture stiffening. "Yes?"

It's someone who has a lovely scent of seaweed. I don't know why I'm thinking seaweed smells good. I hate the sea.

The voice coming from the hallway shakes me to my bones. "I need to see your lady-in-waiting." It's Azur, and the seaweed smell is gone.

I look at the door and see that he's wearing a black hat, like last time.

Of course he was going to demand a price for letting me stay in the castle. I knew it.

Tarlia dips her chin. "I'm sorry. She's busy."

"One minute. I need just one minute of her time, and if she wants to give me more, then it's up to her."

Give him more... He's so pretentious. Still, if I don't talk to him, he'll make everything worse. I add a slight glamour to make my face ugly—just in case—and approach the door. "How can I help you?"

He raises a finger. "One minute. I just want to ask a question."

A question can hide an infinite number of tricks and traps, but I can't say I won't talk to him.

Tarlia smiles. "You can ask your question here." She points at me. "We became friends—and have no secrets."

He raises an eyebrow. "That's great to hear, but this secret's mine, not hers." He turns to me. "In my room. One minute."

I hate this, but what's going to happen if I refuse his request?

"It's fine," I tell Tarlia. "I'll be right back."

"No." She smiles again. "I'll walk outside, then count to one hundred slowly and return. That should be more than enough. Ask your question here."

With that, she walks past him and closes the door.

I'm sure he'll open it again and tell her that his request doesn't work like that, but instead, he walks to the window, so that he's far from the door, and beckons to me. He's wearing a long-sleeved blue linen shirt, his black hat, and leather trousers, in a practical look, with no embroidery or details. The only strange part of his attire is the hat.

I approach him cautiously. When I'm three steps away from him, he whispers, "This is going to sound strange, but remember I can't lie. Five lower fae are in the cells of the Inquiry House in the Jewel City, and have been sentenced to death, even though they committed no crime. They are set to be executed tonight. To prevent that, I need to free them. I can see that you're good with glamours, and I'd like you to come with me."

This is quite confusing, but I try to be fast and ask everything at once. "Why would you care for any lower fae? How do you expect to breach a well-secured royal facility? Do you realize I'm not allowed to set foot in the Jewel City?"

"Your first question is too complex for me to answer right now, but in general, I don't appreciate pointless deaths. I have a plan to infiltrate the Inquiry House, but I'll need glamours. We won't use the gates to get there, so nobody will check whether you're stepping in that city or not. And you'll be using a glamour."

"Is this a trick? A plan to catch me or catch somebody else?"

Azur hesitates. Ha. Of course he does.

He inhales sharply. "I'll have to trick the guards, so yes, it's a trick, but my goal is for you to return here safely by nightfall. You can keep working in the castle as the visitor's lady-in-waiting, if that's what you wish. I don't want you to be arrested, hurt, or killed, and I trust that our combined magic will keep us safe. If things go wrong, I still have power, influence, and Renel's protection. I won't say this will be a mission without any risks, but I can assure you that they're minimal."

"Why do you think I would care for some fae I've never met?"

He glances at my hands, which are unglamoured, the webbing between fingers visible. "You're lower fae."

"So what? Many of my kind will gladly sell even their own family under the illusion that the higher fae will accept them as one of their own."

Having to speak and think fast made me too honest. Well, what's said is said.

Azur gives me the most bizarre smile I've ever seen. It's not bizarre because it's strange or fake. It's bizarre because, in anyone else, I'd find a smile of understanding, admiration even, but that cannot be the case here.

The door then opens, and Tarlia walks in. "Your minute's up."

He glances at her, then stares at me. "What do you think? This will need to remain a secret."

And yet he didn't even make me promise not to tell

anything. I could spill it all to Tarlia right now. And then again, he knows I'm an intruder. At any moment, he could use this information against me.

I turn to Tarlia. "Two more minutes. Please."

She frowns but walks out, and I turn to him.

"I can go with you, but I want a deal."

"What do you propose?"

"You won't tell anyone I don't belong in the castle."

He tosses his hair back. "Haven't I been doing that already?"

"Give me your word."

"I can't do that. If Renel asks, and depending on how he asks, I can't deny him an answer. That's why I don't want to know your name or anything about you. Do not tell me anything that could compromise you."

That... makes sense, I guess. "Fair, then. Promise you won't reveal that I'm an intruder to anyone other than Renel, and that you'll reveal it to him only if he asks."

Azur takes a deep breath. "If you threaten Renel's life or do anything that goes against his orders, I might have to tell him."

"Fine. Other than that, you won't tell anyone else."

"I won't. I wasn't going to."

"But now you're demanding your price."

He bows. "I'm asking. Not demanding."

"Why me?"

"You're good with glamours."

"You said my glamour wasn't working."

"I could still see your talent. Your magic is impressive."

I agree it's impressive, perhaps even more than he realizes, and yet so much of this could be a trap. He could be testing how far my magic goes, could be trying to earn my trust... So many possibilities. I decide to ask another question, just to check his intentions. "If I don't go, what will happen to the men sentenced to death?"

"Foresight is not among my magical abilities, unfortunately, but I'll try to free them from the prison before they're executed

—even if you don't come. And I still won't tell anyone about you."

"Don't you fear getting caught?"

"I trust that my magic will prevent that."

"So you *can* go without me, and the men will still be freed."

He looks up for a second, then says, "Yes, but I'd rather go with you. A strong glamour will make my job easier and improve my chances of success. It will increase their chance of survival."

I ask, "Why these fae? Lower fae are enchanted and enslaved every day."

"Because I'm in a position where I can do something."

Had I been some two years younger, still naïve and pure-hearted, I would follow him even to the fiery gorge if he asked me with those lovely blue eyes staring at me like that.

Now, I'm just curious to understand why he's doing this. I don't believe for a single second that he's some kind of vigilante gallantly saving lower fae, and I'm not even sure I believe he needs me. Well, technically, he does *not* need me.

But curiosity has a way of grabbing one's mind, taking over the parts where fear and caution should exist. And I'm curious. Way too curious.

I smile at him. "I'll go with you."

He returns the smile, looking genuinely happy, then gets serious again. "Let's go, then. We need to hurry."

"I'll need to explain it to the human girl."

"So you're getting along?"

"Yes. I'm happy here."

He gives me an odd look, then walks to the door and opens it.

Tarlia stumbles forward, likely because she was leaning on the door.

Azur doesn't wait for me to talk to her, and says, "I'll need your lady in waiting for a few hours. She'll return—unharmed. You have access to other servants if you need them. Just ask your guard."

Tarlia looks at me and then at him. "No. I need *her*."

Azur smirks. "Unfortunately, it's not up to you to decide."

He sounds so smug and scornful that I almost regret my decision, if it wasn't for the curiosity pulsing in my veins.

I turn to her. "It's fine. Really. No need to worry."

She widens her eyes at me, then I approach her, hug her, and whisper in her ear, "I'll explain later, but know that I'm not being forced or coerced into doing anything." Then, in an even lower voice, I add, "The glamour will hold."

"All right. Be careful," she whispers back.

Azur watches us with attentive eyes—perhaps realizing I already knew her.

Maybe he already noticed that, and might even think I've known her for much longer, under the impression she's Astra. Then why did he put me here with her? What is his goal?

I hope I'm about to find out.

ASTRA

So much happened in so little time that I could barely get my bearings, find myself again, and it's already time to go home.

Home—the place I missed so much. And then perhaps what I missed most was Marlak, and I'll still miss him for a few days. My heart is tight with worry and yet full of gratitude. I'm happy he'll finally free his sister, and happy he escaped that prison.

Nelsin left Ziven by the river and returned to take me back to the island, while Ferer went ahead to wait for us there.

I don't have anything other than the clothes in my body, so this trip will be light—and fast.

Nelsin points to a place in the kitchen, which I suppose is an invisible faerie circle.

"Ready?" he asks.

Not really. Inside me, there's a strange hollowness. I want to ignore it, but it's as if it keeps growing. This is ridiculous. I've lived my entire life without Marlak; I can't let his absence make me feel this way.

And yet I can't change the way I feel.

I smile at Nelsin. "Can't wait to go home."

He stares at me. "Are you sure? We could wait here if you want."

"I need to work on my magic, and it's safer on the island."

"Oh, there will be an eternity—"

"There won't." I don't know where my certitude comes from, but I can feel it, something pressing against me, a strange urgency propelling me, even if it's not propelling me to return to the island, for some odd reason. "I need my magic yesterday, but that's not possible, so let's try to get it today."

Nelsin takes a deep breath, his usual playful face serious for once. "Astra, these things take time."

"So let's not waste it. Let's go."

The moment I say that, I feel as if air magic surrounds me. I know it's not air—Nelsin's magic is water, and yet it feels like a whirlwind turning everything around me blurry.

When it stops, I no longer see Nelsin in front of me, and I'm not by the Queen's River; I'm indoors, in a huge ballroom with an elaborate staircase and ornate windows. For a second, I feel Marlak behind me, his presence grounding me, making me feel at ease—but then he's gone.

It's the Amethyst Palace, I know it is, but it's wrong. The floor is covered with glass shards, and I don't see the balcony I usually see. Something about this place makes my skin crawl— and then, behind me, I hear a hiss. My spine feels covered in ice, a chill spreading throughout my body, and it's not Marlak's pleasant magic, but something wrong, unnatural, corrupted.

My entire body feels stiff, unable to move, and yet I need to see what's making that sound, need to turn and look, even if my eyes want to close.

The glass behind me cracks as something slithers in my direction. I don't want to turn.

I have to turn. My heart is beating loud and fast, loud and fast, while I'm here, overcome with a strange terror paralyzing me. No, I won't be caught defenseless.

I turn—and see light.

Near me, water flows, wind blows on leaves, and birds sing. There's something rough but pleasant touching my back.

"Astra," a familiar voice calls, a voice I trust.

The light is the sun above me, and I'm lying down on dirt. Nelsin's looking at me, calling my name.

"What happened?" I ask, still spooked by what I saw in the Amethyst Palace, but also puzzled and disoriented.

"You fell," Nelsin says. "I caught you—but just barely."

I sit and notice we're on the riverbank by our island. Almost home. While I feel safe here, that hiss, that presence, that feeling that something was wrong, takes over my thoughts. Many questions cross my mind, but I decide it's better to ask them where I know I'll be safe.

I get up. "I'm better now. Shall we cross?"

Nelsin stares at me, then says, "I'll hold you, then."

"Sure." While I don't think it will be necessary, I don't want to protest.

He lifts some of the river water, then freezes it in a disk, much larger than the one he did last time we crossed the river. I'm guessing he's truly afraid I'll fall. We step on it, he places an arm around my waist, then we glide to the island.

I wish my heart were fuller when stepping here, wish I were happy to finally be home and wait for Marlak and his sister, but the uneasiness inside me won't let me enjoy this moment, enjoy this return to the place I sorely missed.

"Everything looks the same," I say as I step off the disk and back onto the firm soil of the island. I'm trying to make some random conversation because I want some levity before I can even dare to bring up what I saw.

"Well, trees don't grow that fast, and it's still summer. It might start to get cool at night, though."

Cool—and with no fire. "How cold does it get here in winter?"

"A little uncomfortable, but we're not there yet."

I nod, realizing we'll probably have to leave this house soon regardless, which makes me sad. Still, seeing the stone walls of the buildings lights my heart again.

We walk into the kitchen, and Ferer comes out of the hallway. "Everything all right?"

"Yes," Nelsin says.

"No," I add, and the two knights stare at me with wide eyes. "I need to ask you some questions. Do you have a moment?"

Nelsin spreads his arms. "All the time in the world for my lady."

I chuckle, and Ferer rolls his eyes.

"Let's sit." I point at a table and pull a chair.

They do as I say, and Ferer has his observant eyes focused on me. "What is it?"

I sigh. "First, before anything, I want to commend you two on working together."

Ferer taps his nails on the table. "It's not like we have a choice."

"But you can leave, right? If you want." I need to make sure they're not forced to be here.

"It would be dishonorable," Ferer says, then shrugs. "But possible, sure. When I say no choice, I mean the company I have to keep." He glances at Nelsin.

The cat-eared fae raises his hands. "I, on the other hand, love everyone around me. Love makes the world a pretty place."

Ferer shakes his head and looks up, and I decide to go straight to the point.

"All right. Are visions common when you go from one faerie circle to another? When you travel like I did?"

"What kind of visions?" Nelsin leans forward.

"It's a place. I know it exists." Terror crawls my skin as I recall that moment. "But there was something wrong with it, as if something... evil was taking hold of it. I saw it now, when we came here."

Nelsin strokes his chin. "Perhaps when you passed out you had a vision, but it's not common."

"But I see things," I say. "Sometimes, often in dreams. Anyway, there's this old castle, called the Amethyst Palace. Have you ever heard of it?"

Ferer narrows his eyes. "Too many small courts ended or were merged. There are abandoned palaces all throughout the continent, but I've never heard of this name."

"Me neither," Nelsin says. "But it's true that it could be anywhere."

I recall the castle at the Court of Bees. That wasn't anything like the palace in my dreams, and there was something different... I know. "I don't think it's a fae palace, but Tiurian." I recall Otavio's reaction, and how he believed I had read about it in a book about Tiuris. "I mean, I'm sure it is."

Ferer looks up, thinking. "Tiurians had some sanctuaries, usually underground. We don't know where all of them are."

"It's not an underground sanctuary. I've been to one and seen another in a dream. The architecture is different. Regardless, I just felt something horrific in this castle, the Amethyst Palace. I think it was a warning."

"Against what?"

"I don't know, but I need to find this castle."

Nelsin nods. "We'll help you. We can bring all the books on Tiuris we can find, and we can read them with you. We'll find it, Astra."

But it's not fae books that I need. The realization hits me like lightning. "I already know where I can find more information about it." I stare at them both. "What I need from you is just to help me get there."

They glance at each other. In a moment like that, I can see a sliver of their love piercing through, the type of love that lets them communicate without words. It's there, despite everything.

Ferer nods. "Sure. Let's plan, and once Marlak is back—"

"I'm afraid it cannot wait."

Their mutual glance is heavier now.

Nelsin lifts two fingers in the air. "Two, three days, Astra. We can start planning, preparing. Remember that you still need to work on your magic."

"Improving my magic could take a month, two months, perhaps a year, or even more. Five years is not a long time to learn magic, but one day waiting might be too much."

"Rushing into things is never a good idea, Astra." Ferer speaks slowly, as if to calm me down. "We can plan, and you wait for Marlak to return. His magic is much stronger and—"

"Not on the other side of the River of Tears," I say. "Now, to be clear, I'm not asking for *authorization* to leave; I'm asking for help, but you're free to say *no*, obviously."

Ferer frowns. "We're not saying *no*."

"Right, so let me explain. I need to go to my master's study. I know how to climb the castle walls to get there. He'll have more information about Tiurians, about me, and I'm sure he'll know whatever there is to know about this Amethyst Palace. After I do that, it will be easier to find it. You don't need to come, but you could take me to the edge of the River of Tears, at least, so my journey is faster. It's all I'm asking."

Nelsin grimaces. "Marlak will geld us if something happens to you."

"He won't," I say. "Now wait, this is actually important. Did he order you two to keep me here as a *prisoner*?" If yes, then I might have to strangle Marlak.

"No!" Nelsin's grimace is worse than before. "From the beginning, we could have taken you off the island if we deemed it important."

Ferer gives him a murderous glare. "A suggestion someone *abused*."

"Hey, mistakes happen." Nelsin turns to me, his eyes pleading. "But I don't want to repeat it. Wait for Marlak, please."

"Fair." I exhale. "I don't want you to get in trouble. I'll wait."

Of course I won't, but there's no winning this argument, and in reality, it might be better not to implicate them.

Nelsin smiles. "Wise decision, my lady. And we'll plan."

Ferer chuckles. "She's lying."

I frown, slightly surprised. "How do you know?"

"I observe more than I talk, unlike some people." He glances at Nelsin, then at me. "You want to go to the human kingdom, I'll come with you. That's much better than you venturing there on your own. It's hasty, but if you say it's important, we'll believe you."

I smile.

"I'll come too," Nelsin adds, looking like he just bit a rotten apple. "Even though I'm dreading it."

"Let's get ready, then." I get up. "And don't worry. I'll deal with my husband."

The man in my dreams would never want me to stay hidden in a house or on an island, ignoring such a strong vision, such a strong urge. The issue is whether Marlak is really that man.

Nelsin has a nervous laugh. "Then make sure you stay alive to deal with him."

Ferer huffs. "She's not going to *die* visiting the castle she knows like the palm of her hand."

Of course not. I won't die visiting the Krastel castle—at least I don't think so.

As to that other castle, the one that plagues my dreams, when I consider the creature I sensed in it, I'm not so sure.

LIDIANE

I don't know why my legs feel soft like honey and my chest feels like a bottomless pit ready to swallow me as I follow Azur down the stairs.

Considering I'm about to join an enemy on a dangerous mission that could get me imprisoned—or worse—fear is not foolish, but wise. But not breathing properly will only make things even more difficult.

He takes me to his room again, and at least this time I don't think he hopes to get between my legs. What *does* he want? Of course I'd love to think that someone is finally appreciating my amazing magic, but why does it have to be Renel's pig?

When we reach Azur's room, he closes the door, then turns to me and blinks, as if confused. "You're afraid."

Why did he have to notice it? Now he's going to think I'm a pathetic coward.

"I'm… surprised." My voice comes out way too weak. I try to speak louder. "Startled, maybe."

I don't know what's going on with me and why my heart feels like a dragonfly wing.

He watches me, his expression indecipherable. "You don't have to come." He sounds so sad, so disappointed.

No! Now he's hitting me where it hurts the most: my pride. "I'm absolutely confident in my magic. And I already said I was going."

His stare travels over my face slowly, as if searching for an answer hidden in my eyes or lips. "You don't trust me."

Did he just realize it now? I mutter, "I barely know you."

He keeps staring, his lips parted, his breath deep and slow. I might dislike him, but I can't deny he's beautiful.

My heart speeds up, and the truth is I can't stand even one more second here, in his dim room, just the two of us standing so close, so I say, "Let's go. I think it's the waiting that's making me anxious."

He tosses his hat onto his bed, then reaches out and holds my hands. I don't know what I was expecting to feel, but it sure wasn't something akin to being hit by lightning and having darkness itself consume me.

I suppose he has a faerie ring right in his room, considering we're already gone, and I feel like I'm being turned upside down even though I'm certain that I'm still standing. I have transcended with Nelsin and my brother before, and it was never like this. *Nothing* was ever like this.

The darkness subsides, revealing bright light and blue sky around us. Beneath me, there's firm ground, but not a lot—just a small circle, smaller than my house. We must be on top of a tower.

From here, I can hear the ocean clearly, that horrific roaring that shakes my bones, a lullaby for corpses, calling me to that infinite depth where claws, teeth, and tentacles lay waiting. A shiver runs from my toes to my scalp.

We're near the shore, probably close to the Jewel City—a horrific place where all lower fae are enchanted. As if that wasn't enough, the dreadful city has to be by the sea, by those nameless and named horrors I struggle to ignore.

For a second, I wonder what I'm doing here, but then

remember this is an opportunity to try to figure out Azur and maybe help five innocent fae. With a deep breath, I tell myself to ignore the ocean and focus.

It's when I realize that I'm still holding Azur's hand—and let it go. The feeling of his fingers around mine doesn't fade, though, and it's not that I'm disgusted, even though I wish I were. I step towards the edge to see where we are, but Azur places an arm in front of me.

"Wait. While most fae won't look up, we don't want to risk being seen—yet." Without the hat, wisps of his sandy hair move with the wind, some of the gold turning silver under the sunlight. He's too annoyingly pretty, and I think he knows it, which makes it a thousand times worse.

"I'm just wondering where we are," I say. "Also, did you just transcend straight from your bedroom?"

"Yes," he mutters, his tone slightly curt, as if refusing to expand on it. "Can you give us a glamour not to be noticed?"

His words are like a bucket of water hitting my stomach. He *knows* I can do that.

At this point, trying to evade his request will only look ridiculous. And yet something about it bugs me. "You saw through my glamour. How do you know other fae won't see through it as well?"

He blinks slowly. "I'm different. There's nothing wrong with your magic."

His magic must be quite strong to see through glamours.

"Right. Let's hope whatever I do now works."

"I'm sure it will."

Absolute confidence in my magic. Why don't I ever get that from a decent fae?

He closes his eyes, his lashes caressing his face, as I hover my hands around his head. I *could* kill him now, and yet the thought dies as soon as it crosses my mind. Killing someone when they lend you their trust is vile and shameful. And this; closing his eyes in front of me, is a type of trust.

Of course, there's no need to close your eyes to get glamour done, but I'm not going to tell him that and miss my chance at a respite from his deep blue, disconcerting stare.

The glamour I do on him is not as strong as what I can achieve with the capes, since it's not bound to a physical object, but I think it should be enough. Once I finish, it doesn't look like it's properly done, though. I can still see him as clearly as before, and I think I would still spot him among a crowd of a thousand, but I decide to trust my magic.

"Done," I say.

His eyes pop open, zeroed in on me. He turns and points to the edge of the tower, then blows some air from the surface near it, I suppose to get rid of the dust there. He kneels, then lies belly down, so that only his face is outside the tower, looking down.

Am I really going to lie beside Azur? Oh, well, it's likely the safest way to look down, so I do what he just did, making sure there's a palm between us, and leaving only the top of my head off the roof, looking down.

All right. I was expecting to see the Jewel City from afar.

It *is* far, but far below us.

We're on top of a tower right in the middle of it. I can see the lazy waters of the Solemn River with the hundreds of houses on its shore, the tall Jewell Wall surrounding the city everywhere but by the river, and even part of the Solemn Port on the other side, with ships far onto the sea. The sea is so close that I can feel it cooling my insides, as I'm closer to it than I ever thought I'd be.

Still, what's surprising is being here, in this city where I'm most definitely not allowed. And the part that's even more surprising is how right this feels, as if I belonged here.

Without looking at him, I say, "I thought you couldn't transcend into the Jewel City."

"*I* can." He says it as if stating he can walk from one room to another, and yet there's a trace of pride there.

I'm intrigued, so I try to pry more information from him, and say, "Most fae can't."

"None other, as far as I know." Again that mild, calm tone, stating something extraordinary as if he was describing the weather.

How powerful is Azur? I try not to let the shock get to me, and decide to use the opportunity to ask another question, under the guise of being playful. "How does it feel to be that unique?"

"Everyone's unique," he mumbles, this time with a slight hint of annoyance, then he points down. "See there? The beige building with two floors and a golden door? That's the Inquiry House."

It's not exactly under us, but two blocks ahead, on a cobbled street with so many trees that they hide a good part of the building. Two fae guards stand at the entrance, but other than that, it doesn't seem to have that much security—which makes sense. The Jewel City itself is the security.

"What's your plan?" I ask.

"Can you see their faces from here?"

"Yes, but... I'm not sure it's enough to do a lookalike glamour."

"We'll go down and look at them from up close. I just want you to know who to notice. Here we won't be overheard, but down there we might, so when we descend, we need to know exactly what to do."

"I can do that. Sure." Something about this situation, about being alone with Azur, feels awkward. "Why are you so certain nobody will come up here?"

He shrugs. "Nobody can fly in, out, or above the Jewel. This is the bell tower, the tallest in the city, too tall and difficult to climb."

"You're familiar with this city." I don't know why the idea bothers me. Of course he's used to the Crystal Court *Jewel*.

"A little." He turns to me. "I'm sure you hate it. I'm sorry you have to see it."

His sympathetic tone confuses me, and I look down again, down at the sprawling city beneath us, intrigued by those cobbled streets filled with people walking by as if they had all the time in the world, fascinated and horrified by the calm and peace down there.

"It's strange," I say, as I'm taking in the sights below me. "I've always heard about the horrors of the Jewel City, the place where lower fae are enslaved, and I thought it would be gloomy, depressing, that it would show signs of its violence. And yet you look down and see fae going on about their lives as if nothing was happening. People sit in restaurants, some of them laugh together, couples walk down holding hands. They live as if they were in a happy little village. Can't they see it? Are they really that blind to the suffering of the lower fae?"

I turn to him and meet his eyes, now glinting with anger—and realize I might have spoken too much. For a second, I want to mumble that I meant no offense, but the words won't come out, of course. I meant every word I said. I might as well finish my thought, so I ask, "Don't they have any shame?"

"Shame?" There's amusement and derision in his tone. "They think the opulence of this city is a sign of their superiority."

His reply stuns me, and yet won't quench my anger, so I ask, "Are they that dumb?"

He tilts his head. "It's not about being dumb—or blind. Not exactly, I don't think. Nobody wants to think they're evil, nobody would want to admit they're morally corrupt. It means they'll believe in the story that will support their moral high ground, that will prove to them that they're the good guys."

I laugh. "They can't think they're good."

"Oh, yes, they're *certain* of that. And this is the Jewel. For them, the sign of their superiority. See, it's safer, cleaner, and richer than any other place in the kingdom. They think it's because they're so amazing, not because of all the enchanted servants, all the slave work."

I shake my head, annoyed at all the citizens of the Jewel, and yet at the same time glad to find someone who understands me, someone with whom I can be honest about the way

I feel. For a second, I imagine us two freeing all the lower fae, changing the world together. For a second, I imagine us together.

Then sanity returns to me and I remember who I'm talking to.

"Aren't you high fae?"

His body tenses and he bites his lips. "I don't think high fae are superior, and I don't think lower fae should be enslaved."

"But you support Renel, the fae making sure—"

"Some things are older than Renel's reign."

"Does *he* think all fae are equal?"

"Careful there." He raises a finger. "As his bound guardian, I'm not allowed to utter any negative words about him, nor tolerate them."

"Aren't you allowed to *praise* him? If he thinks—"

"Don't ask me about Renel." He's practically snarling. "Don't mention him."

"Fine." I shrug.

He waggles a finger by my face. "I mean it."

I push his hand down. "I won't mention your dear master. Don't worry."

Azur swallows. If he's trying to swallow down his fury, he's doing a poor job, as his eyes look like bulging, angry blue flames. At least that makes him look as far from pretty as he can get. Still pretty, though.

The downside is that I'm on top of a tower, in the middle of a city where I'm not welcome, alone with an extremely powerful and now extremely furious fae.

ZIVEN

Looking at the clouds from above as the world zips beneath me was an experience I never thought I'd have. It makes all my effort to stay alive worth it.

Of course, the annoying part is the grumpy fae prince breathing on my neck. Fine, he's not that close, and with that much wind, any air he exhales will be blown behind us. Still, I get the feeling his eyes are burning holes in the back of my head, and that he's furious at me for merely existing.

And yet his reason for traveling is fair. If I had a sister, and if I liked that sister, I would want to rescue her.

We land at a desert beach with coarse sand and angry, powerful waves hitting it. Such a magnificent ocean.

I wonder where we are, but I don't want to ask, since the touchy prince will probably get annoyed. I just hope we reach the tower soon—and that everything goes well. I'm not naïve enough to think it's not going to be dangerous.

Marlak takes a moment to hug Cherry Cake, then it flies and soon disappears in the sky. I have the impression that it truly vanishes, as if skipping into another dimension, but I'm not sure.

"We're in the Icy Lands," Marlak gruffs.

"That's... close, I suppose."

He nods.

The air is warm, and there's no ice to be seen. "I thought—" I give up on asking my question, knowing my companion's temper.

"What?"

I'd better finish my stupid thought. "I thought there would be ice."

"It's summer. There is some ice and snow in the mountains, and some blocks of ice left by the ice golems, and that's it."

"Isn't this too hot for the ice golems?"

"I think when it's warm like this, they take shelter during the day and come out at night, when it's cooler."

"So that's when we'll need to be careful."

"We'll have reached our destination by then. Let's go."

A queasy feeling takes over me. The night is the worst time to get to an ancient, magical prison. Perhaps a cursed prison.

And then not reaching our destination will mean sleeping out in the open, where ice golems and who knows what other monsters can find us.

A chill runs up my spine, even if the breeze is not yet cool enough to be the cause of it. I truly did not think this through.

LIDIANE

Azur might be furious, and murderous thoughts might be crossing his mind. Was it because I said Renel's his master? Why does an obvious piece of truth have to hurt him like that?

I recall then that he promised me I'd return safely to the castle, so if this talk has made him want to kill me, he'll have to wait. On the other hand, I'm not bound by any promise to keep him safe.

Perhaps I could use this opportunity to take down Renel's most valuable ally. It would be a chance to weaken the false king. The question is how, when Azur is so powerful.

Then I consider what he just said about the lower fae and the fact he's here to rescue some of them, and wonder if killing him is a good idea. Perhaps I don't need to decide right now. What I need to do is earn his trust. That way, once I make up my mind, I can strike.

I place a hand on his shoulder. "I didn't mean to upset you."

"I'm not angry at you." His voice is soft.

Azur is weird. He then stares at my hand on his shoulder, and I really wish he didn't make such a big deal out of it, because now I don't know if I can pull it back.

Even though he's lying down, I notice his chest expanding

and contracting in a deep breath, then he smiles and looks at me. "What should I call you? Not your name, but I need to know what to call you."

I chuckle while taking the opportunity to remove my hand from his shoulder. "*You* works."

"Then what am I going to call you in my head?"

"*She*? *Her*? That works too, you know?"

"Fair." A hint of melancholy taints his voice, and for some silly reason, it tugs my insides.

It's not like my name is a big secret, and I'm definitely not one of the ancient fae for whom names carry any power either. It's a great opportunity to make him believe I trust him. I'm about to tell him, but he puts a hand over my lips.

"Don't." A shadow crosses his eyes. "Don't tell me."

"What if it comes out by accident?" My tone is playful, but part of me is wondering why he's so scared.

"Be mindful." His voice is sharp like a dagger. He then points down to the city again. "Look." A tall fae man with long silver hair is entering the building. "That one."

All I see is the back of the man's head. "I couldn't see his face."

"Did you notice his clothes? Blue shirt with silver embroidery, black pants."

"Calfskin leather pants, silk shirt with loose shoulders and a tighter waist, last year's Selise's style embroidery. Yes, I noticed it."

"Right." I don't know if he's surprised, impressed, or if he just realized I might be a dressmaker. It's not a huge secret either. He continues, "I'll poke you when we cross him. He's an important constable and one of the fae we might have to impersonate."

"I'll recognize him."

Azur nods, his eyes focused on the Inquiry House. I look down at the city again, and all the happy, oblivious citizens. Perhaps selfish citizens. Here and there, in corners, almost hidden, I see lower fae cleaning, serving, tending gardens. I always wonder what it's like to be enchanted like that.

Are they aware of what they're doing and yet unable to escape it, as if imprisoned in their own bodies? Is it like a dream? Are their minds numb? Too few fae had their enchantment broken, and it was usually done by their masters. Those fae don't recall much of their time of servitude, but it doesn't mean that they weren't awake, suffering through each second. A shudder shakes my body, and then I notice Azur staring at me.

"You're upset," he says.

"Not upset, just—wondering what it's like to live here. For the people who are enchanted."

He bites his lip, looks at the city, then back at me. "It's normal to feel for others. Once you stop, you lose yourself."

"Do you feel for the lower fae?"

His lips part, inhaling air quickly, then he looks down. "Yes. My empathy is intact, despite my role." He chuckles. "Or is it *because* of it?"

"You don't like to be a guardian?"

"You're truly asking me if I enjoy being bound?" There's a note of sadness in his voice. "I fear your question veers too close to the subject I already asked you not to mention."

The subject being Renel. Is Azur implying that he doesn't like to be a bound guardian? Is that what I'm supposed to conclude? Doesn't make any sense.

"A bound guardian... That's a voluntary role, isn't it?" I ask, keeping my voice light and my tone curious. "They can't force you to do it. Or am I wrong?"

He runs a hand through his shiny blond hair. "Voluntary, of course. And I never said I didn't like to serve Renel."

"So you like it?"

"What do you think?" His glare fades in a second, and he points down to the Inquiry House. "Pay attention. Someone we might need to impersonate could step in or out at any minute."

I look at the entrance of the building, and yet my mind is

not really focused there. Can it be that Azur isn't really Renel's ally? That he dislikes his role? But he confirmed that his position as a bound guardian is voluntary, meaning that he *chose* this. Then again, do I know anything about his life before he became Renel's dog?

Any sane person would let the subject rest, but the right time to poke at embers to rekindle a fire is when they're still hot. And annoyed people don't watch their words as carefully as they should.

"Hypothetically," I say. "And I'm not talking about you. I'm curious because you're the first bound guardian I have an opportunity to talk to. So, hypothetically, can a bound guardian quit their role?"

His nostrils flare, and I can see a line forming on his forehead. I don't think he liked my question. Still, he takes a deep breath, then says, "Bindings can be unbound, of course, but they're always tricky."

"Could you quit if you wanted to?"

"Your question assumes that a guardian would want to abandon their task, and that would contradict the essence of their role. A bound guardian is loyal. Always loyal. It's who we are."

This time, there's a hint of pride in his words. So I guess he *likes* to serve the sham king. It means I can keep calling him Renel's pig. I smile. "Makes sense. Well, it's a fascinating job."

"Yes, enthralling. Now let's focus." He points to the city again.

Apparently, my ability to keep quiet is nonexistent. But I have to try to understand him. "Does Renel know you're here?"

Azur inhales sharply. "Mention him once again, and I'll leave you on this roof."

"You promised to return me to the castle safely by nightfall."

He smirks. "I didn't, actually. I only said that was my goal. Never said I couldn't change it."

Right. Now I'm feeling like the biggest idiot of all idiots, having agreed with his plan without checking his words, perhaps taken by curiosity, perhaps mesmerized by his eyes. I don't even like blue eyes! Except for his, perhaps, but it's not my fault they're so pretty.

I scoff. "Well played, *guardian*."

He stares at me for a moment, as if a calm, friendly stare could erase his words. "I still don't want you to be harmed, and still want to make sure you're back to the castle by nightfall. Just don't mention him."

I nod. Of course I can avoid mentioning his stupid master. Of course I can swallow all my questions. And of course I can let my curiosity itch me until I want to scream. Annoying, but not the end of the world.

"Also," Azur adds, "Don't kill anyone."

I'm sure I make a bizarre grimace. "I wasn't…"

"If things go wrong. You can make deals with living fae, but won't be able to explain or hide a dead body."

"Right." The idea that he has thought this through is disconcerting, but it's another proof he won't kill me—just perhaps enchant and imprison me, which is not exactly a relief.

My attention turns to the Inquiry House, where some more fae walk in and out, none of them wearing any uniform, so I assume they aren't guards, but work there. They tend to wear more delicately embroidered clothes than what I was used to seeing in Serenade, and their cuts are what I would consider a little passe, but it might be because of their walls and isolation.

A young man with long brown hair exits the building.

"That one," Azur whispers. "It should work."

As I'm noticing the style of the man's shirt, I feel Azur's hand around mine, then feel the ground below me disappearing, replaced by darkness, then replaced by dirt, roots, and pebbles. We're under a tree, in one of the city gardens, close to a pebbled street, but none of the passers-by turn to look at us.

I get up and try to swipe away some dust from my dress, when I feel a gust of air around my clothes, so strong that it removes all the dirt at once.

Azur smiles. "There. All clean." Then, in a lower voice, he adds, "Great glamour."

I suppose he thinks my magic is the reason nobody noticed us, but in truth, I wasn't expecting to transcend right in the middle of the Jewel.

"You should have warned me," I say.

He tosses his hair back. "They won't look too much at two fae frolicking in the grass."

Nobody's walking by, so I change my hair to straight and brown, then lighten my skin. I approach him and have to stretch my hands to get near his head, but I turn his hair brown, give him an upturned nose, and make his eyes bulgy. I make my dress looser and give him a silk shirt with that intricate embroidery I saw so much around this city. Something doesn't feel right with the glamour I put on him. Beneath the bulgy eyes, beneath the brown hair, I can still see him, as if there was no way to erase his presence. And yet the glamour was done correctly, the way I always do it.

I decide to trust it, and say, "Now we're good."

"Flawless." He looks down at himself, then raises his eyes and stares at me. "You managed to impress me."

That comment makes me chuckle. "Basic glamour. Let's not exaggerate."

"Nothing's basic about this. Or you."

My heart speeds up, but then he changes his tone and says, "Let's go."

And like that, I'm walking by Renel's guardian in the most despicable fae city ever, still struck by its calm and peaceful sheen.

I realize we're some three blocks from the Inquiry House, in a street with restaurants, all mostly empty except for groups of people casually talking, having a late breakfast.

We turn a corner, and then I feel Azur's hand on my arm. The first man is walking ahead of us—meaning that I still can't see his face, which is a problem.

"We'll cross him later," Azur whispers.

He pulls me to another street and we walk fast, almost running, until we return to that first street just in time to see the man. Aquiline nose, small eyes, even more embroidery on the front part of his shirt. I can create a glamour like him, no issues.

We keep walking, this time slowly, until we cross the second man on another street. This one has a more classic face, which actually makes it harder to mimic him.

"It won't be perfect," I whisper.

"Not a problem. Did you see enough?"

"Yes."

We walk away from that place, turn a corner to an empty street, then he pulls me to a wall alcove where we stand face to face, my heart getting so loud all of a sudden.

"Do it," he says. "I'll be the first fae, and you'll be the second. We'll walk in together."

I bring to mind the image of them, both from behind and the front, the details of their clothes, their body types, facial features, then hover my hands around Azur and make the change. I still see him beneath it all, as if I could never erase his presence, but at this point, I'm thinking that perhaps it's me. Perhaps I'm the one who can't forget what the real Azur looks like, and I don't want to think too much about the reason why it's happening.

Then I change myself. To be honest, it's the first time I'm trying to look like a man. The biggest issue is the voice, especially because I've never heard him, but I'm assuming I won't do any talking.

We're about to break into a high-security building, and the thought makes my heart jump. It also makes me decide to tell him that the glamour isn't quite right. "I... still see you. You're still there."

He looks at his arms and his glamoured long sleeves. "It looks fine. The fact you're seeing through means your sight is good, not that your glamour is bad."

True, but I was never able to see through my own glamour

before, and the idea of this power suddenly worries me. I lower my voice to an almost inaudible whisper. "Some fae can see through glamours or detect them."

Azur winks. It's him, through and through, underneath a translucent layer of magic. "It's why we'll be quick, before anyone notices us. Let's go."

We leave the alcove and walk back in the direction of the inquiry house. It's when I realize I have no idea how he plans to move five fae from that place or how he plans to deal with the guards there.

So many signs that this is a trap awaiting me. So many things that could go wrong, and yet there's no way back now.

Nobody notices us as we walk to the Inquiry House, and the guards don't even blink when we walk *into* it. There's indeed a lot less security than a building like this would have in a normal fae city, which tends to deal with lower fae on a daily basis. They're always trying to find ways to trap us, enslave us, but here, there isn't any new lower fae to be trapped, so I can imagine all they do is deal with petty disputes among higher fae.

The entrance is a circular room with a dark marble floor, with two fae sitting on a circular seat, with large books beside them. One of these fae, a young woman, looks at me as if surprised. "Back already?"

"New orders," Azur says, his voice deeper than usual.

I look at her and shrug as if confirming his words, even if I'm not sure the man I'm impersonating would do that.

Azur keeps walking towards a door on the right, and I follow him. We pass two guards, then descend two flights of stone stairs. Musky air greets me when we reach the bottom, a long corridor with some ten windowless cells, illuminated only by lightstones.

One guard sits at the entrance and stares at us in surprise. "What are you—"

"Orders," Azur says, then keeps walking.

Two cells have young high fae in them, but most of them are empty.

Azur whispers, "Don't worry about the guards. I'm changing the air to make them confused."

"You can do that?" I whisper back.

"Air's my element."

I meant that I didn't know that air magic could make people confused, but this is not the time to discuss magical skills.

At the end of the hall, we reach a small cell containing the lower fae. Five men, wearing guard uniforms, sitting quietly against a wall of the cell, their eyes unfocused, like puppets when you put them back on the shelf. Two of them have purple skin, one is smaller like a pixie, but wingless, and two of them look like high fae but with horns. They remind me of some fae in the village where I grew up. They're also someone's sons, brothers, perhaps even fathers, torn from their lives by some cruel trick of destiny.

I hear a sharp stream of air. The lock clicks, then Azur pushes the door open.

We're too far from the guard at the entrance, who probably didn't notice that Azur used air magic to unlock the door. Another use of air I had never heard before—not that I've met many air wielders, of course, but I'd assume more fae would be aware that they could open locks, if it was something common.

We enter the cell, and Azur says, "Get up." The men obey at once.

I'm still unsure how we're going to get them out of this building or this city, but Azur sounds confident enough—until he looks at me, eyes wide in fear.

Steps echo in the hallway. Someone's coming, and there's something different about this person if they rattled Azur this much.

It can only mean that we're deep in trouble.

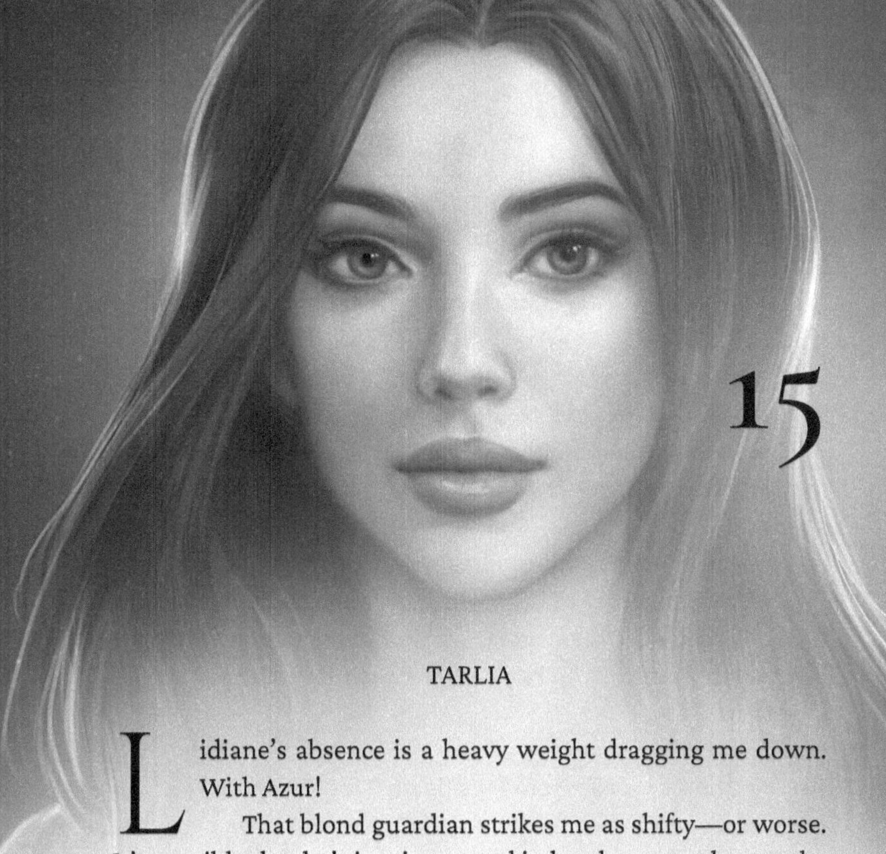

15

Lidiane's absence is a heavy weight dragging me down. With Azur!

That blond guardian strikes me as shifty—or worse. It's possible that he's just interested in her, but even that can be dangerous when there's such a power imbalance between them. Looking back, I should have insisted, should have fought harder for her to stay, but I'm not sure how to overcome Lidiane's stubbornness or even how to defy Renel's guardian. I hate being so powerless.

The door slams open and I turn, expecting to see Lidiane, expecting some terrible news, but it's just Otavio, staring at me with an eyebrow raised. He closes the door more slowly than he opened it and approaches me.

"What was the name of the book again?"

I have absolutely no idea what he's talking about, but I think even Astra wouldn't be so sure. "What book?"

Otavio huffs. "Don't play with me, Astra. The one that mentioned the castle."

"I... don't recall."

"You *do* recall." He waves a thick, green book in his hand.

"You told me it was *Tiuris, the Fallen Kingdom.* There's nothing about the Amethyst Palace here."

And there's no information about any of that in my mind. I bite my lip, as if thinking, then remember that Astra doesn't do that, and stop it. "Maybe it was another edition? Or a similar name..."

"What did it say? About the castle?" There's no desperation in his voice, and yet I can see a glint of it in his eyes.

I should be the one getting desperate, considering I won't have any decent answer. "Well..." I blink. "I might not recall the specifics."

"Just tell me everything you remember."

"It's an old castle." It has to be, if he looked for it in a history book. "Very old." Otavio stares at me, clearly unimpressed. I'll have to improvise. "The book I think mentioned a prince who died there—"

"Prince?" He frowns.

"Yes, but it was a mysterious death." Just based on Otavio's grimace, I guess I'm completely off. "No. Wait. That was another book. Another story. I'm getting confused." I try to think. I've never heard of such a palace, despite having studied all kinds of useless history, so it means that either it doesn't exist or that it's not registered in regular books. "Amethyst... I think I read that it was an old castle, or maybe a castle from a legend."

Otavio grabs my arm. "Tell me what you read."

"I don't remember. I read some stories, some history, it gets all mixed after some time. And it's been stressful."

He sighs and lets go of my arm. "Try to remember."

"Why does it matter?" I'm quite intrigued, in fact.

"History is important, Astra. Lost history is even more important."

Lost. I can use that information. I close my eyes and hope I don't contradict Astra too much. "I think I read about a famous castle with purple walls, which is the reason for its name. I thought it would be a beautiful castle, but then I read that it was either destroyed or forgotten, as if the people writing the history weren't sure about it."

"That's it?"

"It wasn't much."

He waves the book again. "And you read this book?"

If Astra said so, I'm guessing I'll have to say *yes*, right? "There *was* a Tiurian history book in the hut, but I didn't read it much, only looked at some pages. It might have been a different edition—or a completely different book."

He throws the green tome on the bed. "Read it, then. It's a one-sided account, written by the fae. Still, if you look at the gaps in their narrative, you might gleam some truth about Tiuris."

That's Astra's real heritage. I still can't believe she's Tiurian, and I don't know how she feels about it. I hesitate between displaying joy, excitement, or sadness, then decide to simply pretend to be a dutiful pupil. "I'll read it. Thank you." I lower my head.

Astra always carried a sort of quiet resignation—or was it fear? I can't imagine what it must have been to have such a secret in Otavio's hands.

He stares at me. Stares for too long. I don't even know if my glamour is still working well without Lidiane here.

"The time with that villain changed you, Astra."

Indeed. It changed her much more than he realizes, but I'll obviously never say that. I smile. "My hope is that the experience has made me stronger."

"You don't need to be strong. You need to be smart. Snatch that king's heart."

He raises an eyebrow and gives me a look that seems to imply *or else*.

The threat hangs between us, a threat that Astra would also recognize. I always thought he treated her better than us, but it's not exactly true, if he made sure she was always afraid of having her identity exposed. Sometimes her devotion to Otavio and overbearing obedience got to my nerves, and yet now I understand the root of it: fear.

"Don't worry," I say. "The fae king will bow at my feet in no time."

Would Astra sound this confident? No matter. The sweet smile I give Otavio seems to appease him.

Meanwhile, I imagine my hands around my master's throat cutting his airflow until his life fades away.

I'll have my revenge—one day. Either by treachery, poison, dagger, or my hands. And I won't even feel bad for killing Astra's beloved master, now that I can see the invisible chains he used to keep her docile.

I hate this man.

And he's still here, staring at me, examining me. I can see him calculating, thinking, making a decision. Did he realize I'm an impostor? I'll just deny it. I don't think he would deem me capable of infiltrating the castle or that Astra would have somewhere to run to, and still his stare peeves me.

To my relief, someone knocks on the door, ending my torment—at least for now. Otavio opens it and greets a guard standing outside.

"His Highness requests her presence in his lunch hall." The guard points at me. "When she's ready, of course."

I get up, eager to get away from my captor. "Well, I'm ready."

"No," Otavio says, then turns to the guard. "Wait outside." He closes the door and stares at me. "I need to prepare you."

Even one more second in this room is too much for me, and I look fine with the frilly, overly complicated dress he made me wear. I also have three daggers attached to my thighs. I know they're useless against magic, but they make me feel safe.

What does Otavio want to do? More pointless things to my hair, certainly.

"It's better to go like this," I say. "As if I don't care what he thinks, don't need to get ready. *I* took all the seduction classes, and you weren't there. Why don't you trust the skills you made sure I acquired?"

He sighs. "I won't tolerate any mistakes. But for now, I'll trust you and see how it goes."

"Thanks."

"Astra," he says. "I must warn you; keep your legs closed."

Disgusting creep. I jump with my feet together. "Like this? You think it will look attractive if I do this instead of walking?"

"You know what I mean. Wait until you gain his trust."

His words make me want to ride the fae king's cock this very morning, just to spite Otavio. Still, I smile. "You'll have to trust my skills, master."

He pauses, then narrows his eyes. "Never saw you displaying any."

To be fair, I wouldn't believe Astra capable of voluntarily seducing anyone either, but Otavio's barb is unfair.

I smirk. "I made a fae prince venture into human lands to marry me. Do you still think I'm incompetent?"

He rolls his eyes. "Which was completely uncalled for and irresponsible. I still can't believe—"

"I only did what I had to do to save my skin when attacked." Ziven told me about their encounter, and while I'm not sure of what happened between Astra and Marlak, this explanation makes sense. "And I'll do what I have to do to perform my duty."

Otavio nods, for once appeased, for once having no reply.

Funny that the moment I stopped trying to impersonate Astra was the moment I won an argument. Perhaps I should just be myself and hope the glamour is enough to trick him.

I open the door and follow the guard, curious to see the fae king, wondering what he looks like, with a faint hope that he won't ask questions I don't know how to answer.

The guard leads me to the hallway from where I see the main spiral stairs at the center of the castle, illuminated by the Crystal on top of the roof, its rays of light spreading like thin, silver lines. We head to another hallway, then reach a tall, wide silver door, and he gestures for me to enter.

It's a dining room with floor-to-ceiling windows overlooking a valley. The king is looking outside, alone, and turns to me at the same time as the door closes.

I step back and catch my breath.

Fae are beautiful, I'm well aware of that, and perhaps they use their magic to look even more beautiful, to enchant and entrance us. The magic must be working, because I'm fascinated by his dark eyes, his straight nose, his thick lips. He reminds me a little of his brother, but in the same way a polished gem looks like a rough stone. And that might be his only flaw; Renel's perhaps too polished, to the point that his perfect features make him look harsh, cold, distant. And still beautiful.

Old Tarlia would definitely want to get a taste of him before bringing him down, would want him to... The image is clear and tempting, as I imagine myself bent over that table, the king behind me—inside me. And yet it's not a true desire, as I'm still thinking about Ziven, missing his messy hair and lazy smile, still thinking about our kiss. Why is he occupying my mind? I need to focus.

"You summoned me?" I ask.

Renel looks thoughtful, then smiles. "I *invited* you, and I'm glad to see you here. You look... refreshed."

I can't believe even he can notice the difference. I shrug. "Healthy sleep on a comfortable bed does that."

His smile fades. "My brother... didn't provide you—"

"I *had* a bed." I don't think Astra would want me to disparage her husband. "I guess he thought it was decent enough, but it doesn't compare to the beds in this castle."

He raises an eyebrow. "Would you like... to compare what we do on the beds?"

Quite direct, this one. The suggestion would tempt old Tarlia, for sure, but I need to at least pretend to do my job. I decide to ignore the innuendo. "I just did, didn't I? Or are you suggesting anything other than sleeping?" I manage to sound sweet and innocent.

He's wearing a dozen or so thin silver bracelets on his arms and starts fiddling with them. "Well, you can... Read on a bed. Or sit. Stretch."

I wonder if he's trying to be funny and chuckle. "I shall try it, then."

He nods, his shoulders sagging, then points to the table, where there's a large bowl with some small bright pink fruit.

"Sleepberries. They only grow on the southern hills of the Crystal Court, before we reach the Endless Mountains. Sometimes, when I was young, my mother would take me and my—" He pauses and swallows. "My family, and we'd spend the entire morning picking and eating them. It was our meal for the day. That's... a typical fae food. Like you asked." He looks down.

I approach the table and pick a berry, admiring its minuscule size. "Why the name?"

His chuckle is natural and relaxed. For once, I can gleam the person beneath the king. "The villagers of the area gave it the name, and claimed that eating these berries could make you sleep forever—just so foreigners didn't eat it."

The idea sounds ingenious, except for one detail. "But fae can't lie."

"Straight up lie, no. But we can deceive, play with words." He lifts a shoulder, a hint of playfulness in his eyes.

"I'll keep that in mind." I stare at my pink berry. "So I can eat this and I won't sleep."

"You will sleep, of course. Later, at night. You won't fall into an endless sleep, no. Not because of the berry, at least."

I put it in my mouth, and Renel leans forward. "Don't!"

Too late. I've already bitten it.

LIDIANE

Azur holds my hand, and in a second we're in the cell across from the one where the fae are held, the door still wide open. He pulls me to the back wall, behind him, and then I sense some strange magic around us, almost like a glamour, except that this feels different.

I move my head just enough to peek and see a tall fae with black hair entering the corridor with the cells. Two guards follow him.

The man turns to the guards. "Go back, please. I'll be fine here."

His voice is commanding with the authority of someone used to giving orders. From here, I can sense a current of power, magic, even if I'm so close to Azur, who's already incredibly powerful.

In fact, Azur's body is touching mine, pressing me back against the wall, and I can feel it trembling. He's afraid. I don't know why he can't simply transcend us away, or what exactly he fears.

The man walks to the cell with the lower fae, stares at the wide-open door, and snorts. "Incompetent guards." He enters the cell and addresses the prisoners. "Well, now, why are you standing?"

"Orders," the lower fae mumble in unison.

The strange man chuckles, then points at one of the fae. "You. I release you."

One of the purple-skinned fae stares at him in confusion, then steps forward, as if to attack the newcomer, but then falls to the ground, quivering and grunting.

"Silence!" The high fae yells. There is enchantment lacing his words, that horrible command that will make people do things they don't want, that will make them exert their bodies more than they should.

The purple-skinned fae convulses. In front of me, Azur shudders.

"You," the high fae says, pointing to a horned fae. "I'll release your mind, but you shall not move against me."

The poor horned man looks around, his eyes wide. "What's happening?"

"I'm Zorwal, leader of the Crystal Court Council, and here to learn the truth of what happened."

Zorwal. I had heard the name, but had imagined he would look older.

The fae nods, and Zorwal asks, "Who broke the walls of the desert keep?"

"Desert…" The fae closes his eyes, I assume struggling to recall what happened, then he sees his colleague on the floor, still suffering.

I'm disgusted and yet powerless.

Zorwal places a hand on the fae's head, around his curved horns. "This should help."

The fae winces. "It hurts."

"It can hurt much more." There's no question about the menace contained in these words. "Now, what happened last night?"

"Giants," he says between groans. "Giants broke walls, took us. We had no chance. We tried. No chance."

Zorwal emits a sound that should be a chuckle, but sounds like a snarl. "Of course you had no chance. Who was in the keep?"

The man looks around and sees his companions. "Us. The guards."

"Who were *the prisoners* in the keep?"

The fae squeezes his eyes shut, as if in pain. "I don't remember."

Zorwal presses his hand harder. "Break the bonds, break the bonds. And don't scream."

"Can't," the fae mutters, visibly in pain.

If they have sworn an oath not to reveal something, pulling this information will break their minds. I doubt it's a concern for the fae questioning him.

"It's there, in your mind. Find it," Zorwal coos.

Azur shudders, and for some odd reason, I can sense his panic. So much panic. He then mutters, "Shit."

A stream of air pushes Zorwal against the wall, and he hits it with a thud, blood spattering behind his head.

I shut my eyes, overcome with revulsion, but Azur holds my hand and then we are standing among the lower fae.

"Obey me," Azur says. "Stand up and hold hands in a circle including us. Now."

Steps echo in the hallway, while even the fae who was convulsing gets up. Zorwal's body on the floor makes me shudder, while the steps terrify me. There's no way this will end up well.

The lower fae close the circle while the steps approach us. Before anyone reaches us, darkness surrounds us, and I realize Azur's transcending all of us.

All of us.

He might be the most powerful fae in the Crystal Court—or the world, apart from Marlak, maybe, but I'm not sure.

The extent of his power terrifies me, even if he's saving me and some lower fae.

But there's something that terrifies me much, much more. And now we're right in the middle of it.

The ocean.

We're on the deck of a merchant ship, no land anywhere around us, just water, the water above those dangerous depths, the water my adoptive mother always warned me never to get anywhere near.

Azur's in front of me, and I plead with my eyes as I say, "I can't be here."

He raises a hand as if to mean *one moment*, but even one second is too much.

An arrow zips by us, reaching the middle of our circle, and I notice an archer nearby and three fae advancing in our direction with swords and daggers.

Azur raises his arms. "We're here in peace, and you'll forget how we got here."

There's enchantment in his voice, but I'm not sure how much it can do against so many at once.

"No, we won't." A high fae man advances at us, sword in hand. "What's your purpose?"

"Take these travelers with you across the ocean, and I'll pay you three hundred golden swans."

"We have no food for them, and don't want fugitives."

"Fair," Azur says, then adds, "Hold hands."

The lower fae and I redo our circle, and I sense darkness around us again. We land on another merchant ship, this one much smaller, so small that our circle is squeezed, and I bump against the deck. This is even more terrifying, since it puts me closer to the water.

"What's this?" A fae woman yells. She's wearing a simple tunic and pants, and I'm not sure if she's high fae or lower fae.

Azur raises his arms again. "We're friends. Take these five fae to the Nowhere Lands, and we'll pay you one hundred golden swans."

A fae with green skin approaches us. "They're enchanted." He sneers at Azur. "What's the meaning of this?"

"Innocent men escaping execution," Azur says. He's still glamoured to look like the constable from the Jewel City. "I can break their enchantment now, or make it happen once they reach their destination."

The green man grimaces. "Oh, just free them already!"

"Can you take them?" Azur asks. "The money should be enough—"

"Three hundred golden swans," I say. I don't like that Azur lowered his price because this is a smaller boat, and I'm hoping there will be no long negotiation. "If you don't need it all, it can help them start a new life." Then I turn to Azur. "I need to *go*."

He nods, as if to tell me he understands—but he doesn't. He doesn't know.

"Five hundred," the woman from the boat says.

Azur rolls his eyes and gives me a mild glare, then turns to the woman and man on the boat. "All I can offer is three hundred. If you don't want it, we'll find another boat."

There's something shifting in the air, in the water, and the waves are getting higher, but I don't think anyone else's noticing what's about to come.

"Who will take these fugitives?" The woman laughs. "Nobody."

The boat jerks as if hitting a rock. It's not a rock, but something much worse. My body is a pool of terror, frozen on the spot and yet yearning to run, even though there's nowhere to go.

Nowhere. We're trapped.

I'm so nervous that my vision is blurry and all sounds are muffled.

What a way to meet my end. What a stupid way.

LIDIANE

I should never get near the ocean, but here I am, on a small boat—and I'm sure they're coming for me.

In the midst of that confusion, I hear Azur's voice.

"Behind me," he says, then pulls me against the wall of the cabin and stands in front of me, like we did in the prison. I think this is some kind of glamour that doesn't change our appearance and yet still disguises us. I doubt it will work.

Amidst my horror, I still have enough presence of mind to be surprised at Azur's power. How many magical skills does he have? Why is he so incredibly proficient in all of them? Unfortunately, unless he transcends us away right now, I'll be dead before I get any answer.

"They're after me," I whisper, right as I see a gigantic tentacle rising above the waters. "Get me away from here."

"Stop your magic. Now," Azur whispers. "And don't leave this wall." I do as he says, and see his normal face with blond hair. He then adds, "I can't transcend. But trust me."

Trust me. I do. Strangely, I do, even if I don't know how I'll survive this.

Another gigantic tentacle envelops the boat. The five fae are too stunned to do anything, while the boat owners are stepping back, thankfully not making any foolish attempt to fight the beast about to pull us to the depths of the ocean.

Azur then raises a hand. "Royalty of the Sea," he yells. "This is Azur, guardian of the acting king of the Crystal Court, Renel Goldenstar. I request an audience, and that you hold back your Kraken until we reach an agreement."

Slowly, the largest tentacle unwraps the boat.

I gulp some air, and yet my chest feels empty. First, an audience with any royal from the Sea Court is not going to help me. Second, I don't know if they'll listen to Azur. The best he might be able to do is save everyone else on this boat—and doom me. I should really start establishing a no-sea rule before agreeing to do anything. Right. As if I'm going to have the chance to make any deals after this.

My only solace is my internal snigger at his use of the term *acting king*. He can't refer to Renel as king, as it would be a lie—he has never been crowned. Not that my snigger will help me in any way.

Perhaps I should step forward and deal with the Sea Court, and yet I'm paralyzed. All my life, I was told to avoid the sea. All my life, I heard its roar deep inside my mind as a constant threat. How can I give up on my life after everything my brother and I went through? It would betray the woman who raised me, betray the memory of my mother. And then Azur's words echo in my head: *don't leave this wall. Trust me.*

There was no enchantment in them, no command, no deal, and yet for some reason I feel compelled to listen, compelled to do as he said—as if I trusted him. He's still standing in front of me, his touch grounding my body, perhaps reminding me that this is a horrific reality, and not one of my nightmares. And yet his presence also calms me, as if part of me thought he was a match for the Sea Court.

The kraken disappears, submerged back to the depths from where it came from. All that's left is the roaring ocean and the wind. The couple from the boat hug each other, eyes closed, while the five fugitive fae stand in a circle, unaware of the reality around them, or perhaps aware and yet horrified that they can't even cower. I fear my heart will punch a hole in the wall behind me, or perhaps push Azur away from me, as it keeps punching his lower back.

All we can do is wait. Interminable seconds while I wonder if they'll just disintegrate the boat or send something worse than their previous monster.

Interminable seconds while my life hangs by a thread.

"Trust me," Azur whispers again, then reaches back and pats my arm.

Of course I *want* to trust him, want to believe that everything will be all right, want to believe that there's someone who could care about me, protect me, but real life is not like that.

Everyone protects their own skin first.

Perhaps this is my destiny. I've evaded the sea long enough —eventually, it was bound to find me.

Anticipation is almost killing me with anxiety, when something stirs in the water, then three forms jump onto the boat, facing Azur. Three male sea fae. Two of them are guards, looking like any normal high fae except for some scales on their exposed chests, and tubes with water around their necks, mouths, and noses, connecting to a circle around their waists— containing seawater, as they can't breathe air. They only wear golden trousers and no bow, spear, sword, or any other weapon. The man in the middle has no scales on his light brown skin and wears no tubes, meaning he's one of the sea fae who can breathe air. With a boyish face and a golden comb pulling back his curly black hair, he must be a young royal.

He looks around. "Who dares request *an audience?*" He spits those last words. "Who dares disturb Prince Machiel, crown heir of the sea?"

Prince. *The* prince. Just a kid, some two or three years younger than me, and yet he's the sole heir of the Sea Court. This is not good.

I notice then that he has webbed hands just like mine—the

hands I usually have to hide, and yet he flaunts them with no shame.

"I requested it," Azur replies, his voice calm.

The young man advances toward him in hard steps. "This boat carries something that belongs to the sea."

Azur shrugs. "Ask for it, then. No need to terrorize anyone with your little pet."

I can't see the young man's face anymore, now that he's right in front of Azur. "Pet? You call our ancient kraken a pet?"

"What should I call him?"

"It's a she, you ignorant git. And I'll call her back if you don't give me what I'm looking for."

"What *is* it you're looking for?" Azur asks.

I shut my eyes tight, bracing for his reply, wondering what he's going to say.

"One of our own."

Azur raises a hand. "I was not aware of any sea fae here—other than your highness and your distinguished guards, of course—but you can look."

The prince laughs, then yells, "Search the boat!"

His guards approach the fae on the prow, looking at their faces, hovering their hands around them, I guess to check for glamours, and yet the prince doesn't move.

A guard approaches the prince. "Nothing. Should we kill them?"

"Not yet," the prince replies, then changes his tone. "There is a sea fae here. Where?"

"You're free to look," Azur replies, his voice even calmer than before. "Like I said, I was not aware of any sea fae, and you can ask everyone on the boat. We can't lie."

The prince huffs, then yells, "Check the cabin."

The two guards enter through the door beside me. I hear them moving things, then descending stairs. Other than that, all I hear is my heart and the ocean. Would this prince hear my heart?

The guards return after a couple of minutes. "Nobody downstairs."

"There is a sea fae here!" The prince yells. "Where is she?"

How can he know I'm female? It could be my brother here.

I feel like stepping forward and ending this. I'll confess nobody knew what I was, and that it's all my fault. And yet I can still hear Azur's words. *Trust me.* I should *not* trust him, but for some odd reason, I still want to give him a chance, still want to see what he's planning. I doubt this prince won't notice that he's hiding something, and then everything will be worse. And yet I remain here, silent, waiting, perhaps curious about what Renel's guardian wants to do.

"You've searched the entire boat," Azur says. "Could it be that you're mistaken?"

"I'm not mistaken," Prince Machiel barks. Then, after a few seconds, he asks, "What's behind you?"

There. It took long enough, but he figured it out.

Azur chuckles. "Is your vision that poor? Can't you see the cabin wall?"

Oh dear. I want to evaporate. This is not going to end up well.

"Truly?" the prince asks. "Then step away from it."

Azur sighs. "I represent the Crystal Court Crown, on a sovereign vessel, gliding above your court, having paid its dues. Our peace accords state—"

"Step away!" The prince roars. "Or I'll kill you."

"You can try." Azur's voice is still calm. "On a one-to-one duel. The problem is that one of us might end up dead, and then our courts will have a tricky, tricky diplomatic situation."

"Not if you enter the duel willingly."

"Unfortunately for me, Renel will still be upset if I kill you."

I can't believe Azur's threatening the Sea Prince.

The prince's laughter chills my marrows. "Not me. You'll duel *my pet.*"

"Same problem. Renel will be upset if it dies. And you can't say it entered the duel willingly."

That's it. Azur's insane.

"You think you can kill our ancient Kraken?"

"I do. And I can't lie." Bonkers. Azur's completely bonkers. He continues, "You may think I'm delusional, of course, and that's your prerogative. From your distorted point of view, I still think you don't want to kill the acting Crystal Court King's guardian. Bad business. And I want no quarrel with the Sea Court. Same issue."

"Then step away from this wall. Now!"

"What exactly do you think's behind me? A portal to a hidden compartment?"

"Step. Away."

"In exchange for what?"

I want to poke Azur and beg him to stop dragging this. He's only making everything worse.

"I could crush this boat with one snap of my fingers."

"Technically, you'll snap your fingers and call your ancient Kraken, and she'll do the work for you, isn't that right?"

"Step away!"

"Why don't you ask nicely, and maybe I'll consider—"

"Grab him!" the prince yells.

The two guards approach Azur from the sides, but he pushes them into the ocean with his air magic.

"Do you even understand *nicely?*" Azur asks. "You know what? I'll do it, just so you stop annoying me."

With that, Azur steps away from me. With his warmth gone, I feel a chilly breeze covering me, a void where he was. I shiver but refrain from shutting my eyes.

If I'm going to face this prince, I'll face him head on.

ASTRA

I'm finally comfortable again wearing trousers and a shirt made by Irene, even if I also packed a light dress in case I need to blend in a Krastel village.

The terror from the vision hasn't left me, that dreadful feeling that something unnatural and evil looms, but there's no point dwelling on that. What I need to do is find answers—and find the Amethyst Palace. Even if it's in ruins, I have to find it.

Ferer and Nelsin are in the kitchen, dressed and ready to go. In the end, convincing them didn't take long.

I smile at them. "You know, you're two of my favorite people."

Nelsin places a hand on his heart and smiles, while Ferer rolls his eyes. "You're too forgiving, Astra."

"I'm glad I am. Bitterness poisons our hearts."

Ferer shakes his head. "Caution keeps us alive."

"*Love* keeps us alive," Nelsin says. "Or else we'd be walking corpses."

Ferer glares at him. "Love makes us cautious, so our loved ones remain alive."

Tarlia's words come to mind. *Careful is boring. I'll be reckless and wild.* Perhaps I agree with her, even if I also agree with Ferer. Truths can be paradoxical.

"We're all alive," I say. "And that's what matters."

I was hoping to end an interminable debate, but then Nelsin adds, "And full of love."

"Right." Ferer's expression is anything but loving. "Let's go."

We approach the edge of the island, then Nelsin forms an ice disk, while Ferer jumps into the river.

We cross over to the bank, then Nelsin leads me to the faerie ring. This time, he holds my hands while I feel that odd gust of wind twirling around me, transporting us through a large distance in a way I would have thought impossible just a few days ago.

So many things seemed impossible then.

The wind stops, and I find myself in a forest, still holding Nelsin's hands, and I let them go. Ferer shows up a few seconds after us.

"Where are we?" I ask.

"Silent Woods," Ferer says. "Once we cross the river, it's a straight path to the human castle, but we can still avoid the main road."

He takes a path in the forest, and Nelsin I follow him.

I realize then that he sounds as if he knows Krastel's roads. "Was it the way Marlak took when he came to…" I almost say *take me*, but it sounds offensive. "… marry me?"

"No." Nelsin's the one who answers. "We came from further south, so we could take smaller roads."

"Were both of you with him?"

Nelsin laughs. "Oh, yes."

"You know, I have many questions about that day, but there's one that plagues me; where did he get that carriage?"

"Oh, I wondered the same," Nelsin says. "We met him, and he had that garish vehicle. I was thinking we'd be a little more discreet entering the human kingdom, but no, he had that ostentatious carriage. He bought a horse in a small village, then later I sold it."

Perhaps one of my guesses was right. "Is the carriage… a royal relic? Like the suitcase?"

"I suppose so," Ferer says.

"Weren't you surprised? Puzzled?" I chuckle. "Horrified?"

Ferer takes a deep breath. "I made an oath to Marlak a long time ago, and yet he never accepted my offer to help him, even if he came by sometimes and tried to help me and my sister. Then, out of the blue, he asked me if I would like to be a knight, but not for him, for his queen. I was curious, obviously, perhaps surprised that he had chosen a human wife, but… I understand wanting to protect the people you love."

"He didn't love me then."

"Then how do you explain what he did?" Ferer's tone is curious.

"Well, we have a mind connection, as you must have noticed, and he feared I'd find out his secrets, so he decided to make sure I'd never be able to tell anyone. And that was it." It all sounds so silly in retrospect, and I chuckle. "*Not* romantic."

"Oh no, not at all," Nelsin croons. "He took a carriage and walked into a human castle without knowing if they would be allies or foes, or if they'd sell his location to his brother. He made changes to the island house."

"And he accepted my help," Ferer adds. "Marlak is a loner. I used to think he was too proud to work with others, but the truth is that he fears he'll put the people around him in danger. He was willing to change."

"Because I could find out his secrets." Odd how my words ring false even to me, but I don't think there was any love at that point. "He didn't even know me."

"You don't believe that, do you?" Nelsin laughs.

Not really, but then... "You think he was in love with someone he had just met?"

Ferer shakes his head. "Have you considered that whatever he saw in this mind connection of yours could have been enough to convince him?"

My legs pause as I take in his words. *What he saw in the mind connection.* Marlak was the man in my dreams, sure, but I was also the woman in his. "I guess you have a point."

The thought makes me flustered and giddy, and missing him even more, and I want to change the subject, so I turn to Nelsin. "And you, had an oath too?"

Nelsin points to Ferer, "When Marlak asked him to be his knight, I volunteered as well, and here I am."

Volunteer. Anger rises up in my stomach. "He had no right to say he could have killed you. Had no right to treat you like that."

"He did, actually," Ferer says. "Nelsin made an oath as well, a very amicable oath, let's say, and didn't have to do much other than keep you safe—which he fumbled."

I click my tongue. "Not a good reason for Marlak to suggest killing him."

Ferer frowns. "Is Nelsin dead? Hurt? No. So I don't see the issue."

Nelsin's top ears are hiding in his hair, even if his steps haven't faltered. He turns to me. "The good thing is that now you have a wiser, more experienced knight."

"She already had one," Ferer says.

"I'm glad you're both here." I almost add that I wish they'd start getting along again, but I decide it's none of my business if their relationship needs time to heal.

We walk some more, then reach the River of Tears Canyon, and cross it over a tree trunk. Such a thin stream compared to the Queen's River, and yet dividing the land like that.

"Did you test?" I ask. "If your magic really doesn't work here?"

Ferer raises his hood and chuckles. "Rest assured, it does not."

"Your lack of magic most definitely doesn't assure me."

"We can still fight, and have swords." He pulls back his cloak and shows me a silver hilt.

The sight makes me miss Downshadow, but in truth, I'm better with daggers, and I have a few of them in my pockets, even if I hope I won't need them.

We walk through woods bordering a road for about an hour, when I see the walls of my tower at a distance, the tower from where I stared at the scenery below me, hoping that one day I would explore the forests and fields that I only saw from afar.

When we approach the Krastel City, we take a detour to avoid it, then reach the castle walls from the quieter side.

"Lots of guards inside," Ferer murmurs. "Are you sure about this?"

I point to the wall. "There's a hole at the bottom, amidst those bushes. I'll go in and out, and you two can wait here."

"No," Ferer says. "One of us is coming with you. The other waits here. You can choose which."

"Can you climb that tower?" I ask.

"Yes," they both reply at once, and Nelsin adds, "You forgot I have cat traits."

Ferer then says, "Fae have more balance and physical—"

"Right." I point at Ferer. "Come, then. Follow me and do what I do."

With ears turned down, disappointment clear on his face, Nelsin says, "I guess I'll wait."

Ferer grimaces. "Oh, don't be dramatic."

"We'll be right back," I say.

I hate to make Nelsin feel like that, but one of them had to stay.

I crouch and go through the hole under the wall. It seems tighter than the last time I tried it, when we were training to find ways in and out of buildings. It's funny that we should practice it in our own castle, as if they never considered we could use these skills against them.

On the other side, there are more bushes, giving us cover. I wait for a guard to pass, then come out and gesture for Ferer to follow me. We move along the wall until we're on the north side of the tower, where the wall is closest to it. The sun is high up so it will make it uncomfortable to look up, and since the outer wall is so close on this side, no guards will see the tower from an angle.

Climbing this tower is easy, familiar, perhaps even easier after I tried climbing down that weird, shaky Crystal Castle. I glance down and notice that Ferer is following me with ease as well. If things go wrong, it will be good to have someone with me.

When I approach Otavio's window, I can't help but recall the last time I did this, when I heard his conversation with Andrezza. It's clear now that he never revealed anything to her. I wonder about the princess, and if they're still making her sick.

Regret fills my chest when I consider that I never tried to warn her. Could I do it now?

The first part is getting in. I listen attentively, to see if the study is empty, and after a couple of minutes with no voices or other sounds, I sneak through the window and find myself in that place I know so well, with the familiar smell of books and tinctures that accompanied me throughout my childhood.

Ferer comes right after me, and I put a finger over my lips to let him know we should be silent. There could be guards near the hallway, and I don't want to risk anyone coming in and finding me.

The first place I look is the bookshelf behind his desk, but I see only ordinary books, and in fact, not all of them. Even the Tiurian dictionary is missing, along with some history books.

My stomach sinks.

I go to the other side of the room to check his cabinet with potions, poisons, ointments, and herbs. Only the common— and innocuous—substances remain. Even the calapher is gone, probably because it's rare.

Ferer stands in a corner, his eyes alert, and I return to Otavio's table. Then, slowly, not to make any noise, I pull a drawer. Empty.

Empty, empty, empty. Everything mildly important is gone.

"Hide," Ferer whispers, but I'm right behind Otavio's desk, and there is no way to do it silently or fast enough.

A guard enters, one I've never seen before. He asks, "What are you doing here?"

I smile and walk to him. "Hi, I'm Astra. I suppose you're new, right? Do you want to help me find a book?"

He frowns, puzzled.

I lift my shoulders. "I suppose not. Sorry. If you come across Master Otavio, tell him I'm still looking." I turn around and check the book spines on the bigger bookshelf. Ferer is hidden somewhere, and I'm acting naturally enough not to raise suspicion.

"Where's your master?" the guard asks.

I look around. "He was here just—well, I guess I don't know."

The guard is too silent and still hasn't moved. This is not good. Since my time might be running up, I decide to keep trying to find something, anything, but all books on Tiuris or its languages are gone. It means Otavio took them with him, perhaps even means he'll never come back.

The guard turns around and leaves, and I finally breathe properly. Ferer sticks his neck from behind a curtain by the window and whispers, "We should go."

I agree, but there has to be something. Some sign, some... I check to see if the drawers have false bottoms, then open the thicker books to see if they hide anything in them. It's as if he knew someone could come in here when he was gone. No. There has to be something. I close my eyes, trying to focus, trying to sense something.

I decide to check the bottom of the largest bookshelf, and open some books. In one of them, I find some loose sheets of paper. They could be meaningful. I hope this is something he forgot, rather than useless papers he didn't bother taking with him.

One paper has some names and a family tree, but the writing is hard to read. As I'm trying to decipher it, someone clears their throat behind me. Shit.

I turn—and see Sayanne.

She smirks. "Well there, did you already forget your training? If I wanted to stab you, you'd be dead now."

She looks the same; auburn hair, rosy cheeks, brilliant eyes. Even with Otavio absent, she still has some of that artificial beauty he sometimes gave us with his products, and yet something is off about her.

I smile. In a way, I'm glad to see she's fine. "Good to see you."

"Is it? Is it really good, Astra? Or were you thinking I'd be dead?"

I realize what's so off about her. On her neck, she has a gold necklace with rubies, matching her earrings, and her dress is made of fine dark silk. Quite fine. I blink, then, taking in her words.

"Why would I think you would be dead? Did something happen?"

There's malice and pain in her laughter. "Oh, nice little Astra. I sometimes wonder if you're truly naïve, if you're dumb, or if it's all part of your sick little game."

I don't understand what's happening, but most of all, I'm worried about her. "Stop it. We were raised like sisters. If something's wrong, maybe I could—"

"Oh, please. You think you can humiliate me? Offer me your help? I don't need it. I don't need you. I don't need Otavio. I'm a survivor, Astra."

"Well, great. I'm happy for you."

"Are you?" She narrows her eyes. "Why are you here then, instead of fucking the two fae brothers? Did they already ditch you? It was bound to happen, wasn't it? Tell me, Astra, did they at least pay you more than the Tirenzy guard did?"

How does she know that?

Well, she might have been listening at the time. The odd thing is that I don't care, and strangely, it doesn't hurt. It no longer hurts, and I would laugh with joy if I wasn't worried about Sayanne. Still, I can't let her insult remain unanswered, and smile.

"This time, I got paid in sex. Very good sex, I must say. Quite worth it."

She sneers. "Of course. You were always a slut, weren't you? The only reason you didn't fuck all the guards is that they didn't want you."

I look at her and see no trace of the girl who grew up with me, the girl I loved, and I wonder what happened to poison her heart. "Sayanne, are you all right?"

She laughs. "More than all right. Survivor, remember?"

I'm trying to decipher her words, untangle her bitterness. Was she left to fend for herself? "Where's Andrezza?"

"In prison, where traitors go."

"Why?"

"Oh, you don't know. You don't know anything. Neither her nor Otavio are welcome anymore. And I'm afraid I have more bad news. You came here to beg him for protection, didn't you?"

"Beg who?"

She giggles. "You pretend to be so silly. Quin, of course. And I'm assuming you don't know what happened to him."

I recall his warm smile, his friendliness. For some time, he was a bright light in my life. "What happened?"

"He eloped with the princess. The real one. The one he truly wanted."

A knot in my heart untangles in relief. It means Driziely wasn't killed, isn't being poisoned. It means Quin is alive. "They escaped?"

"They did." Sayanne chuckles. "I can't wait for that stuck-up bitch to try to make a living on her own. What is she going to do? Become a peasant? A cook? Perhaps a whore?"

I frown. "You have a weird obsession."

"It's reality, Astra. Reality's cruel."

"*Your* reality certainly is."

"Right. You, on the other hand, live among clouds and stars and rainbows. So privileged, the preferred substitute, except that *I* was always the best. I can turn men into my slaves."

"Sounds exciting. I wish you good luck."

"You don't get to end the conversation! I haven't finished. Do you want to know what happened to former Queen Cecilia?"

"Let me guess. She fell from a window." Perhaps I'm trying to test her, see if she shows any reaction. As much as I hate it, I can definitely see this Sayanne pushing Tarlia down a window.

Sayanne smirks. "So you *do* know."

I'm stunned. "She died?"

"No. She flew away. What do you think? The queen is dead, Astra. The princess ran away and became disowned. The two older princes died from a mysterious disease." Her smirk is chilling. "Ziven died, along with your dear Tarlia, on their way back from the fae territories."

"They could still be on the road."

"They're not!" she yells. "There's nothing here for you. *Nobody* for you. And now you'll be arrested like the worthless little traitor you are. Guards!"

Six men rush into the room.

I laugh. "Funny, isn't she?"

The guards pay me no mind, and Sayanne roars, "Arrest her!"

The guards advance.

"Wait!" I yell. While the guards pause, I see no friendliness in them. There will be no way to get out of this using cunning words and pretense, but I can try to appeal to her pride. "Six, Sayanne? Do you think I'm that much of a better fighter than you?"

"I don't care. Arrest her!"

Oh, this is bad.

LIDIANE

The sea prince stares at me. Not *at* me. Through me, as if he can't see me. He stares some more, then turns to Azur. "Very funny."

Did Azur manage such an incredible glamour that it hid me?

Azur shrugs. "What's funny? You asked me to move, I moved. What are you even expecting to see on that wall?"

Prince Machiel bites his lips, visibly seething, while the guards jump back onto the boat.

"Raid the boat!" the prince yells.

"Oh, no, you don't," Azur says, then pushes the guards again. He sends a gust of air on the prince, but it doesn't affect him.

Above us, dark clouds convene. Some sea fae can manipulate water and clouds—and create lightning.

Indeed thunder crashes near us with a terrifying roar. I understand part of Azur's plan—to glamour and hide me—but I still think there's no way out of this.

More thunder crashes above us, and then another figure steps on the boat. It's a man, his chest covered in silver scales, his skin dark, his hair black and silver.

The freaking Sea King. In person.

If I puke here, will it ruin Azur's magic? What if I faint?

"What's going on here?" the king's voice sounds like thunder, and yet he's addressing the prince, not Azur.

"We felt it," the prince says. "The magical signature—"

"Did you find anyone?" His voice is kind even if it's deep. His eyes rover over the boat as if searching for someone.

"Not yet." The prince lowers his head, all his haughtiness gone.

The king then turns to Azur. "Was it you that called us?"

"After they sent the kraken, yes."

"Hmmm." The king closes his eyes. "Is there anyone hidden on this boat?"

Smart question.

"Everyone's on the prow, your majesty. You can look." Azur's answer is also smart.

"Is anyone under a strong glamour?" This king is asking all the right questions.

"Nobody here is looking like someone else," Azur replies. "Everyone you see has their own appearance."

Will the king notice the gaps in this answer? I don't look like someone else; I'm invisible, I suppose. And everyone *he sees* isn't enchanted.

The king looks around, his eyes pausing in my direction, but then moving about. "Apologies, then." He extends a closed hand. When he opens it, there's a purple pearl on it—the rarest one. "Take this as an apology. And go in peace." He turns to the prince. "Son, let's go."

The prince glares at Azur, but jumps into the ocean after his father. Sunlight pierces the clouds and illuminates the boat again.

Azur gives the pearl and a bag of coins to the couple. "As you can see, they won't bother you again. Forget about me or how I got here."

The woman takes it.

He turns to the lower fae. "You're unbound now. May your new life bring you joy."

The men blink, but I barely have time to see them, as Azur takes my hands, and then darkness surrounds us until we're back in his room.

He lets my hands go, staggers back, then sits on his bed and closes his eyes. I know those symptoms: magic fatigue.

"I'll let you rest," I say, surprised that I found my voice after those terrifying events, and disappointed that I can't ask him any of the questions taking hold of my mind.

He puts his hat on and gets up. "No." His voice is slurred. "I need to find Renel."

"You can't go anywhere like this. You're about to faint. I don't know what you did to your magic, but—"

"Fainting is much better than being convicted of murder. Let's go." He waves a finger in front of me. "Drag me if I pass out." He pauses, then stares at me. "*What* are you?"

The question reaches deep inside me, stirring troubling memories, troubling words. I see my mother's body, my brother pulling me back, and hear the words over and over: *avoid the sea.*

With effort, I keep any trembling from my voice. "I thought you didn't want to know."

His stare pierces my soul, but then he looks away. "True. It's best that I don't. Now, let's go." After two steps, he stumbles back. "Wait."

"You can't walk anywhere, Azur."

He leans on me and takes my hand. "Hold me, then."

Darkness sets in the room. "You can't be planning on transcending."

"Not planning, no. Doing it."

Then everything's dark.

MARLAK

The prince hasn't complained yet, even though we've been climbing hills for hours to get to the plateau where the tower is located. The images are so clear in my mind; both Astra's vision and my own memory of when I came here, still so young and hopeful, thinking it would be easy to find my sister.

I fear I might still be that person, fear it won't be as easy as simply finding the tower, and yet I'm here, rushing to Mirella's rescue—because it's what I wanted to do the moment I learned she had been taken prisoner. The moment I learned she survived.

This is a rocky area with some dangerous hot pools, so every step we take needs to be careful. The blue tower is in the middle of a basin, hard to be missed. And yet I can't believe I missed it so many years ago.

The human prince has been following me, voicing no complaints, and keeping a steady rhythm. So far, not as much of a hurdle as I expected. I turn to check if he's behind me, and he gives me a tight-lipped smile.

Then I crouch, pain consuming my entire body.

Something's wrong, wrong, wrong. So wrong that I can feel it grabbing my heart and shredding it into thousands of pieces. The ground around me turns to ice, my magic materializing the cold dread within me.

"Marlak, what's wrong?" The prince manages to look serious, but I can't answer.

My mind is spinning. Someone I love is in danger. Astra must be in danger. I can feel it.

"Marlak." Ziven crouches in front of me. "Let me help you."

"Astra," I mutter. "Something's happening."

"We can hurry and come back. We can save her."

It's my worst fear; being far from her, unable to do anything. "Too late."

"Astra's strong," Ziven says. "And powerful. You need to trust that she'll survive. Meanwhile, we can go back."

I don't know if I can reach her. It's just so much darkness, like a horde of monsters attacking me, but it's obviously not me, and even if I create walls and walls of ice, they won't save her.

TARLIA

This berry is the bitterest thing I've ever tasted. Renel stares at me with panic in his eyes, while I wonder if I have poison in my mouth.

I spit it. "Is it safe or not?"

"It's bitter. You need to peel it." He takes one and removes the pink skin, revealing a dark red, semi-translucid, tiny interior. He then extends his arm and hands it to me. "Like this; it tastes much better."

"Thanks." I try it. A little sour, but with some mild sweetness. I glance at the bowl with dozens and dozens of those berries and can't imagine peeling them all, can't even imagine that anyone would lie just so other people wouldn't eat it. "It's nice."

"Glad you like it." Renel takes three more, peels them, and passes them to me.

I admire the deftness in his fingers and can't help but imagine what else they can do. Why do I have to be like that?

I need to make conversation, so I try to say something nice. "I wish I could see these hills where these sleepberries grow."

He sighs. "I haven't been there in years."

There's a blanket of sadness around him, enveloping him in a strange, cozy discomfort he can't escape. Or maybe it's my impression. Not that I care that he's sad, considering all he's done to Astra, Marlak, and the lower fae.

Renel gives me a clearly forced smile. "Do you know the difference between ignorance and apathy?"

Bizarre question. "I guess—"

"I don't know and I don't care." He stares at me, as if expecting something.

"Right." I nod.

He narrows his eyes. "Do you know what one tray told the other?"

"I can't imagine."

"Dinner's on me."

I'm wondering if this is some secret fae code talk, when it finally hits me.

They're jokes! Terrible ones.

Still, there's no greater offense than not laughing at someone's joke—except that it's too late now.

"Oh! I'm so slow!" I giggle, hoping some self-deprecation will salvage this. "They're jokes. You know, you figure out who's an idiot by noticing who's too slow to laugh."

He's serious, his posture stiff, except for a hand running through his hair. One of the combs pulling it back falls on the table. "You can also identify an idiot by the pathetic jokes they tell. I... was trying to..." He closes his eyes.

I wave a hand. "Making conversation can be strange, especially when we don't know each other." To be fair, talking to him feels like trying to extract juice from a stone.

"Yes. Of course." Renel looks like a spring ready to snap. "I... have a gift for you." He takes a sword in a scabbard from the chair beside him and passes it to me. "My... Marlak gave it to you, and I believe it should be yours."

I pull part of the hilt and realize it's some kind of fae treasure, just based on the quality of the gems and the craftsmanship. Shit. I know this hilt.

This sword looks just like Downshadow—except that it has clear quartz instead of rubies. Or are these beacon stones? I notice my fascination and try to tone it down, considering that Astra would have seen this sword before.

I decide to ask a question I'm curious about.

"Isn't this part of the Crystal Court treasure? Was Marlak allowed to gift it to me?"

"It's yours now. That's what matters."

I put the sword back in its scabbard, place it on the table, and smile.

Renel then asks, "Do you know why he gave you that?"

All I can imagine is that it was a hint, hoping she'd also be interested in his *other sword*.

I swallow my chuckle and focus on peeling a berry. "You'll have to ask him." I'm glad I manage to erase all the bite from my voice.

Renel leans back and strokes his chin, his bracelets clinking. "I cannot. He escaped last night." His eyes are set on me as he says that, I assume to check my reaction.

"Truly?"

The news hit me like a storm wind. Marlak... escaped. Was Astra that fast? Something else hits me; Renel is not threatening me. It means that he didn't bring Astra here as some kind of bait for his brother, but rather because he wants something from her, just like she told me.

The fact that Marlak's free means I could walk away if I wanted to return to Ziven. Ziven, who pushed me away. I'm spinning, with no sense of direction, and yet I'm sitting by a king—a king with a prize on his head, a prize who would grant me the freedom I desperately need.

I notice then that Renel's still watching me, and ask the first question that crosses my mind. "Is it that easy to escape your prisons?"

"It shouldn't be, but he had help from giants."

This story is getting quite bizarre. "Can they cross the Charmed River?"

"He was in the Shadow Lands." Renel's stare is still curious. "Did you ever hear anything about giants?"

"We didn't talk much." I notice that I have a berry in my fingers and go back to trying to peel it.

He tilts his head, and then asks in a soft voice, "Astra, did he hurt you?"

Oddly, the *name* hurts, the idea that I'm an impostor's impostor. I like Astra, but I don't want to walk in her shoes, don't want to keep pretending to be someone I'm not. I tap on the table. "Not really, but I have a request."

He raises his eyebrows, visibly surprised.

"It's something simple," I say, before he protests. "And it's a favor, so it's up to you. I want to start anew, forget my past, so I want a new name. Something different. Can you choose a nickname for me? Another way to call me?"

He shoots me a panicked look. "What if you don't like it?"

"If it's horrible, we can try to come up with something else. Come on. There's no right or wrong."

He stares at me, focusing, thinking, actually taking the question seriously. Then again, he seems to take everything seriously. After a few seconds, he says, "Tar."

My breath leaves my chest in a fraction of a second, and I drop the berry I was holding. "What?"

He runs his hands over his bracelets. "I can think of something else."

"Where did you get that from?"

"Star. Astra, star, then for some reason I thought Star was too obvious, and then I decided to leave it just *Tar*."

I'm shaking from head to toe.

Renel closes his eyes. "I didn't mean like pine tar. I wouldn't call you slimy. You don't look slimy at all—or sticky. I don't know what came over me."

"Tar is fine, actually." Sure, sounds a little ridiculous, but then, it's almost my name. "In fact, I like it." His lips form a faint smile. Then I add, "Just don't say it near my master."

He stares at me in a way that might make me shake again. "You don't like him."

"It's... a complicated relationship."

He runs a finger over his bracelets. "Lots of relationships are complicated. It doesn't mean there isn't love deep down, underneath it all. But that doesn't look like it's the case here."

I shake my head. "No love."

He presses his lips together, thoughtful. "I would send him away if I could. Unfortunately, my deal with him was that he would look over you, make sure you're safe."

"I thought fae couldn't make deals with humans."

"I thought the same, and yet I just learned that this law doesn't include Tiurians. Perhaps I could make a deal with you."

Would the deal not work, or would Renel notice there was something wrong? Whatever. I smile. "What deal would you like to make?"

"None yet. How much do you know about your magic?"

"Didn't Otavio tell you? Nothing. I never trained. Wasn't even aware I had magic."

Renel looks down at his bracelets, then back at me. "How does it feel? To find out you have it?"

"If I could understand or use it properly, I guess it would make me happy—or powerful." The idea is fascinating, but dwelling on it is as useful as wondering how I'd feel with wings.

Renel looks out the window, thinking. I want to act natural, try to find a way to have a pleasant interaction with him, but I'm stuck. Why did I ever think I could seduce him, when he's so... odd.

Go, Tarlia, seduce a piece of wood. That would likely be easier. He's distant, immersed in his own worries, or perhaps plotting some evil deed. Evil. All I see is a tense but handsome fae fiddling with his bracelets, hair, and comb, as if sitting on a chair was something new and uncomfortable.

I try to bring up a topic that might cheer him up. "What was it like? To pick sleepberries with your family?"

His eyes dash quickly to me, and then he takes a deep breath. "Calm. No fears, no worries. Calm. It didn't sound like much. I appreciate it now, even if it's so... Distant. Like it was other people."

His voice is normal, casual, and yet I can feel that mantle of sadness enveloping him, becoming a cloud taking over this room. I could swear it even dims the light coming from the window.

What was I thinking? There can't be any topic worse than his family, considering his parents are dead and his brother has become his enemy. To be fair, Renel was the one who mentioned it first.

And hey, you know what? I don't see why Renel's so sad, considering he's still living like a king, and he's the one who captured his brother—even if he escaped. Perhaps that's what's bothering him, but he doesn't seem to care that he no longer has Marlak under his clutches.

Renel might be pretending, trying to gauge my reaction. Then again, he might want something with Astra's magic, something I'll obviously never be able to give him—but it will be fun to disappoint him.

I finally manage to finish peeling a berry and put it in my mouth, wondering if that's all the food I'll get for lunch. This one's so sour that I want to spit it, but I swallow it.

Renel's still silent, thoughtful, watching me. I need to come up with something to say, something smart, perhaps funny, or something that will cheer him up and make him trust me, but my mind is blank.

Behind me, I hear a thud, like a heavy step, and turn quickly, ready to fight in case it's an attacker. To my surprise, I see Azur leaning on Lidiane. She nods at me, quickly, as if to say she's fine.

Azur smiles at Renel. "It's time for fun! We're going to a festival. Take my hand."

"Now?" Renel asks, then points to me and Lidiane. "But they'll—"

"Have fun. They can come." Azur laughs. "Now. It's really, really, really important. Now." He widens his eyes and I'm not sure if it's a plea, an order, or what.

Renel approaches his guardian while Lidiane extends a hand to me. Despite her previous nod, she's anything but relaxed. Something's wrong, perhaps something happened, and yet her look is encouraging. I'm assuming we're about to transcend, like we did with Nelsin, to get near the castle.

I take Lidiane's hand, then Renel's. His fingers are cold, and holding his hand feels strange, the gesture too intimate for someone I barely know.

The room turns dark in less than a second, and I feel like my stomach is about to be turned upside down. There's light again right away, but we're inside an old wooden cabin. I let go of Renel's hand and look around. Behind me, someone screams. I turn to see an old fae woman with bark-like skin, her eyes wide, staring at us.

Azur laughs. "Apologies. Wrong house. Please forget this." He turns to us and says, "Let's drink some more."

He opens the door and we follow him. A cobbled path in front of the house leads to more houses down the hill. There's something else down there, as I hear some distant music and voices.

Renel somehow looks even tenser than he did before, a quizzical expression on his face as he stares at his guardian. "Summer End Festival, really?"

"Fun, Renel, fun. Let's have *very public fun*." Azur's voice is slightly slurred, as if he had drunk too much, and yet there's intention in the emphasis on the last words.

Renel shakes his head but keeps walking.

Azur still has an arm around Lidiane, as if leaning on her. She doesn't look happy, but not as if she's upset at him. Did they become buddies in the few hours they've been together? More than buddies?

Down there, I see a large valley and many wooden stalls, some of them covered in canopies. Delightful scents of meat and spices hit my nostrils, making me hungry. The music is clearer now; drums and strings in an entrancing melody. A fae festival!

If we weren't coming here in such puzzling circumstances, I guess I would be thrilled.

Renel grunts. "Are you trying to get me assassinated?"

Azur chuckles. "I can't, Your Highness! You know well I can't."

"You sound like you would if you could." Renel's definitely looking grumpy.

Meanwhile, Azur's reply is a laugh.

The guardian then stops and says, "There are guards. We'll get you some." He then turns to me. "Wait."

He waves a hand and does something that tickles my ear. I touch it and feel no difference.

Lidiane glares at him. "You can do glamours?"

He grins at her. "I'm multi-talented."

She pushes him away from her. "I'm sure you can use your talents to walk on your own."

Azur's legs wobble, then he leans on Renel, who rolls his eyes. "I hope there will be a great explanation for this."

Lidiane steps beside me and whispers, "He gave you fae ears." I touch them again, and she adds, "It's an illusion. You won't be able to feel them."

"Are you all right?" I whisper back.

She nods. "We'll talk later."

We walk in between a booth selling mini sculptures and a closed tent and step inside a large circle of booths, stalls, and tents. In the middle, there are wooden tables and an empty place in front of the band where three fae are dancing.

"Guards!" Azur yells. "Guards!"

All the fae around us stare at him and Renel, but soon two guards run to us.

"What is it?" One of them asks.

"Bow, you idiot!" Azur says. "Can't you recognize your acting king? He's stubborn but needs protection. Get some of your colleagues to form a perimeter around us."

The guards bow, then one of them whistles, and two more guards approach us. As far as I know, a retinue of four is hardly enough for a royal, but with fae, things are different, since they have magical rules and deals.

We reach one of the wooden tables in the middle of the festival, followed by curious glances and angry glares. Lidiane sits beside me, but then Azur sits by her, so that she's sandwiched between us, with Renel alone across from us.

I realize then that the place is mostly empty, with more than half of the stalls and tents closed, even if there are vendors selling food, drinks, clothes, and more objects. Many guards are walking around, so I assume coming here is not that dangerous for Renel.

Renel places a bag of coins in one of the guards' hands. "Bring us some wine and water."

"And food," I say. My stomach is growling.

"Bring some skewers," Renel adds with a smile.

Lidiane turns to me. "I've never been here before, but this has to be the Summer End Festival at Caraneya. We're near the Solemn River, southeast of where the castle is currently located. Fae—both high and low—come from around the area, and this festival will probably be full at night and in the early hours of the morning."

"Why are we here?" I whisper.

"For fun." Her smile doesn't reach her eyes, but this is not the moment to try to get any answers from her.

A guard comes in with a jug and four cups. Renel himself serves them and passes them to us.

Strangely, he looks like a different person, with none of the tension I saw earlier. Instead, he looks regal, confident, and powerful, even sitting at a simple wooden table. Either this or what I saw in the castle was an act, or perhaps they're different sides of the same person, and this is Renel when he's in a public appearance, acting as the Crystal Court King.

The wine is delicious, with a fresh, zesty taste. I wish I could drink a lot of it, but I need to keep my wits. A guard brings a bucket with some kind of meat skewers and places it on the table.

Renel points at it and smiles. "More fae food, like you wanted."

I take a skewer and taste some of the meat. It's juicy, well-seasoned, and delicious. My stomach growls again, I think in approval or excitement. The meat has some thin bones and I'm assuming it's some kind of small bird.

Renel and Azur take second servings of wine, while I take another skewer.

"What's this?" I ask no one in particular.

"Mountain rat," Renel replies.

"Rat?" I stare again at my skewer, unsure if I should feel disgusted. "They must be huge. But delicious." There. I made up my mind and decide to keep on eating.

Azur gets up and climbs on the table, then yells, "We celebrate. Summer end!"

Lidiane leans her head on her hands, as if trying to hide, while Renel has a quick grimace, soon replaced by laughter. Fake laughter, I realize.

More people stare at us now.

"I can sing," Azur says from the top of the table. "And dance!"

He takes off his shirt and tosses it to Lidiane. A quick glance tells me he's well-defined, but I look away. I don't want Renel to think I'm thirsting after his good-looking guardian.

Renel takes a slow sip of his wine, while Azur—I can't believe what he's doing. I glance again quickly, just to make sure I'm not imagining him unlacing his trousers, and catch him lowering them, so that I'm greeted with the sight of his dong. I look away quickly, and my eyes meet Renel's. He looks more puzzled than vexed and shrugs. Beside me, Lidiane stares down at the table, as if refusing to acknowledge the spectacle in front of her.

I take another piece of my rat skewer, still impressed with the seasoning, when I feel strong, rough arms around my arms and torso, pulling me back.

Someone's trying to kidnap me—or kill me.

ASTRA

Six guards? Why did Sayanne call six guards to arrest me? And I can't even try to use my magic. First, I don't know if it will work. Second, what am I even going to do? Dazzle them?

I step back, then jump over the table and push it with all my strength. I just want to push the guards and Sayanne out of the room. Beside me, I see a large strip of cloth moving—the curtain. Ferer throws it on the ground like a jumping rope, and trips some of the guards.

I pick books from behind me and throw them, managing to hit Sayanne's head. She steps back, then turns around and leaves the study. Beside me, someone else is throwing more books.

Nelsin! He's much faster and much more precise than me. I can't believe he's here, and I'm thankful for his disobedience.

With another stroke of the curtain, Ferer trips two more guards, while Nelsin pushes the table against them, and gets them out the door.

"Retreat," Sayanne calls from the hallway. "They can't go anywhere."

"Thank you, sister!" I yell, partly being sarcastic, but partly in earnest.

All I needed was for them to retreat.

My heart feels heavy and swollen after seeing Sayanne ordering my arrest. As much as Tarlia had told me Sayanne had tried to kill her, I had a small hope that it had been some kind of misunderstanding.

No. Sayanne is beyond hope—and will never be my friend again. Of course, that's the last item on a long list of problems.

At least the guards are outside, and then Nelsin and Ferer push the door and bolt it. For once, I'm glad Otavio had so many locks in it.

Ferer turns to me, his face grave. "They'll surround the tower, perhaps launch arrows."

"We'll wait," I say, not too loud but not softly enough to prevent being overheard. "They'll get tired."

I put a finger over my lips, point to the adjoining room, then tiptoe there, while Nelsin and Ferer walk normally. Of course, fae don't make noise when they walk.

We pass by the chair where Otavio colored my hair black before my wedding. It's strange to look back at that time, look back at my fear, and yet, in retrospect, I wasn't that afraid of Marlak. Could it be that part of me already yearned for his company? I don't know.

Outside, the guards are quiet. That's not a good sign. For all I know, they could be planning to bring the door down or something, and that's why they quit. I pull a bookshelf and reveal the secret passage from where Otavio wanted me to escape all these days ago. When I try to open the door, I realize it's locked.

Nelsin steps ahead, looks at the lock, then pulls a long metal filament from his pocket and works on it. I hope he can unlock it. Outside the room, the silence is ominous. Of course they're planning something—unless they truly think we're going to try to scale down the walls, in which case, it would make sense to place everyone downstairs.

Nelsin is focused, concentrated, and keeps moving that piece of metal. Ferer and I watch him in silence—partial silence, as I'm sure my heart is making a racket.

After many agonizing seconds, the door clicks, revealing that hallway with narrow steps where I made the decision to marry Marlak rather than become a fugitive, the decision that has led me to where I am today—back here.

We go in, then Nelsin does the best to pull the bookcase, and then locks the door again, even if we're in the dark.

We step away from the door, Ferer in the front, touching the walls and descending slowly, carrying a dim lightstone.

Behind me, Nelsin whispers, "Do you know where this leads?"

"No," I reply. "But it should let us escape the castle."

It has to, or else Otavio wouldn't have tried to sneak me away through this passage. I wonder how come he found it, if there are other passages like this, and if the guards know about it.

And then I recall that nobody would have expected me to escape that day, whereas now, they know we're fleeing—and it could make all the difference.

I add, "But I'm not sure if the exit will be clear."

We could end up trapped here, but then, what's the alternative? Scaling down the walls would make us easy, slow-moving targets.

When I decided to come here, I knew there would be some risks, but in truth, I largely underestimated them. How could I have guessed everything that happened in the castle? I'm not even sure I believe Sayanne's words that the two princes and the queen died, that Princess Driziely escaped, even if I hope she did. And why is Sayanne giving orders as if she had any authority here?

My only consolation is that at least she's alive, even if she's drowning in bitterness.

We keep descending slowly those dark stairs. A few times, I sense some movement by my feet—probably mice or other creatures. The stairs have a musty, damp smell, and eventually I hear water.

Ferer stops and extends his lightstone, its brightness reflecting on the floor below. Not floor, water.

"It's submerged," he says. "I can go in first, and check if it's safe for you. Do you want to hold this?"

He offers me the lightstone, and I point to Nelsin. "Let him carry it. I don't want to do any magic by accident."

"True."

Nelsin takes the stone, then says, "Be careful." His voice is shaky, afraid.

Ferer chuckles. "It's water, Nelsin. You surely don't think *I'm* going to drown."

"We don't know what's in there," he says.

"I'm going." Ferer turns and descends the last steps, then dives into the water.

I'm carrying the loose pages taken from the middle of the books, and not looking forward to ruining the only thing I got from this expedition.

Since Nelsin has a bag, I ask, "Do you have anything water-proof? For these?" I show him the pages.

"In fact, I do." He opens his bag and pulls out a waterskin, then rolls the pages, puts them inside, and grins. "Genius, right?"

"I'm glad they fit."

He shrugs. "We couldn't have known we'd need to swim." His tone is light, but I can sense his tension as he looks at the water below.

"My master was going to make me escape through here," I say. "So I don't think it's dangerous."

"Let's hope it isn't."

His eyes are focused on the water, waiting for Ferer to return. Even in the dim light, I see his top ears perked up, as if trying to hear anything from his companion.

Seconds and seconds pass, and even I get agitated. When I'm thinking one of us should jump after Ferer, he finally emerges.

"It's safe," he says, still submerged up to his chest. "It leads to a small river, but it's a long tunnel. You'll have to hold your breath and swim fast, or else I can pull you." He says this last part looking at me. "If you're not a strong swimmer."

"Can you pull me?" I feel slightly embarrassed saying that. "I can barely swim."

Ferer nods, then looks at Nelsin. "You?"

"I can go on my own," he says.

I descend two steps on those submerged stairs until I have water up to my thighs, then Ferer turns around. "Hold onto my waist, and don't let go. You'll need to relax, all right? Make sure you don't try to breathe."

I laugh. "I'm not going to try to breathe water!"

"You say that now, but when your lungs start to burn—"

"I'll be careful."

I take a deep breath, filling my lungs with air, then hold his waist. He takes off right after that, his feet moving fast through a dark underwater tunnel. I would never be able to swim at that speed.

There's an opening ahead, with some faint greenish light, and what I'm assuming is the unnamed river that runs by the Krastel castle. It's a long tunnel. I'm exhaling slowly, but eventually, all my air is gone, and my lungs beg for more. It makes sense that some people would breathe water by mistake.

Air, air, air.

My lungs are screaming, and I interlace my fingers so as to hold Ferer tighter. We cross the opening, and I feel the current pushing us. Pushing a lot. I want to come to the surface, but the water won't let me. I could swear it snatches my hands, then drags me away from Ferer. I still can't breathe. All I need to do is reach the surface—and yet there's a swirl spinning me, and I can't get away from it.

A swirl. I've done this before, but with Marlak, who used air magic to make me comfortable underwater. With no air, this is torture. And then I don't even know if it's a swirl or if it's just that I'm such a terrible swimmer that I'm doing something wrong.

And yet it stops, and I find my feet touching soft sand, with nymph guards armed with spears all around me. Ahead of me, on a throne, their queen.

I'm out of air and feel as if I'm breathing something, but it burns, and I can't speak. I need to ask for air, or for them to let me go to the surface, but I don't know how.

There is a way. I recall that the queen can do that mind-talking thing.

"Air," I say, in my mind. "Air. I need to breathe."

She just stares, and I realize Nelsin and Ferer aren't anywhere around me. I'm all alone here. So far, I trusted the nymphs, but this time, there's something wrong about this.

"Air," I try again.

My vision gets blurry, then everything is black.

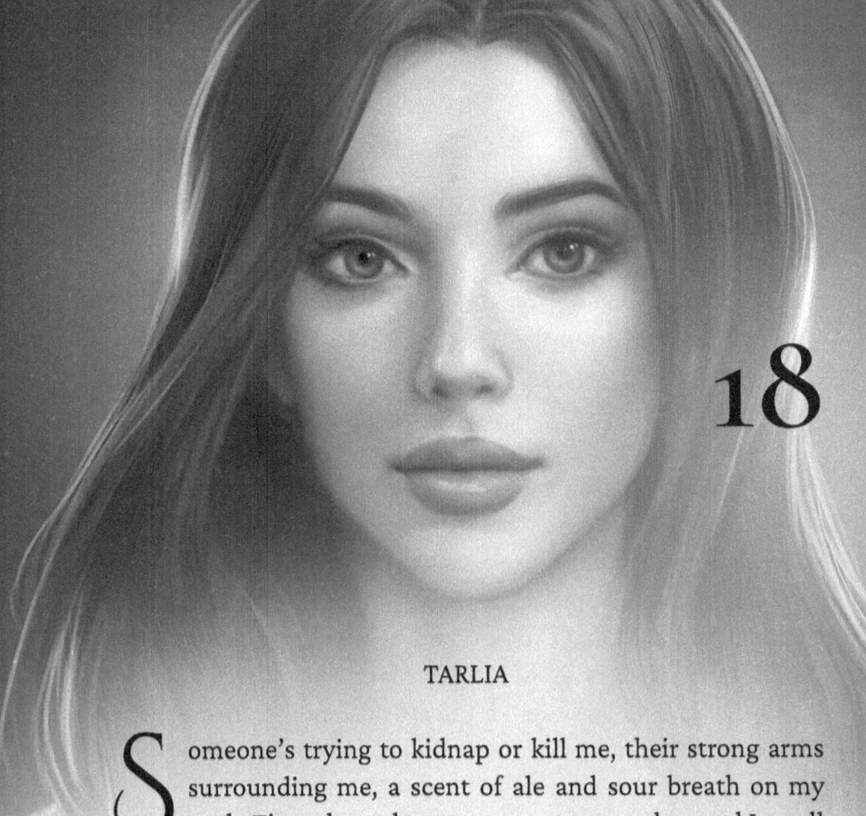

18

TARLIA

Someone's trying to kidnap or kill me, their strong arms surrounding me, a scent of ale and sour breath on my neck. Time slows down as my senses awaken and I recall what I learned about escaping a situation like this.

Instead of resisting the pull, I push my weight back, then put a leg behind theirs and trip them. We both fall to the ground, and I roll away. Renel is beside us, a sword pointed to my attacker's throat—an old fae man. Two more attackers are coming from both sides and I raise my skewer, ready to stab anyone, but the attackers gasp for air. Meanwhile, two guards approach us, stepping between us and the men, who are now on the ground.

I look back and see Lidiane, her eyes wide staring at us, and then Azur collapsing and falling from the table. The only reason he doesn't reach the ground is that Lidiane slows his fall, and then a guard grabs him.

The three attackers are unconscious, and I think Azur just used air magic on them, and must have used so much of it that it made him faint.

"Today is a day of celebration," Renel says, his voice incredibly loud and confident. "Therefore, I ask for clemency, and that their lives be spared."

He's addressing the guards, but not only the guards; everyone around us, probably to make them think he's some kind of compassionate king.

With a lower voice, he asks the guards, "Is there a flying carriage nearby?"

A man nods.

"We'll have to borrow it," Renel says, then turns to me. "Would you like to fly over the Solemn River?"

"Sure." In reality, the idea of going anywhere above ground spooks me, but I'm not the one making the decisions here.

Renel nods, then picks up Azur and throws him against his shoulder, his guardian's long blond hair hanging behind him. With his free hand, he grabs his guardian's hat.

Beside me, Lidiane looks thoughtful and worried. Is she worried about Azur? I can't wait to have a moment alone with her and ask what in the world that is all about.

This whole trip is so strange that I don't even feel scared or traumatized anymore. Perhaps I got numbed after the Krastel guards attacked our carriage, after thinking Ziven was dead. *That* pain is still raw, torturing my flesh.

In comparison, whatever happened now feels like one of those strange dreams that makes no sense when you wake up. I glance at Renel carrying his naked guardian and change my mind; this is more like a feverish, never-ending weird dream.

Five guards surround us as we walk away from the festival until we approach a large, two-story wooden building. In front of it, there's a strange, round carriage. I suppose that's the vehicle Renel is going to borrow. I can't imagine what magic makes it fly, until I see four winged pixies, their faces gaunt and tired—and realize they're going to carry us. I don't want to imagine what will happen if they falter. Maybe it's better not to imagine it.

A guard opens the door and Renel gestures for me and Lidiane to enter, and we sit on a luxurious, cushioned velvet seat. Renel sits across from us, then places his guardian beside him, covering his private parts with a shirt.

The carriage rises, and I shut my eyes tight as if it could change the feeling that there's nothing beneath us.

"You don't like flying?" Renel asks.

"I'm not used to it."

He looks outside. "It *is* strange."

Beside me, Lidiane fidgets, then asks, "Doesn't it bother you? The pixies?" She's staring at Renel.

I'm wondering if she's had enough of all this insanity and wants to be expelled from the castle. That's the only explanation for this provocation.

His expression is thoughtful. "You mean because they're enchanted?"

"That's part of it, yes." At least she toned down her voice and now sounds only curious.

"The tradition of having enchanted workers goes down a long way, from the time fae enchanted humans." His tone is polite and friendly. "Since I came to power, I made changes, and now only convicted criminals can be enchanted."

She raises an eyebrow. "And who convicts them?"

Why is she irritating him when we're up in the air?

"You should know that," he says, his voice level. "There are courts everywhere, and in fact, most courts have at least one lower fae. That wasn't always the case either. What's your name?"

She hesitates, then says, "Lidiane."

"Lidiane, if your concern is for the lower fae, you should know I share it."

"I was curious."

He nods. "Your questions are fair. I suppose I'd ask them too, if I had the chance to speak with the acting monarch." He turns to me. "Do you have any questions?"

"I wouldn't even know where to start. Do you like being king?" Maybe the question is silly, but it was the first thing that popped into my mind.

"I do my best to honor the responsibility I hold. Now *I* have a question." He points at us. "How come you two know each other?"

I have to answer that, since I can lie. "We bonded right away, from the moment she was assigned as my lady-in-waiting."

Renel looks more carefully at Lidiane. "Oh. So you…"

Azur opens his eyes and sits up. "What happened?"

"It depends. What's the last thing you remember?" Renel asks.

"I need to think." The guardian glances at me and Lidiane, then adds, "But I'm fine."

For some reason, my eyelids feel heavy. This is some magic, I know it is, and I have to fight it—but my body is feeling so soothed, relaxed, so at ease…

"Sleep," I hear in my mind, and I realize it's a brilliant idea.

ASTRA

I feel water being pulled out of my chest, then take a deep breath as I lie on the ground of a strange, small cave, illuminated with some kind of lightstones. An odd, fae-looking nymph sits by me. I realize then that his eyes look like fae—or human eyes, deep brown and shaped like normal eyes, while his body looks like a nymph's, with green skin and fins. I take another look at the cave and see water outside it, as if we were in a gigantic air bubble.

"Where am I?" I ask.

"Near the Nymph throne. You swallowed some water. Our queen apologizes for her oversight." He passes me a strange contraption, with a tube and something to put over my mouth. "This will allow you to breathe for a few minutes down there."

After almost dying, perhaps I should be more careful, and yet for some reason I trust him, and still trust the Nymph

Queen. Either way, if I'm deep underwater, I have worse things to fear. And I have one question.

"Are you half-fae?"

He nods. "Yes. And before you ask, it's extremely rare. Few couples like my parents have children."

"But they can…" Oh, what kind of inappropriate question was I almost about to ask? I smile. "Be couples?"

He smirks. "Yes, intercourse is possible, Astra. With humans too."

I truly hope he's not offering, and he's so strange that I don't think I would be able to know. "Interesting. But fae and nymphs don't interact a lot, do they?"

"No. Most of us can't breathe outside the water for long, and most fae can't breathe underwater. The exception is the Sea Court, but they're no friends of ours."

"You don't need to be friends to… I mean, relationships can happen, right? People sometimes pick… weird partners." I don't know if I'm making any sense.

"True. But the Sea Court is known for killing anyone who disobeys their rules, so it would be dangerous."

"I see. What's your name?"

"Ether." He extends a webbed hand. "Humans shake hands, right?"

I take it and shake it. "Yes, we do."

I put the tube around me, then he helps me place the part that should cover my mouth and nose.

"You'll be able to breathe using this, but not for long." He stares at me. "Do you need anything? Have any questions? Otherwise, we're on our way to the Nymph Queen."

"Why is she helping me?"

He tilts his head. "You'd need to ask her that."

"But can't you give me your opinion?"

He takes a deep breath. "We don't interfere in fae business or the business above the ground, but everyone can benefit from allies. Are you ready?"

"What's the queen's name?" I feel that it would be polite to know her name, even if I'll probably still address her as Her Majesty or something.

"Nymph Queen. For us, being a monarch is a sacrifice of the self in exchange for the greater good. We don't keep our names."

I blink. "That's... different."

"I suppose." He then asks, "Can we go?"

"Sure." I'd rather make this fast, as Nelsin and Ferer are probably worried. I even regret asking questions and wasting time.

Ether pulls me by the arm and we dive into the water again. My heart speeds up as I hold my breath, the memory of passing out still fresh with the horror and fear of drowning, of not being able to breathe.

As we descend, he points to my nose, to that strange thing around it. Despite my body's protests, I force myself to inhale—and it's air. It's safe. Being submerged so deep still spooks me, but the queen didn't exactly give me a choice on whether I could choose to see her or not.

Rude, I suppose.

We keep going down, then he takes me by the hand and the now familiar swirl spins me. This time, without Marlak or someone I trust, it's somewhat terrifying.

My heart is at full speed when I find myself in that same strange chamber, in front of the Queen's throne. There are no guards around us, just Ether, who stands at a distance.

"Apologies for forgetting you need help under water," the queen says. "We have no time for cordiality, no time to wait until you decide to come to us. No time, Astra."

I can feel her hurry, her desperation, and yet I don't know what she means by *no time*. I don't understand what she fears. "Why?"

Her dark eyes narrow. I used to think they were expressionless, and yet now, the feeling they convey is sadness, despair, not anger.

"Something stirs in the Shadow Lands. I do not know what.

We can't get near that place, and haven't been able to find out. The giants are scared, and few things scare giants. Something's about to happen. I can sense that old forces are converging, and moving faster and faster."

"What forces?"

"I do not know, Astra. What I know is that you'll need to be ready. Do you know who you are?"

"I'm Tiurian—but I know little about my magic."

"I'll tell you one thing: Tiurian magic hasn't been seen or felt for about one hundred years."

"That's... around the time of the River Treaty."

I feel the weight of her eyes on me. "Do you know how the humans managed to secure part of the continent for themselves? Make sure the fae would never enslave them?"

"They... fought." At least that's what I learned in the Elite Tower.

Her chuckle sounds odd and bitter. "If they had any fighting chance, it was thanks to Tiurian magic. Without the Tiurians, the humans would never have gained their freedom. And yet once the humans won, they turned their back to their supporters, declared them their enemies, despite their help. Or maybe turning their backs to the Tiurians was the condition the fae imposed to agree with the river treaty and grant humans their freedom. Interesting, right?"

"I... didn't know that."

"I don't know the details either, but what I know is that the Tiurians disappeared. A few of them were caught and murdered, but overall, they vanished. And one of the ways in which they vanished was by suppressing their magic, so that their descendants would not be discovered."

What she's saying is surprising and isn't, but there's a part of it that doesn't make sense. "How come there are creatures who can sense Tiurian magic? I was found because of it."

"Fae used to live three hundred, even five hundred years, and there are still fae and other creatures from the time when they had long lives. Another possibility is that the knowledge on how to find Tiurian magic has been passed through generations. The thing is, Tiurian magic is extremely rare, practically extinguished. While there are many Tiurian descendants, their magic is dormant. But yours isn't."

Her words make my heart speed up. "You mean that even if they try to use it, they won't have magic?"

"Exactly."

"I always thought Tiurians suppressed their own magic either due to fear of being found or shame because they were told it was dark."

"That's not completely wrong. The magic *was* suppressed— intentionally, I believe. But it was done collectively. It was hidden. But not completely. And now we'll need it."

"How? I'm trying to connect with my power, but I don't even know where to start. Can you... give me some advice?"

She gets up from her throne and approaches me. "Magic is not something external you connect to. It's not a trick you learn. Magic is you, the essence of your being. It's like breathing. You don't need to figure out how it's done. You just do it."

Her words sound wise, but if I think about them, they sound shallow. "Walking is like that; I just do it. And yet there was a time when it wasn't the case."

"I'm sure you didn't read a book on how to walk or had anyone explain it to you. You simply did it when you were ready. There's no question you're ready, or you wouldn't have used your magic before. Now use it. Be ready. Find what you need to find. Time is running out."

"Can you please be less vague?" I plead, aware I'm sounding whiny.

"I'm not trying to be wise or cryptic. I'm being vague because I don't know the details of what's about to happen, so all I can tell you is to be ready. Be the powerful Tiurian you are and trust your magic. Self-doubt is a luxury, Astra, one you can't have."

Wow. I'm feeling so luxurious.

I heard that, she says in my head, while staring at me with a smirk.

"Should we just talk without talking?"

"No need. We're alone. Now go. You're probably the most powerful Tiurian alive. *Be* that powerful Tiurian."

"I guess all I need to do is trust myself, and then boom!" I know it sounds snarky, but if she'll hear it in my head regardless, what can I do?

"Glad to hear you understand."

"Please explain more." I'm absolutely whiny now. "Tell me about my kind."

She shakes her head. "I just told you all I know. I don't understand your magic. It's up to you, Astra."

Ether approaches me, takes my hand, and then pulls me back up, through strange swirls, and then up again, until we're back in that cave.

He says, "I'll need the breathing mask back, but the way to the surface is short. You won't run out of air."

I take off that tube, inhale a deep breath, then he pulls me by the hand again—and brings me down.

Why are we going down? We swirl and swirl, and then he pulls me up, and I see the rocks surrounding our island—and take a deep gulp of air. Goodness, I love air.

As I'm pushing myself up the rocks, Nelsin comes running and extends a hand to help me climb.

"Finally," he says.

"I'm so sorry. I bet you were worried."

Ferer approaches us. "The nymphs told us you were summoned to an audience, but it was so unlike them, so sudden. Are you all right?"

"Sort of. The nymphs fear something, but they don't know what it is. The queen told me I had to figure out my magic soon, that there's no time, and yet she wouldn't explain why."

"You'll figure it out." Nelsin waves a hand. "Also, time for them is different. When they mean something's going to happen soon, they probably mean in ten years or so."

Ferer frowns, his expression troubled. "Not necessarily."

I sigh. "Well, I'll do my best for my magic to..." I snap my fingers. "Come alive! Not that it's dead. Or living. I don't even know."

Nelsin chuckles. "We'll help you figure it out. But you should eat and rest first."

Do you know who you are?

The queen's question is still in my mind, getting louder and louder. Who *am* I? I've never even seen myself, the way I truly am.

An idea comes to me. "I need to wash my hair first, then I'll eat and check the books. Do you have lime, vinegar, or both?"

Nelsin places his hands on his waist. "How do you think we season your salads?"

"I need some for my *hair,*" I explain.

He raises an eyebrow. "Hair salad?"

"To get rid of the color, at least the one Otavio used to find me. By the way, what did you do with the hair coloring bottles?"

"They're still here," Ferer says. "Tarlia used some."

Tarlia. Shit. But she's in the castle now, so he won't try to find her.

I turn to Ferer. "Throw the liquid from the bottles somewhere where nobody can find it. It's how Otavio located me, so we need to get rid of that." I touch my hair. "And I'll get rid of my fake color—as much as I can, at least. Before you say anything, if we ever go somewhere, I can wear a hat, a wig, something. I need to be myself. Find my true self."

"Your true self is not your hair color, Astra," Nelsin says, then points to his chest. "It's here."

"For me it is. My hair color was always about hiding who I am. I'll no longer hide it."

The two knights stare at each other, perhaps worried.

Ferer sighs. "We'll get you some lime and vinegar. And I'll bring hoods, hats, and wigs next time I go to a village."

"Thank you. And thank you both for your help in the Krastel castle."

Nelsin smirks. "I have your papers. They didn't get wet." He then clears his throat, his top ears perked up. "Also, I'm not bragging or anything, but did you notice how disobedience can be useful sometimes? Aren't you glad I didn't wait outside?"

Ferer rolls his eyes. "Your disobedience, this time, was not a reckless decision that almost got you or Astra killed, so there's a difference."

"Of course." Nelsin's tone is playful. "We learn, evolve, and all that. It's why we should forgive." These last words are laced with a deep sadness, almost like an open wound.

"I forgive you," I say. I know he doesn't want to hear it from me, but I feel bad seeing him sad like that.

Ferer turns to me. "I'll get you the lime and vinegar. Nelsin, can you fill her bath?"

"Of course!" His smile is wide even if his eyes don't match his lips, and if his top ears are now hidden under his hair.

I follow him inside the house.

Now, I have no idea if removing my fake color will change anything. I obviously don't even know how to awaken my magic or whatever. And then, while the nymph's warnings were clearly urgent, they were so vague that they gave me nothing.

All I know is that there's some kind of imminent danger, and that I should trust myself and use the magic I don't know how to use.

Then again, perhaps the nymphs are mistaken. They can't be counting on me to prevent or defeat some big evil, right? I mean, that doesn't make any sense.

If the wellbeing of the world will soon depend on my magic, then we're all doomed.

19

AZUR

My magic is gone and I'm naked in the middle of nowhere—or everywhere. I want to transcend away, escape, but I'm stuck. Suspended between consciousness and sleep, all I feel is nothingness, strangely calming nothingness calling me.

Until I feel a tug. There's a bond pulling me, pulling me back to that dreadful place full of pain. Not a dreadful place, but a carriage with my master, the human girl, and *her*.

"What happened?" The words roll out of my tongue somewhat slurred.

"It depends. What's the last thing you remember?" Renel asks, and then memories assault me at once.

Murder, danger, blood. Why do I feel so horrible after getting rid of that vile leader of the council? And how come I passed out from magic fatigue? How did I get to that point? I need to speak to Renel in private, and I have postponed this for too long.

"I need to think," I say, still stunned, still shocked. "But I'm fine."

Only a faint trace of my magic still runs in my veins, but it should be enough. I change the air around the human girl and the pretty fae, even if my heart tells me that it's wrong.

Renel exhales. "Good. I thought I would have to carry you into the castle."

The idea of someone hauling me is so humiliating that makes me cringe.

Her breathing gets steady, deep, and so does the human girl's. They're both asleep.

"Oh." Renel sounds appalled. "Did you just make my human guest pass out?"

I turn to him. "Both of them. We need to talk."

"Very much so, but it could wait."

"If you want, I can wake them."

"Now it won't change anything. What is it? The explanation for all this?" He gestures to me, and I realize I'm naked with only a shirt covering me.

Right. More memories assault me like punches, but I need to start from the beginning.

"I went to the Jewel City, and the task you assigned me was accomplished."

"That's... great to hear."

"But there were problems." I swallow. If I could, I'd never confess what I've done, and yet I feel my bond pressing me, which doesn't even make sense. It would be safer for him not to know any of that, but magic is magic, and for some reason, it wants me to tell him the truth. "I was about to transcend with the prisoners—when Zorwal arrived."

Renel catches a breath and his relaxed expression turns serious at once.

I continue, "I hid, and I don't think he saw me, but he was trying to extract information from those men, and wanted to know who was in the Desert Keep."

His eyes are enormous and his breathing shallow as he stares at me. "What did you do?"

"I was duty-bound to keep that information secret, so I had no choice." The remaining words get stuck in my throat. In my mind, it was already horrific, a sight that stains my memory with blood and death, and yet now, when it's time to voice it, it's as if I'm about to make it real, permanent.

"Azur, just tell me what you did." Renel's voice is gentle. "Whatever it is, I'll understand it."

"I killed Zorwal." The confession comes quickly, like coughing out something that was choking me.

Renel's eyes widen even more, then he blinks. "How?"

"I threw him against a wall, and he hit his head."

His finger touches his bracelets. "Are you sure? You know he has healing abilities."

"There was blood—a splatter." That disgusting image has been carved in my mind. "And his eyes... I glanced at them, and they were empty. He was no longer breathing. He was dead, Renel. I'm absolutely sure of it."

Renel's lips part, and the sound that comes from his mouth is what I least expected; laughter. Pure, joyous laughter.

He notices me staring at him, and says, "It's not—" His laughter resumes, and he can't finish the sentence. After a few seconds, he says, "Not that I delight in death." And yet hysterical laughter takes hold of him again.

It's odd. I always thought Renel was thankful to Zorwal, who helped him gain and maintain his position, even if the relationship wasn't the most friendly. That's clearly not the case.

When Renel chokes what I think might be his last laugh, I say, "So you like the news?"

"Not..." His shoulders sag. "Well, yes. I can't believe it. Killed him. I could kiss you right now."

"That's hardly necessary."

Renel shakes his head, a wide grin spread across his face. "I know! I'm just... Can't believe it."

"Right. Now, the issue is that I don't want to be sentenced for murder, and there will be a body along with five missing prisoners in the Jewel's Inquiry House."

His smile fades. "Were you able to free them?"

"They're on a boat, going to the Nowhere Lands."

"You killed the leader of the council then went to the Jewel Port with the fugitives?"

I often want to strangle Renel, and in moments like this, the want is a thousandfold. "Of course not. What do you take me for?"

"An incredibly efficient guardian. It's just a question, Azur. How did you get them on their way?"

"I transcended straight onto a boat."

He stares at me open-mouthed. "In the middle of the sea?"

"Where else would it be? Among clouds?"

"A port. Does your magic even work in the ocean? Not to mention the scare you must have given the crew. And it's Sea Court territory. I'm not sure they wouldn't notice that much magic."

"What was the alternative? And I promised you to do my best to save their lives. It meant that if someone else's life was on the line, I would not be able to save them."

I can't transcend. I still remember being stuck on that boat, unable to escape, the Sea Court threatening her.

Renel rolls his eyes. "*Do your best* means trying within the limits you think are right. Your best, not your impossible."

"That's not how magic bonds work, Renel."

He runs a hand over his head and almost drops one of the combs holding back his hair. "Was anyone else in danger?"

I sigh. "That's not what I'm talking about. I'm just saying I had no choice."

"You did well." A strange chuckle leaves his lips. "More than well."

I lift a finger. "So you should trust me."

"Funny you say that. Didn't I come to a festival *to have fun* just because you said so? Almost got killed, but that's a minor detail, I assume."

I roll my eyes at the absurdity of what he just said. "Those desperate villagers were nowhere near killing you, and you know that. And there were tons of guards around you. I can't—

it's physically impossible for me to put you in danger. And you know why I brought us to the festival."

He squares his shoulders. "Yes, sure. So people will say they saw us far away from the Jewel City. Not sure why *I* had to be there. What you aren't taking into consideration is that you never dance, never get drunk. I think you barely ever laugh, Azur. All of a sudden you're stripping naked on a table."

"Excessive wine makes people do stupid things. I won't be the first one. The attendees who saw us will think I had been drinking for a while. Nothing strange in that."

Renel nods. "Did anyone see you in the Jewel City?"

She did, but he doesn't need to know that. "I was disguised and glamoured, then used air magic to make the guards lethargic and confused."

"They'll know the murderer was an air wielder."

"Not necessarily. Few fae can use magic to change the air people breathe. They might not identify the element used, or even realize there was any magic. They won't know how Zorwal was thrown against the wall. I mean, air doesn't leave signs."

"Which is a sign in itself."

"Sure, but someone could have pushed him or something. Now, as to the prisoners disappearing... They don't know I can transcend."

"Marlak knows." He points to the girls in the carriage. "They also do."

"The human has no idea it's anything special." I point at the pretty fae, sleeping so peacefully. "And she won't tell anyone." At least that's what I hope, considering she has her own secrets to hide.

Renel glances at her. "Now, I do have a few questions about this fae, Lidiane."

The name surprises me. I've heard it before, but I don't recall where, and yet I'm sure the information is stored deep down where I'm not sure I want to reach.

"I mean," he continues, "When you said you had chosen a

lady-in-waiting for the Tiurian, I was thinking of something more pragmatic."

Renel's uttering nonsense while I'm here, pushing and pulling my memory, wanting to know and not know who she is.

"Azur," he mutters.

The word gets my attention. Of course it does. I'm barely different from an enchanted fae, unable to escape my commands. "Yes?"

"Did you place her as the human's lady-in-waiting just because you're smitten?"

Stupid questions deserve no answers. "I'm not reckless, Renel."

"Where did you even find her?"

"She was *already* in the castle, and I placed her where I thought she could be useful." I point at the two young women asleep. "Was I wrong? The human seems to trust her."

Renel glances at them. "Why is a high fae even acting as a servant?"

"She's lower fae." I look at her hands and notice that her glamour is holding even when she's asleep. No surprise—her magic is powerful. The question is why. And why was the Sea Court after her?

"Fine." Renel sighs. "But do you see the problem in placing your lover to guard my human guest?"

I make no effort to tone down my glare. "Your question contains an incorrect assumption. How can I answer it?"

"Isn't she your lover?"

"She is not."

"But you'd like her to be."

No is at the tip of my tongue, but won't come out, obviously.

"She's gorgeous," I say in a matter-of-fact non-answer.

"There are thousands of gorgeous fae in the crystal court. Would you want to sleep with all of them?"

They're not like her, but I obviously won't say that. I raise an eyebrow. "Maybe I wouldn't mind it."

He takes a long, deep breath. "Listen, I can see the merits of showing your junk to the girl you like, but you should pick somewhere more private."

"Is this supposed to be funny?"

"I don't know. My jokes suck, Azur. Nevermind me. Now, if you like her, great, but maybe try not to get her involved in all this... mess."

Too late. She's neck deep. I hope I never have to tell Renel that. "I didn't say I liked her."

"Do you *not* like her?"

"I barely know her."

"That makes no difference. I always remember my father telling me about when he met my mother."

Renel hangs to the memory of his father like some deity. His father and his love at first sight. His father and his beautiful love that eventually got him killed.

"Your father's case is unique, Renel. Regardless, I'm a guardian."

"My father was a guardian."

"Not a *bound* guardian."

Renel throws his hands in the air. "I swear, if people hear you, they'll think I walk around with you on a leash or something."

I chuckle. "That will fuel quite a few fantasies."

He laughs as well. "They'll be lining up for threesomes."

I lean back on the seat. "I'm sure they would be doing that, if they knew where to line up." I point to the human girl. "Now, since you've become an expert on seduction overnight, how is it going?"

"I didn't read any books; you did. You should be the expert, but after today's display, I'm not so sure. Regardless, she's human. I thought she would be just like a fae woman, you know, minus the pointy ears. No. It's as if she's from another species."

"Come on. All high fae have human blood."

"But humans have *no* fae blood, and I'm pretty sure there's something missing there." He stares at her as if she was some kind of weird food he doesn't know how to eat.

He'll obviously never manage to make her fall in love with him. Doesn't surprise me. "Maybe that's the trick. Find what's missing."

He stares at her, his expression thoughtful, likely concocting a foolish plan. His desperation reeks through every pore and I inhale it like perfume.

Then, all of a sudden, the memory hits me, and with it, a wave of fury. My fists clench as if they had a will of their own.

I know who Lidiane is. Oh. The truth is so revolting I might feel sick.

Consumed with distress, I look outside and realize we're approaching the Crystal Castle. I change the air the girls breathe, then tell Renel, "Silence now. They'll wake up in a minute or so."

He nods and looks out the window. "There are lots of guards at the Royal Terrace."

"Hmm." Probably because of Zorwal's murder. A thrill of fear runs through me, but I decide to convince myself that they cannot know what I've done.

Across from me, Lidiane opens her eyes, and I glare at the little traitor. She manages to frown as if confused, and yet I keep my stare.

"So you enchanted us," she says.

I smirk. "Got a problem with a nap?"

Renel stares from me to the window. I look again and have to admit that the amount of guards at the terrace is not normal. I decide then that if they come for me, I'll transcend away. I can't leave Renel, though. I guess I'll just have to bring him along.

My heart is beating fast, and I can feel it pushing my chest. Even Lidiane's face changes from defiant to worried. She's deep in the same mud that I am, and now I'm not even sorry for that. Meanwhile, the human girl is just waking up, looking around and stretching, so oblivious and ignorant.

I can't transcend yet. My orders are to keep my magic secret from the fae guards in the castle. The exception is if I absolutely have no choice, so I'll have to wait. I'll have to bring Lidiane along, since our secrets intertwine like knotted thorns. More than just our secrets.

When I feel the thud of the landing, my heart matches it with its own thud. If things go wrong, I'll have to be fast. How am I going to do it, coming out of a magic depletion?

A guard opens the door.

"Your Highness." The guard bows to Renel.

Too calm, too respectful. I don't think they're here to arrest me, at least not yet, and it doesn't seem that they're going to announce the death of their council leader, since his tone is not grave enough.

I'm puzzled for a second, until he continues, "Lord Zorwal summons you."

Lord.

Zorwal.

I feel like I'm falling into a bottomless hole.

ASTRA

Purple. So purple. I had no idea that all the fake color would come off like that, and yet I've looked at myself in the mirror more times than I should, just to see my hair again. It's bright, colorful, not a light lilac or a deep purple.

It's pretty.

It's what I've been hiding all these years.

It's me.

Perhaps I had to see that, see myself. Now, every time I look in the mirror, I want to giggle and cry and yell and cheer.

Hello, Astra. It's nice to meet you after all this time.

I'm not sure my hair is going to tell me who I am or how to

connect with my magic, though. What *might* help me is to check the papers I got from Otavio's office, and that's what makes me stop staring at myself and head to the kitchen.

I sit with Nelsin and Ferer, checking those pages.

The first one has a list of family trees, with names I don't recognize, only two or three generations deep.

Ferer pulls the paper to look at it from a better angle. "They sound Tiurian to me."

His comment surprises me. "You know the Tiurian language?"

He chuckles. "A little. Very little. A few words here and there, and that's all. It's just that they don't sound like fae or human words or names."

I look back at the paper. Why would Otavio make a list of families? Under most of them, he wrote *ended* or added a question mark.

"So perhaps he was looking at Tiurian family lines. But why?"

Nelsin taps his fingers on the table. "If Tiuris had a monarchy, I'd bet he was looking at what happened to the royal line. But it didn't."

Ferer's expression is thoughtful. "There are claims that the Tiurian Kingdom *had* a monarchy, but that was a long time ago, like more than five hundred years, and we don't even know if it's true. Now, it could be a different line. A lot of magic is passed on through blood, so he could be looking for someone with a certain kind of magic, I suppose. Or maybe not necessarily magic, but a specific family line."

Family. I'd love so much to learn about mine, and yet there's nothing on this paper about it. "It could relate to me or not. It's possible I was just the first obviously Tiurian child he found, my origins clear because of my hair color."

"The hair color could also mean something," Ferer suggests.

"Maybe. The Nymph Queen said Tiurian magic has been suppressed for a hundred years, and yet I have it. I'm not saying it's the hair... I just don't know." I can't understand what it all means.

Nelsin looks at me. "At least we learned something with the first paper; he was paying attention to a family—or many families. And these were family lines that ended."

I'm trying to untangle this puzzle. "It *could* be related to me, either because of some magic, or maybe my family line has some significance. He could be trying to figure out who my family is, or maybe this is from before he found me. Maybe he was already... looking for someone."

The possibility stuns me, and then again, a list of families proves of nothing.

Ferer takes a deep breath. "What did he tell you? About how he found you."

"Someone in an orphanage called him when my hair started to grow, asking him to disguise it. He's a beautician, so it makes sense. He brought me to the castle, and then the orphanage caught fire and all the records were lost." I roll my eyes. "How convenient. Nowadays, I think he might have caused the fire either to hide his steps or to protect me, I don't know."

"Hold on." Ferer raises a finger. "Was he already the royal beautician at the time?"

"Yes."

"Then it *doesn't* make sense that they'd call him. Why would they trust him? How would they know he wouldn't turn you over to the king?"

"I have considered that, but in my mind, it was someone who knew him, or perhaps who knew he was Tiurian, maybe even another one of us."

Nelsin snaps his fingers. "Ha. A Tiurian, for sure. Unless the whole story about the orphanage is a lie. Do you have any proof it existed? That there was an orphanage that burned when you were a baby?"

"He showed me a royal record once." I sigh, my previous naivety managing to stun me. "Who knows if the record's even real."

Nelsin looks at me. "How old were you when he took you?"

"He says I was eight months old."

"Who was hiding you before that?" he asks.

"I didn't have much hair before. Again, that's what *he* claims, but I've seen some hairless babies. It makes sense." I think back to the Nymph Queen and her hurry. "You know what? I don't have time to focus on this right now, even if it's interesting. Let me see the other papers."

A quick glance tells me that they're cosmetics recipes for lip coloring and lash thickener.

I don't even know what to say. "I'm so sorry. I guess it was foolish to go to Otavio's office. I learned nothing, and it's not going to help me with my magic, which is what I need to focus on."

Ferer nods. "All right, so what do you want to learn?"

"First, there's something I need to find. Have you ever heard of the Amethyst Palace?"

"Yes," Ferer says, while Nelsin says, "No."

"You've *heard* of it?" I don't hide my surprise.

Nelsin stares at Ferer, who sits up straight.

"Stories," he says. "Legends, perhaps. It was the Tiurian's castle, where their king and queen lived."

"What happened to it?" I ask.

"Disappeared together with most of the Tiurian civilization. But that might be a story, you know? But I've heard about it."

Nelsin turns to him. "How come you know all that?"

"Sea Court. We had some books from there."

I'm quite intrigued. "So they know more about Tiuris? Is it possible to go there? To research?"

Ferer's laugh is bitter. "They'd kill me on sight. And they're not very welcoming of strangers. The only reason they allow boats to float above them is due to some old treaty or something."

I remember what the half-nymph told me. "Because the sea court punishes relations with other fae, is that it?"

"I suppose. They killed my mother, and I guess my father too."

Oh, this is horrific. "I'm so sorry. And they kill children?"

Ferer shrugs. "I suppose. You said Krastel could kill Tiurian children too, didn't you?"

"That's what Otavio told me, but I don't even know what's true anymore. We do learn that darksouls are evil and dangerous, so I suppose Tiurian children could be killed." My voice cracks. "I used to believe Tiurians were dangerous."

"What made you change your mind?" Nelsin asks.

I stare at the wood patterns on the table. "So many lies… It's like I was immersed in them, and once I was out, I could look back and see them for what they were. I won't say I'm free and perfectly confident that there's nothing dark or dangerous about my magic, but I can see the manipulation for what it was."

Nelsin stares at me. "It might still affect your connection with your magic."

"Certainly." I chuckle. "As if I didn't have enough problems." *Find what you need to find.* The queen's words come to mind. "You know what? I need to find that castle."

Ferer raises an eyebrow. "You think it's hiding somewhere?"

"I do. Didn't Marlak spend years looking for a tower? A castle is just a little bigger. It can also be hidden. And I need to find it." I remember the books Marlak gave me. "Have any of you read *Tiuris, the Fallen Kingdom*?"

They both shake their heads.

"I'll check it now."

Ferer strokes his chin. "What about your magic?"

"The castle first. And it's urgent."

"We'll help you. And we can bring more books for you."

I click my tongue. "I'm afraid we might be out of time."

The Nymph Queen's fear was palpable enough. And I'm starting to worry about Marlak.

And then, I don't even know what I'm looking for—or why.

Trust yourself.

It sounds so clear, inspiring even, but when my head is a mess of tangled thoughts, which of them should I trust?

LIDIANE

Zorwal. I saw him dying in front of me.

Now, apparently, he's summoning the false king. I don't look at Azur, fearing my eyes could betray his guilt. Renel walks out and doesn't look back either, perhaps with the same thought.

Azur didn't make me sleep like he thought. I was pretending, and now I'm trying to make sense of everything I heard, including the fact that now Azur knows my name. It shouldn't make much difference.

Beside me, Tarlia says, "Interesting trip."

I think she can feel the tension in the air and yet doesn't understand what's happening, but no casual conversation can erase my shock.

Still, I smile at her. "At least you enjoyed the roasted rat."

She grins. "Very much."

Azur is still glaring at me for some bizarre reason.

"Lidiane." His voice is full of venom. "Follow me now."

I point at Tarlia. "I need to walk her to her room."

"A guard can do that."

"No." Tarlia holds my hand. "Don't want a random guard."

Azur doesn't even glance at her and takes my arm. "Come."

I push him away. "Let me escort her. I'll see you after."

"Five minutes, no more." He leans over and waves a finger near my face, then walks out of the carriage, holding a shirt over his crotch and yet standing tall as if he was covered in finery.

"Moody, this one," Tarlia says, her voice much lighter than her face.

"Yes." There are so many thoughts crossing my mind at the same time that none of them are intelligible. "Let's go."

We walk into the castle, strangely undisturbed by any guards. Nobody stops us, nobody asks us anything. I guess arriving in the company of the sham king has its advantages.

I try not to worry about Zorwal or whoever summoned Renel. I'll soon find out if he's dead or alive, and then I can wonder if he remembers anything.

Chills are creeping up my back, even if I try to remain calm. And then I'm also wondering why Azur was so strange, so *angry*. Do I need to wonder? He killed a man who's apparently summoning his master now. Something's wrong, something's odd, and things don't make sense. And yet I still think Azur was unlike himself—as if I even knew him.

She's gorgeous. I still remember what he said when he thought I was asleep. Then again, I know what I look like, and agree with his assessment.

Still, he avoided some of Renel's questions, when he could have said *no*. Does he like me? This line of thought will never lead to a positive outcome and makes no sense. I came to this castle to find a way to bring down Renel, and I'll never be able to do that if I change my mind about his bound guardian—even if he might seem nice sometimes.

This is my first time walking into the castle from this door, and it takes me a few minutes to recall where Tarlia's room is, but I remember it when we get to the central part of the castle around the spiral staircase, under the crystal. From there, I find her hallway easily.

We barely enter her room, and she asks, "What happened?"

"A lot." I look around to check if we're truly alone, and see no one, but then I'm not even sure what to say or from where to start.

She steps close to me. "Did he threaten you?"

"Who?" I'm thinking about Zorwal, but then I realize she means Azur. "No."

"Why did he need you?"

Odd. Only now I notice that I made no promises to keep anything secret, and yet the truth of what happened at the Jewel and then later at the sea is too heavy, too dangerous. "I can't tell you all, but—" I was going to say Azur's not so bad. Am I sure? Does it matter?

"What?"

"I'm not afraid of Renel's guardian and I'll go see him now. Still, if by any chance I don't return in three hours—"

"Oh, no. If it's getting that bad, you need to tell him *no*."

"Nothing's..." *Bad*, I was going to say, but it makes no sense. "I mean, Azur's not dangerous."

Tarlia stares at me as if I had just hit my head.

"At least I don't think so," I add. "If things go wrong, look for Serenade. It's a village in the north, where I live. Ask for me. Eventually, my brother will find you."

"What's happening, Lidiane?"

"I'll probably be back, but I can't tell you everything." I take her hands. "Trust me that I want to keep you safe."

"Do you even want to defeat Renel?"

I let go of her hands. "Why would I change my mind?"

"You trust his guardian."

"Not completely, no. And they're two different fae, in case you haven't noticed."

Her look is still suspicious.

"I have to go now," I say as I walk toward the door. "But I'll be back—I think. Your glamour will hold until the evening, at least."

"Good luck," she mutters, when I'm already outside.

I don't turn back to reply to her.

You trust his guardian. Why do her words gut me?

I *had* to trust him. We worked together, saved some innocent fae, he protected me. I do trust him to a certain extent, and yet the admission bothers me. And then I recall what I heard, and the fact that he went to the Jewel City under Renel's orders. Why did I have the impression he was rebelling or something? Perhaps moonlighting as a hero? No, it was just part of his job. Of course he was following orders. What was I thinking?

And then there was the glare he gave me, so different from everything that came before. I dread this meeting as much as I'm eager to see him and understand what's going on.

And then there's the worst part: Zorwal. Is he truly alive? And if yes, can he identify who killed him?

20

Azur is standing outside his door, arms crossed, one foot on the wall, his posture deceivingly casual. He's no longer naked, thankfully. Instead, he's wearing a sleeveless leather tunic and trousers, perhaps to match his carefully prepared dashing, careless look. He's also wearing his black hat again.

When he sees me, a flash of fury in his eyes betrays his true state of mind. I'm starting to wonder if he thinks it's my fault Zorwal isn't dead or my fault he summoned Renel. I don't know, and I hate having to wonder.

I enter his room in silence, unsure if my greeting should be friendly or cautious.

Behind me, he closes the door, then grabs my arm and pulls me away from it.

"Stop it." I push his hand away. "I haven't given you the right to lay your fingers on me."

"Oh. You had no problem holding my hand earlier."

"To transcend? That's different."

"To steal my secrets. All my secrets." He approaches me and

raises a finger. "I know who you are, Lidiane, and I know who your master is."

My name shouldn't have led him to deduce anything, and I don't understand why he's talking about a master.

"Listen, not everyone's like you. Me, for example, I don't serve anyone."

His laughter is sharp like a knife. "Oh, the privilege! And yet you chose to work for that creep."

Does he mean Larjax? I haven't seen him in such a long time, and he was never my master. "What creep?"

"Marlak."

That's his problem? I chuckle. "I do *not* work for him, nor is he my master."

"Is that so? Astra came to the Court of Bees coronation wearing an incredible dress that was one of the talks of the ceremony."

My chest swells with poorly-timed pride. I'm sure Azur isn't praising my craftmanship.

He continues, "Now, who made that dress? Astra was seen coming from Serenade, and there's only one dressmaker in that village with the skill for such a dress. Lidiane, a pretty fae with dark skin and hair like clouds before rain, just like yours."

His comparison is terrible. "My hair's not gray."

"I meant black—like rain at night. And I appreciate that at least you recognize that it's you I'm talking about. Spare me your denials and non-answers, and you'll save us both time and patience." His eyes lock on mine, as if expecting an excuse, a denial, or even an apology. All I can give him is defiance.

He breaks the eye contact and runs a hand through his hair. "Astra's dress was made to measure, there's no doubt of that, which meant you spent time with her. Now she's here, and it's clear you're quite comfortable with each other." When his eyes find mine again, the blue in them is a spark of anger. "You're under Marlak's orders, aren't you?"

With his power, Azur can intimidate anyone, I suppose, but

I'm not going to cower, not to him. I roll my eyes. "Marlak disappeared, in case you weren't aware."

"He's always hiding. Why would you claim he disappeared?" The finger he points at me is an accusation.

"Whispers."

"Spare me. Spare me. Do I have to remind you how many secrets of yours I hold? Do I have to threaten you? Spare me and tell me the truth. Are you Marlak's ally?"

"Yes," I say it clearly, with no shame, because I have none.

Azur exhales and looks down, his features downcast, as if disappointed. Wasn't it what he was presuming?

I continue, "But I didn't come here on his orders. I don't know where he is. I was worried about Astra, that's why I came. There's no big plan, no conspiracy."

Azur snorts. "Such hypocrisy. You seem all worried about the lower fae, then you serve Marlak."

"I don't *serve* him."

"Making a dress for his wife counts as serving. Or what was it?"

"I'm a dressmaker. I can choose to make clothes for any client I wish. I don't *serve.*"

His anger is replaced by something akin to shame. "Serving is disgusting, right? Is that what you think?"

I swallow, regretting my previous words that reached him like a splinter poking at his pride. "I think it must be uncomfortable."

Azur bangs a hand on a wall. "What are you here for? Tell me."

All my regrets about making him uncomfortable are gone. "To protect the human guest. It's obvious, isn't it?"

He waves a finger in the air. "No. Oh, no. That is not true. If you were protecting her, she would be far from the castle by now. Why is she still here?"

"Her husband disappeared. Her master's here. Where do you think she can go?"

He sneers. "You do take me for a fool, don't you?"

I wonder if he realized I never said she's still here, but I'm also getting tired of his questions, his accusations. "You *knew* I wasn't a castle servant, and yet you let me stay. What's *your* plan?"

"I'm the one with the questions here."

"You know my secrets, but I know yours too."

"Don't even try going there, Lidiane. Your secrets are far more numerous and greater than mine, and where my life is in danger, so is yours."

"Shouldn't you be worrying about that? About whoever summoned your master?"

He waves a hand. "I'll soon find out. I want to know who you are first."

"Fair. Want to know? I was raised by a dressmaker, a lower fae. Difficult childhood, even more difficult because of my status. My dream was to become the biggest, most famous dressmaker in the kingdom, and yet it makes no sense to try to do that, to try to keep fighting just for a small, tiny chance. It makes no sense to create beauty when everything around me is ugly. I want a better world for the lower fae, and for a moment, when I was with you, on that tower, looking at the Jewel City, I thought you wanted it too, but it's not true. You were just following your master's orders."

He stares at me, mouth open, eyes wide. I'm thinking he's about to stop his questioning, but then he goes back to his accusing mode. "What part of *bound guardian* don't you understand?"

"The part where you pretend to care about the fae your master oppresses. Were you trying to trick me?"

"No." He looks down. "When everything happened..." He closes his eyes. "And then everything after that. I regretted bringing you. I wanted to see your magic, wanted to see who you were, that was all. I thought it would be an easy, straightforward task. That was why I brought you along. I was wrong, and I regret it."

"You didn't even ask my name."

He shakes his head. "If I recognized it, and depending on who you were, I'd need to tell Renel. In fact, I'll have to tell him. What I don't understand is how you thought you could just saunter into the Crystal Castle, stay here and spy on us, and not be discovered. It sounds either dumb, naive, or else you counted on my help." He frowns. "Perhaps... manipulated me."

"The true answer is that I trusted destiny. Sometimes you trust, let go, and the flow of life takes you where you need."

He rolls his eyes. "Naïve, then. But I just want to know one thing: why would you be Marlak's ally? Marlak, of all people?"

"Why not? A lot of lower fae like him."

Azur laughs. "It's absolutely ridiculous. Marlak has no love for lower fae, or for anyone he considers *beneath* him."

"So you know him?"

"Have you met his beloved sister?"

"You're going to slander the dead now?"

"Not my plan, no. I stick to truths. Take the most degenerate villain you can imagine, and you still won't come close to Mirella."

I can't believe what he's saying. "Are you really accusing *a child* of being evil? A dead child?"

"She was thirteen when the family deaths happened. Evil people show signs early."

"Well, I don't commune with spirits, so I'm not *her* ally."

"But you support her dear brother, who stood by her when she mocked and intimidated anyone she could. You may not like Renel, but I assure you, he's a saint compared to his siblings, and I'm not saying that because I'm bound."

"Lower fae are being enslaved under Renel's rule, and you think he's great?"

"I didn't say that. What I mean is that Marlak's horrible."

"Marlak was a *child* when his sister was alive."

"A child who chose to align with the powerful people around him, who chose to align with his horrible stepfather, with his vile stepsister. A child who ignored his brother."

"The keyword here is *child*, Azur. I met Marlak before the

accident, and he was already kind and has shown nothing but kindness since. Still, I don't work for him on a regular basis other than maybe a favor here and there. I'm not following his orders or enacting any plan for him. I'm just trying to protect the human girl."

"Because she's his wife, isn't it?"

"No." It can't be, since I'm talking about Tarlia, who's *not* his wife.

Azur frowns. "Does he love her?"

"Most definitely no."

He pauses, takes a deep breath, then looks up, thinking. "Something here isn't right. If you wanted to protect Astra, you'd get her out of the castle as soon as you could. I saw her trying to escape, so don't come up with that story that she has nowhere to go. Perhaps she doesn't, but she was risking her life trying to get out of here." He stares at me. "What changed?"

"I came."

He frowns. "And convinced her to stay?"

"I wouldn't say that."

His stare is deep and piercing, and then he breaks into laughter. "Did Astra leave the castle?"

Oh, no. I think he's catching on. Still, I shrug. "Yes, obviously. You were there when we came to the festival."

"The old fae trick of unrelated sentences. You won't fool me, Lidiane. Did Astra come to the festival?"

There's a chill at the tip of my fingers moving to my body. I don't know if I can still save this, but I can try. "You brought us. You saw who was there."

"I'm asking. Was *Astra* there? Did I transcend Marlak's wife to the festival? Or was it an impostor?"

I try to come up with an answer, but I take too long.

Before I have a chance to reply, he says, "Your silence is quite persuasive—and damning. Your main magic is glamours, isn't it? It makes total sense." He laughs. "An impostor. Can't believe it. I'd say the plan is ingenious, if it wasn't so frail. So

Astra escaped, perhaps already met Marlak. Why is the impostor still here, risking getting caught? What's the point?"

"We want to make sure Astra's safe, and Marlak as well."

He narrows his eyes. "Is that all? Or are you perhaps hoping to dig some secrets or even dig into Renel's skull?"

"I don't plan to kill him."

"What of the girl?"

"I don't think she wants to kill him."

"Think." Azur snorts and shakes his head, then points at me. "You deceived me."

"Did I? What did you think I was?"

"Not Marlak's ally." His anger has dissipated, and he's thoughtful now.

I don't know what he plans to do to me, but if he's smart, he'll kill me—and get rid of the only person who knows what he did to that council leader.

I consider my options, but soon realize there are none; I have no chance to win a fight against him, and I can't escape the fae who's likely the most powerful transcender in the world.

He's calmer when he asks, "Do you want to protect the human impostor?"

"Yes."

He raises an eyebrow. "Do you care about your life?"

I stare at him, unsure if he's threatening me.

"I'll take it as a yes," he says. "You're going to escape this castle. Go. Nobody watches the servants who leave, and you can use your glamour. Take the impostor. Or don't take her. I don't care. After sunset, if I find out you're still here, I'll tell Renel who you are. I don't think you'll like it. Oh, and do not try to use glamor to evade me. I can see you. I can sense you anywhere you go. So leave."

"Am I supposed to believe you'll let me walk away and face no consequences?"

"You want a deal? Leave now, and I promise I won't tell Renel you're Marlak's ally, unless I don't have a choice, but at that point, you'll be far away, and you'll face no consequences for that."

"Why?"

"Why?" He chuckles. "This castle's a dangerous place, and I don't mean just Renel. There's Zorwal or whoever is impersonating him. You talk of destiny, but the flow of life sometimes throws you against a boulder."

"I mean why are you letting me walk away like that? Facing no consequences?"

He blinks. "I'm not going to state the obvious. Now go."

Nothing's obvious, but there's no point trying to understand his motivations. I approach the door but turn around before I reach it, as I still have a question hanging on my mind. "Who do you think summoned Renel?"

"I don't know."

"Do you think… it was someone else pretending to be him at the Jewel?"

Azur shakes his head, his face grim. "His magic's quite unique, in the way he can extract information and break bonds, break minds. I'm sure it was him." In a lower voice, he adds, "I'm also sure he was dead when we left that prison. I've seen people dying before, and I know what I saw."

"So who summoned Renel?"

"I don't know. It's one more reason you should leave while you have time. Go away, hide, and don't come back. You're free to leave, and freedom is a treasure not to be squandered."

A treasure he doesn't have.

I wonder what kind of person he could have been if he had never been bound, then realize there's no point in wondering what could have been. I nod, and he reaches for the doorknob.

There's a knock right before he opens it.

A guard stands in the hallway.

"Sir, His Highness Renel summons you." He glances at me. "And lady Lidiane."

Azur looks at me and grimaces, then turns to the guard. "I'll be in his quarters in a moment."

"Not his quarters, sir; the council chamber. He's with Zorwal."

Zorwal.

I guess life's about to throw me against a boulder.

RENEL

Zorwal's summoning me. Of course he is. Of course he's alive, and most definitely not dead, like Azur thought. Who even dies from hitting their head? Fine, some fae and humans do, but not Zorwal, obviously.

Azur must have sent him a soft puff, pushed him, and for some bizarre reason decided he was dead.

Great.

Got my hopes up for no reason, and now I'm falling face down toward reality. Zorwal has helped me, and for a long time, I appreciated his support, except that now the hand that guided me has gotten tighter and tighter, and it's strangling me—but I don't know how to escape.

The relief I felt when hearing Zorwal was dead caught me by surprise, but the more I think about it, the more it makes sense; he makes me feel trapped, and if he were dead, I would be free. The issue is how to kill him when his magic is so strong.

This will be the worst audience with him ever, now that I worry about whether Azur was spotted, and how it will implicate me. All because I didn't want five random fae to die. They'd die because of me, though. Saving them was the right thing to do—right, but risky.

The guard opens the door leading to the council chamber and I walk in, keeping my demeanor calm, my face relaxed, even if my mind is about to catch fire.

Zorwal stands by the high chair, facing the back of the room, and I take a long look at his head. No bandage, no wound, nothing. I make a mental list with a few profanities to tell Azur when I see him next.

I killed him, I'm sure.

Right. Unless an impostor was in the prison. Maybe I can hope?

The door closes behind me and I flinch, waiting for the blasts to come.

Zorwal turns, his eyes narrowed like slits. "What exactly were you and your guardian doing?"

I pretend not to notice his tone and smile, keeping my voice relaxed and casual. "We went to the Summer End Festival in Caraneya. It was a little slow at this time—"

"Quiet," he hisses.

I don't feel any cut, as I was expecting. No cut at all. Far from relieved, I'm terrified of what he'll do next, and struggling to keep all that fear buried deep where it cannot come to my face.

Zorwal steps from the dais and stands in front of me, so close that if I were just a little more foolish, I could try to strike him.

He asks, "Why would a king go to a peasants' festival?"

"Isn't it a good idea to commune with my subjects? Show them I'm like them?"

"Idiot." This time, I feel a cut in my arm. "Are you like them?"

"High fae also go—" A cut on the back of my hand makes me want to scream.

"Foolish child. You don't want to look like *them*. Your subjects need to see you as their ruler, as better than them."

I lower my head. "That makes sense."

"Makes sense," he mocks me. "You talk like a bird, knowing nothing of what you're repeating. Listen to me, Renel. Is it the plebs you need to please? Are they the ones keeping you in power?"

"Your advice, Your Grace, is that it's the powerful families that keep me where I am, that if they were to oppose me, I'd topple like a rotten tree. I know that."

"Then why sully yourself in a festival like that? Why would you go anywhere with your bound guardian as if he were your friend? Your bound guardian should *serve* you, not make a fool of himself."

Even though Zorwal is angry, I'm relieved that he hasn't mentioned the escaped prisoners yet. "You're wise, Your Grace."

He lays a finger on my face as if examining me. I close my eyes, wondering if he'll inflict some new type of torture.

"And who were the females accompanying you?" Malice and threat lace his gentle voice.

I don't want him paying attention to Tar, or realizing what she is. Why did I have to bring her to that festival?

"Pretty girls." I shrug.

"Hmmm." He wrinkles his nose, and I brace myself for the worst. "There's something else; the Desert Keep guards. Have you heard anything about them?"

All my silly hopes to be spared of that subject evaporate in a second, but I manage to hide my worry and say, "I sentenced them to death this morning."

"And that's all you know?"

"After the council meeting, I soon went to Caraneya. Is there anything else you'd like to inform me?"

"They escaped."

I frown, as if confused. "I thought they were held in the Jewel City."

"They were."

"It's the safest city in the kingdom, walled and protected on all sides. If someone steps out of a prison, they'll still be in the city. Haven't they been found?"

"Alas, no. Do you know anything about it?"

I pretend to think, then say, "It could be related to whatever happened at the Desert Keep. Giants could help them escape, but they wouldn't—"

"Nitwit. No giants would come so far south."

"Fair. What about the guards keeping the prisoners in the Jewel City? If they weren't enchanted, they would have seen what happened. Were they questioned?"

Zorwal exhales. "What do you think?"

"I'm wondering what they said, what they saw." Yes, I'm most definitely wondering about that.

"Nothing out of the ordinary. Nothing. It's as if the prisoners vanished."

I blink. "Is that possible?"

"Apparently it is."

"What if there's a secret passage in the inquiry house? That could be a good explanation."

"Hmmm. I will investigate." He waves a hand over me, healing my cuts. "Now, I'd like to have a word with your companions. I haven't spoken to your guardian in a long time, and I'm eager to meet the girls who caused your foolishness. Summon them, please."

It's sheer will that keeps me from trembling. While it's possible that Zorwal hasn't connected the prison breach with my trip, there's a chance he's aware that something's wrong. Now, if I protest or refuse to summon them, it will only make things worse.

"Of course. I'll bring them here."

I'm heading to the door when I hear, "Stop."

I turn and see Zorwal smiling at me, a friendly, jovial smile that now chills my blood. "I want you to stay and wait for them. Just tell a guard to summon them right away, on your orders."

My orders—which Azur cannot refuse. And Zorwal wants me to wait here, so we won't even have time to agree on a story.

"Of course."

I do as he said, and tell the guard to summon Astra, Azur, and Lidiane.

If Zorwal finds out Azur can transcend like he does, we're doomed. If he finds out Astra is Tiurian, I don't know what will happen.

I'll have to think fast—and hope Azur and the girls understand what I mean.

21

AZUR

How dare that foul council leader summon Lidiane? Why would he want to see her? One thing I know: he has no right to do that, but at least sending only one guard was imbecilic.

I pull the air from the guard's lungs and throat, then the part of the air about to flow to his brain. As expected, he faints.

"Azur!" Lidiane sounds shocked, and I truly don't understand why.

I drag the guard inside my room and close the door, then turn to her.

"You swore no oath to Renel, so there's no need to attend his summons. Escape this castle and never return. Right now."

Her stunning face has a mix of fear and worry. "It will be worse. Refusing an acting king's summons is a crime."

"So what? Do you think they need a reason to convict you? Aren't you Marlak's ally?" The thought still cools my skin and heats my head, but I suppose everything has a good side. "Hide like he hides. And I doubt Renel will hunt you."

"It will be worse *for you*."

For me. She's worried about me, despite my outburst, despite my hate for her sordid *ally*. For the first time, I see a glimmer of something more in her brilliant eyes. One more reason she needs to escape while she can. "I'll say you left and I don't know where you are."

"Not suspicious at all."

Fury is a constant companion, stirring my mind, driving me mad. Why do I have to be bound like that? Why did I have to bring her with me? Little mistakes, big consequences. I consider begging her to leave, perhaps telling her everything, but I can't risk any hesitation.

I keep my face hard and let all that repressed fury emerge to my eyes. "Either you go now or I'll make you unconscious and lock you somewhere, but then, if they ask me your location, I'll know the answer." To my dismay, my voice comes out far less threatening than I intended. Her stare disconcerts me, just like everything about her.

She considers me for a moment, then says, "I'll go, but I'll take the human visitor with me."

"Do it quickly."

I want to touch her hand, her face, kiss her goodbye. I want so much. Too much. Everything out of reach. She stares at me, lips parted, and for a fraction of a second, I wonder if she's thinking the same—a thought that needs to be buried.

"Go." This time my voice is the cold steel I've become a master at wielding.

Perhaps one day, when I'm free, if I'm free, I'll find her. This is not the time.

She leaves the room, and I sit on the bed, taking a big gulp of breath, then head to the council chamber.

I killed Zorwal. I know I did, and it *was* him. He's the only fae who can tear memories and break bonds from people's minds. Apparently, Marlak can access memories as well, but Renel says it's different and doesn't hurt.

Who's in the council chamber? An impostor? A double?

Two guards stand at the entrance, but I pay them no mind

and open the door. Zorwal sits in his high chair, as smug as always.

"Your Grace asked to see me?" My voice is casual, uninterested.

"Yes, yes." Renel sounds calm as well. "I was explaining to His Grace that Tar wanted to fly over the Solemn River."

Tar? Oh, the human girl. I smile. "A beautiful day for flying."

Zorwal—or his impostor—stares at us in silence, as if waiting. He looks like Zorwal, but it could be an impressive glamour.

The silence and the waiting are unnerving me, so I say, "I suppose Your Grace wanted something from me."

"In a moment." Zorwal's smirk is eerie. "Once everyone is here."

Everyone. Hopefully Lidiane will never come close to this man, whoever he is.

Renel smiles at me, his tone jovial. "He's interested in our trip to the festival."

"Really?" I turn to Zorwal and grin. "Would Your Grace like to come next time?"

He descends from his chair with so much flair that convinces me he's the real leader of the council—a chilling conclusion. With slow steps, he approaches me, sniffs, then glares at Renel.

"You need to teach your guardian to behave. Does he always ask more than he should?"

"Azur takes his duties seriously, Your Grace, and that often means asking questions so that he can better serve me."

Zorwal snorts. "Teach him to respect authority, Renel, or else I'll have to do that myself. He needs to know his place."

I refrain from rolling my eyes. Fae like him have a sick pleasure in telling themselves they're better than others. I'm so used to it that it doesn't even make me angry anymore, it just strengthens my will. One day, they'll all pay.

Renel lowers his head. "I appreciate your guidance."

Can't Zorwal see through Renel's words? He's not saying which guidance or even that he'll do it. Unless this is an impostor too worried about faking being the council leader, but I doubt it.

At least Lidiane's gone. Wait. If Zorwal summoned everyone, he would summon the human girl—and Lidiane might have gone to her room.

Cold dread settles in my stomach, a horrifying cold spreading to my heart.

Why didn't I make her leave the moment I found out she was an intruder? Why, Azur? The stupidity of it stuns me.

Please be gone, Lidiane, please. Please, be far away, be happy.

My plea sounds hollow, while fear crushes me with the weight of a thousand castles.

When the door opens behind me, at first I don't want to look; I want to hope that they didn't find the girls, or tell myself that it's just the human impostor. And yet I need to be sure.

I turn—and see the human girl, followed by Lidiane, who gives me an apologetic look. Cold shivers prickle my skin, poke my mind, and stab my heart. I would transcend her away if it wasn't for the dreadful bond to Renel enslaving me like heavy, unbreakable chains. I've never hated this bond so much.

But it's all my fault. I'm the idiot who brought her into this mess, and now I need to get her out of it.

She's wearing no glamour, which is smart. If this is Zorwal, and if it was him in the Inquisition House, we wouldn't want him to recognize her magic.

"Oh, look at that." Zorwal's voice is both mocking and threatening. "The guardian's in love."

Love.

The word echoes in my head, dancing with all the fury that resides in it. Love.

It hadn't crossed my mind. I can sense a bond with her, and yet it's just a constant tug, a calling. What I have is a deep yearning, but I yearn for so much I cannot have that I'm used to burying it all.

I don't dare utter anything to soften or challenge his words, considering *I'm not supposed to speak when it's not my turn.* I don't dare look at her anymore, and turn to Zorwal, my expression neutral.

Renel chuckles. "Azur? Lady friends always surround him. He's quite a loving fae."

He's trying to help, but the effect is feeble. I bet he agrees with Zorwal's opinion, therefore can't even contradict him.

Is she horrified, disgusted? Or could her feelings be anywhere opposite from revulsion?

No point thinking about her reaction. I need to focus.

To my horror, Zorwal approaches her. It takes all my self-control to keep my feet in place and my magic reigned in.

I hate the way his calculating eyes focus on her, hate it that he's anywhere near her.

"What's your magic?" he asks.

"Air." She displays no hesitation or fear. It must be her elemental magic, likely weak, or else I'd sense it.

He doesn't move and asks, "What about glamours?"

I want to push him away from her, distract him, but can't figure out a way to do it without putting her in danger.

"I'm trying to get better at them." Her tone is light, with no hint of fear, even if I can sense her discomfort.

"But you can do them?" Zorwal insists.

"When I focus, yes, but they're not perfect."

Her magic is more than incredible, but I'm glad her opinion is different, allowing her to give him this vague answer.

He then points to Tar. "What about her? Can she do any magic?"

"She's human," Renel says.

"Some humans have magic." Zorwal approaches Tar and places his hands around her head, as if trying to sense her magic.

He probably suspects she's Tiurian. I bet Renel's panicking even if he doesn't show any hint of fear.

Zorwal steps away and chuckles. "An ordinary human. Is she good in bed, at least?"

"I'm right here," Tar says. This won't end up well. "And yes, I'm an incredible fuck."

The council leader eyes her up and down. "I doubt it, but you're welcome to try to prove your point to me, and I'll decide if you can stay in the castle."

"I'll—" She's about to say something, but I block the air flowing around her vocal cords and silence her. While I sympathize with her backbone, talking back to Zorwal won't help anyone.

"She's *my* guest, and it's *my* castle," Renel says. "I can inform you of her prowess in bed myself."

Zorwal stares at Renel and narrows his eyes. "So protective, and yet you're not in love. What's your interest in her?"

Renel shrugs. "She's pretty."

The council leader looks at her, his eyes full of glee, having found one of Renel's weaknesses. What does he want, though? What more can he want, when he has so much power already?

He turns to Renel. "She's *human.* While the Treaty prevents them from serving us, it doesn't change her nature."

I'm still keeping Tar silent, when Zorwal steps in front of Lidiane. "Now this one, here, there's no treaty preventing anything."

"There are laws," Renel says. "Unless she commits a crime—"

"We can *find* a crime." Zorwal puts his hand over her head, to pull her thoughts, pull her memories, then break her mind.

A tremor shakes me—inside *and* outside. The castle's moving again.

I shouldn't have let this go so far. At least now her secrets are Renel's secrets, so my servitude bond won't get in my way.

This time, I hope I kill him right. I pull the air from Zorwal's lungs and head at the same time as I send my sword flying to his neck.

Horror seizes me as I realize my air magic isn't affecting him. Not only that, my body feels wrong. At least I see the sword beheading him, and yet there's some kind of mysterious magic at work, weakening me. With the last of my remaining power, I make a transcending circle from where I pull Renel, Tar, and Lidiane. It's always harder without holding hands, and much harder when my magic's drained.

Then, it's as if my vision—and my senses—stop working. Still, I have to finish transcending or we'll get lost or ripped apart.

Anywhere. And yet I'm so weak, and it's not magic fatigue, but something far scarier. Even though I'm empty, I manage to pull from the last drip of power still coursing in my veins—and finish transcending.

My body hits the ground with a thud. Even through the haziness I'm feeling, I look around to see if Renel is safe, if Lidiane's safe. The bonds tug at me. The human girl is also here, as I couldn't leave her behind. We're safe, far from that horrific magic. I don't feel like myself, though. Something has gone horrifically wrong.

"Who silenced me?" Tar asks.

Lidiane frowns. "*That's* what you want to know?"

"Yes. I was going to tell him that I'd love to prove my point. I could get him alone and then kill him."

Renel shakes his head. "That would be a futile and dangerous attempt. He's too powerful."

"Not anymore, I guess," Tar says.

"I think he's dead this time." Renel's voice is quiet, a hint of fear piercing through it.

I'm not sure I agree with him. "I... beheaded him, or at least it looked like it, but—"

"I felt it," Lidiane says. "Some strange magic, still active even after he was hit."

I nod. "Exactly. He did something to me."

Tar grimaces. "What do you mean, *dead this time*? What kind of fae is he?"

It's a valid—and important—question.

"Is he even fae?" I ask. "We don't usually survive beheadings or having our skulls cracked." I look at Renel, who's been his protege for years. "Do *you* know?"

"He's a healer—unusually talented. But still... Even the Witch King was killed when beheaded, so he has to be dead." He sounds as if he's trying to convince himself. Then he covers his face with his hands. "And the castle moved."

I don't share his worry about the castle's trajectory, but I nod. "It did."

"Where did it go?" Tar asks.

Renel's visibly disturbed. "It should be south now, close to the Endless Mountains."

She raises an eyebrow. "Aren't you the one who controls the castle?"

"It's far more complex than that, like I told you."

I always want to laugh when Renel gives this pathetic explanation, but there isn't anything funny about our situation.

Lidiane is the first to get up, then looks around. "Are we where I think we are?"

Tar gets up too. "While I can't read your thoughts, the air here is obviously dry, and the vegetation rather... arid. The only place like that is..." She swallows. "The eastern part of the Shadow Lands—as far as I know. Perhaps you have this vegetation somewhere in the Crystal Court."

Renel's eyes dart around, then settle on me. "Is this where we are?" He knows well the answer as we came to the keep in this region just a few days ago, but I think he's still holding on for some form of denial.

"Yes." I exhale, but it's defeat, not relief. "Shadow Lands. Be thankful I was able to finish transcending while affected by whatever magic Zorwal cast on me."

Renel presses his lips together. "If he survived, we'll have to return to the castle and face him. *If* he lets me return."

He annoys me sometimes—all the time, in fact—but in times like this, the annoyance is unbearable. "*You* are the freaking acting king, Renel. Expel him from the council or something."

"Yes, I'll kick out a fae who can survive a beheading. Can't see where it will go wrong. And he knows... secrets about me."

Zorwal is aware that Renel has no right to be king, and unlike me, he isn't bound to keep it quiet. The grim truth is that what Renel fears the most is losing his power.

I shrug. "Now you know some of his secrets too. Maybe it will all balance out in the end."

Maybe Zorwal will kick Renel out or even kill him. That would be quite sad, as I'd also die.

Renel points at Lidiane. "He wouldn't have found anything in her mind. You didn't have to—"

"She was with me," I say. "When we went to the Jewel City. I had no choice." Not to mention that Zorwal could have hurt her, but I doubt Renel cares about that.

He runs his hands over his face, then asks, "Why?"

"She's good with glamours, and her magic came in handy."

"Everything, Azur," Renel's voice cracks with dread, fear, anger; I'm not even sure. "You almost made me lose everything. Let's hope Zorwal is indeed dead."

"Yes, let's hope." I'm out of words, out of excuses or explanations.

"Anyway," Tar says. "Shouldn't we leave this place as soon as possible?"

"Indeed we do." I look at the dry soil under me, unsure how to even explain how deep in trouble we are, feeling the walls of my throat closing in.

When I meet Lidiane's eyes, I find worry there. She knows.

"Why are you two sitting and talking?" Tar asks. "Isn't this the land of monsters?"

Lidiane turns to her, her voice mild. "It's fine, actually. It shouldn't be too bad during the day."

Tar rolls her eyes. "Are we going to have a picnic or something? I mean, picnic without food or drinks. Perhaps we'll go sightseeing."

"Azur needs to catch a breath," Renel says, then turns to me. "How are you feeling?"

I cross my arms. "Awful, but thanks for asking."

Renel chuckles. "Take your time. There are still many hours before nightfall."

"Indeed," I say between gritted teeth.

Part of me is gone, as if having another piece of me ripped away, and yet to admit that... I'm perhaps hoping it isn't true.

Lidiane says in a quiet voice, "We should get moving. We might reach the Charmed River before sunset."

"*Might* reach the river means we might not," Renel replies. "Then we'll be trapped here, where foul creatures *will* attack us. It's wiser to let Azur rest until he feels better and can transcend us away." He turns his focus on me. "Do you agree?"

I don't, and yet for some reason I lack the guts to explain why, as if voicing it would materialize my shame. I'm not sure who I am anymore.

Lidiane looks at me as if wondering if she can reveal what she knows. I give her a subtle nod, dreading the words about to come from her lips.

"His magic's gone," she says, her tone grave.

"That much is obvious." Renel chuckles, then turns to me. "You can rest. Sit, relax. Still a long time until the sun—"

"Gone, Renel," I finally confess. "There's nothing. No trace of it, as if I was a weakling." His face shifts, visibly hurt, and I realize what I said. "Not weakling, but like... a human, not myself. No magic left. Imagine you lose an arm. There's no waiting for it to become less tired, waiting for it to heal. It's gone."

I hate everything about this, hate everything.

Renel stares at me with wide eyes. "But it will come back, right?"

"I don't know." I make an effort not to yell, even if I want to scream until my voice is gone like my magic. "Maybe it will, maybe it won't. I can't even sense the air around me, as if it didn't exist. It's like losing a sense all of a sudden. Perhaps my magic will return before nightfall. What if it doesn't?"

"It's fine," Lidiane says. "We can walk."

"Can we?" Renel asks. "Are we close enough?"

Lidiane closes her eyes, thinking. Her expression is glum when she opens them. "Actually, I can hear the sea. In the north. It's about an hour walking or so. We're far from the Charmed River."

"Can we go to the sea?" Tar suggests. "Escape from there?"

Her idea means that she doesn't know about Lidiane's issue with the Sea Court.

"There will be no boat," Lidiane says. "Even if we were to improvise a raft, if there was enough wood for it, we'd be lost in the sea."

"All right," Tar says. "So let me know if I'm understanding this correctly. We're in the Shadow Lands, too far from the Charmed River to reach it before sunset. We can't escape by sea either. It means we'll be in this dreadful land when night falls and monsters roam, right?"

"It seems you're correct," Renel says, then asks me, "Any suggestion?"

Right. I'm the one supposed to save Renel, bound by magic to prioritize his safety above all else—and yet, this time, I failed.

"Can you recite any prayers?" I don't have any better idea.

TARLIA

Astra would pray if she were here. She'd trust the Almighty Mother with all her heart.

Unfortunately—or fortunately—I'm not her. Instead of praying, I need to come up with a rational solution. As if reason could get us out of the Shadow Lands. Still, I have to try.

"We need to plan," I say. "We'll think together, use our minds, and find a solution." My words were so inspiring in my head, but now they sound ridiculous.

Renel is still sitting on the ground. "Our minds are all we

have, right? Let's use them." He glares at Azur. "Better late than never."

Azur puffs. "I did the best I could with the orders I was given. And why was Zorwal even interested in our journey to the festival?"

Renel strokes his chin. "He must have noticed that something was wrong, or maybe even suspected that you were in the Jewel City. He can do that sometimes, skirt around an issue and pretend he doesn't know it."

"Why would he suspect me?" Azur asks. "He doesn't even know—didn't even know—I can transcend."

"Now he does." Renel's face is somber.

"Right," I say. "If we try to find the reason we're here, we'll go back to a fated moment when our father and mother did the deed, and it won't bring us any closer to a solution."

"We need to know what Zorwal wants," Azur says.

"The decapitated guy?" I can't believe he's worried about that. "I think surviving is a tad bit more important. We need three things: water, shelter, and food. There's little of those around us. I still think going to the shore might be a good idea. There will be fish. If we make a raft, we can paddle along the shore."

"The currents are too strong," Lidiane says. "We wouldn't be able to paddle against them."

"We can let the currents take us wherever they want. Even if it's the Nowhere Lands, it's better than here."

Renel clicks his tongue. "I need to get back to the castle. If I disappear like that, the court could plunge into an internal war."

"Right, but you need to survive first." Why can't they focus on the basics?

"A raft wouldn't work," Azur says. "There's no wood around here, just thin branches, and we have no tools. Can you make a raft with these bushes?" He gestures around us.

"And I can't go to the shore," Lidiane says, then shows her

webbed hands. "My father was from the Sea Court, and I have no idea what he did, but they want me dead there. Sorry."

There goes the easiest idea, even if it's true that we wouldn't find any material to build a raft. "Fair, so we stay inland. I have some daggers. Does anyone have any weapons?"

Renel points to his hip. "A sword."

Azur shrugs. "Nothing."

"Me neither," Lidiane says.

I pass a dagger to Lidiane and another to Azur, leaving only one for me. Great. I'm arming my enemies now.

"What about magic?" I ask.

"Still gone." Azur looks down as he pockets the dagger.

"My magic is fine," Lidiane says, "But all I can do are glamours."

Azur looks at her. "You said you had air, back in the council room."

"It's very weak. I can't use it to fight, for example, or even to float."

"Few fae do," Azur says. "Air is a flimsy, tricky type of magic."

The way he looks at Lidiane makes me want to agree with Zorwal's assessment. *He's in love.* But I'm not sure about her. What kind of person falls in love in one day? Then, they're fae. Maybe it's different. I can't imagine what her brother would say if he saw Renel's guardian giving her these longing looks.

To be fair, I wish someone would look at me like that. Anyway, first I have to survive.

"So," I say, trying to get their attention. "There must be some kind of plant here with water. We need to find it, or we'll get dehydrated soon. For shelter, if we can't find anything, we could dig a hole in the ground. It will keep animals out. Food... We can try to find an edible plant."

"A hole in the ground won't work," Lidiane says. "The worst type of monsters are soulsuckers. They feed from fear, and physical barriers won't contain them."

I don't know what to do anymore, so I laugh. "Well, isn't that great?"

"We could try to find the giants," Renel suggests.

Azur's eyes are lost in the distance. "Yes, except that we don't know if they'll help us or *eat us.*"

"They didn't eat the guards," Renel says.

Azur glares at him. "Maybe they weren't hungry."

Lidiane shakes her head. "The giants will find us if they want, or hide and never let us get anywhere near them. But they don't eat people."

"I could shout." Renel waves both arms, as if trying to draw attention. "Giants! Awesome deal for you! You can't miss this offer!"

Azur chuckles. "Giants don't do deals. And they can lie."

"But we can't," Renel says. "There must be something they want. I'm sure they didn't free Marlak out of the goodness of their hearts."

Azur points at him. "Great reminder. They freed Marlak, your enemy. If anything, they might want to help him. What better way to do that than killing you?"

Renel waves a hand. "Smart politicians always play both sides."

Azur rolls his eyes. "You think there's a chance giants are scheming and shrewd?"

This conversation isn't going anywhere. I recall what Renel told me this morning. "Marlak was brought to a prison here, you said. Is it far?"

"Way south," Renel says. "Close to the Charmed River. If we could make it there, we could cross the river."

"Are there any other prisons or buildings further north?"

"That's the only one I know."

"How far?" I insist. "In hours walking?"

"Nobody measured that," Renel says.

Azur narrows his eyes, thinking. "The keep is some two, three hours by foot to the river. The distance between the keep and the north shore would be about four, five times that distance. We're somewhere between five and ten hours from there."

I try to think. "Will that place have water? Will it protect us against the creatures outside?"

"The walls had a magical barrier," Renel says. "But I'm not sure how much damage the giants made."

Azur is thoughtful. "They wouldn't have broken every single wall. At least one room might still be standing. If we run, maybe…"

"I can't run for six hours straight," I say. "I'll run a little, then walk a little."

Lidiane takes a deep breath. "We can't run that much either, but it might be the only solution."

Renel grimaces. "That's what the sum of our minds can come up with? Run and hope for the best? That's a wild creature's solution."

Azur raises a finger. "Nature is wise, after all."

I'm still considering our chances. "It will be tough to run without water."

"We'll have no time to look for it," Lidiane says.

Renel strokes his chin, looking thoughtful. "I could still try to yell; giants, awesome deal!"

"What are you even going to offer them?" Azur asks.

"Whatever they want. It's a once-in-a-lifetime opportunity."

Azur sighs. "Right. Let's hope they're in a good mood and ask for something you can give them. If we even meet them." He gets up. "I think running it is."

The desert ahead of me looks infinite, with a far-away horizon and nothing beyond it, not even mountains. And then, perhaps I should be glad that we're in the desert, and not in the jungle part of the Shadow Lands. We could have been devoured by now.

Renel gets up as well. "What if we don't reach the keep by sunset?"

Azur snorts. "We'll be tired, thirsty, and have to fight whatever attacks us."

"My illusions could help," Lidiane says.

Illusions. While I found them impressive when she got us into the castle, I don't think they'll really help us now, but I'm glad she's optimistic. I'm not looking forward to running, but here we go. Again, I'll have to be thankful to Otavio for all the rigorous, pointless training he made us go through. It might help me reach the keep—and survive.

And then it hits me. With Azur's magic disabled, Renel's defenseless. I can kill him tonight, escape in the morning, find the Owl Inn, and claim the prize.

Hope lies ahead of me—and gives me courage and resilience. My legs move with newfound determination.

Freedom, here I come.

RENEL

The earth passes beneath me in a blur as I dash forward. And forward. Only horizon ahead of me, as I run among low bushes in this arid vegetation.

To my right, the sun makes its way to kiss the horizon, seeming to move faster than we do.

A few times, we slowed our pace to a walk and even took two small breaks to get rid of the wine we drank earlier.

I wish I had drank more water, juice, anything. My mouth and throat are so dry that they hurt. While I tried to call the giants and offer my incredible deal, none of them has shown up so far, and I decided it was better to save my voice—and my dignity.

Tar runs well, despite being human, and has kept up with our pace. Perhaps everything I heard about humans being weaker isn't true after all, or else she's stronger.

Running south is no guarantee we'll find the keep, but

Lidiane claims that if the prison has magic wards, she'll be able to sense them. At least *one person* in our group has magic—not that I have any right to complain.

There were moments when I considered stopping and resting by some bushes, unable to do this anymore. I would sit down and wait gracefully for death—but then my brother wins, my late stepfather wins. They'll get rid of me like they always wanted, and I can't let them do that. It's the pettiness in me that gives me strength when my legs are about to give up. I don't know how the others can keep running and haven't collapsed yet.

Then again, if Azur is in love, that will give him more than enough resistance to run all the way to the Icy Lands and back. Lidiane, I don't know what pushes her, or if she feels the same. Tar is pretty focused.

It's odd to think that even for mere survival, we need a destination, a focus, a reason to keep going.

For me, it's staying alive and spiting them all. Take that, Mirella, I'm still here. Odd. The memory of my stepsister brings me more sadness than anger. Tainted memories that I push away, that I'd rather not face. I did what I could with the charge I was given. Never enough, no. Of course it wasn't enough.

For now, I run, even if the distance feels interminable and my legs want to falter, even if the sun gets closer and closer to the horizon. Each minute that passes eats more of my hope that we'll find shelter before nightfall.

We'll be in the middle of the desert, exhausted and thirsty, surrounded by monsters. And yet I don't dare suggest this possibility or try to see if anyone has a better idea. At this point, perhaps the only thing that will save us is speed—unless the giants decide to show up.

"Giants!" My voice is feeble. "I have an amazing offer!"

I was thinking that it doesn't hurt to try, but the truth is that my throat is so dry that talking hurts.

Beside me, Azur sniggers. Right. I guess trying to prevent our impending death is ridiculous now. I glare at him.

"We'll get there," he says between sharp breaths.

"Still a little far," Lidiane says. "Let's keep going."

Far. The question in my mind chills my bones. I can't be the only one with that question, and I hope someone else will ask it. After a while, I decide I'll have to be the one.

"Do you think we can make it? Before nightfall?"

Lidiane runs in silence for some seconds, then says, "Maybe."

Her breathless and gloomy voice sounds like *most definitely not, but I don't know what else to do.*

"Worst case, we fight through the last stretch," Azur says.

I'm not sure how he intends to fight creatures that can invade our minds, but there's no point in doubting his resolve. I mean, pointing out the impracticality and hopelessness of our very tiring plan could be worth it—if we had an alternative. As it is, all we can do is run forward.

The shadows of the bushes are getting long, illuminated by tilted rays from a descending sun as the clouds take an orange hue. I've never wondered whether night creatures come out only when it's completely dark, or if dusk is enough.

Despite the shadows, I see a form moving towards us.

"Watch out!" I yell and pull my sword, then cut through a wild rat coming in Tar's direction. It's a big one, almost as big as a wild pig, an odd type of rat that only exists in the Shadow Lands.

She pulls a dagger too, and so does Azur.

Two more of those critters advance towards us, and I manage to kill them both. Three more, and I need some swift sword moves.

When I look around, I realize we're surrounded. Dozens and dozens of those gigantic Shadow Land rats. While they are small compared to us, in a group like that, they can overwhelm us quickly.

A roaring sound shakes the ground, and I stop breathing for a second. The creatures run away, and yet I'm terrified of whatever else is coming.

"It was me." Lidiane raises a hand. "Sound glamour. Let's go."

Tar runs beside me and looks at the creatures disappearing in the distance. "I thought it was safe during the day."

"Wild rats are just critters," Azur says. "Wait until you see the monsters."

"She won't see any," Lidiane says, then adds, "If we hurry."

"You mean if we fly?" Tar asks. "Run at an impossible speed?"

I'm pretty sure I'm already running at an impossible speed, but I decide to keep quiet.

"Because if we're going to die," Tar continues. "I could at least rest."

"We're not too far." Lidiane's voice comes from behind me. "We'll get there right after nightfall."

After nightfall.

Am I the only one who sees the problem here?

I think I am the only one, or maybe nobody wants to state the obvious: only sheer luck will keep us alive.

22

ZIVEN

I watch Marlak as we continue on our way to the tower island.

His worry about Astra subsided and he told me he thinks her danger is over, or else he was just overreacting.

Witnessing his pain was when I finally saw him as a real person; someone with feelings and a heart.

Still gruffy, though. And jealous of his unicorn. Jealous of Astra, too.

He thinks I already forgot he overheard her conversation like an insecure teenager. I could mock him all night for that, but I didn't spend years striving to survive just to risk my neck for nothing. He's got a temper and I don't want to tempt it.

At least I'm relieved to know that he no longer senses Astra in danger. I have few friends, but I like to think she's one of them, and my life's already too lonely as it is.

Only the stars light our way as we walk on rocky hills with sparse vegetation. On our way, we encounter a few carcasses, looking like seagulls or other birds, some of them still emitting a putrid smell.

The sight gives me the creeps. "Who's eating them? Ice Golems?"

Marlak turns to me and huffs. "Golems don't eat food. They're magical beings."

"Then who's eating the seagulls?"

He shrugs. "Bigger birds?"

"How big? We walked all the way here and I didn't hear any birds. And these are fresh. If there's a predator out there—"

"We're almost in the tower. We'll be indoors soon."

"You say it as if we'll just stroll in."

He raises an eyebrow. "*I'll* walk in. You can help me open the door, if necessary, then do whatever you want."

"The ferocious giant bird could be *on* the island, Marlak. Have you considered that?"

"We're bigger than birds. And you can't expect to infiltrate a magical prison if *this* makes you afraid." He points to the carcass.

"I'm just wondering."

He keeps walking, and I follow despite my misgivings. I'm not *just wondering*, no. It's a basic precaution. If there's a dangerous creature out there, we need to be careful.

Regardless of his opinion, I decide to keep my ears perked and my senses alert to any danger that may come my way. Marlak and his inflated self-confidence can deal with whatever comes his way.

Then again, he's so powerful that monsters might be no threat to him. I wish his abnormal magical prowess would make me more at ease, but everything about this place puts me on edge, and it's not that I'm a coward, like Marlak's suggesting.

We climb a rocky hill, and the air changes, becoming warmer and more humid, with more water dissolved in the air. So much water.

He pauses at the edge of a cliff. When I look down, I understand the reason for the humidity—and realize we reached our destination.

The cliff is a circle surrounding a lake with hot water, white steam billowing from it. In the middle, a green island and a tower, strangely slim in the middle and wide on top, made of a dark stone. My entire body wants to turn around and run, while part of me is fascinated by it.

"It's here," he says. "Except that the island is invisible."

I blink, wondering if I'm imagining things. "I can see the island and the tower, Marlak. Can't you?"

He frowns. "No. All I see is a gigantic hot spring."

I look down at the lake surrounding the island. "There's magic in that water, keeping it boiling. It's not just the fire of the earth."

"I know. It's why I can't just freeze it and form a bridge."

"There *is* a bridge." I point, then realize he can't see it. "It's on the other side of the island. I'm not sure if it's made of wood or metal, but it's covered, perhaps to prevent travelers from getting hot water spilled on them."

Marlak nods. "Let's go."

Uneasiness takes hold of me as I observe the rocky cliff. While I think I'm a good enough climber that I could descend it, I'm not so sure about doing it in the dark, in a magical place, and with whatever is killing those birds out there. Plus, I have a gut feeling telling me not to go, that it's not safe at night.

"After the sun rises," I say. "It's too dangerous to go there now."

He rolls his eyes. "Oh. I knew it. Scared of a little cliff."

"Mock me all you want. You're not going to make me step into that island at night. Strange magic surrounds it, and night-time brings out the worst in curses and creatures. You've waited years; you can wait a few more hours."

He huffs. "Truly? What's your plan then? To sleep out here?"

"We have a tent, don't we?"

"Ice golems roam this area, not to mention the evil, terrifying bird-killing monster." His voice is deep and mocking, then goes back to normal. "Do you prefer to spend the night out here in the open, or indoors?"

Valid question, no doubt, and yet...

"Not in that tower." My spine tingles just looking at it. "And I'm not descending this cliff now. I don't know it well enough, and I don't want to risk being attacked while hanging from it."

He sighs. "I can make ice steps. A nice, cute staircase for you, if you're so afraid of the cliff."

"Ice stairs?" I chuckle. "Not slippery at all, I suppose."

"I don't care how you're getting down there. We're going to that tower tonight."

"You're free to go. I'll wait until tomorrow."

He pauses, then narrows his eyes. "Ziven, let me make one thing clear. You said you had nowhere to go, right?"

"Yes. And if you say you'll never harbor me again and you'll forbid all your allies from helping me, I'm still not going to that island tonight. I don't care. I'm not going, Marlak. If you're so desperate to go, I'm not stopping you."

He clenches his fists, then takes a deep breath. "Please." His tone is different, I suppose because he realized he can't mock or threaten me to do what he wants. "I need to see my sister. One night is an eternity. I'm also anxious to return home to my wife. Astra still worries me, even if I don't sense any danger right now. Please. You wanted to help me; help me."

"Tomorrow."

He looks down. "Just show me the location of the bridge. You don't need to cross it."

"I think it needs to be opened, and there's no guarantee I can unlock it more than once, that it will work if I don't go through. I'm going tomorrow. You can either wait or try to do it yourself."

Marlak sighs, rolls his eyes, then says, "Fine then. Have fun with the bird killer."

He steps into the cliff and soon disappears as he descends it. For a second, I consider trying to convince him not to go, tell him it's dangerous, but I know he won't listen.

That island feels wrong, eerie. While I should walk away

and find a safer spot to sleep, I prefer to stand still, as I doubt his stubbornness will help him find an entrance he can't see.

Sometimes I wonder how Astra tolerates that royal asshole-ness. Hearts make no sense.

I sit on a rock and wait, hoping no monsters find me. Despite Marlak's grumpiness, I hope they don't find him either.

LIDIANE

Far, far ahead, I can sense a faint trace of wards. It could be one hour, and then it could be three, four hours away. Perhaps I should tell the others that there's a chance we'll never make it, but I'm clinging to the sliver of hope that we might—somehow—defy death.

Beside me, Azur runs, but I can sense his uneasiness, even his fear. Earlier, I felt his lack of magic, and there's no point pondering what any of that means when we might die at any moment.

We have to survive first, and then later I can decide what to do, perhaps even decide how I feel. For now, I'm terrified of what we might face.

We've come across two groups of wild rats, and my sound glamour scared them away. I'd rather not encounter any more of them, as I'm not sure what my sound will attract—or awaken. A chill covers my skin, and it has nothing to do with the cooling dusk.

Shades of orange, red, and pink paint the sky as the sun slowly disappears on the horizon. Less than an hour of daylight —and no sign of the keep.

My brother will be furious if I die here. I wonder if anyone will know where we are, or if we'll be an open question forever haunting our loved ones.

Beside me, Azur mutters, "We'll make it."

His face is slick with sweat, his blond hair messy around his face, and yet he knows I need some cheering, some hope. When I look at him, I have no doubt that we can cross the Shadow Lands at night, that we can defeat any monster, that we'll fight together to the end.

Now, if everything goes wrong, that will be a worthy way to die, but I'd rather live and see what future awaits me when the sun rises.

Purple has taken over the sky, while the sunlight gets dimmer and dimmer. Stars already peer at us from between angry, red clouds.

My legs are weak, but I keep pushing them. Just a little more, just a little. Considering the wards are likely far ahead, in reality I'll have to keep going a lot more, and yet I need to tell my legs that it's right ahead, or else they'll falter.

My breath catches when the last hint of daylight disappears.

"How far?" Azur mutters.

I can sense wards up ahead, not *too* far. "One hour or two."

"What?" Tarlia asks.

"We'll hurry," I say softly. "Silence now. Let's avoid calling attention to ourselves."

Our feet against the earth and our ragged breaths are already noisy enough. From what I've heard, the monsters from the Shadow Lands don't all attack together, meaning that only one type might find us.

Soulsuckers are the worst. It's hard to fight something that attacks our minds. Sand Sprites can be tricky because they are hard to kill. My hope is that earth ghouls find us. They're humanoids, but made of some energy of the earth, not really alive, not really dead, and easy to kill.

In truth, I hope nothing finds us. If I ever needed luck, it was today.

"We'll make it," Azur says again, and for some silly reason, his confidence makes me smile.

Am I falling for him? Have I already fallen?

In one day. I need to be less gullible and more careful.

Azur stops running, his eyes brilliant against the darkness surrounding us. "Lidiane, I love you. I'm sure I do. Can you feel our bond?"

What I feel are my heartbeats accelerating, my legs weakening, by hands trembling. What else do I feel, other than a mix of excitement and terror?

He pulls my hand to his chest, where his heart is beating so, so fast, its rhythm matching mine. Our eyes meet, and it's as if time stopped—nothing else in this moment but him and I.

His blue eyes draw me in, pull me, his brilliant eyes promising more than I dare hope—until their spark suddenly fades. Or is it the world fading around me? Something sticky covers my hand. His blood. It can't be. This can't be real, can't be.

"Azur," I call him, as if my weak voice could undo his wounds, bring back his life.

Across his chest, three prongs protrude. A trident.

I tremble from head to toe.

The Sea Court has found me.

Azur falls, his eyes looking at nothing, while tridents surround me. Meanwhile, a fae holds a man with a fish tail; my brother. I didn't know his body looked like that.

The sea court is about to kill him. I know they are.

"No!" I scream and scream and scream. "No!" As if my screams could do anything.

"Lidiane!" a girl calls. "Lidiane!" The yell is desperate, but it sounds so distant, so... "Azur! Renel!"

I know those names, I know that voice.

"You want to sleep *now*?" Her voice cracks with anger. "I'm also tired, but really? What's wrong with you?"

Someone touches my shoulder. "Lidiane!"

My eyes snap open, and I see Tarlia beside me, a dirty dagger in her hand, her clothes all spattered with mud—or blood.

"What's happening?"

She exhales. "You all decided to take a nap. A fucking nap!"

Only then do I notice I'm lying down—right in the middle of the Shadow Lands. I get up and see some kind of giant slug cut in half. And then I realize what happened. "A soulsucker. Did you kill it?"

"I cut it in half. Let's hope it's enough."

"Should be—for now. Wake Renel, and I'll wake Azur."

She crouches by Renel, showing him her rich vocabulary of expletives. I can't believe we survived this.

Azur is lying down, his face peaceful.

I touch his shoulder. "Azur. It's an illusion. Everything's fine."

He sits, his eyes wide, glances at me, then darts his gaze.

"A soulsucker," I explain. "Somehow, Tar killed it."

He blinks as he gets up, still looking away. "Unbelievable."

Renel gets up slowly, his entire body trembling.

"Shall we run?" Tarlia asks everyone. "Or do you want to wait for giant rats? More sleepy slugs?"

"Let's go." I take a deep breath, hoping it will give me the strength to continue.

I still can't believe she was able to kill the soulsucker. Either the creature couldn't affect us all at once, or else it underestimated her and was feeding on her real fear of being in this place alone, with her companions asleep.

At least *some* luck graced us.

As I run, I consider my bizarre vision.

I love you. The words warm and chill my heart at the same time, even if I know they are fake words from a vision meant to draw my fear.

Falling in love *is* terrifying, so I can understand the soulsucker strategy. It was just an illusion. A strange illusion.

At least the cool night wind and the fear of facing any other creatures give me renowned strength. I can't believe I've run so much. The magic of the wards feels stronger now, almost within reach.

Then I hear it; the sound of wind moving sand.

"Sand sprite!" I yell. "Let's bundle together!"

I pull Tarlia in front of me, and then Renel and Azur flank us. Sand sprites prefer smaller targets, and might hesitate to attack a group of people together.

They can be incorporeal like sand carried by wind, or solid like a boulder. The issue is that they can hit us, and if they're solid, they can do a lot of damage. For now, it's just circling us. I make the roaring sound, hoping it will scare the creature, but it makes no difference.

Unsure what to do, I create an illusion of myself running away from the group.

The sprite becomes solid and attacks the illusion. I use glamour to make us unnoticeable, then create another illusion running in another direction. The sand sprite attacks it but then returns, as if sensing us.

I recall then some old tales about tubular bells in windows, and create that sound. The sand sprite stops moving.

I don't know how long I can keep that sound going, but I whisper, "Let's walk slowly."

We move forward cautiously, while the creature is solid but motionless. We pass it, then I create two illusions of groups of people going in other directions, and mutter, "Run!"

Tarlia runs in front of me, and I create sounds of steps going in other directions while muffling ours.

I can't be sure we lost it, but I can't keep the sound so far back anymore. Then I hear a growl—and another.

Ghouls.

Renel's sword reflects the moonlight as he decapitates one creature, then another. They're uglier and more terrifying than I imagined. Even if they look like they're made of earth, they have eerily realistic faces with no hair but with eyes, pointy or round ears, noses, mouth, and even teeth. The strange teeth are the issue, as they can bite fast and eventually kill. One or two ghouls is not a problem, but we're not dealing with a couple of them, but many, many more.

I turn and see another one behind me, which Azur stabs. Tarlia crouches and tries to evade one ghoul, but without much success, until Renel decapitates it. He's mostly fighting on his own, with some help from Azur.

I create the roaring sound, but it has no effect. Tubular bells don't affect them either, and neither does any illusion. I'm not good with light illusions, but I try one, just to see how many surround us. Too many. Hundreds, coming from all directions.

Where did they come from?

There's no way, no way we can defeat them all. No way we can escape. No way we can reach the keep.

In a matter of seconds—or perhaps minutes, depending on our fighting skills—we'll be dead.

RENEL

So. Many. Ghouls.

Too many, and they aren't susceptible to glamours, so Lidiane's magic is useless. All we have is my sword and Tar's daggers, hardly enough against this horde.

Two creatures jump at me at once. I kick one and stab the other. Dark blood pours from his wound. Beside me, Tar is over-whelmed, trying to keep three of them at bay. I push one, decapitate two, then turn and elbow a ghoul coming for me.

Behind me, Azur grunts, and two ghouls push him to the ground. He's barely keeping himself alive with that silly dagger. I jump in his direction, pull the creatures away from him, then throw them across more attackers.

My movement left the girls exposed, and five ghouls encircle them. I move to their side and keep the creatures at bay with broad swings, then turn back to do the same, as Azur can't really block them without a proper weapon.

I turn again, block, kill a couple of ghouls, turn—and I don't know how long I'll last.

As long as it takes.

There are four lives on the line here. I don't feel my arms, my body, my legs. All I focus is on pushing the creatures away, trying to keep us alive for one more second, then one more, then another one.

This second is all that matters.

And yet the creatures are getting closer and closer, pushed by the ones behind them, so they can't even step back when I hit them.

I let instinct take over, that fighting instinct after years of practice, so that I don't even know what my arms are doing anymore, just that it's keeping the ghouls from reaching us.

As much as I tell myself I can keep resisting, I know that death is watching us, ready to take us the moment I make the smallest mistake, or maybe when no amount of fighting will be enough. I don't want to die now, and for once, it's not only my pettiness talking. This would be a stupid ending in the middle of nowhere, after a meaningless life. So empty, and yet I cling to it with all my might.

I strike and strike, unwilling to yield, too stubborn to accept defeat, fighting against all odds. Still standing, despite everything. I could use some luck now. A lot of luck. I can't do this.

"Giants! Help!" Can anyone even hear me amidst the growls?

My screams disappear into the night.

"Somebody! Anybody! Help!"

One last strike, and one more. I don't want Azur to die. Don't want those girls to die either. But I can't hold back the ghouls.

Too many. Too fast.

Four ghouls are coming at me, while I see that they're overwhelming Tar. I want to help her, but they're also pushing Azur, who has Lidiane behind him. I... I can't defend them all.

Can't even defend myself.

I swing my sword and yell, "Aaaaah!"

The ghouls pause, then turn around and run.

Fuck. I'm strangely proud and embarrassed at the same

time. I scared the creatures, but if I had known a yell was all it took, I could have saved so much anguish, so much effort.

A relief chuckle comes to me. "Did you see that?"

Azur is checking if Lidiane is all right and doesn't even have the courtesy to acknowledge me. Me, who saved them, not to mention the fact he's supposed to protect me.

Tar at least stares at me, eyes wide, lips parted. At least *one* person is impressed.

Wait. She's looking *behind* me. I turn quickly, ready to face another threat, but there's nothing threatening about the creature approaching us.

Nothing at all.

At once, I'm overcome with memories of a different time, memories of my brother, my father, the family I once had, the *happiness* I once had.

It's the dark unicorn.

And yet he has a name, a name that had almost faded from my memory: Cherry Cake.

I thought he had disappeared or even died. Sometimes I wondered if he was just a figment of my imagination, if the time when I flew on him with my brother was nothing but a dream. In retrospect—it *was* a dream. A childish illusion.

No. He's real. He's here. This time, he has no saddle like he did so many years ago, and it doesn't matter. He saved me. Saved us.

I told Azur that I could take his horn to get his magic, but my stomach churns at the idea of anyone hurting him. I would never bring myself to do it, and I don't even think it's possible. He's more powerful than a horde of ghouls. Who am I to try to defeat him?

He approaches slowly, then gets close enough and touches my forehead with his nose, just like he used to do years ago. I reach out to caress him.

"Don't!" Azur yells.

Cherry Cake steps back, and I turn to my guardian. "I'm not

an idiot." I point to the unicorn. "He's my friend. Or maybe was, a long time ago."

I caress the unicorn's flank. "Thank you. Thank you for still being a friend."

He neighs, then turns around and trots away, going south.

"We have to follow him," I yell at the others.

Lidiane gets up, and we get moving. Cherry Cake's pace might be a slow trot for him, but for us, it means more running. I'm positive that my legs are disappointed that they didn't get their deserved eternal rest back there.

But at least it isn't far. The issue is whether the keep will be safe. It could be overrun with giants, for instance, who might not want us there.

Stupid giants. Imagine the deal they could have gotten if they had shown up when I thought I was about to die. A once-in-a-lifetime opportunity. I yelled, but did they listen? Nope.

Now, *if* the keep is accessible, I hope the wards are still standing—or else we'll have no place to spend the night.

23

TARLIA

I think I'll want to lie down for a week after this—if we make it. But I think we will. Even if I'm completely illiterate in magic, I can feel the powerful, soothing energy this unicorn emanates.

I can't believe I'm still alive, though. Thanks to Renel, and to a minor extent, Azur. I thought I was aware that fae could move with inhuman speed and skill, but whatever I had in my mind was nothing close to what I witnessed.

Renel moved his sword so fast that I could barely see it, slaying those creatures in a manner that would be impossible for any human. Fae. Somehow, with his hair messy, his focus on the battle, he looked human—and yet even more beautiful.

And he seems to be friends with a majestic beast.

I'm not sure if I can kill him.

How can I bring myself to kill the man who saved me? True that he was saving his own skin—and his guardian's. I wonder if that unicorn will be upset if I kill his fae friend, but at the same time, if it loved Renel that much, it could have shown up earlier.

I suppose there will be no unicorn after me if I murder him.

The issue is there's no way I can defeat Renel in any form of hand-to-hand combat. I doubt I could even stab him when he's distracted—his reflexes are too good. It will have to be when he's asleep—if I can muster the courage.

After that, I can wake up early in the morning, run to the fae territories, find the Owl's Inn, claim my prize, and then gain my freedom. I feel queasy planning to murder a travel companion, but then, I didn't even want to be here.

Astra won't harbor me forever. Ziven… He's on the same boat as me, if not on his own. I'm all alone, and I need to safeguard my future.

If we make it.

"There!" Lidiane says.

I can't see anything. Wait. It's part of a wall or something, but still so far… I hope my legs don't collapse before we get there. I almost feel like slowing down, but I'm too proud to accept the humiliation of trailing behind. And I don't want to think what kind of creatures could snatch me if I run too far behind the others.

The walls grow bigger and bigger ahead of us, tall fortress walls of what I hope will be our shelter. As we're about to reach an enormous gate, the unicorn flies away, a strange, eerie, wingless flight.

There goes our protection.

And the heavy gate is closed from the outside.

"I'll go in and open it," Azur says, then proceeds to scale the wall.

The ease with which he does that is worrisome. For a moment I imagine those ghouls doing the same.

The only sound is the wind on bushes as he steps on the other side, only stars illuminating us. After a moment, the gate screeches and moves up, but just about some five palms.

Lidiane and Renel crouch and slide in, and I do the same.

The gate then slams closed behind us.

Azur turns to Lidiane. "Is it warded?"

"It feels safe, but…"

"What?" he asks.

She shakes her head. "The magic feels different, old."

"Can we spend the night here?" I ask. If she says *no*, I might just ignore her, lie down and quit. Please no more running.

"Yes." She nods.

Renel exhales, clearly relieved. He must be thinking *no more sword fighting*, then says, "I'll go in first, see if the place is clear."

Many small buildings border the walls. He enters the first of them, where a table is turned upside down and the floor is covered with ripped papers and shattered glass.

Azur huffs. "Messy giants."

Renel crouches. "The footprints are small. These were fae, probably trying to figure out why the giants came."

"Right." Azur has a mocking chuckle. "Do they think enchanted guards would write down confidential information? Idiots."

I'm not in the mood to figure out what happened here. If it's safe, it's good enough. "I need water," I say. "A bed, too. A massage, maybe. And a hot bath, definitely."

Renel turns to me. "The keep has quarters, but I'm afraid there isn't enough water for a bath." He actually sounds apologetic.

"I was kidding. But I do want at least a pitcher and a cloth to get rid of this soulsucker goo."

"We'll find it."

The second building has a large kitchen with many stone tables, and a hearth that still has some embers burning. Azur manages to rekindle the fire.

Some jars of water are broken, but we find a container, cups, and even some cheese, bread, and dried meat and fruit. Lidiane activates some lightstones, so that we don't need to light candles.

Azur finds a lavatory with basins and jars, and Renel brings us clean uniforms, including a dress that I guess hasn't been worn in some fifty years. Better than sticky, slimy clothes.

I find a closed booth in the lavatory and rip out my disgusting dress. As I run the wet cloth over my skin, I can't believe I'm finally able to get rid of the gunk, sweat, and most importantly, ghoul mud and soulsucker slime. I still need a hot bath, maybe a hundred baths, ideally with alcohol, but this will do for now. I've never been so glad to put on clean clothes, delighting in the feel of the linen against my clean skin, even if it's a little musty, and even if I have no underwear. I'm alive—and clean. Starving, too.

We all sit in the kitchen for a much-deserved dinner. They all wear black shirts and pants, from some kind of uniform they found. I guess there was only one dress. Azur's hat was destroyed fighting the ghouls, and his hair is all messy and loose.

There's no hiding the exhaustion on our faces, but there's also relief, and even some joy. We survived.

Azur, Lidiane, and Renel eat mostly dried fruit and nuts, while I attack the bread and the dried meat. I suspect this is rat meat, but I don't want to ask. It's nothing like the meat at the festival, but it's food.

The festival—a lifetime has passed since then, and yet it was only a few hours ago.

"Is there wine by any chance?" I ask.

Renel gets up. "Of course." He points to large wooden barrels in the corner. "Not the best, though."

I shrug. "At least we can celebrate. We should, after surviving what we did."

"Who wants some?" Renel asks as he lifts a barrel and places it on the table, then fills a cup under its tap.

Azur raises a hand, and Renel slides a cup to him.

"I'll have some," Lidiane says.

"And me, of course," I make sure to remind him.

"Obviously." He passes a cup to me, then to Lidiane, and finally takes one for himself.

Lidiane's sitting across from me, beside Azur. I'm not sure what's happening with these two. All of a sudden, they're like great friends—or lovers. Well, if she's happy, that's what matters.

The wine's dreadful, but it's wine—vinegary wine. I drink and then feel guilty that Renel got it for me. Renel, who I want to kill. But what else am I going to do with my life? Where am I going to go without a single coin in my possession? And killing him could help Astra. I don't want to get distracted with these thoughts, and get up.

"I propose a toast. To everyone's bravery."

Azur snorts. "I did nothing. And got us stranded here."

I disagree. "You killed the creepy old man back in the castle before he could hurt Lidiane. That counts."

He tilts his head, unconvinced, then we all toast, and he chugs down his wine.

Renel takes a sip from his cup and looks at me. "How did you kill the soulsucker?"

Lidiane chuckles. "I want to know that too."

"You were all fallen, that disgusting thing slithered toward me, and I stabbed it, stabbed it, then cut it. It was easy, actually. The thing didn't fight back."

Lidiane shakes her head. "You didn't really think we were taking naps, did you?"

I shrink my shoulders, the terror of that moment seizing my body. "I feared you were all dead, but I thought... I decided it was better to believe you were taking a rest, because I would do that if I could, so it was believable."

"You saved our lives," Renel says.

"You saved ours, so we're even." I point to Lidiane. "She did a lot, too."

"When I could," she says, her voice quiet.

Azur opens his arms. "For once, I was a useless guardian."

"You fought too," I say. "It's not your fault all you had was a dagger."

He raises a finger. "It *is* my fault. I'm the one who threw my sword."

"I can't believe Cherry Cake saved us," Lidiane says, I suppose wanting to change the subject.

What a bizarre name for a fearsome magical unicorn.

Renel stares at her, his eyes wide. "How do you know his name?"

She blinks, then Azur asks, "What name?"

"Cherry Cake." There's a hint of annoyance in Renel's voice.

Azur shrugs. "You said it."

Renel frowns. "I did?"

Sneaky Azur.

Renel had not mentioned the name of the unicorn before. I would have remembered it. He only said it now. How does Lidiane even know it? It must have something to do with Marlak—and Azur is covering for her.

Interesting.

I decide to give her some more help, since I can lie.

"Don't you remember? You were yelling: *Cherry Cake, come and help me! I have an awesome deal!*"

Renel frowns. "I wasn't calling Cherry Cake."

"Right." I take a sip of my wine. "You were calling the giants. You said the unicorn's name when he showed up. I'm all confused."

Azur sighs. "It turns out that the giants had no interest in any deal."

"Too bad for them," Renel says, then furrows his eyebrows. "Then again, they don't like the fae and mistrust us. Perhaps we were lucky." He pauses, then turns to Azur. "You feared I was going to try to take the unicorn's horn?"

"I thought you wanted it."

"I might have thought so too." Renel looks down, then faces his guardian. "But I wasn't going to try it now, when he came to save me, and I don't even think anyone can do it."

Azur shrugs. "I wasn't sure about your intentions. I'm still your guardian, right? As useless as I've been in the last few hours."

Renel clicks his tongue. "You're never useless."

"I am. Having no magic is the worst thing ever."

"So now you know how it feels." Renel's snort is bitter.

I almost protest that their words are highly offensive considering I have no magic and tend to feel fine when not surrounded by ghouls, but then I remember that Astra *has* some magic, even if I don't know what it is, so I decide to be quiet.

"I was scared," Lidiane says, perhaps again trying to change the subject. "I thought at any moment one of us would die, especially Renel, fighting those ghouls."

Azur strokes a lock of his hair. "Then I'd die, and I don't know how you two would survive—no offense."

"None taken." I chuckle, but something he said makes no sense. "Why do you think you'd be the first to die after Renel?"

"Bound guardian," Azur says. "The moment my charge dies, so do I."

Lidiane tenses, her eyes wide. She's worried about Azur. And if I kill Renel...

Maybe not.

I ask, "What if it's not your fault?"

"It's *always* my fault. My role is to protect him. My soul life purpose."

I'm not sure if he's being sarcastic or not.

Renel looks up and shakes his head. "You say it as if *I* made the deal."

Lidiane turns to Azur. "Didn't you volunteer to be a guardian?"

"Yes, I volunteered." There's an edge to his voice. "When I was ten years old."

"My stepfather created the bond." Renel puts a hand on his chest. "If it had been me, I'd make him a normal guardian—like my father was. I do try to be careful and not die, though."

"What if Azur dies?" I ask.

"I'll be replaced." Azur chuckles. "What a tragedy."

"I'm not going to replace you." Renel sounds irritated, which is odd. He isn't the one with a life bond.

I can't kill Renel, not if Lidiane is in love with Azur, but then again, maybe I'm seeing love where there's just some mild attraction or friendship.

"I have a question." How am I going to make this sound natural? I clean my throat. "Many, in fact, but this is a curiosity I've always had, since fae are so different." They all stare at me, eyes wide. "Considering you are all so... *free* concerning intimate relationships, do you ever form attachments? Like romantic attachments?"

"Of course," Renel says. "Fae love deeply, be it for a night or for a lifetime."

I'm not sure that makes any sense. "But if it's always deep, then it's never deep, is it? How would one know if it's a night or a lifetime?"

Renel takes a sip of his wine. "When we decide to get married, it's usually for a lifetime. Vows are serious for us."

I think about Marlak rushing to our castle to marry Astra, and wonder if he was thinking it would be for a lifetime, or if he didn't count a wedding in human lands as a real vow.

"What about soulmates? Is there a sign or something, a way to recognize them?" I look at Azur and Lidiane, hoping to hear *their* answer, and hoping it's better than Nelsin's *you'll know it when you know.*

"Yes." Renel sits up, his eyes bright. Does *he* have someone? "It's a tug, as if you were pulled by an invisible chord."

"Not necessarily," Azur says.

"How do you know?" I ask.

Azur's face is a mask. "It varies from person to person."

That's unfortunately similar to Nelsin's non-explanation.

"My parents were soulmates," Renel says. "He saw her and knew it right away, and that's how he described it; a pull." He looks down and takes a deep breath. "He liked to tell us about the day he met her, as if destiny had a hand in their story."

A story with a sad ending. This would be a great time to change the subject, but I still want to understand what's going on with Lidiane and Azur.

"So the sign is that you'll know it right away?"

Lidiane stares at me with a puzzled face, obviously not understanding why I'm bringing up this subject.

Azur shakes his head. "Most people misread signs and wouldn't know it immediately."

"Right. So... basically..." I shrug. "You guess? How do you know it's not just some infatuation?"

Azur gets up and refills his cup. "There will be some kind of magical manifestation. I'm not sure what happens when you don't have magic, though."

"You know a lot about it," I say.

He snorts, then sits down again. "I'm a guardian. I know a lot about many things."

I'm going to guess that Lidiane and Azur are *not* soulmates. I think I'd see them exchanging some looks, right? Something.

It means I *can* kill Renel. My heart freezes in my chest.

Nobody mentioned Zorwal and whether by any chance he survived a beheading. Perhaps it's too much for now. If I escape, collect my prize, and go somewhere far away, it won't matter.

My hand trembles as I take another sip of the wine, but I decide I need to go ahead with my plan, so I say, "We're safe here, but it would be safer if we didn't sleep on our own. Lidiane and Azur can share a room, and I can share another with Renel."

My plan is to catch him when he's asleep.

Lidiane gives me a weird look. I'm wondering if she thinks I'm interested in Renel, or if I'm pushing her towards Azur. I hope she doesn't realize I'm a potential murderer.

Renel glances at his guardian then turns to me. "That's a wise idea."

Lidiane stares at her cup, while Azur drinks from his. They don't even glance at each other. Can I kill Renel? My heart beats with uneasiness inside my chest.

We're all exhausted, so we soon leave the kitchen and go to the quarters. Renel picks a room with a bunk bed, a small table, and two chairs, and I find myself alone with him, aware that he still has a sword—and all I have is a dagger.

I don't wait for an invitation and sit at the bottom bed, then lie back on it, with my feet on the floor. I think my body is going to ache for weeks.

"You were quite interested in soulmates," Renel says.

I sit up. "Just curious."

He pulls a chair in front of me. "Do you still want a massage?"

"I was joking. Are you offering?" I hope not. I can't kill someone who offers me a massage, I just can't.

"I'm trying to make you feel better. I know it was a hard day, Astra."

"Tar," I say, dreading this farce.

He shakes his head. "Sorry."

I wonder what he would do if he found out I'm not her. Kill me? But I don't think he'd do it now. He'd sentence me to prison or to death. In fact, if he gets angry, that will give me a good reason to kill him. I could even claim self-defense. Right now, he's being too nice, and I don't think I'll be able to move forward with my plan.

"There's something I need to tell you."

"Yes?"

I feel the air and the courage whooshing from my chest. No, I have to say it. I'm tired of living a lie.

"I'm not Astra." Once I start, the words flow. "I'm not Tiurian. I was just raised with Astra. Like her, I was trained to replace the Krastel princess. My name's Tarlia."

He stares at me, his jaw hard, a manic glint in his eyes.

I deeply, deeply regret the words I just said—but there's no way to take them back.

ASTRA

Pages and pages flew by, and yet *Tiuris, The Fallen Kingdom* didn't bring me any answers. The book was written by a Crystal Court fae, describing one of the sanctuaries and theorizing that Tiuris must have been the most important kingdom on this continent before the arrival of the fae and humans from across the sea. The text doesn't have much *information* other than speculation, even if it sounds plausible.

If Tiuris was an important kingdom, then it probably had a castle, perhaps many. The Amethyst Palace must have been real, and yet I don't understand its significance or why it's calling to me.

I decide to take another look at the book about the Shadow War, interested to see what it says about the defeat of the Witch King. He was a dangerous enemy because he could absorb magic, absorb life force, and use it against his enemies. Sending armies to fight him could mean giving him more ammunition.

Still, his enemies positioned their armies to surround and overwhelm the witch king's allies as a last attempt against him. Last indeed, and these were people marching to their deaths. At the time, fae and humans were allies. What I find interesting is the absence of Tiurians. Tiurians are generally considered human, and therefore would be accounted in that group, but why no mention of their magic?

If it's true that later, during the Treaty War, Tiurians were instrumental in assuring victory and survival for the humans by giving them magic, how come they're not mentioned here?

The book then says that the alliance killed the Witch King's children, and I can't help but feel disgusted. Sure, the guy was bad, but his family was likely innocent—I think.

I'm not sure reading these books has been a fruitful use of my time. Perhaps it's just that all my life I was told to find answers in writing, and I want to do the same now, but if there were any text detailing the location of the Amethyst Palace, it would have been found by now.

Perhaps I should go to the river and seek the Nymph Queen. I'll beg her for a sign, a direction, a clearer explanation. This is so frustrating. And then, if she doesn't know, what is she going to do?

The worst is that I can't even think straight. The entire day, Marlak has consumed my thoughts, not with longing or desire, but with worry. So much worry. I keep telling myself that he has spent a lifetime dodging enemies and likely has magic more powerful than any fae alive, and yet my heart feels wrong and tight and painful.

And then I can't stop thinking about Lidiane and Tarlia. By nightfall, I could barely breathe. Ferer was agitated too. I'm wondering if we should try to get them out of that castle—but I also need to find the Amethyst Palace. Why does everything have to happen at the same time?

Falling asleep is a struggle. When I do, I find myself in a thick forest, calling for Marlak.

Marlak, where are you?

My body feels cold and taut and my heart feels like it's being pulled, stretched. Everything's wrong.

And then I'm in the Crystal Palace, on that balcony, looking at a starry sky above a forest, when I hear steps behind me.

The woman walking in my direction is calm, collected, confident. Every step she takes exudes power. Her hair is purple and shimmery and her face glows with inner light. She looks like me, if I were gorgeous and powerful, that is.

"You're not a girl anymore," she says.

"I know."

"Of course." She chuckles, then runs her hand through her incredible hair. "I'm sure you also know he's in danger."

It's like a bucket of ice in my stomach. "What danger?"

She tilts her head, her look somehow mischievous. "Do you *need* to know?"

"Obviously."

"You don't need to *know*, little Astra." Those words remind me of Andrezza, both caring and belittling.

The strange Astra smirks. "You don't like *little Astra*, do you? Then don't be little Astra." She grimaces and pretends to cry. "Poor little me. I don't know what to do."

"Why don't you help me instead of mocking me?"

"What do you think I'm doing, *little Astra*?"

"You're telling me the obvious, big Astra."

"I disagree. Look around. Look. Truly look. Now, if you want your husband to live, find me." She disappears, and yet I hear her voice one last time. "Find me."

I realize then that the vision was not some strange, super powerful and yet snarky version of me. It was the Amethyst Palace.

Find me.

What does she think I've been trying to do?

I'm still staring at that forest, that sky, when a horrible screech reaches my ear, then gigantic tentacles surround the balcony. I turn to retreat inside, but the rooms are filled with grisly humanoid forms—ghouls. And yet Marlak's the one in danger. I need to find him.

"Marlak!" I yell. My voice echoes through the hills, spreading far into the night, and yet there's no reply.

"Marlak! Husband!"

Nothing. All I feel is empty, terrified.

And still with no answers.

24

LIDIANE

I walk down the hall of the Desert Keep's quarters with Azur, imagining all the ways in which I'll strangle Tarlia.

Soulmates! Wink, wink, soulmates. So, how do you find out when someone is your soulmate?

She didn't even have the decency to try to look away or pretend she wasn't talking about me and Azur.

Soulmates.

The word feels heavy, strange, alien. I haven't looked at him since we left that kitchen and came to find a bedroom.

A bedroom. For us.

That's on Tarlia too, who came up with the ludicrous suggestion. Perhaps that's on me as well, who was too stunned to protest.

Soulmates. Really?

I want to tell myself that the idea is absurd, and yet, even in my head, I'm unable to say it.

Denial would be a lie.

I know what I felt when I sensed his magic gone. He said it was as if he had lost part of himself—but at that moment, I could swear it was part of me too, as if we were connected. Connected by an unbreakable bond.

And yet it's still strange. I don't even know how to feel about it. And I don't know what's going to happen.

Azur opens a door and looks inside. "Is this good?" His voice has an odd harshness.

"Looks clean enough." It's just a simple, small bedroom with two bunk beds, a small, round table, and two wooden chairs. I chuckle. "Better than perishing in the desert."

"Good." He gestures for me to enter, not even a hint of a smile on his lips, then slams the door shut and turns to me.

I don't like his demeanor. "What's the attitude for?"

His fists are clenched. "Since when?"

"Not sure. Since when can't you ask a complete question?"

"You know what I'm talking about."

"I don't." Is he upset at Tarlia? Still angry that I know Marlak? Annoyed for some other reason? "And you know what? The keep is safe. I'll find another room."

He crosses his arms and stands in front of the door. "No."

"So you think you can give me orders?"

"No. But I can stop you."

This is all wrong and I'm too tired to argue. I sigh. "Can you explain what you want to know? And if there's something I did to upset you, tell me what it is?"

He blinks and his expression softens. "You didn't do anything wrong, and I'm not upset at you."

"That's not what it looks like."

He takes a slow, deep breath, then swallows. "Since when have you known... about our bond?"

Do I even have an answer for that? Was it when I sensed his lack of magic? When he appeared in the soulsucker's vision? Or was it even earlier, when I saw him for the first time? My heart feels strange in my chest.

"What difference does it make?"

He looks away. "None. No difference at all." He frowns, then looks back at me. "But you do know what we are, don't you?"

I can't have a serious conversation right now, so I chuckle. "Two exhausted fae who just survived the impossible."

"True." The corners of his lips lift as if about to smile, but then his face hardens at once. "But it will only get more and more dangerous. And I don't know if luck will save you next time."

I lift a shoulder in a half-shrug. "If luck were certain, it wouldn't be luck."

"You don't care. Don't care about anything that happened today."

"What do you want me to do? Sit and cry? Actually, sitting is a wonderful idea." I take a chair by the table.

He sits across from me and places a lightstone between us that casts an eerie glow on his beautiful face.

"Lidiane, I want you to listen to me." At least his tone is soft now, with none of that previous anger. "When the sun rises tomorrow, I want you to leave this place and walk to the Charmed River. I have no doubt that you're more than capable of surviving the Shadow Lands during the day, and I think you'll do fine once you're in Fae Territories. Go. Don't come back. This mess... isn't for you."

I know what he's saying. *Escape. Disappear.* His suggestion makes sense, but it feels like a splinter digging into my heart, even if my mind still can't comprehend why. I don't want to push that splinter, cause unbearable pain, don't want a serious conversation, and smirk. "Are you planning on taking residence here or something?"

He glares at me, his blue eyes reflecting the lightstone. "Obviously not."

"Then you're *also* going to cross the river. While I agree with you that I can fare well in the Shadow Lands during the day, I'm not so sure about you and your master, no offense. We can part ways *afterwards*, since you can't wait to get rid of me."

Azur gets up all of a sudden and kicks the chair. "I want you gone. Gone."

"Funny. You were telling a completely different story this morning."

"I was an idiot! A reckless, mindless idiot. I should never, ever, have brought you to the Jewel City to rescue those fae. I made a mistake. Now I'm looking into fixing my folly."

"*Why* did you ask me to come with you?"

He crouches and puts the chair back in its right position. "You know why." His voice is quiet.

"No. Was it because you sensed the bond? And yet now you're pushing me away, and it seems you abhor that bond, so no, that doesn't explain it."

He sits again and places his hands on the table, his fingers interlaced. "I thought... A soulmate bond is supposed to be good, right? It's a great omen and great luck to find your soulmate. And I knew it. The moment I saw you, I knew it. And I thought..."

He presses a lock of his hair between his fingers. "I look back and don't even understand what I was thinking. It was as if you were a key to open *my* shackles. That was completely selfish, but at that moment, I saw you as a sign, a gift. I was thinking of what you could bring to me, wondering what would happen once you also felt the bond. I wondered what it would be like to kiss you, to hold you in my arms, to look at you and see the same feeling reflected in you. I imagined all that. Foolish, foolish dreams, as if I wasn't a guardian, as if my life wasn't bound."

He closes his eyes, and when he opens them, they're brilliant with unshed tears. "I can say sorry a thousand times, a million times, and it won't fix my foolishness. I let myself dream for a moment, let myself imagine a different life, a happy future. And then Renel asked me to save those fae. An easy task. And yet..." He snorts. "Some women like flowers, some women like a nice walk together, some like a delectable dinner. And yet I knew in my heart that what you would like most would be to do something meaningful, to make a difference for the fae who can't do anything for themselves. I could feel it."

As if he could look into my soul, and yet something in it still feels wrong. "Except for the part where you were actually working for the person oppressing those fae."

He leans forward. "*Bound* guardian, Lidiane. I can't help it."

"You could have been honest."

He looks at me, then looks away. "But I chose to be foolish."

I consider our mission this morning. Odd that the truth only hits me now. "You didn't need me at all, did you? You could have transcended straight into their cell, then taken them from there. Bringing me was nothing but a sham."

"Yes. And no. I wasn't sure if there were any magical wards in the prison area, and if I could transcend there. Using glamours was a good strategy not only to gain access to the Inquiry House, but also to cause some confusion as to who actually released the prisoners. It felt like a good idea, and if Zorwal hadn't shown up, they would have taken a long time to notice what happened, and I could have secured a boat for the fugitives at a port. Easy. Of course, I didn't predict any tribulation. First, Zorwal, then whatever happened with the Sea Court. I don't want to know what you are, even if I'm here thinking you're a bastard princess or something."

"I'm no princess, Azur."

He looks at his hands, his eyes so sad. "It's best if I don't know."

All my anger at him evaporates like water on dry soil, and I feel like explaining some of my truth to him. "There is nothing to know. My father was from the Sea Court, but my mother wasn't. I don't know who he was or what he did to piss off the king so much, but I assume it was bad. In a way, I don't know my story either. They killed my mother when I was just a baby, and would have killed me too, except that I was well hidden in the Crystal Court, living with the lower fae. Well, I *am* lower fae there."

He rolls his eyes. "*Lower* is such a ridiculous word."

"It doesn't bother me. I'd be more ashamed of being a

Crystal Court high fae, considering what most of them do. No offense."

"I'm not high fae."

"But you look like one, live like one. The fact that you may have some distant ancestor—"

"It wasn't my choice. My parents were from the south-western coast, near Clare Beach. Do you know what the original fae from that area look like?"

"I'm not sure."

He draws imaginary circles on the table with his finger. "Some of us have colored skins; blue, purple, while others have the regular high fae and human shades from beige to brown. We also have small, pointy black horns." He looks at me.

"But you don't."

"They cut them." The casual, detached tone he uses barely disguises the buried pain seeping through.

My hands cover my mouth as if they could contain my horror. "I'm sorry."

He looks down and shrugs. "No need. I suppose they did a good job. My hair even grows where the horns used to be." He snorts. "I'm so lucky I have no stumps."

I understand now why he wears a hat whenever he can. It's just... "Wouldn't it have dulled your senses? Or your magic?"

"At the time, my magic suffered, yes. But then, slowly, it came back. The worst was the pain, and then looking at myself in the mirror."

"I'm sorry."

"I don't want your pity."

"It's not—"

"I don't want anything from you, in fact." His tone is harsh again, as if he just remembered he absolutely needs to be a prick to me. "I just want you to leave when the sun rises."

I roll my eyes. "We're all going south. There's no need for me to escape like a fugitive. We can split after we cross the river and you're on your way to... wherever you're going."

"No. I want you gone, gone before I do anything foolish." He puts a hand on his chest. "For now, all I feel is the pull, the bond. You feel that as well, I think. But there's nothing more. No friendship, no loving moments together, no memories."

"Surviving what we did together is kind of hard to forget."

"Fair. There will be *some* memories, but there's no love in them, and there will be nothing more. A soulmate is a *potential* for something, a seed. We can choose never to plant it. The bond is still weak. The only way to solidify it is by doing something we can choose never to do. Leave while you can, escape. In fact, I don't know why you didn't escape at the castle when I told you so."

"A guard summoned me."

"So let's not take any chances anymore. Go south right after the sun rises."

I think about Zorwal, about the dangers Azur's about to face, and taste something bitter. And there's another problem. "I won't leave Tar."

"Take her with you. Go to her room and call her. I doubt Renel will suspect she's about to escape. Go."

Go, go, go. As if I was an unwanted dog. "I already understood that you want to get rid of me. No need to keep repeating yourself."

Azur nods. "Great. Now, if by any chance, I find that you're still here in the morning, I'll tell Renel that your friend is an impostor. I don't think it will go well for her."

"So you're threatening me now."

"I'm glad I'm being clear."

I get up and walk to the door. "Don't worry. I'll be gone tomorrow. And you won't see me anymore tonight. Or ever, I suppose."

Azur pulls me back, preventing me from touching the door handle, his chest touching my back. "You'll sleep here."

"You have no right to give me orders."

"Does this make you hate me?" he whispers in my ear, his arms clasped tight around me.

His voice is a spark that lights a fire in me and raises goosebumps on my skin. Suddenly, I don't want those arms to let me go; I want them to squeeze me tight, want more whispers, want him to explore my skin with his hands.

I grit my teeth and force myself to forget the horrifying images that just came to me. "It has a different effect, Azur, one that I thought you wanted to avoid."

He turns me around to face him and holds my hands. "Stay," he pleads. "Just in case. Please. If there's something in this keep… I won't sleep not knowing if you're safe."

"Get used to it. That's going to be the rest of our lives."

"But you won't be in a building in the Shadow Lands. That's the difference. Stay with me. Just tonight. I'm strong; I can resist the pull."

"You, you, you. It's all about you. It's what *you* feel, what *you* want, what *you* fear. I'm still not a person to you." And I can't believe I'm bonded to this idiot.

He lets go of my hand. "Then hate me, hate my selfishness. There's only ruin ahead of me. The days of the Crystal Court are counted, and when it collapses, I'll be among the first to burn with it. I'll have a short life, perhaps even shorter if my magic doesn't return. I don't want you entangled in any of that."

"Then let's be rational. The Shadow Lands are not too dangerous during the day, but we could still benefit from reaching the Charmed River together. We can all leave right after sunrise. Once we're in Fae Territories, we part ways."

"I want a promise."

"No," I say. "I don't owe you anything. You may have saved my life on that boat, but you were the one who put it in danger, so it doesn't count. Also, you know what? I dare you to tell Renel about Tar and not implicate yourself. Finally, this bond of ours, it's a curse, it's destiny mocking us, that's the only explanation. And I *will* find another room for me."

"Don't go, please." He pulls me before I turn and wraps his arms around me, so that we're facing each other. "Let me feel that you're close—just once. I know it's all about me, a selfish wish."

"If you liked me just a little, you'd wonder what *I* wanted."

"What do you want?"

To be left alone. The words won't leave my lips, though. I can't utter such a lie.

The horrifying truth is that I want Azur. Stupid bond.

I would rather face insurmountable obstacles with him, even if he's an idiot, than run away and live a safe but empty, uneventful life. Except that he doesn't feel the same.

I say, "If there's no future for us, I'd rather split sooner rather than later. I'd rather have nothing than a taste of something that will never happen. Believe it or not, I have a heart too. I have feelings, and the bond messes with them. I'll sleep in the room next to this one. If something happens, I'll scream really loud, so please don't worry. Tomorrow we'll cross the Charmed River then part ways forever."

"Not forever. We'll still find each other in this life or the next."

"I won't be sitting around waiting. And if we ever meet again, I doubt it will be during some idyllic dream. There will always be challenges, always uncertainties, so there will *never* be a future for us. We'll be condemned to roam apart. Forever. You know, people love and persevere together, despite all odds. When they love. But you're right that there's no love here, just a pointless, useless bond."

His jaw clenches but he stares at me, speechless, and finally unwraps his arms. I feel cold without his touch. Strange.

Part of me is glad he's finally letting me go, part of me wishes he had insisted, wishes... Why are wishes so foolish? I turn around, walk away, and find the next room. This one has only one bed and doesn't even have sheets, but I said I'd sleep in the room next to his, so I have to keep my word.

I want to scream. I'm so frustrated. I want to cry. And none of it makes any sense. I don't even know him.

My brother would be horrified if he heard about me and Azur. Marlak would probably think he had enchanted me or something.

In a way, this is for the best. My family matters more than this one random person whose feelings are like mine, whose magic I can feel, who knows what kind of things I like...

I sigh.

A fae who serves Renel. Not truly his choice, but still.

Parting ways might be for the best. But why does it have to hurt so much?

ZIVEN

As I wait for Marlak, my anxiety grows. Too many things could have gone wrong, and I even wonder if I should have insisted that he wait here with me—as if he wasn't more stubborn than a rock. Still, I regret letting him descend to that lake. Astra will never forgive me if something happens to her husband. I have to believe nothing happened, though. Marlak's quite powerful. Even knowing that, my heart won't rest.

The air is getting chilly, and I open the bag to get a coat. As I'm pulling it, I hear steps and look up. It's Marlak, finally. I would be relieved—except that he's looking more furious than ever.

"All right," he says. "What can I offer you to open that bridge now?"

"Nothing. We'll die if we walk there tonight. I don't know how I know it, but I do. I want to live after this, even if it's for a pointless, aimless life, with nowhere to go. I still want to survive. I want you to survive too. For Astra. A few hours, Marlak. You have way more magic than me, meaning that you must also know that you shouldn't go there now. You can feel the wrongness of the place."

"My sister's there."

"If she survived this far, she can survive a few more hours. You know I'm right, Marlak. You have to know."

"When you ask me for a favor, I'll remember your refusal." His tone would be terrifying if I weren't more terrified of this place.

"That's my hope. That we'll both come out of this alive to ask and refuse favors, and maybe be assholes to each other."

He huffs. "I'm friendly. Patient. You're the one who's not helping."

"I know." I don't even roll my eyes. *I'm* the patient one here, but I don't want to brag. "Let's find a place to set camp."

Marlak glares at me as if it would somehow make me change my mind. After a few seconds, he nods. "Fine."

We walk back to where we came from, to a flat area by a slope, so that it's protected from some of the wind. It's also far from any carcass.

I look at the ground, searching for twigs, but there aren't many. "Can you set the tent?" I ask. "I'll find some wood."

"Wood for what?" he spits.

"Why do people who camp gather wood, Marlak?" I turn, thinking of going back to where there were some trees, then feel his hand grabbing my arm and pulling me back. "What?" I ask.

"No fire. No fire." His eyes are wide and almost wild. "It will attract all kinds of dangerous things. Do you want a beacon for the bird eater?"

"Fire scares dangerous beasts." I can't believe I have to explain this basic fact to him.

"It does not. It's a beacon for great horrors. No fire." He's so absurd.

"Great. Then we shall be eaten in our sleep."

"We can keep watch. Or use magic." He's finally saying something decent.

"That might be an idea. We could create a thick ice layer over the tent, like a shield. That way, we won't be noticed or attacked. Can we at least light a lightstone, though? Or we'll be in pitch black."

"Why would I have a problem with a lightstone?"

Perhaps because he thinks fire is some great danger? I just shrug. "No idea."

He pulls a tent and opens it on the ground. It's a rough leather thing with a flexible pole to hold the top. Quite small. I'm almost suggesting I can sleep elsewhere, but then I remember that horrific tower, this bird-killing monster or whatever, and then the ice golems, and decide it's better to sleep with Marlak, and enter the tent.

In one second, we're immersed in darkness, surrounded by a thick layer of ice, then he lights the stone.

"Let's sleep, since you're so afraid of the dark."

"I'm prudent."

He shrugs. "Makes sense. With such weak magic, you definitely need to be careful."

While I understand he's worried about his sister, it's getting too much. I can also make fun of him. "Impressive, right? You and your powerful magic couldn't even see the island."

"That's not magic. That's a silly rule because you're a king's son. Doesn't count."

I smile. "And yet I was right; you need me."

"Only to get me to the tower, no more."

"*Only*. If I were half the jackass you are, I'd be making you beg me to get you to that tower, and I'm not. I'm here out of my own free will."

"Here in the *tent*. Waiting until sunrise. And I'm absolutely not a jackass. If it was anyone else in my place, they'd have encased you in ice."

"Technically, we *are* encased in ice." I chuckle. "And you encased me and Astra, when you didn't even know her. Then you locked her hands and feet in ice. Is that how you flirt? Kidnap women, then hold them with ice?"

Marlak smirks. "Let's agree it works. Don't despair, human prince, you also have water magic, and can encase your own special lady one day."

I huff. "Not interested."

Marlak lifts a shoulder. "Your special guy, then."

"Even less interested."

He stares at me. "Nobody special, then? Astra's friend, maybe?"

"Tarlia's a good friend, that's it. You know, some people are perfectly capable of having *friendships* with the gender they're attracted to. I'm not sure you understand the concept."

"That's not true. I have a female friend."

"Then why were you thinking me and Astra…"

"I would never think that. She has me, half-roasted and scarred, right? Why would she want a perfect prince?" He sighs. "I'm just kidding. I trust her, and I know that what we have goes deeper than looks."

I nod. I could tell him he's good-looking, but we're alone in a tent and I feel that would be weird. "You did overhear her that day."

"I didn't trust her at the time. In retrospect, it wasn't one of my brightest moments."

Funny that just mentioning Astra improves his mood—except when he's worried about her. I can perhaps understand what they see in each other, even understand how their love makes them better people.

"I'm glad you trust Astra now. She has a good heart, and it seems you make her happy."

"And you? Nobody, really?"

I find it weird to discuss my love life with the grumpiness expert, but at the same time, at least he's not teasing me now. "I thought Tarlia, maybe. But it's strange. She's pretty, smart, kind. I like her, I truly do. And yet I feel nothing. Nothing romantic, at least. I think she feels differently about me, and I fear losing a friend."

"If she's your friend, she'll understand."

"That's what I hope." I still recall our kiss, her anger, her words, our goodbye. I'm not sure I can tell her she's special and yet not *that* special, and how to do it without hurting her.

"So tomorrow you'll get me to that tower, right?"

"Yes. During the day. It's safer."

I see his chest rise and fall. "One more night without my sister."

"I'm sorry. For all that happened to you. But I'll help you rescue her. That's a promise."

"Thank you."

He sounds earnest. Perhaps the exhaustion of the trip took some of his edge, and then perhaps he feels what I feel, senses the eerie magic in that lake, and knows it's not going to be that simple. He may realize that waiting until daylight is the best course of action.

Of course, I can't fault him for being worried about his sister. I can't imagine what horrors she's facing right now, what horrors she has faced for twelve years.

Tomorrow we'll see. I hope we come out alive.

25

TARLIA

Renel stares at me in silence, his entire body stiff. I wonder if I can take back my words, pretend it was a joke, but I don't think he'll believe me.

"Not Astra." His chuckle is maniac and bitter at the same time. He raises a shaky hand and points at me. "You know what's the worst? The very worst? I knew it. It was this morning, wasn't it? That you switched. You were different. I knew it. Why? Are you here to *mock me*? Some prank sent by my brother?"

"I got to the castle last night. Marlak didn't send me there. I only found out he escaped when you told me."

He shuts his eyes as he takes a deep breath, then looks at me, his face raw with pain.

"Astra was my only hope. My *last* hope. Not for me, for my kingdom. For an entire city. You know what's going to happen? Three more moves, and the castle will end up in the Fiery Gorge. That will create a fissure that will split the land in two. It will destroy the Jewel City, kill almost everyone there. Why did you do this? Why?"

He's not angry; he's desperate. I'm feeling almost... regretful. Ashamed. But I don't think I did anything wrong.

"I thought Astra was in danger."

"Let me guess; you thought I would cut her hands and send them to my brother." He glares at me like someone capable of doing exactly that.

I don't know what to say, and I suppose he assumes that's an answer.

He snorts. "Right. That sounds like something Marlak would say. What else did he tell you? That I bathe in the blood of the lower fae?"

"I never had a conversation with him."

Renel rolls his eyes. "Your excuse is absurd. If I were capable of torturing Astra to pressure my brother, what do you think I would do to an *impostor*?"

I swallow. "I... thought I could escape if things got dangerous. Perhaps thought you wouldn't figure it out."

"Who sent you?" I'm sure his voice makes the walls tremble. "Give me the truth, or you'll find out what I'm capable of."

I don't want to implicate Lidiane or her friends, so I pretend to hesitate, then say, "A fae called Stromplax." Renel grimaces, and I think I might have exaggerated the weirdness of the name. Too late now. "He knows Marlak and was worried about Astra, then found me. I was in the fae territories doing some work for Krastel, pretending to be the princess. This fae found me, told me Astra had been kidnapped, suggested the switch, and I thought it was a good idea. Astra escaped."

"You stayed in the castle to spy on me, didn't you?" His glare is murderous and his voice is a terrifying hiss.

"What difference does it make?" I keep my voice level. "Astra herself could have spied on you. You knew the risk in capturing your brother's wife."

Renel gets up and wiggles a finger. "No. Oh, no. I was approached by her master, who told me she had been *kidnapped* by my brother—against her will. He begged me to rescue her.

That's what I was told. And then I learned she was Tiurian, and thought destiny was finally gracing me with luck. I didn't set out to capture or steal anyone's wife. She came *willingly*, or at least pretended to do so, and Marlak claimed over and over that he didn't care for her."

"And you believed it?"

His eyes narrow so much that they become slits. "You think I'm an idiot, right? That's the joke."

I'm so exhausted that I decide to be honest. "I just wanted to save Astra. She's my friend. A sister, almost. And if I could get some information, that would be good too. I can't go back to the Krastel castle. The truth is that they attacked my carriage on my way back, but I fought and escaped. But they attacked me. I have nothing to return to."

"I'm sorry for that." Much of his fury is gone, and he tilts his head and stares at me. "Why did you decide to tell me the truth?"

"I was tired." That's the truth, actually, or at least part of it. "Tired of being the substitute's substitute. That's what we do. We were raised to replace Princess Driziely, for safety, so we were substitutes, both me and Astra. And that's what I was doing; pretending to be someone else. I'm tired of being nobody. Not that I'm anybody. I know that. And I'm useless to you, and maybe I wanted to hear it said to my face." Yes, because then if I kill, him I'll have no regrets.

"You saved my life, *Tarlia*." The mocking tone he uses for my name makes me feel even smaller and more insignificant than I already am. "That's the *only* reason I won't put you in one of the cells downstairs to sleep on your own. You shouldn't have played with me. There are bigger wheels at work. Bigger needs. Many lives in danger." His tone has such a desperate edge that it makes me believe him more than the fact that fae can't lie.

I sigh. "What is it you need from Astra? Because if it is something important, something that could save lives, you could ask her."

He shakes his head. "If she's in love with Marlak, she'll think I'm a monster. She won't do anything for me."

"*I* could explain it."

He sits on the bed and rests his face on his hands. "A Tiurian can give magic to someone they love. She'll obviously never love me. And yet she can give magic to my brother, my brother, who has more magic than anyone can dream of."

"Is there another solution? To your problem?"

"Yes." His voice is laced with bitterness and sarcasm. "I can get a unicorn's horn. Do you think it's even possible? And do you think I'd hurt Cherry Cake?"

"So that's why Azur shouted? He thought you'd try to get his horn?"

Renel snorts. "Azur's an idiot sometimes." His eyes are misty with tears. "The only person I trust, though."

"It must be nice to have somebody bound to you."

"I didn't bind him." His tone shifts to anger, and I can't even explain that I didn't mean it like that because he keeps talking. "It wasn't my choice. I was a kid too, and heard that a powerful fae boy wanted to be my guardian. Who wouldn't be thrilled? I had no magic, Tarlia. You have no idea what it's like to grow up like me, powerless, vulnerable, when everyone around you has magic, when your family happens to have an insane amount of it. When I heard I'd get a guardian, I was ecstatic. Who wouldn't be? I'd have someone to protect me. I didn't know it would tie his life to mine. I didn't know that."

"I'm sorry."

"It was my stepfather's fault. He's dead and I still hate him, still hate him to this day. Sometimes I'm filled with so much hate that I think I'm going to explode, and yet I have to get up and take care of the kingdom, get up and hold meetings with the most despicable fae in this court. Every day. No respite for me. No running away. That castle is a shackle, that throne is a shackle."

I don't want to provoke him, but what he's saying makes no

sense. "You do know there's someone else interested in your position, right?"

"Marlak thinks I'm a monster. The moment he becomes king, he'll put me in a prison—or worse."

"Didn't you just do that to him?"

"And yet he escaped. Am I hunting him down? No. I let him live his life in peace. Does he let me live mine? Oh, no."

"What has he done to you?"

"He wants to depose me."

"I barely know him, and I'm not from your court, or even fae, so I have no stake in any of that, but my understanding is that he believes he should be king, and some fae agree with him."

Renel snorts. "The problem is that he would kill me if he could. Oh, he would. That's the issue number one. The second problem is that he wouldn't know how to maintain the peace in the Crystal Court, wouldn't know how to manage the powerful families. Zorwal has always told me—"

"Wait. You mean the creepy man Azur beheaded and might or might not still be alive? The reason we're here?"

"I have no affection for him, but he gave me good advice, made sure I kept the court united. There has been peace for years, thanks to me."

I'm having trouble digesting what he just told me. "No, no. Hang on. You're telling me that you get advice on how to *run the court* from the sinister man who almost killed Lidiane?"

"His advice is wise, despite everything."

Oh, wow.

I don't need any effort to understand why Lidiane, Nelsin, and Ferer hate Renel and why he must be a disgraceful king. I guess he deserves to be murdered in his sleep after all.

I nod. "Well, help is help, I suppose." What am I going to say?

"I understand your disapproval, but the thing is, if you are going to govern a snake nest, you need to understand the snakes.

You can't act like a helpless little mouse. And I won't give Marlak the throne. I won't. He always had everything. And you know who appointed him heir? My stepfather, the same filthy fae who condemned Azur to be bound to me for life. You're complaining that I get advice from Zorwal, but you want to support a decision made by *my despicable stepfather.* Does that make any sense?"

"I don't know." I think back to what he said about an entire city being destroyed. "What are you going to do now? About the castle? The city? Is there another solution?" Perhaps I need to know if he has to remain alive.

He pinches the bridge of his nose. "It wasn't for lack of trying. I researched everything. Read all the books I could. I'm the castle master and need magic to steer it, but I don't have it."

"What if you named someone else as the master?" I know he dreads the idea, but if it's the only solution, he should cast his pride aside.

"The castle can take five, ten, fifteen years to adapt to a new master. Meanwhile, it will keep moving out of its own will. I don't have that time."

"I'm sorry." These are pointless words that don't change anything, but I don't know what to say. "If it's any consolation, even if I hadn't replaced Astra, your plan would still not work. She loves Marlak."

He chuckles. "Incredible consolation."

"I mean it's not my fault."

"It's your fault you're here mocking me, pretending I don't know the difference between two very different women."

I have to laugh. "I look like her! And I had glamour."

"Glamour." He sneers. "No, don't tell me. Lidiane is your accomplice, isn't she?"

I can't compromise her, so I lie. "Not her. Another fae did it."

He glares at me. "Tarlia, just because you're human and can say any crap you want, it doesn't mean I'm going to believe it. It's obvious that it's Lidiane."

I had given up on killing him, but I might have a good reason now. "What are you going to do to her?"

"What do you think I can do? She's Azur's soulmate. Can't you see it?"

"Of course not. I have no idea what I'm supposed to see. How do *you* know?"

"She sensed his lack of magic."

"She also sensed the wards. Is the keep her soulmate?"

He shrugs. "You look at them and you know it."

I suppose we're back to *you'll know it when you know*. But it also means maybe there's hope for her. "Are you planning on punishing her?"

Renel closes his eyes. "*Tar*, let me make one thing very clear: whatever horrific stories you heard about me, they're not true. I wouldn't dream of hurting the woman Azur loves. He's like a brother to me. *More* than a brother. I'll talk to them and we'll find a solution."

I exhale. "What are you going to do about the castle?"

"I'll have to give evacuation orders to the entire area of the fissure. Everyone will hate me. I guess I'll be deposed after all. Perhaps murdered. Who knows?"

"What if you don't return? Can't other people give those orders?"

He shakes his head. "Nobody believes me. Nobody. Not even Azur, in fact. But I know I'm right. I've predicted the trajectory of the castle for the last three years."

"Why won't they believe you, then?"

"I don't know. Zorwal underestimates me, I suppose. Azur... he says there might be something I'm missing. He doesn't believe a castle would self-destruct. I think he sees the castle like a person, and thinks that nobody could ever self-destruct, or choose death, but it's not true. I myself, often considered... often wanted..."

He pauses.

"To die?" I'm not shocked or horrified. I understand him.

He looks away, looks down, then takes a deep breath. "Yes. But then my brother wins, my stepfather wins, everyone who thought I was a worthless burden wins. And Azur dies. So here I am. Very much alive, as you can see." His honesty surprises me, and perhaps the way his words resonate with me. "To be fair, even before Azur came into my life, I decided I didn't want to die—just because I wanted to spite them all."

"I know what it's like to cling to anger. They say it's poison, but sometimes it's a tonic. Keeps you going."

There's relief in his chuckle, and we stare at each other in silence for a moment. A moment of understanding. I can imagine this boy without magic clinging to anger, hoping to spite everyone who wronged him, and I respect that.

"Who do *you* hate?" he asks.

"My master, Otavio. The one who trained me and Astra, prepared us to be substitutes. The person who practically raised me. Every single day of my life, for the last ten years, I've been dreaming about killing him."

"He doesn't look hard to kill."

"No. The thing is that killing him is easy, but surviving the deed is hard. I may not love my life, but I still wouldn't want to waste it for him. I want to outlive him, kill him, and still come out of it alive. Come out of it... somehow... victorious. Dying after killing him doesn't sound fair, when he took everything from me."

"What did he take?" He looks at me like he truly wants to know the answer, which is rare. So many people talk over each other, or just ask questions to keep the conversation going, and he's here, interested in my past.

I don't know if I want to stick a knife into those memories and feel that pain again, don't know if I want to become vulnerable, and yet the words flow.

"I was just a little girl. They think children have no memory, but we do. I saw him visiting my house, then leaving. At night, someone came and killed my family. I watched them, and yet I ran away, like a coward." Coward, coward, coward. "The guilt still gnaws at me. Otavio found me running and took me to the castle. I was only five and thought it was curious. Little as I was, I felt there was something odd about it. Only years later, the sequence of events made sense. He wanted another substitute, and I happened to look like the princess—or like Astra, I'm not sure. He killed my family, then took me to the castle as if to *protect* me. The worst is that I had to grow up under his protection. I was an orphan, a child. What was I going to do? Where was I going to go? I *still* have nowhere to go. I walked away from the prison where I was raised, and yet without means, without a family, I haven't found any freedom."

And won't collect any prize, since I obviously can't kill Renel. I can't. I was deceiving myself thinking I could murder anyone.

"If Astra's your friend, she'll help you, won't she?"

"How much? Until how long? She's married to a fugitive, and has to worry about her own neck. What can she do for me?"

He runs a finger over his bracelets, then looks at me. "Is that why you replaced Astra? You were trying to gain some favor with some rebels or something? Find out some big secret, then sell it?" His guess is close.

"I wasn't sure. I just wanted to do something. Otavio always said that people will keep you alive as long as you're useful to them."

"Otavio." He snorts. "The one you want to murder. So you follow his advice?"

I hope he's not implying my situation is similar to *his*. "No. Almost everything he says is imbecilic. It doesn't mean that a drop of wisdom can't fall out of his mouth from time to time. But most of it is nonsense. I don't even understand what his plan is."

"It sounded like he wanted to protect another Tiurian."

I shake my head. "People don't kill families just to protect someone. I'm not even thinking about the morals of it, but the logistics. It's too complicated, risky, laborious. Everything he's done with the substitutes in Krastel is too complex. Nobody puts that much time and effort into a plan if they don't hope to get something out of it."

True that I know *part* of his plan; he wants Astra to marry

Renel or at least seduce him. But that still doesn't explain his end goal.

"If Astra's gone, then his plan will flop. It should give you some satisfaction."

"A lot. Deceiving him is quite satisfying."

Renel nods.

I wonder if he's assuming I enjoyed tricking him too, and say, "I took no pleasure in deceiving *you*. And I didn't even deceive you that much, considering I was too busy trying to survive. I even forgot to act like Astra."

He has an amused smile. "What would she act like?"

"Hopeful, sweet—not sarcastic and bitter."

"I don't think you're bitter."

I laugh. "I'm sweet?"

"You're practical."

"I'll take it as a compliment."

He pauses, then sighs. "I appreciate your honesty. I exploded just now, but it has nothing to do with you. It's not your fault that some strange magic controls the castle, or that I can't steer it. I suppose you were just helping your friend, and Marlak, to a certain extent, but I can't fault you for that. Anyone in your place would keep the charade, would perhaps use it to try to gain some advantage, perhaps even try to seduce me. You did none of that."

I chuckle. "So I wasn't seductive?"

"You know you weren't."

"Ouch." I laugh. "Straight to the heart. What about you? If you needed Astra to fall in love with you, shouldn't you try to... romance her? Me?"

He stares at his hands, then looks at me and smirks. "It sounds vile, right? Of course it does. Despicable, perhaps. I wouldn't trick her. Not too much, at least. I'd just try to get some magic, and then I'd explain everything. That was my plan."

"But you didn't try."

He blinks. "I... did? I was terrible, I know. I tried to tell you jokes."

"Oh." I can't believe he thought that was in any way seductive. "Is that how fae flirt?"

His laugh is warm and relaxed. "No. I don't know how anyone flirts. How am I supposed to know? When I went to revels, women tugged at my clothes, and if I liked them enough, I took them to a corner and let them take it all off. I don't think that counts as flirting."

"I suppose not." He's too good-looking. Of course he needs no effort. "I had *classes* on seduction."

"Really? I would *never* have guessed."

I laugh again. "I wasn't trying. You were all weird in the only time we had alone, with the berries, and then... I mean, how do you try to seduce someone and run through a dangerous landscape at the same time? It doesn't work. And if I were to try to seduce you the way I learned, it would take weeks. I don't know if I could do it. There's a lot of manipulation involved in it."

"How do you flirt? When you're interested in someone?"

Ziven comes to mind. "I suppose when it matters, I don't know what to do."

"There's someone who matters, then?"

"Maybe. You? Anyone special?"

"I think people need someone to pull them out of their pits of pain, make them forget their agony, but I cling to it like a lifeline. I don't think I can love, even if I could be kind to someone in love with me. I would try not to hurt Astra, if by any chance she ever... But now that I think about it, even if she hadn't escaped, even if she wasn't in love with my brother, I'm too deep in my own agony, in my own anger. I can't pull anyone up, rescue them from their misery. I would never have seduced her, and the reality is that I had a witless plan from the start. That's what desperation does to you."

"Desperation can do worse than addling your minds." I

think about my stupid plan to kill him, my willingness to do something despicable just for money.

He looks at me. "And you're desperate."

It's as if he's reading my mind, and the thought fills me with shame. "No. I... I'm confused, maybe. Lost, perhaps. Certainly lost."

"Like a leaf in the wind? Will go where it takes you?"

"No. I want to take charge of my life. I just..." I can't finish the sentence and sound even more pathetic. The truth is that I don't know what to do and I *am* lost.

He strokes his chin, his expression thoughtful. When he stops and looks away like that, when I can look at him without his accusing or astute eyes peering into me, I'm stunned by his beauty. Of course, he's fae.

He turns to me. "I *have* a solution to your desperation. You could live in the castle, be my human guest. As yourself, not Astra. I'll figure out a way to get rid of your master. And you can live there."

It has to be some kind of trick. "After I deceived you?"

Renel smirks. "I'm not being nice, Tarlia. I'm being strategic. If you have somewhere to go, you'll have no need to deceive me, sell my secrets, perhaps even kill me."

"Kill?" My mouth makes a bizarre noise that barely sounds like laughter. "I saw you fighting with your sword earlier. Killing you would never be possible."

"There are thousands of ways to kill someone, and most of them don't involve sword fighting. Now, I can make a vow, a promise. It can't be broken. I can't make a deal with you or give you employment because of the treaty, but you can stay as a guest, and do whatever you want, except betray or murder me. You get along with Lidiane. No need to worry anymore."

Why is his offer squeezing my chest? Can everything be that easy? Can I be saved like that? And then, it makes me want to crawl into a hole to hide away from my shame.

Before I say anything, he grimaces. "I mean, until the castle falls into the Fiery Gorge. I suppose I do *not* have any solution for you, other than even more desperation."

My shoulders sag. Of course nothing can be that easy.

Still, I smile. "Look at the bright side; I don't think I've discovered any scandalous secret about you. The issue with the castle will soon be public knowledge. No need to fear any betrayal."

"No." His eyes are unfocused, distant. "And yet all that lies ahead of us is uncertainty. Still, for now, you're welcome to remain in the castle—if you want. You can tell me tomorrow what you decide." He gets up. "I'll let you rest now."

I watch as he climbs the ladder to the bed above me. I know that his offer might not last long, and yet it felt sincere. He wants to help me, asking absolutely nothing in return. The thought warms my heart, the idea that someone can do good just for the sake of it, with no ulterior motives.

He claimed it was so that I didn't betray him, but he could put me in a cell. That would be much easier—and much safer.

"Renel," I say.

"Yes?"

"I really appreciate that you don't even want to have sex with me."

"You *appreciate* that?" He sounds puzzled, even perhaps offended for some reason.

"It's refreshing. If any other man were offering me a place to stay, it would be because they'd want to fuck me. Sorry for the word. I'm tired and I'm crude."

"You're practical." His voice is quiet, coming through the mattress above me. He's silent for a moment, then asks, "Would you be upset if I did?"

"Did what?"

"You're beautiful and quite brave. Of course I'd have sex with you—but only if you wanted it, and since it's not the case, it's not the case."

Oh. He *would* have sex with me. The image then crosses my

mind; his chest against mine, the feel of his hard cock inside me, his hands caressing my skin. Those hands.

I recall him fighting those ghouls, recall his skill and speed with that sword. I think about the sweat dripping down his face. I didn't even know fae could sweat, but he looked majestic doing it. I imagine him sweating above me, looking at me with desire in those beautiful eyes. I wouldn't mind having sex with him either, and now that I planted the image in my mind, I might even crave it.

Ziven comes to mind. Ugh. Why does Ziven have to show up in my thoughts *now*? Ziven, who rejected me. Ziven, who asked me to return to him—but made no promises. I could have died today. Who knows if I'll be alive tomorrow?

"Are you tired?" I ask.

"I'm feeling better. We don't tire as much as you."

"Is it true that fae love fiercely, be it for a night or a lifetime?"

He's silent for a moment, then says, "Yes."

"I'd like to try it—if you're not too tired."

He jumps from his bed and sits by me. "There's no need for that. Unless you're saying the truth."

"But I want it. And I realize this is sudden, perhaps too straightforward, and not at all seductive, but I don't want to be seductive. I don't even want to be sexy. I almost died. I'm tired. My body hurts. And if your body hurts too much, we can leave it for another time, or for never, but if not... This is perfect. We don't feel anything for each other, nor will we start getting clingy, jealous, or emotional. It's freeing, you know? To simply have sex, without any expectations. I suppose fae do that, but humans don't. When humans do, the man acts as if he's using the woman, taking something from her. I *have* been in that position, knowing well that the man saw me as a *thing* being used for his pleasure, knowing well that the morning after, he'd call me names and laugh behind my back. And yet when that gloomy darkness came over me, I just wanted a cock inside me to appease my anger, to make me forget my family, my past, the life I never had. Not that I want to forget anything now. The day was too hard for unwanted thoughts to get hold of my mind— for any thoughts, in fact. I just want to experience you. Tomorrow you won't laugh at me, and none of this will bother us or change anything. And I suppose I talk too much."

He chuckles and shakes his head. "Can anyone ever talk too much? When we voice so few of the infinite thoughts that cross our minds? How many people dare to speak their minds? And yet you do. Fearlessly."

The fervor in his eyes makes him look even more stunning than he already is.

There's none of the tense king I saw this morning, none of the anxious fae who spoke to me just now. All I see is confidence and grace, like when he fought out there, when he didn't hesitate even for a second, when he showed no hint of fear.

His hand touches my thigh, deft fingers sending a rush of desire through my body, while he looks straight into my eyes, with the kind of look that can bare one's soul. Such incredible eyes.

I'm not sure if I'm truly fearless. I've been bold before, but never like this, never with someone like him.

My heart is beating faster and faster while my core is getting warmer and warmer.

RENEL

S
he has wild, playful eyes and a look that drives me mad. Tarlia. An impostor.

A beautiful, bold impostor. A fearless woman who held her own against a horde of monsters. A beautiful woman who gave me the strength to keep going, keep fighting. How long would I have resisted if it weren't for her?

Tarlia. A solace in this moment, a respite from my dread and pain.

I want to get lost in the feel of her body, forget my past, ignore my future. Soft as a feather, I run my hand over her thigh. The skin is so smooth, inviting, and her body quivers in response, while her lips part. I keep moving my hand and find nothing under her dress, just bare skin.

She smirks, giving me a challenging look, her eyes pure fire. Beautiful, fearless Tarlia.

From light, my touch turns heavy, a squeeze, and she gifts me a soft moan.

What we've been through together tonight might equal a lifetime, but I still don't know her well, know her body very little, and she's human, so I ask, "On a scale from extremely gentle to brutally rough, how do you want it?"

She gives me the prettiest smile ever and chuckles. "I can choose?"

I caress her face and look into her gorgeous eyes. "Always."

"I'm not made of glass." There's a lovely playfulness in that smirk. "But I'm also exhausted. Other than that, as long as neither of us gets hurt, anything goes."

Not gentle, I suppose. I grab the hem of her dress and pull it all at once, ripping the straps, revealing her naked body. Her breasts are round, perky, with taut, inviting nipples.

I lie on top of her, then give her light, fast bites, first on her neck, then on her breast. Her back arches, her lips part, and her moans are better than any song.

I'm rock-hard already, and we haven't even started. It's as if she knows it, as she caresses my chest, then brings her hand down, under my trousers, her soft fingers seizing my cock. Her touch is just right, and I gasp as she caresses my shaft, her eyes brilliant with desire, her smile mischievous.

"I want this," she says. "You know what? I wanted it since this morning, when I first saw you."

I trail a hand from her face to the plain between her breasts. "I wanted you too. You. Not your friend. That's why I said you're two completely different women."

She tilts her head. "How did you imagine fucking me?"

I trail my hand down until I'm caressing her inner thigh, then I move slowly to tease her core. "I'd spread you on the table, then taste you like the berries until you screamed my name so many times my ear hurt."

"Ouch. Poor ear." Her chuckle is light, lovely. There's no sound more delightful than her voice, her laughter.

My finger reaches her entrance, and I feel my cock quivering. She's so wet. So, so wet. "How did *you* imagine fucking me?"

"You'd push my head against the table, lift my skirt, then fuck me hard from behind, so hard that I'd whimper in pain."

"And yet you said you didn't want to get hurt."

She narrows her eyes, teasing me. "Imaginary pain is not pain, Renel."

I caress her entrance, and then, slowly, find her sweet spot.

Her entire body arches and trembles.

"You like that?" I ask.

"Yes," she moans.

"Then say my name."

"Renel," she whispers.

I caress her there again, and she closes her eyes, biting her lips. Such lovely lips. I move back, away from her hands' reach, and unlace my trousers, then remove them.

Her eyes sparkle when she sees my erect cock. Her eyes are so amazing already, they look incredible with that glint, that desire.

I get out of the bed, then pick her up and put her on the table.

"The table's hard, Renel," she complains even as she laughs.

"So am I. We can imagine we're back in the castle, back to this morning. And now we can do what we wanted. But tell me to stop, if I do something wrong."

I lift her legs, press her gently, then harder, my finger half inside her. I adore the sound of her moans. It's like an instrument I'm playing. With deft strokes, I create the most amazing sounds. Her body is already quivering as I kneel, then trail my tongue around her entrance. My reward is her loudest yell yet.

She's all mine in this moment. Mine to please. Mine to tease. Mine to lick and taste and adore. Mine, if only for a night.

For now, all I want is to see what I can do with her body, hear her different moans, make her tremble under my touch.

And yet I haven't forgotten what she said she wanted. When I feel her body trembling the hardest, when I hear her moans peaking, then slowing down, I get up.

"What now?" she asks, her brilliant eyes staring at me with expectation.

I take a moment to admire her body, the curve of her breasts, her navel, her waist. I take another look at her entrance, so wet, so ready.

The corners of her lips lift in an adorable smile as I caress her body slowly. Then she closes her eyes, her mouth in an adorable o shape, her back arching again.

I pull her up, push her legs down, then turn her around and press her face against the table. I feel her entrance with my finger, then enter her halfway. She's warm and tight and wet. It's as if I've always belonged here. In another stroke, my entire cock is inside her. Her moan is a half whimper. At first, I move back and forth slowly, delighting in the feel of her inside, delighting in the sounds she makes, caressing her lovely, round ass.

I caress her neck and grab a handful of hair, then enter her hard, harder, faster. I want to hear her scream all night. Even if I know we can't do this forever, I wish we could. When I feel she's about to have a second explosion of pleasure, I finally yield to mine, and fill her with my seed.

My body feels weightless, free, all my muscles relaxed.

I carry her back to bed, then lie beside her, wrapping her close to me, her warm skin against mine such a comfort.

"Was it all right?" I ask.

"It was quite terrible, Renel."

"You're a horrible liar, Tar."

She laughs. "Fair. It was *a little* more than all right. What about you?"

"Same. More than all right." Unlike her, I can't lie, but I don't need to say all the truth either.

I kiss her neck, and she giggles softly. Holding her tight like this, I can believe my life's not doomed, I can believe I'll find a happy ending.

It's a magical, perfect moment.

I know it's not forever, but then again, nothing is, so I might as well enjoy what I have now. Is there even anything other than now?

26

AZUR

hat's sleep? Nothing but a few hours here and there when I drift away from my pool of pain.

She's beside me, only a thin stone wall between us. If I were a bit more coward, a bit more selfish, I'd get up, knock on her door, and plead forgiveness. I'd tell her I love her, tell her I want to spend every last second I have with her.

But that would be selfish.

I thought having my horns removed was the greatest pain I could ever face, but I was wrong; nothing compares to this. To stay in this room, away from her, to let her go and perhaps never see her again feels like ripping out my heart.

And yet I'll do it if it keeps her from feeling a fraction of the same pain, if it keeps her from risking her life trying to be near me and all the innumerous dangers surrounding me. If at least one of us can have a happy life, it should be her.

I'm too poisoned, bred with bitterness too deep, never even hoping to escape this prison. The end might be near, but it will be my end too, and I'd never dare bring her with me into this bottomless hole.

Revolving on this empty, cold bed won't bring me any more rest, so I get up and put on my old leather tunic. The hallway outside is a balcony leading to a reddening sky. Is it also bleeding like my soul? Do I have one, or am I beyond redemption? Why did life grant me such a gift just to tear her away?

I hear steps going up the stairs and reach for my sword—except that there's nothing in my scabbard. My magic is still gone, and all I have is the dagger Tar gave me.

Coming up the stairs, the first thing I see is the lovely hair that frames her beautiful face like mist. Lidiane.

She pauses when she sees me and places a hand over her heart. "It's you."

"I thought you were going to stay in the room beside me."

"I *slept* there. When I could no longer sleep, I got up. Weren't you the one who told me to leave as soon as the sun came up? Had I done what you asked, I would be out in the desert at this time, so don't come and say it's dangerous."

"I wasn't going to say anything."

"Great."

She's angry. That should be good, and yet it brings me pain instead of relief.

I say, "We'll leave soon."

She snorts. "Really? You think they're about to wake up? They sounded... occupied last night."

"I'll wait two hours, then wake them if they sleep too long."

She rests on the railing and stares at the sky. "It's beautiful, isn't it? All full of color. Despite everything, a new day is coming. Like life and death."

"Death was quite close last night."

"Yes. But it wasn't our time yet." She looks at me, then looks at the top of my head. I wonder if she's trying to imagine what I used to look like, but then she waves a hand, and I feel the tickle of a glamour. Such a familiar glamour, as if it was my own.

I touch my head, even though I know glamours can't be felt. "What did you do?"

"Gave you a hat, Azur. It should last until noon or so. I could fix the other one if I had the tools, but I don't. I'm sorry it ripped."

I shake my head. "I have other hats."

She has a lovely light chuckle. "A whole collection?"

"A few. Just in case."

"Well, at least you won't be hatless on your way to the castle, and once there, you can get back to your collection."

I take a deep breath. "I thought you were angry at me."

"I am."

"And yet you're giving me a hat glamour?"

"One thing has nothing to do with the other, Azur. We can care about people even when we fight."

I stare at her. "We didn't fight. Did we?"

"There needs to be something before the fighting, right? We're nothing—other than having this strange bond."

"I'm sorry, Lidiane. Sorry for the pain I brought you."

She shakes her head. "Your pain is because you only see the bad side of things. You hold on to your fear."

I look back at the sky. "I do. And it's why you should stay away from me."

"Don't worry. I will." Her laugh is strangely melodious and cutting at the same time, then she turns to me and frowns, pointing at my vest pocket. "What do you have there?"

I know what she means, but I'm not sure if I want to reveal it to her. "Here?"

"There's some... magic. Feeble, and yet it's your magic."

I don't think I can hide anything from her, so I pull a piece of old, enchanted parchment.

Her eyes widen. "It was you! You! I can't believe it."

"What do you mean?"

"The transcending letter! At the Owl Inn. That's your part, isn't it?"

I don't know why I feel foolish, and yet I'm more curious about her side of the story. "So you know some rebels."

"What about you? Sending information to them!"

A thrill of terror runs down my spine. If Renel learns about this, I don't know what could happen. I put a finger over my lips and point back at where my master's room is. "It was... a test. I never sent anything compromising. And I would never be able to jeopardize Renel's safety. It doesn't mean anything."

"I know! I mean, I'm not sure I understand why you did it, but the information was quite bland. I stole the other side of the letter, Azur, and left them with a replica. I don't know who you thought you were communicating with, but they claimed to serve the Nether Court. They're not nice fae."

Her words shake me, but I try not to show any reaction, and ask, "Have you considered that my plan might have been to set up a trap for them?"

"Obviously. Everyone considered it." She narrows her bright eyes and stares at me. "But that wasn't your plan, was it?"

"Fine. I didn't have a plan. I just... It was a small act of rebellion, of defiance. As if I wanted to prove to myself that I wasn't completely bound, as if I wanted to..." The truth is that my motivation is cloudy even for me. "I don't even know, to tell you the truth."

"Fair." The look she gives me is far from reassuring, as if she could peer into every corner of my soul, smell every piece of hatred lodged there. "But I stole it, so that I checked the information before passing it on."

A horrible thought crosses my mind. "To protect Marlak?" She doesn't deny it, and I feel fury rising up and filling my heart. "What are you to him?"

She sneers. "Don't tell me you're jealous. You have no right to be."

"He has a wife now."

Lidiane rolls her eyes. "Of course he does. And he's a friend. And it wasn't just to protect him that I stole the transcending note. I did it because I could, because those fae in the Owl Inn are obnoxious and don't even deserve stupid information everyone can easily get. How did you even know there are rebels there?"

"I just left the note. My little act of rebellion."

She nods. "I understand." I feel that she truly does, like she can see me for who I am. She continues, "The thing is, I gave the other side of the note to my brother."

"You have a brother?" I'm not sure why it intrigues me.

"Yes, and you'll never get any family introduction, since we're nothing. But can you write to him? Tell him I'm safe and returning home? Just because—"

"Of course." I would never deny her something so simple. "But it's better to avoid names and places, just in case. Notes like these could fall into the wrong hands."

"I doubt it, but sure."

I stretch the note and point my finger at it. "What do you want me to say?" Then I realize this is not going to work and shake my head. "I'm sorry. With my magic gone... I can't." I feel so useless!

"Makes sense. Sorry for asking you that."

"At least when my magic returns, I can write to you." It was supposed to come out as some kind of joke, but it isn't. The truth of it hits me, the truth that we'll never be apart.

"Except you won't, right? Because you want nothing to do with me."

I almost tell her that it's not that. I want to explain that I want nothing more than to hold her close, but will it change anything? All it will accomplish is to make our parting even harder. All I do is look away.

"Right." Her voice has a sarcastic cheerfulness to it. "Well, I'm going down to eat now. Do you want to come, or would you rather starve?"

"I ate last night. I'm far from starving. I'll..." I wanted to say *be fine*, but I can't voice the lie. "Stay here."

"Whatever suits you. I'll find something downstairs."

I hear her steps retreating then turn to see her head disappearing in the stairs. The distance hurts.

People talk about a bond like a pull, and it sounds pleasant, but nobody mentions the pain of resisting the pull.

There's too much darkness ahead of me. Darkness that shall never touch her.

And now I don't even know what to do with this transcending note; if I should burn or relish it, a reminder of what will never be, but also a constant temptation to contact her.

I fold it and put it back in my pocket, telling myself that if I can ever use it to warn her against some danger, it will be worth keeping it.

MARLAK

My dreams were weird tonight.

Strange, dense forests, then Astra calling my name as I called hers. I also saw my brother wielding a sword like a grandmaster, keeping a horde of monsters at bay. That was definitely the strangest part.

Hopefully my nights will go back to my old, happy dreams when I return home.

I melt some ice from the top of the tent just to check if there's sunlight yet, and faint rays peer through the canvas.

Beside me, Ziven stirs. "Hey." His voice is slurred. "I guess it's time."

"Yes."

I recall my anger last night, my anxiety, then recall the moment I approached that strange lake, the feeling of having my magic gone, the feeling that something was wrong.

"Maybe you were right," I say, even if it takes all my strength to admit it.

"You're worried about your sister. Feelings muddle our logic." He smiles. "But we'll rescue her now."

He picks up his shirt and puts it on. I can't believe he slept without it, not that it's that cold, but I wouldn't sleep half undressed by a stranger.

I use my water magic to push the ice away from the tent. More sunlight comes through, and I pack my things and go outside. Ziven leaves the tent right after me, and I fold it and put it in my bag.

As much as I'm eager to see my sister, the memory of that lake revolves in my stomach.

I turn to the human prince. "You know it's going to be dangerous, right?"

"Most likely. I'll be alert."

We approach the cliff carefully. I decide to climb it down without any air magic. Last night I climbed too, even if a few times I thought I was about to fall. It was some strange compulsion to go see my sister right away. An understandable compulsion, when I consider that she had to spend the night in that dreadful place.

We approach the lake, and even though I can sense the water, something's wrong.

I turn to the prince. "Do you feel your magic weakening?"

His eyebrows contract. "I'm not sure if it's my magic or if it's this water." He then creates a ball of ice. "I can condense some of the steam, though. Can't you?"

"I'd rather not even try. Not yet. I can't grasp the water like usual. Nevermind the air. I still feel it, though."

The prince nods. "We still have swords."

"Yes," I mutter.

Swords can do very little against certain types of magic. I'm sure he knows it, and I don't need to mention the precarious situation we might encounter.

We edge the lake until he stops and looks at me. "Can you see it?"

There's nothing, not even some haze, some blur in the landscape, just the mist from the vapor of the lake water. "I see nothing at all."

He presses his hand over something, and then, slowly, a metal gate appears in front of me—just the gate. In the middle, where there should be a lock, there's a plaque—a familiar plaque. It has an engraving with a heart, a teardrop, or a drop of blood, and an eye. The eye makes a lot of sense now, since whatever magic's in here controls who's able to see it.

Ziven's hand touches the bottom of the plaque.

"I see the gate now," I say.

"Do you know how to open it?"

"Blood, I suppose. It's what the drawing is saying, isn't it?"

He grimaces. "If I were to follow the drawing, I'd need to cut my eye."

I lend him a dagger. "Just make a small puncture on your thumb, then press it on the plaque."

"Phew." He chuckles. "I thought you were going to ask me to poke my eye. Let's hope it works, even if they didn't draw a thumb."

"It's the blood that matters."

Stupid blood that can determine so much.

He pierces his skin with the tip of the blade, then presses his bloody finger on the drawing of the eye.

A rush of power stirs around us. The gate vibrates and opens, the sound of its hinges loud like a roar. I finally see a wooden bridge, closed off on top and with small, high windows on the sides.

"Here we go," he says. This time, there's no mistaking the hesitation and trembling in his voice.

I don't want to force him to go in there. "You opened the gate. You can wait for me here."

He shakes his head. "I don't think it will let you go through without me. And I'm here to help you. Believe it or not, I'm not a coward."

"I'm not saying that. It's just... It's my sister, right? Not yours."

"We don't know what's on that island, Marlak. We need to be ready for the worst." He takes a step. "Let's go."

Worst. I'm not ready for the worst, nor do I want to imagine it, but I step onto the bridge.

The wood boards creek as we walk. Beneath them, I see a metal base blocking the steam from the hot lake—I suppose otherwise we'd be cooked here. It's still quite warm, but not enough to hurt or kill us.

The bridge is a lot more solid than I expected—and somehow longer as well. I still can't see any island, and I'm wondering about the type of magic used to create—and maintain—this place.

We walk some more and reach another gate, identical to the first one, with vertical bars and a plaque in the middle. Ziven presses his slightly bloody thumb on the drawing of the eye, and the gate moves.

I finally see an island with some trees, bushes, flowers, and, in the middle, a black tower, made of a stone so smooth that it reflects part of the sky.

Blue tower—I see.

The tower reaches up into the sky like the curved spine of some animal. At its bottom, stands a humongous metal door.

"The bridge's gone," Ziven mutters.

I look back and indeed don't see it, but that's expected. "Even for you?"

He nods.

I swallow, a taste of ash in my mouth. "We'll figure it out later."

My hope is that it just turned invisible, but that we can still use it to escape this place.

A stench of decay reaches my nostrils and I soon identify its source: a seagull's carcass, similar to the ones we saw outside. This is a good sign; something's flying in and out. I don't mention that to the human prince, preferring to keep our silence and remain attentive to our surroundings.

The more we step onto the island, the more I feel my magic returning. I can sense my connection to the humidity around me and even the air.

I was going to pull my sword, but I'd rather use my magic if something happens.

We finally reach the steps leading to the humongous door, and I pause, taking in the enormity of the task ahead of me.

Will my sister be there? Will she be alive? It's so hard to even fathom what so many years in a place like this could do to a person.

Before we climb the stairs, the door opens, and Mirella steps out.

Mirella.

Alive, well, healthy.

My sister.

My heart leaps with joy and I finally exhale all the anxiety bottled up in my chest for years.

She looks the same. Older, yes, but the same Mirella, with black hair and blue eyes. She's even wearing a pretty tiara.

"Marlak!" She stares at me, eyes wide, an emotional laughter coming from her mouth. "You came!"

The next thing I know is that she has her arms around me, and I'm hugging my sister again. After all these years, we're reunited.

It's the end of a long nightmare.

"Aw!" she yells, as I feel a jet of water on my back.

A dagger falls behind me, and she rushes towards Ziven, but he locks her feet in place with ice.

"Filthy human!" she hurls, her face contracted in hatred.

Ziven raises his arms. "She was about to stab you."

It takes me a few seconds to understand what happened, to grasp the truth of what Ziven prevented. Perhaps I should have predicted this.

I turn to her. "Mirella, it's me. And he's here to help. I'm not an impostor or a hallucination. It's me."

She blinks as if coming out of a daze, then looks at me and touches the burned side of my head, horror in her eyes. "What happened?"

Shame fills my heart, and I look down. "You know what happened."

"Marlak," she mutters, so much sorrow and pity in her voice that it constricts my heart. She then blinks and looks confused again, and asks, "What are you here for?"

"To rescue you. Get you out of here."

"I like it here." Her smile is friendly, happy, innocent even.

While it's great to see she's not suffering, I fear she might not be in a good mental state.

"Do you want to live here forever?" I ask cautiously.

I understand attachment, fear of change. She might not be ready to leave her prison.

"I just want to sleep." She moves her feet, trying to free them from the the ice locking it in place.

"Don't attack us," I say.

She shakes her head. "I just want to sleep. I was going to bed when I heard visitors. I never get visitors."

"Are you alone here?"

She nods. "They all died. All of them. Let me go," she pleads. "I need to sleep."

"Promise not to attack us." It pains me to say that, to treat her like a threat, but I need to be careful.

"I'm going to sleep now." She shows her empty hands. "No weapon. No magic. We can talk later. I like visitors. Good visitors, not the nasty ones."

"Who did you have as visitors? Did anyone bring any supplies?"

She shakes her head then wiggles her body again and manages to free her feet. Before I can say anything, she rushes up the stairs and closes the door. In normal circumstances, I would have followed her, but this time, I didn't want to startle her.

A feeling of powerlessness overcomes me. I don't know what happened to her in the last years and I'm not sure how I can convince her to leave this place—unless she's truly happy. That should be a relief, I suppose.

I stare at Ziven, wondering what he's thinking.

He gives me a tight smile. "She's alive and looks healthy. The rest can be fixed."

"Yes." Hopefully.

We climb the steps, but there's no handle to open the door

from the outside, nor can it be pushed inward. I'm considering opening it with air or water magic when Ziven suggests looking for another entrance.

We walk around the tower, coming across another carcass, this one much older and no longer fetid.

"None of these birds are from here," Ziven says, echoing what I thought before. "Or even from the surrounding area. Something's flying in and out."

"Which is good news."

He raises an eyebrow. "Or bad, depending on what it is."

"It eats *birds*. I don't think it will confuse us with a bird. And it hasn't hurt her."

Ziven doesn't look convinced. "With magical laws in place, anything is possible, but you're right that we're no birds. Now, if she gets visitors, someone has come in—and *has left*."

Someone has come in. Of course. Someone even threatened to bring me here.

"I'm thinking it might have been Azur, my brother's guardian. First, he has an unnatural ability to transcend. I've never seen anything like that, or even heard about it, in fact. Second, when I was captured, they considered bringing me here. So he *can* come here." I sigh. "I'd rather not wait for his visit, though."

"No. I don't want to spend months here." His tone is playful, but there's a hint of fear in his words.

A fear I share. I have to go home soon; Astra's waiting for me.

On the back of the tower, we find a door. This one is open ajar, full of dried leaves, dirt, twigs, and all kinds of things that wind and rain could have blown through such a passage.

We step into it to find a room with tables and counters, all of them covered with dirt, dust, and leaves. Huge spider webs cover every corner. Against a wall, there are two piles of jute bags. Flour—enough for ten people for a year, I suppose. And yet untouched.

"Marlak," Ziven mutters, his voice shaking.

I turn and find him pointing to a corner. Instead of the expected spider or other animal, I see two skeletons, both wearing scraps of red clothes that might have been uniforms.

I recall my sister's words. "She said they died. I suppose that's who she meant."

"There could be more." Ziven tilts his head and looks at the corpses. "Why would they die in the kitchen? You know, not on a bed or something?"

A chill fills my stomach. "It could be a fast-acting poison, or else they were attacked."

Ziven approaches one of the bodies. "The clothes are ripped."

"They were exposed to the elements. But they could have been attacked, yes."

"It's clear why she doesn't use the kitchen."

"This place can kill anyone's appetite."

Ziven turns to me. "But why wouldn't she move the bodies? Bury them?"

I swallow. "She was born a king's daughter. I got along well with her. We practiced magic together, challenged each other. I like her as a sister, but—" I don't even know how to explain it.

"You think she would be too shocked to touch a dead body."

"Yes. Shocked, yes." The word that had been crossing my mind was *spoiled*, but it's hard to say that about someone who had to live years on this cursed island.

Ziven glances at the flour. "She didn't even pick up any supplies, by the looks of it."

"Perhaps she did, and not everything is here."

"I'll check if there's anything outside."

I'm not sure if it's a fruitful course of action, but follow him. Indeed we see wooden barrels and boxes by the outer wall.

He turns one of the barrels' taps, puts a finger under it, then smells it. "Water," he says.

"I'm glad you didn't taste it, considering the possibility of poison."

"Had I been an idiot, I wouldn't be alive."

"Didn't you say you saved your life by pretending to be an idiot? What if part of it was your own personality?"

"Who knows, right?" He chuckles.

I need some levity, need to relax instead of wondering what happened in this place.

I say, "Let's check the rest of the tower, then I'll come down and bury the workers."

"I'll help you," he offers.

Beside the kitchen, there's another room with a large, broken table and chairs, as well as a fallen chandelier. Shattered glass from a large window covers the floor.

Ziven looks around, then smiles at me. "I'm sure the rest of the tower isn't all like this. I mean, she doesn't want to leave, so I'm sure there must be some cozy, comfy part we haven't seen."

The dining room's door leads to a huge hall where statues and furniture lie broken. We're on the other side of the humongous entrance door from where my sister greeted us, at the base of spiral stairs that climb to the top of the tower.

"You know," he says. "I'm quite disorganized myself, so I can relate."

He's trying to make me feel better, and yet, if any of this was normal, there would be no need to say anything. Still, I chuckle.

He continues, "I tell myself to clean it later, and later. And it's never later, you know? I'm sure that's what's happening here."

"Or else she expects someone else to clean it." That's the most likely explanation.

"We can help her arrange it a little."

"We'll look for an exit first."

"Yes, that. But in case—"

"No case. We're leaving this place soon." I don't want to consider any alternative.

"What if she truly wants to stay?" Ziven asks.

"Of course she doesn't, despite whatever nonsense she might tell herself."

We climb the stairs to find broken furniture, broken

windows, and spiderwebs everywhere, with no sign that a person has been living here. We see no other kitchen or any place where Mirella might have prepared food, and no food, in fact.

Another skeleton lies in the hallway on the third floor, this one also with ripped clothes. I feel bad for the servants who were likely sent here to help her. Or were these her visitors? I'm not sure.

There are a few bedrooms. Some of them have just a wooden bed and what used to be a hay mattress, while some of them show signs of nicer beds and covers. We don't even find her room—or her.

"She could be outside," Ziven says. "We can look for a shack or something."

As much as I appreciate his optimism, I know it's unrealistic. "There would be a trail leading to the back door."

"There could be another door. Or else she hides somewhere to sleep. It could explain why she survived for so long."

My chest is tight with worry. In a way, I should be relieved to see her so healthy, but it's hard to understand what's happening here and hard to digest the fact that she's been living in a filthy tower unfit for anyone to live in.

Ziven stares at me. "What do you want to do now? Keep looking for her? Try to find a way out? Bury the bodies?"

His question reaches my mind but finds only emptiness there. What do I want to do? What can I do?

He takes my silence as an invitation to keep talking. "She said she was going to sleep, so that's what she's doing, right? Just because we haven't found her, it doesn't mean she isn't comfy somewhere, resting, *like she said she would*." He stares at me as he emphasizes the last words. "When she wakes, we'll talk to her. Meanwhile, let's look for a way out and give the bodies a decent resting place."

"You're right." I'm so dazed, so stunned. I can't even believe that the irksome human prince is the one talking sense to me.

We descend the stairs, then he tries to find the bridge again, walking in the area where it was last time, and then around the island.

"It's gone, Marlak. Unless it shows up again at a specific time or something. I can watch it."

His theory is quite unlikely. "But it was there all the time, wasn't it? Since last night. It disappeared after we crossed it."

"Yes."

"So it doesn't have to do with the time of the day, but our location."

"Perhaps it might still be visible from the other side. Who knows? Perhaps another person with king's blood will stroll by." He stares at the lake. "What about air magic? Can't you float across the lake?"

"If I could float across, we would be able to create an ice bridge. Something in this lake blocks our magic."

"What if you floated really high? Truly high. Far from the lake?"

The idea is quite disturbing. All I can picture is a fall right into the weird, hot water. "My air magic is not... I can't sustain myself well mid-air."

"What if we had some kind of rope, hook? Something to connect with the cliff on the other side?"

I narrow my eyes. "Maybe."

We return to the kitchen and the tower, then bring the bodies outside. There are gardening tools and the remains of what must have been a vegetable garden many years ago, and we find a plot of soft soil to bury the remains.

Ziven doesn't complain about any of the work or about being on this island. If he keeps acting like that, I might have to admit he's decent company and not a hurdle. I'm not ready for that yet, though. And I'm too worried about our precarious situation.

When we finish the burial, I decide to touch on a matter that I'm sure has been in his mind.

"The carcasses," I mutter.

He grimaces. "You want to *bury* them?"

"No." I don't know how I manage to chuckle. "But I was thinking something. Why is whatever killing the birds coming here? Bringing seagulls all the way from the ocean?"

"Maybe it's warm and cozy? It's a bird-eating monster sauna?"

"True. I hope it's not a monster, though."

He gives me a playful smile. "Didn't you say it won't confuse us with birds? Not sure about you, but I have no feathers."

He's right that I dismissed his worries earlier, but that was before seeing the bodies. He saw them too, and I'm sure the idea has crossed his mind, even if he's being flippant now, likely just to contradict me.

"We haven't seen it yet," I say. "We need to be on the lookout; it might show us how to escape this island."

"We'll watch." His nod is as shaky as his voice.

Other than that, too many questions burden my mind.

Where's Mirella? What's happening to her?

And most importantly, how are we going to leave this dreadful place?

27

ASTRA

My stomach feels upside down when I wake up, still in my old room where I slept so many nights dreaming about Marlak.

This time, it was a nightmare. I felt him near, and then I couldn't feel him anymore. I still recall that weird Astra telling me to find the Amethyst Palace. Something's wrong. I don't know if it's me being paranoid and missing him, or...

I take a slow, deep breath. Or what?

Perhaps one of a thousand things that could happen to him in the Icy Lands or in that mysterious tower. Is the answer really to find the Amethyst Palace?

Not that I know how to find it.

I could perhaps return to that sanctuary and try to find some clue, something. A chill runs from my head to my toes. I won't have time to go to the sanctuary. I need to find the Amethyst Palace as soon as I can.

But how?

Even my inner voice won't tell me how. Even the strange Astra in my dreams won't tell me how. The Nymph Queen herself couldn't tell me how.

All I have is a chest full of panic and anxiety about to overflow.

I get up and head to the kitchen, where Nelsin is sitting at a table.

"Good morning!" I think he's trying to sound cheerful, but I suppose my worry is like a shroud above his house and everyone can feel it.

I grab a piece of bread and a bowl of fruit from the counter, then sit with him. "Where's Ferer?"

"Outside. Practicing magic or sword forms. Or moping. Something like that."

"I'm moping too, and I need to practice magic. I suppose I should join him."

He presses his lips together. "Did you figure out anything?"

"No! Except that I dreamed that I have to find the Amethyst Palace immediately. Now! I don't even have time to research." I can't keep the annoyance from my voice.

Nelsin plucks a grape from my plate. "Why do you think that is?"

"No time? I fear Marlak might be in danger. And I know you're going to say I'm making no sense. He went to the Blue Tower. What does it have to do with that Palace? And then I'll tell you that I don't know."

He chuckles. "Sometimes you don't need to know. You feel it."

"Yes. I *feel* we're in trouble. And in case I don't feel it enough, the Nymph Queen almost drowned me just to tell me I'm about to be in some big, big trouble if I don't *find myself*. Did she have any advice for me? Of course not. Just warnings. You know, do they think that if they glare at me a lot, my magic will be scared into showing up?"

Nelsin narrows his eyes, but he looks smoldering rather than glaring, and at least he makes me laugh.

He doesn't change his expression. "Me thinks you don't take my warning seriously."

"There are too many *serious* warnings already. And no explanations. At least if you're not going to give me an explanation, don't scare me."

He leans back, his expression relaxed again. "But that's the thing, Astra; some things don't have an explanation."

"And then how do you figure them out?"

"You feel it. You don't think. How do you know you have to find that palace? What's the explanation?"

I pause, mulling his words. "It's different."

"All things are different from each other. It doesn't mean you can't transpose your experience."

"What should I do, then? To find that palace?"

He plucks and eats another grape, then says, "First, you have to connect with your magic. See, that's the thing; if it was a matter of looking at a book and figuring it out, the fae who wrote that Fallen Kingdom book would have found it already. Anyone would have found it. It needs to be a Tiurian with magic, which seems to be you. So you need to look inward."

"That's literally what the Nymph Queen told me. She said I should find myself. I'm here. Then what?"

He looks up, thinking. "I saw you using your magic. It was quite powerful. Can you bring yourself back to that moment, remember what you felt?"

I recall those strange creatures, recall that I didn't want to die or to let Nelsin die. "Fear. Do I need to be terrified to use my magic?"

"Was it fear?" His blue eyes are bright. "I still remember that moment, and you seemed quite confident, Astra. I'd even say that you were absolutely fearless. So I don't know if I agree with you."

"Fearless?" My chuckle is sad and hopeless.

"Something else, then. Try to remember, Astra. What were you feeling when you created that light?"

Light. It had always been my companion, back when I accepted what Otavio said, when I even accepted that I was tainted.

"I grew up in a human castle, and they believe in the

Almighty Mother. I used to believe in her too, with all my heart." The memory makes me cringe.

"What changed?"

"They call Tiurians darksouls. This Almighty Mother has this protective light against darkness, and we are part of that darkness." Saying those words feels like jabbing my heart. "I… feel ashamed that once I believed that I was somehow unpure, corrupted. I'm angry too, that they should teach that. After being away from Krastel, after seeing things from a distance, I started to understand that so much of it were lies. Lies, lies, lies. How can I be old Astra, with that pure trust in a creature from a religion that hates me?"

"Hmmm. You don't speak Tiurian, right?"

"I don't think the language has been spoken in many years —not that I would learn it."

"So that's the thing. Everything you describe uses the human and fae common tongue, not your own language." He points to my plate. "What do you have in there?"

"Bread?" I'm not sure what point he's trying to make.

"Yes, and yet, in your own language, it would be called something else, right?"

"I wouldn't even know what."

"Maybe one day you'll learn the word, and maybe you'll even learn about a special type of bread and its significance to your people. Meanwhile, are you going to stop eating bread just because it has a name that was given by people who hate Tiurians?"

"The bread isn't preaching that I'm dangerous, Nelsin, so I'm not sure I agree."

"The Almighty Mother is not a Krastelian invention. It's a bigger force, spirit, deity. Who knows if we can even define it. I saw you, and I have no doubt that it was real. So perhaps you're using the wrong name. If it gives you power, fearlessness, why should you turn your back on it?"

I sigh. "It's not on purpose. It's just that I don't see things the same way anymore. But maybe you're right. I used to have her as a constant companion. I always said my protective words before sleeping, and it's true I haven't been doing it anymore, as if I looked back and thought it was something silly, childish, something from my past, and I *was* gullible. And yet now that you're saying it, I do feel... ungrateful. But it comes with so many complicated feelings."

"Uncomplicate it. Think about your connection here." He points to his chest. "Don't think about all the people who exploited that connection to spread lies. If the Almighty Mother is the key to your magic, and it's the only key you know, you have to use it. One day you may call her something different, maybe use a Tiurian word, but for now, it's what you have. Don't starve just because the bread was made by the fae and our kind targeted Tiurians."

I take a piece of bread and cheese while I consider his words. He is right. At the same time, I don't know how I changed like that, how I flipped, or maybe I do. It's a strange thing to confess, and yet saying it feels like disentangling something from my chest.

"You're right. And the bread is good. And I think there's something else to it. The Almighty Mother was one of the things that helped me, that gave me strength, resilience. The other thing was my kindred soul. And I suppose it's stupid that just because I found him, I should ignore a piece of myself. And you're right, no matter how tainted with lies my faith was, it was part of who I was."

"Romantic love sometimes takes over your mind, heart, and body. It's normal."

"But that's not good."

He leans his head in his hand, his face dreamy. "Oh, I disagree. It's absolutely incredible."

His words make me laugh. "Yes, but I also need to care for myself, right? Romantic love is not everything. It can't be my sole source of solace and strength. But it wasn't all that, it was really that I look back at Krastel and see how they manipulated me. But at the same time, my faith was something good. Even the priestess was good. She always helped me—which is strange. She'd hate me if she knew what I was."

"She probably wouldn't hate you. She would think you are not like the other *evil dark souls*." He exaggerates his voice. "Like you, she was also told lies, Astra. It's true that she repeats them, but... I don't know. I can't imagine what it's like to be you, let alone this random person I've never met."

"I don't think it's right to claim an entire group of people is evil, but that's for her to learn—or not. You're right that my faith is my own." I think back to that moment in the plains by the cliff. "You said I was *fearless* back then, and I can see now that it's partly true. The feeling was *surrender*. I trusted in a greater power, trusted in it with all my heart, and in that absolute trust, there was no place for fear. I need to find that trust again."

"I'm sure it hasn't gone far."

"Let's hope so." I smile. "But let me eat first, then I'll find it."

He narrows his eyes, his face playful. "Are you sure you want to eat grapes grown by the fae? Some of them would capture you or kill you."

"These grapes are no match for my might. Let them try!" We both laugh. "How did you know what to say? How to explain it to me?"

"We have similar issues. I also don't know much about my parents—or my people. Ferer is a half sea fae, and yet has never gone to the Sea Court, nor will he. Sometimes I look at myself and ask: who am I? But I think I'm also all these pieces I grabbed on the way. The Crystal Court has not been kind to my people, and yet I can take what they have and make my own. We're not static stones."

"And even stones allow the wind to carve them. Thank you. For showing me the way."

"See? I'm useful sometimes." He looks adorable with his cat ears pointed forward and a crooked grin.

"Being a friend is useful enough."

I finish eating, then go outside to think, to try to reconnect with that faith I had most of my life.

It's *my* faith, not Krastel's, and it will allow me to connect with my power—if I let it.

And maybe that's the secret; to trust. Let go and trust.

I take a deep breath, admire the mountains and the sky, then close my eyes.

It's hard to trust when I'm so stressed, when the solution is not clear. That day with Nelsin, all I had in my mind was how to protect us; there was no confusion, no doubt.

Find me, the castle told me in my dreams.

If I'm going to trust, I have to trust fully. I ask the Almighty Mother to show me the way to the Amethyst Palace and wait. The answer is coming, and I don't even need to worry.

My eyes snap open at once when it hits me. Oh, the answer's so obvious!

Extremely dangerous, quite reckless, and yet utterly obvious.

Can I be that bold?

TARLIA

Peace. So much peace. A quiet contentment fills my heart, pervading my body as the dim light from a wakening sky enters through a murky window. There's something warm on my back, around me...

My breath catches in my throat. I want to sit up, but strong arms hold me tight. My heart jolts.

Renel. Renel's behind me. Renel's arms are enveloping me.

The night's over and he's still here. Then again, there is nowhere else to go—other than the bed above us and all the other rooms in this keep, that is. Then again, we were exhausted.

And yet there's something in the intimacy of waking up like

this, something that stirs in my stomach, something about to induce a wave of panic.

I push his arms—and he holds me tighter.

"Tar?" he mumbles, sounding half asleep.

"It's morning," I say.

He kisses my shoulder. "I can see that."

His hands then caress my belly. That simple touch ignites a rush of desire through my body.

"You said you loved deeply for *one night*. The night is over."

His mouth moves to my neck, then my ear, where a stroke of his tongue makes me moan.

"It's dessert," he says. "Don't you like dessert?"

"I'm food now?" My chuckle sounds wrong, but it's still passable for a chuckle.

"Aren't we both? We can devour and taste each other." One of his hands cups my breast while the other holds me firmly by the waist. "What's your favorite dessert?"

At least this talk is making me hungry and distracting me from the urge to ride his cock again. "Drusils. I don't think fae have it."

"I suppose not. What is it made of?"

"Coconut, milk, and honey. Don't ask me how it's made. All I know is that it's soft on the inside, crunchy on the outside. But we rarely had it, and when we did, they never let me eat more than two." I recall Astra saving her portions for me. Astra. Marlak's wife. Renel's enemy.

"I'll get the recipe. We'll make mountains and mountains of drusils, and you'll eat until you need a break, then have some more and repeat it all over."

That would be child Tarlia's dream—but I'm not a child anymore. "I'll gain weight if I eat too many."

He pinches my belly. "Then you'll get all soft, wiggly, and still pretty. I'll have more places to hold you." He kisses my neck again. "And kiss you. But I like you all lean and firm just as much."

An old bitterness stirs within me. I don't want to believe in an illusion, get carried away with fruitless feelings.

"You talk as if…" I'm not sure what to say. He stops kissing me, perhaps to listen, and I continue, even if it tastes bitter. "As if we had a future."

"Well…" He pauses, then leans his forehead on my back. "True. How can I ignore my dysfunctional castle, right? Soon I'll be bathing in lava, and won't be able to hold you anymore."

He talks as if he wanted to keep holding me. I shouldn't pay attention to that. Men make many promises when their minds are addled with lust. It doesn't mean anything. And yet something he said caught my attention.

"Can't you just stay away from the castle? When it's going to the fiery place or something?"

"A moment of self-destruction like that would call back the castle master. I'd be sucked right back in, I suppose to bear witness of my faults." He sighs and cups my breast. "I'd rather talk about holding you. Last night you made me forget about the castle. Make me forget it again."

"There must be a solution, Renel."

"I'll try to find it." One of his hands moves down, between my legs, the touch so soft, so enticing. "But I want to find something else now."

"Sure, let's ignore our problems."

The tip of his finger caresses my entrance. How does he know how to touch it so right? How can a touch do so much? I suppose the problems *can* wait.

A moan escapes my lips as I try to say, "Let's… ignore them."

"Hmmm, you're already so wet. Is it for me or for the drusils?"

He presses his finger again. I thought I hated fingers down there. But I love *his* finger—and I can't really form coherent sounds anymore.

"Yes," I half moan.

I feel his chest moving with his chuckle on my back. "I suppose you like this?"

His finger makes a light pressure and friction just on the right spot. There's something slightly different now. All I know is that it shoots a thrill of pleasure through my entire body. I'm not sure what sounds I'm making, and if they're loud or not. I'm not sure where I am. Are there stars above me? Around me?

Renel. There's only Renel embracing me, a cocoon of warmth and pleasure, taking me to a strange place beyond all senses. Renel.

Any control's escaping me as my thoughts become nothingness.

No. *I* want to be the one in control.

I push his hand and arm and turn around to face him. He stares at me with surprise at first, but soon a corner of his lips lifts, and he holds my face with both hands, a fervor in his eyes.

I sit up and push him against the bed, so that he's lying flat, staring at me in curiosity and expectation, an eyebrow raised.

We're both still naked, except that the morning light lets me admire the muscles on his chest and abdomen. Such absolute beauty, like a sculpture by a masterful artist. I want to delight in my moments with this absolute male perfection. He emits a soft moan as I kiss the trail of hair leading to his already erect cock. I clasp it with one hand, then look into his eyes as I lick the tip.

"Tar," he mutters, his breath ragged.

"You like this?" I ask, then swirl my tongue around the head of his cock.

"Too much."

I surround his cock with my lips and glide down slowly as my other hand caresses the base, feeling him getting even harder with my touch.

Someone knocks on the door. From behind it, comes Azur's voice. "Renel."

Just to mess with him, I don't stop what I'm doing. On the contrary, I move my tongue even more.

"What is it?" Renel asks with difficulty. He can barely speak.

"We shouldn't linger."

"Is there an emergency?" Renel sounds more annoyed than anyone I've ever heard.

"There could be."

"Then leave," Renel roars. "Leave."

After a few seconds, when I'm sure his guardian is gone, I say, "That was rude."

He caresses my hair. "Rude of him to interrupt this moment."

I'm about to take his cock again, when Renel pushes me against the bed, then mounts on top of me, between my legs.

I pretend to be mad and frown. "You interrupted me."

He runs a finger over my lower lip. "No. As much as I love this warm mouth, I want to come inside you. One more second and you'd taste my seed."

I suck his thumb. "Maybe I would like that."

"Another time. I want to hear you scream a little more."

"Do you think—"

He's inside me—in one thrust. Whatever I was saying gets stuck in my throat.

He pulls out, slowly so that only the head is inside me. "What were you saying?"

"Nonsense."

I want him inside me, and push up my hips, but he moves back, so that all he's doing is teasing me. "I want to hear it," he says.

"I was wondering if you thought the second round could be as good as—"

He's inside me again, and the only sound I can make is a loud moan.

"What was that?" he asks, his tone teasing. "As good as what?"

"If you're not going to let me say it, don't ask."

He chuckles, then thrusts again, even harder. "I might not. Does this compare to drusils?"

"Not quite," I say, just to provoke him.

"Oh, no." He kisses my neck, then nibbles my ear. "I'll have to step up."

He thrusts hard, and between whimpers and moans, I say, "You need to be sweeter, perhaps."

"I'm sweet." He kisses my cheek.

"Then let me taste you."

"Another day. Now, I want you to say my name."

"Renel?" I don't know why I chuckle.

He pulls back again, teasing me. "Again."

"Renel." This is a half moan, as he thrusts inside me.

Renel, Renel, Renel, Renel. I lose track of the times I moan, whisper and yell his name, lose track of the way my body feels, lose track of where I am. There's just us, an explosion of sensations, and another, and another.

Renel, Renel, Renel. Why does it have to feel so good?

I get ahold of my senses again and find him on top of me, looking into my eyes, a tender expression in his eyes.

"Tarlia. You're beautiful."

"I know."

He laughs, then pulls his cock from inside me, kisses my shoulder blade, and holds my hand.

The gesture is so intimate, loving even. Perhaps that's just the way fae are, and it doesn't mean the same to him as it means to me. I pull my hand.

"I thought it was just dessert."

"It was." He kisses my shoulder. "If I could spend the entire day with you, I'd lead you through a seven-course banquet."

"That's a bold promise."

He looks down, sadness marring his eyes for the first time. "It's *not* a promise. I don't know if I'll ever..." He takes a deep breath. "I don't know if we'll ever spend time together again."

I shrug, pretending not to care. Wait. Do I care? Regardless, I have to say something. "It was just one night."

He nods, then kisses my neck and runs a finger over my cheek. "Thank you. You made me forget every single affliction weighing over my head."

"The sex did, Renel, not me." I keep my tone flippant, even if my lips are trembling. Why is he messing with my heart?

He caresses my hair. "It was *you*. Had we spent the night just talking, I'd still forget everything. I wish... I wish things were different, but they aren't. I'll never forget you." He sits up. "We'd better go."

Yes, go. That's the part I need to focus on. I pull my dress, wondering if I can just tie the top straps. He already has a pair of trousers on. "Wait here," he says. "I'll bring you new clothes, a pitcher of water, and a cloth. So you can wash."

He leans down as if to kiss me, but I lower my head, so that he kisses the top of it. Perhaps I'm like a drusil, all soft inside, touched just because we had a night of decent sex.

More than decent, but still.

Perhaps it's just because he's so incredibly beautiful.

I don't know what it is. What I know is that whatever pathetic feeling has come over me, it's new—and terrifying.

28

RENEL

Azur is leaning on the railing of the balcony corridor, his back to the building.

I punch him lightly. "What was all that knocking for?"

He doesn't turn to me, too busy staring at a single cloud in the sky. "*Go away, Azur*. Sometimes I agree you treat me like a dog."

"Oh, please. I was busy. Don't tell me you didn't also—"

He turns with a glare that lets me know everything there is to know about his mood.

"Oh." My tone changes, even if I'm puzzled. "I guess you *didn't*." But it doesn't make sense. "Not even some kisses? Lovely time together? Holding hands?"

Sometimes I fear he'll murder me with his stare, and this is one of those.

He sneers. "I don't have time to trifle with idiocy."

"Time? What exactly did you do with your time? And you were supposed to trifle with your soulmate, not anything else."

"Right. Would that make it easier once we go separate ways?"

"Then don't go separate ways. Bring her with you."

He rolls his eyes. "To the castle? The one you think is going to be consumed in flames soon? The one where Zorwal might be waiting for us? Why would I do that?"

"I don't think Zorwal's alive, and you're not the castle's master. You'll be able to leave when it's about to get destroyed."

"And then die because of our bond. How helpful."

"You know, for someone whose skin is at stake, you don't seem too interested in stopping the castle."

"What do you expect me to do?"

"Nothing. There's nothing to be done other than bracing ourselves for impact and hoping for the best. I spent so long trying to find a way to stop that castle, when perhaps there was never any solution. I'll face it head-on."

He glances back at the room. "I thought you were seducing the human."

"She's not Astra." I scoff. "My plan was stupid, Azur. She's an impostor. But she has a name, and it's Tarlia. And if you thought that was Astra, why would you interrupt us?"

He runs a hand over his hair. "This place gives me the creeps. And if you want to seduce someone, there's no harm in leaving them wanting more."

"*I* want more and yet I'm here, getting ready to leave. Look at how responsible I am."

He raises an eyebrow. "Congratulations." I feel he's just being sardonic, but there's no point arguing.

I sigh. "Now let's go back and face our doom."

A muscle in his jaw ticks. "I'll be right there beside you."

I rest a hand on his shoulder. "Thank you."

"It's my duty."

I know he's saying it just because he's bound, but for me, it still matters a lot. "A duty I appreciate, Azur. And I understand..." I look down, trying to come up with the right words. "I understand it must hurt to send her away."

"No, you don't," he mutters. "Be glad for that."

I want to tell him that there's no greater luck than finding one's soulmate, and yet I doubt it will bring him any consolation. I simply nod and go on my way to the bathing chambers to get a pitcher for Tarlia.

Tarlia. I was so ready to bring her with me to the castle, to hear her laugh every night, to taste more of her, to make love to her on a decent bed. I'd even find a way to make her that dessert she said she likes so much.

But if by any chance Zorwal is alive…

He can't be. But what if? The thought makes me shudder.

ASTRA

In my head, my idea made total sense, but now that I'm looking at Ferer and Nelsin, I'm wondering if I'm a lunatic.

To be fair, I considered *not* telling them my plans, but realistically, I need their help. The problem is that I'm second-guessing my decision.

Nelsin's ears are perked up, while Ferer rests his chin on his hand, both of them staring at me, waiting.

I should tell them slowly, so as not to shock them, and yet I'm not sure how to explain it gradually.

Finally, I take a deep breath and say, "The Amethyst Palace is in the Shadow Lands. In the forest."

Oh, that was the opposite of eloquent.

Ferer gives me a slight nod. "It makes sense." He pauses, then asks, "Do you want to go there?"

"Yes, I do."

Grim doesn't even come close to describing their faces.

Ferer swallows. "It's a dangerous area. At night, especially. We could brave it during the day, if we're careful. Can you wait until Marlak returns?"

Of course he'd ask that.

"The Nymph Queen pulled me into her court to tell me I had

to hurry, that I needed to find myself and my magic immediately."

"I understand the hurry," Ferer says. "But he should be back soon. He's one of the most powerful fae alive, Astra. If anyone can help you walk safely over there, it's Marlak."

Nelsin taps on the table. "Not necessarily. A soulsucker almost defeated him, did it not?"

Ferer sighs. "During the day, Nelsin. I'm not suggesting we go there at night. What I think we should do is plan well, and then go as soon as he's back."

"I agree," I say, even though I disagree. But I need to make my point. "I think waiting for him is a great idea."

Ferer exhales, clearly relieved, while Nelsin narrows his eyes staring at me, I suppose wondering if something hit my head.

I continue, "That said, his presence is no guarantee against some of the creatures in that area, at least as far as I've heard. And there's another problem." Just the thought of mentioning it squeezes my chest and stirs my stomach. "Marlak's in danger. I don't understand why, but I need to find that castle to save him. I know, it makes no sense, but the queen said magic was about feeling. This is what I'm feeling."

I remember then my trip to the Krastel Castle. "I know you trusted me, then we ended up going to the human castle for no reason and faced dangers there."

"Pfff." Nelsin waves a hand. "Some human guards. Please. That's nothing."

"Agree," Ferer says. "The human castle was a kid's play. What made it tricky was that we didn't want to kill those guards. Still, *tricky* is quite different from *dangerous*. And you found *some* information, Astra. Now, the Shadow Lands is a different story. Quite different."

"I know, but I have a plan. My magic kept bloodpuppets away. Nelsin saw it. I'll use it again, and I think it can keep dangerous creatures away from us. Am I completely sure? No. Now, as to waiting for Marlak; I don't think we can. I'm positive that he's in danger. What does it have to do with that castle? I don't know, but I know I have to find it. If I wait for Marlak to return, I might wait forever. There's a chance he'll never come back." My voice doesn't even crack. It's a truth I've felt for over a day now, that instead of terrifying me, pushes me into action.

Ferer and Nelsin stare at me, eyes wide. I'm wondering if they think I'm delusional, completely insane, or if they're considering locking me up before I do something stupid.

"I have to find this castle," I insist. "The Nymph Queen told me so, not exactly in these words, but said I had to find myself, and she was worried. I don't expect you to go into the Shadow Lands with me. Just get me close enough."

Ferer huffs. "You know we'd never abandon you or let you face dangers on your own. That's not a possibility."

"And yet what I'm asking you—"

"Is not too much." Ferer fists the table. "But we'll leave right away and get out of there before the sun sets. Is that clear?"

"Unless we find the Amethyst Palace," I say. "It would be safe at night."

"You don't know that."

"I only see it at night, in my dreams. And before you say they're only dreams, I used to dream about Marlak. I saw his chest scar and everything, and he's real."

Ferer leans forward. "Was he *exactly* like you dreamed? No difference at all?"

"He was. Is. It took me a while to realize it, but he's the exact same person from my dreams."

"And you think the palace will be the same?" he asks, an eyebrow raised.

I pause. "That one is more complicated. I've seen it in different conditions. Sometimes it's safe and peaceful, sometimes abandoned, sometimes there's something dangerous lurking in it, but even then, I felt I had to find it soon."

Ferer and Nelsin look at each other, I suppose to decide what to do. Even if they're no longer together, they still can communicate without words.

Nelsin turns to me. "I'll come with you. First, I trust you. Second, I owe you my life. Ferer can stay."

"What?" Ferer grimaces and turns to Nelsin. I'm assuming this was not what he got from their shared look. "You think I'd leave you both? I made an oath to protect her, and you…" He looks down, then turns to me. "I'll come. But we'll do everything we can to get out of there before night falls."

"Unless we need to stay," I say.

Ferer's shoulders move up and down in a stressful deep breath. "We'll see what happens. In principle, we'll try to make sure we aren't out in the open after the sun sets."

I exhale. This was easier than I expected, and maybe I should have trusted them more. "Right. So what do we do now?"

"Get weapons and supplies." Ferer points at me. "Wear the most comfortable shoes you can and clothes that will let you move easily, but long sleeves are preferred. Make sure you have pockets for daggers."

I get up, almost astonished that they agreed so quickly, that we're about to leave, perhaps even astonished that Ferer is taking the lead.

After I dress quickly, I meet them in the kitchen, and we leave. Nelsin helps me cross the river, and then the three of us use the faerie circle to transcend to some village in the north, close enough to the Shadow Lands.

I wish I had more certainty; a clear direction, a clear clue. Moving blindly into unknown, dangerous lands is terrifying, and yet if I wait for the way to be clear, I'll never move. The only answer is to figure it out as I go, even if I understand so little of what I'm doing.

The circle where we transcend reminds me of the area where we met the Nameless, with a thick forest. I wonder if I'll ever meet her again, if I'll ever have the chance to ask the right questions. For now, it seems that I have to figure things out on my own.

At least I have two friends with me. Then again, it's one more reason why I can't fail.

Ferer points to a trail amidst thick vegetation and trees. "We'll walk north from here. The Charmed River divides fae and Shadow Lands, but it is but a rivulet in this area and we might miss it. We'll be in the Shadow Forest at any moment." He looks at me. "Then I suppose it will be up to you."

I feel as if a cold wind blows me from the inside. What am I supposed to do once we reach those lands? There's still time for me to change my mind, to quit. We could try to get some maps of the area, maybe go to that sanctuary and find answers. I could ask the Nymph Queen, could even try to find the Nameless.

Part of me knows I'll have no time for that. I'll have to trust the light to guide me, trust it, and never falter.

I take a deep breath, then say, "Let's go."

My voice doesn't waver, and neither will I.

TARLIA

I end up putting on a clean uniform Renel brings me, even if the fact that he's bringing it to me makes me shudder. It's as if he knows he's setting a trap for my corniest feelings, for my most ridiculous delusions, so that he'll have me within his grasp. The worst is that I'm not even sure if he needs any effort to trap me.

I'm such a sappy fool.

Tarlia, Tarlia, falling in love after one night. Really?

I don't think it has happened before. I liked Fachin—I suppose. I'm not sure. And I liked Ziven, after many nights of doing nothing.

Liked.

The truth is a spear to my heart.

Liked. In the past.

The pretty false king really left an impression, I guess. But I hope it will pass.

When I open the door, he's waiting for me.

"Is everything all right?" he asks.

"Should it be? Isn't your castle about to self-destruct?"

He smiles. "I meant with you." He looks at the uniform I'm wearing. "Does it fit?"

Why does he have to sound so concerned? It's disconcerting. "It's not like I have a bunch of choices. Better than being naked, don't you think?"

"No." He frowns. "I much prefer you naked."

"Oh. Why didn't you say so?" I undo the top button of my shirt and start undoing the next one.

He places a hand on top of mine. "Naked just for me. I find I'm more possessive than most fae."

Strange words. Does he think he'll keep me as his lover?

He smirks, then looks down at my body as if ready to undress me. "And while I'd love another *dessert*, we'd better leave this cursed place."

He's obviously thinking he'll get to fuck me whenever he wishes. The worst is that I doubt I'd say *no*. I try to change the subject. "This keep was our salvation. Other than Strawberry Cake."

"Cherry Cake." He chuckles. "But I mean the Shadow Lands. Something's wrong here. All those ghouls…"

"There shouldn't be that many?"

"As far as I've heard, no, but then again, if anyone ever encountered a horde of ghouls like that, they would never live to tell their tale, would they?"

I laugh. "No. And if by any miracle they did tell, I doubt anyone would believe them. *I* barely believe we survived."

"And yet we did."

He stares at me with those magnificent dark eyes and makes me tremble from head to toe.

"We should leave." I turn and head for the stairs.

"True." He follows me.

I want to curse the moment I decided to have sex with him, curse every little pointless, unwished feelings coursing through my veins.

Lidiane comes out of the refectory and gives us a thin smile. "Ready to go?"

"More than ready," I say.

She turns to Renel. "Where's your grumpy guardian?"

"Upstairs, I suppose." He turns to the building. "Azur! We're leaving!"

"Are you, now?" Azur shouts from the balcony. "Unbelievable."

"He is indeed grumpy." I turn to Lidiane. "Did something happen?"

She shakes her head and rolls her eyes. "*Nothing* happened."

Nothing. Strange.

I don't understand why she didn't spend time with Azur and give her a questioning look. She waves a hand, and I suppose the explanation will come later. Despite her apparent cheerful disposition, there's a certain sadness in her eyes. I wish I could talk to her, try to understand what's wrong and support her, but I hear Azur approaching us, somehow wearing a brand-new hat.

"We have a long walk," he says, his tone curt.

I want to smack his face for being such an ass to Lidiane.

"You don't say." I roll my eyes.

He glares at me, and I glare right back.

Renel stands by me and touches my arm. "Ready?"

I nod, and then he kisses my cheek. It's so... sweet—and makes me uncomfortable, vulnerable, weak, as if I'm losing control.

We leave together, Renel walking beside me, Azur beside Lidiane, but at a huge distance, as if he wanted to avoid her or vice versa. The desert looks the same as yesterday, and yet I still tremble remembering what we faced at night—and during the day too. I hope we come across no more rats. My legs are trembling, still exhausted from the walk last night.

I wish I could collapse on a bed and sleep for five days straight—unless I could do something else in bed... Why even exhausted do I have to think about that? But then, Renel is walking beside me, his hair loose, slightly curled, and I can still remember our moments this morning, his touch, his words. Perhaps all that goo from the sleepy slug went into my head. That's the only explanation.

I want to ask if the river is far, but of course it is. Two hours walking sounded like so little last night, and now it's an eternity. A freaking eternity. And I can't believe we ran as far as we did yesterday.

In front of me, Azur pauses. "Wait."

He turns to Lidiane, who smiles. I realize her hair is moving slightly, as if caught by a strong breeze. Air magic.

"It's back!" Her relief and her smile make her even prettier than usual, and the look she exchanges with Azur makes both of them seem like different people, especially him.

There's wonder and love and joy and marvel on their faces. It's obvious that whatever's between them, runs deep. And yet, most of the time, all they do is scowl at each other. Odd.

Renel smiles. "Do you think you can transcend?"

Azur's about to say something, but Lidiane's faster. "Not a good idea. This place messes with our magic."

"Was that what happened?" Renel frowns. "The Shadow Lands affected your powers?"

"I don't know." Azur shakes his head. "And it's still quite weak. I'm not sure I'll be able to transcend any time soon. Or ever."

Renel shrugs. "It's fine. We'll find another solution."

We get back to our steady pace. At least nobody suggests running. I hope I never have to run again.

After a long time, we come across a rivulet barely covering its stone bottom.

"Is this *the river*?" I ask. "The important one?" I can't imagine that this thin, shallow thing could contain ghouls or any of the other monsters we encountered.

"There's magic in it," Renel says. "Like the River of Tears."

"That one's deep," I reply, not seeing any similarity. "Requires bridges."

Lidiane turns to me and chuckles. "To be fair, not a lot of people live this far north in the fae lands. Perhaps they don't trust the magic either."

"I wouldn't. But then, we saw what's out there. I guess that changes us."

Lidiane crouches to remove her shoes, then Azur says, "Wait."

"What?" She frowns.

"I'll carry you." Azur manages to sound sweet.

"No." She looks down at her shoes.

I guess they're back to their mutual scowls.

"Fine, then." He rushes across the river, his boots splashing water around him, then sends a gust of wind in our direction.

I'm thinking he's planning on getting some revenge for his rejection, but instead, he lifts Lidiane.

"My magic's back," he says. "I can bring you across without touching you."

"No!" she yells. "I'm perfectly capable of crossing this river. Save your magic. You'll need it."

"Magic is not wheat that you can just store," he says, but puts her back on the ground, and she walks across.

I crouch to remove my shoes, and Renel crouches beside me. "I can carry you."

"Why? We both have feet and legs."

"We both have feet that might get wet and dirty, and if only one of us needs to do it, why not? I didn't mean to imply you couldn't cross a tiny rivulet."

I smirk. "Why didn't Azur offer to carry you? Isn't he your guardian?"

"He protects my life, not my feet."

"And you protect my feet?" I chuckle.

"No—but I'd like to."

The image of being carried by the Crystal Court king, pretense king, or whatever, tickles a vain part of me.

See? I'm not nobody, I would say. *Renel himself carried me.* I'm so ridiculous sometimes.

I stand up. "Fine. Carry me if you wish."

He throws me onto his back and crosses the river. I was expecting something more... careful, let's say, but I suppose this can be etched in my mind to cheer me up in those days when I'm feeling too insignificant.

When we reach the other side, he sets me in front of him and doesn't let go, holding me by my shoulders.

"Renel," Azur says. "I think I can transcend."

Renel doesn't move his eyes away from me. "A moment," he yells, then takes a deep breath.

I chuckle. "I know, I know. Goodbye. It was fun and all, and goodbye."

He looks down. "Yes. And no. It's not... I meant it when I said I wanted you to come with me, and that I'd give you all the dessert you want. I meant it. In fact, I couldn't have said it if I didn't mean it."

His eyes look sad and apologetic and are making me anxious.

"It's fine."

"It's anything but fine. I don't know what's going to happen, but I don't want to see you in danger. Find your friend, find my brother, ask them to protect you. He's been well-hidden for a long time. He can keep you safe too."

I could protest that this would mean depending on a stranger's goodwill, but going to the castle with Renel would be the same. I just nod.

He runs the back of a finger over my face so softly. "You made me forget my anguish, but this is not the time for forgetting; I have to face it. If I survive this, if I survive the castle and the Fiery Gorge, I'll find you."

His tone, his look, his gentleness are grabbing my heart—

and squeezing it. And it hurts. It hurts to be trifled with. "Don't make promises you don't mean."

"Tar, I'm fae. Words bind me. I'll find you, and if you want me, we'll see what happens."

Both his hands are holding my face as if he's trying to look at me one last time. I shouldn't believe it, shouldn't fall for his words, shouldn't let my heart get into this, and yet, when I feel his lips touching mine, all my hesitations are gone.

I wrap my arms around him and kiss him back, as if I could capture his essence, his being in that kiss, as if I wanted to dissolve into him. I wish I could kiss him forever, stay in his arms forever, remain trapped in this infinite bliss.

My eyes are blurry and wet when we part, and he runs a finger to wipe away a tear from my face.

"It's for the best, Tar. If Zorwal is dead, and I think he is, I still have to evacuate an entire city, and I don't know what the council will do. I don't know what will happen. If you're there… I don't even want to think what they could do to you. It's a risk I can't take. We might not see each other again, but when I die, it will have been worth it."

"You can't talk about death like that, as if it's nothing."

"All lives are precious, but death is coming for us all, and when it's time, it's time. I have to face it head on, and be the king my court needs."

He kisses me again. A brief, soft kiss on my lips, then he takes my hand and kisses it.

All I want to do is cry. I don't look when he turns to Azur and tells him they should go, don't look when they disappear.

The truth of what I'm feeling is buried deep.

It hurts too much for me to admit it, so all that's left is the enormous pain taking hold of my body.

29

Tarlia is turned to the other side when I look back at her.

"Where to?" Azur asks, his voice drier than the air in the Shadow Lands desert.

"Are you sure you can transcend?"

He rolls his eyes. "I wouldn't be offering if I couldn't."

I ignore his unbearable mood and say, "The castle will be near Clare Beach. We can try to approach the royal fort, then get a flying carriage."

There's a flash of anger in his eyes, fury even, but I understand that he's upset that he has to leave his soulmate.

Everything around us turns dark, and when there's light again, it's filtered through tree leaves above us. We're in the woods by the ocean, and I can hear waves crashing and smell the salt in the air.

Azur walks ahead of me, and we soon step on a beach with rough sand and wild, angry waves. Clare Beach. The fort here is older than the Crystal Court, made of marble blocks, shining in the sun.

I look back for the castle beyond the trees, beyond the fort

—and find nothing. I pause, staring carefully at the landscape, trying to make sure I'm looking at it right. It makes no sense; the castle should be visible from here.

"What?" Azur turns to me.

My throat feels dry, my chest cold, my head warm. Am I worried? Relieved? "The castle's not here." My voice comes out weak and cracking.

He follows my line of sight. "Oh. Indeed. Dit it not move?"

"Of course it did." My heart is frantic in my chest. "We felt it."

He pauses, thinking, then says slowly, "Perhaps you were mistaken."

Was I? Were my predictions wrong? Can it be that the Crystal Castle will not end up in the Fiery Gorge? Can it be that there's hope for me? That I'll survive? There's a wave of relief about to crash over me, but I hold it back. The truth can't be that simple.

"I was never mistaken before."

"There's a first time for everything, isn't there?"

I bite my lip, thinking. "Yes, but there are other possibilities. One; the castle did *not* move. That's good, and will give us more time, even if I'll have to figure out what happened. Two; the castle went somewhere else, and my predictions are wrong. That might be good too." A dreadful bitter taste takes over my mouth. "And then there's number three."

"What?" He chuckles. "It disappeared?"

"That would be number four. I suppose we could add some random possibilities, such as it going to another court or even continent, but I doubt it."

"What's your dreadful theory number three then?"

My heart's positively banging on my chest, perhaps wanting to escape this doomed body. "I hope I'm wrong. Can you transcend again? If yes, let's go to the Southern Hills, near the New Mountain Village."

He narrows his eyes. "You think..."

"I don't know. Let's eliminate this possibility."

Azur nods, then walks back to the woods, so as to stay away from prying eyes.

As soon as the trees protect us from view, he transcends us, and then we're in the south, near the fields I visited with my parents as a child, the fields with the sleepberries.

And near the Crystal Castle, rising above the trees.

I think I want to vomit.

Azur stares at it, his face pale. "Maybe the castle came straight here, and your prediction is wrong."

When it comes to the Crystal Castle, it's as if he's unable to understand the gravity of the situation, as if he can't trust my findings—and I don't blame him. Denial is comforting—but won't solve anything.

"What are the odds? This was the place it was supposed to go after Clare Beach. It moved twice." Even voicing the words makes my entire body go cold. "Twice."

"We'll check."

"It means two more moves, Azur. Two more."

He swallows, then stares at me, eyes wide. "Is it one more move, and then the Fiery Gorge, or two, then the Fiery Gorge?"

"The Fiery Gorge is the second move, and if it moved twice in one night..."

"We'll see. You said you feared the castle would move faster if you spent too long away from it. Maybe that's why it moved twice—if it's true that it did."

I shake my head. I want to scream, yell, punch something. I want to turn back time and undo so many of my choices, and yet I keep my voice calm. "Perhaps it moved twice because I wasn't there, sure. It still means it will face its end in one year at most. But it could be a matter of hours."

Azur smirks. "Look at the bright side; your anguish will be shorter."

"I'm worried about the Jewel City, Azur. It's right on the path of the fissure."

"You could be mistaken." Why is he so stubborn?

"Yes, there's a chance I'm wrong about everything. And then there's a chance I'm right. I'll have to be smart and strategic."

"What do you want to do?"

"Evacuate the city, of course."

"I mean now. Do you want to find an outpost?"

"We're walking in. There's no time."

"Hmmm. You do realize Zorwal might be there, right?"

I huff. "While I believe your insane theory has *some* merit, I have good reasons to believe you're wrong. If he's there…" I'm wondering if he would do anything against me other than the regular torture. Does he still need me? Would he dare kill me? Then I stop myself from wondering about something so absurd. "Pointless thoughts, Azur. He was *decapitated*." I say it slowly, hoping the obvious fact will finally settle in his mind.

"I smashed his head against a wall," Azur says in the same tone, slowly. "And yet he was still in the castle a few hours later. But maybe you're right. Maybe decapitating him was enough."

I don't think I'm going to convince him that Zorwal is dead, and to be fair, his certainty makes me second-guess my own opinion. And I have an idea. "I'll wear the Shadow Ring. If we meet him again, it will block his magic."

Azur exhales. "Let's hope it works. When we get near the castle, I can lift us both so we arrive by the Royal Terrace."

Being suspended in the air brings me some dreadful memories. "I don't trust other people's air magic."

"My bond would never let me hurt you."

"Intentionally. I won't risk falling to my death, at least not before I do what I have to do. We can walk up the stairs." And something else intrigues me. "How come your magic's working fine like that?"

"I don't know, but I feel fine."

"It doesn't mean your magic is *completely* fine."

"Transcending like I do is the highest and rarest form of fae magic. Instead of fearing some air floating, you should have been afraid of transcending, as we could have ended up split in two, or maybe gone somewhere unintended."

"Like yesterday."

"Yes. Zorwal did something, that's why." His anger is palpable, and his discomfort too. He's obviously unused to making mistakes or seeing his magic failing, and this must have been a great blow to his pride.

"You still got us out of there in time. I'm thankful for what you did, Azur."

He snorts. "Thankful for a night in the Shadow Lands? For almost dying?"

"Keyword being *almost*. And my night was great. Now, this morning is getting awful. And I'm sorry for our bond, sorry that you... might die when I do—which will probably be soon."

"Is your sorrow supposed to make me feel better?" He sounds playful, and yet his question makes me think.

"No. I guess it's for *me* to feel better. I can't say I'm sorry, right? Since it won't help. What I can say is that I didn't think it would come to this. I always thought I'd find a solution. I thought I had more time."

Azur stares at me, every second of his silence hitting me like a condemnation. Finally, he says, "Maybe there's something you're missing."

"Oh, yes. Pointless hope is hard to get rid of."

"At this point, what's left to do?"

I glare at him. "Is that even a question? Evacuate the Jewel City!"

I'm not sure if the look he gives me is pity or disbelief. "In how long? A week, two? Perhaps a couple of days?"

"People tend to value their lives, Azur. It's just a matter of convincing them."

He raises an eyebrow. "You're the acting king, after all. Your word should be worth something."

I don't know if he's trying to incense or encourage me, and frankly, does it even matter?

"Let's get to the castle. For now, that's all I care."

And yet Tarlia comes to mind. The echo of her laughter is my only comfort, and yet the feeling overcoming my senses is worry. And perhaps it's pointless worry. She was with Lidiane, who knows the fae territories well. Even then, my chest feels tight. I glance at Azur but all I see is his regular cranky expression. He would notice if Lidiane was in danger, and she's with Tarlia.

I'm overthinking this—right when I need to focus and save countless lives. And yet I wish she were here with me, I wish I could be sure she was all right. More than anything, I wish I could survive and see her again. I can't even count on the certainty that I'll see her after this life, when we have no bond connecting us. Our time together was too little. Too little even for us to fall in love, and yet I wish I had that time.

But none of this matters now. My past, my future, my death, none of this compares to the thousands of lives in danger, lives I have the duty to protect.

The castle looms larger and larger as we approach it. Two guards open the front door for us, then we climb the interminable stairs to the living area. Azur's steps are heavy, his hands fisted. I think he's still worried about Zorwal, even if his survival is impossible, even if I'll have the Shadow Ring to counter him.

I'm glad to be rid of the council leader, but I'm not so sure how I'll convince the members of the council to support me. Then again, Zorwal would probably scoff at my idea of evacuating the city, so his absence is an advantage—if he's absent, of course.

I don't want to think what might happen if by any chance he survived a decapitation—or what it means. What does Azur think Zorwal is?

When we reach the common level, I approach one of the main guards. "Any news?"

The guard's eyes widen when he sees us. "What do you mean by news?"

"Anything out of the ordinary."

He swallows. "No, unless I'm missing—"

"It's fine," I say. I think he would mention a dead council leader. Shit. He'd mention it.

Azur gives me a worried look. We go to my room, then I open the onyx cabinet. I'm relieved to see that the Shadow Ring is still there. I take it and put it on my finger, and still find it odd there, as if it's mocking me, letting me know it doesn't belong there. No matter.

I turn to Azur. "Let's go to the council chamber."

A guard unlocks the chamber door for us, we enter it, and find the place empty. No body, no sword, no blood. But someone would have cleaned it by now, I suppose.

"You might have to ask," Azur says as he looks around the room.

"I just did, didn't I? Or do you want me to ask if anyone carried any body from this room? Let's check his private chambers."

He takes a deep breath but follows me to Zorwal's office. I knock at first, and when nobody answers, get a guard to open the door for me. No sign of Zorwal. Some papers lie on a desk, and in his private chambers, the bed is made. Nothing out of the ordinary.

I walk then to the royal guard station by the Royal Terrace and ask the guards there if they've seen the council leader. They haven't.

When Azur and I are back in my room, where I'm sure we're alone and can't be overheard, I finally say, "He's not around."

Azur sits in my armchair and raises an eyebrow. "Nor is he dead, in case you didn't notice."

I try to think. "Somebody might have gotten rid of the body. Perhaps they'll blackmail us or something."

"Or else Zorwal is hiding somewhere and recovering."

"How do you think he'd do it?" I chuckle, the idea so absurd. "Do you think he left the council room holding his head in his hands? You think nobody would notice it?"

"No. He would put his head over his neck. Would anyone stop him to ask why he was walking like that?"

"And where did he go?"

Azur shrugs. "Some hideout. I don't know."

"It's much more likely that somebody came in, saw his body, and decided to hide it. Either way, now I need to assemble the council and convince them to evacuate the Jewel City."

Azur gets up. "Call me when you need me."

"You'll have to come with me." He blinks, confused, and I continue, "I'll be alone, with no magic, facing a hostile council. I'll need you by my side."

"You've always told me my presence in those meetings would convey weakness."

"Zorwal had my back. Now he's gone."

"And you miss him dearly."

"Not really. But I still can't face the council on my own." It is humiliating to always depend on someone else, but caution matters more than pride. "Come. I'll summon Silvan first, then the rest."

Azur frowns. "Silvan? Isn't he the most scheming fae in the council?"

"The most ambitious. He'll seize the chance to become the new leader. I need allies, Azur. If I can't convince the council, I can't evacuate the Jewel City."

"What if they insist on staying?"

"Then I don't know."

I don't know anything. I'm on the brink of disaster, watching death approach me faster and faster, and I don't have the slightest idea of what to do.

For a moment, I'm again the kid with a dead mother and wounded brother; I'm alone and lost and scared. Not even Azur is any help.

Every life matters, my father always said, and yet I failed. I can't save my life, can't save Azur's.

But I can still save a city.

TARLIA

"Tarlia, let's go." Lidiane's voice snaps me out of my self-pitying daze.

I realize I'm still by the Charmed River, and that Renel and Azur are gone. Gone. Renel's gone, and I can't let that thought bring me down. Can't let my mushy heart addle my mind.

I smile at her, trying to erase all traces of pain. "Sure. Is there more walking?"

She frowns, her face overcome with worry. "Are you in love with Renel?"

"Love? No. It was just a night, a lovely night, and yet a night." My words are all wrong. "What about you? Are you in love with Azur?"

"It's just a pull. We can accept it or not. You know when you're starving and smell the tastiest food ever, and it makes your stomach growl? That's the soulmate bond. You can decide not to eat it, except that you can't eat anything else, and will starve forever."

"That sounds dreadful. I'm sorry."

She laughs. "I was trying to make it seem not so bad, but I guess it *is* terrible. At least you and Renel are not soulmates. Look at the bright side."

"There's nothing bright about it. If Zorwal doesn't kill him, the council might, and if everything goes well, he'll perish in a fiery volcano. There's no bright side. No, I'm lying. The only bright side is that I don't need to explain to Astra why I'm in love with the person who's keeping her husband from taking the throne. So yay, I suppose."

"She'd understand. What about me? With Renel's dog?" Lidiane's chuckle is bitter. "I can't imagine what my brother would think. So yes, bright side."

"You're still his soulmate."

"But I'm fighting the bond. That's valiant, you know?"

"You'd rather not fight it."

She pauses, thinking. "I've always wanted someone who would consider me an equal, who would have me stand by their side. Azur seemed to be that person—until he wasn't anymore. And maybe that brings me even more sadness than lamenting the fact we never got to spend *any* time together. But he's right that it would have strengthened the bond and perhaps made it worse. I'll just go back to Nameless Blob. That one never lets me down."

At least she makes me laugh. "If I could wipe Renel from my mind, I'd do the same."

"What about Ziven?"

"Oh, one positive right there. I'm cured from my one-sided, pathetic obsession. But he's a good friend, and I'll be happy to see him again, give him a friendly hug, and reciprocate his beautiful non-romantic feelings." I sound so jaded, and it wasn't my intention. "I'm not being sarcastic. A friend like him is a treasure."

"And you'll come back, just like he asked you to."

"I suppose." The thought of returning to that house where I don't belong, not knowing what to do with my life, fills me with little joy, even if I'm incredibly thankful for the shelter and food. "And I'll need to plan my future."

Lidiane sighs. "I don't know. I used to want to have it all figured out, but sometimes we need to flow where the current takes us. There are moments in life when we're in between things, when trying to force destiny is a wasted effort. You have friends, Tarlia. That's more than what a lot of people have. We'll find a solution."

"True." The smile that comes to my face is genuine. Friends *are* precious. "I need to be more thankful, but you're right that I'll find my way. I'll just miss Renel." There. I confessed it even to myself, even if the idea makes me cringe. "And if you think it's ridiculous, you're right." I chuckle.

"There's nothing ridiculous about it. Fae are renowned for falling fast and quick."

"That would be a great excuse." I touch the top of my very round ear. "Unfortunately, I'm not fae."

"But he is."

I shrug. "Well, he's not in love."

Her laughter is light and amused. "Tarlia, are you *that* oblivious? That man is completely obsessed with you. Even at the festival, why do you think someone tried to kidnap *you*?"

"He thought I was Astra then, and was trying to seduce me." The memory brings a bitter taste to my mouth, the idea that he was courting me—unsuccessfully, but still—thinking I was someone else.

"How did he find out you were an impostor?"

"I told him." She looks at me, her eyes wide, and I add, "I was tired of pretending. And now you're going to wonder how come I didn't use all my training to deceive and seduce him. The issue is that I hated all that training. I hate Otavio, hate being used as a pawn by a disgusting, sinister old man."

"Was Renel upset when you told him?"

"A lot. He was hoping Astra would fall in love with him and give him magic."

Lidiane bursts out laughing. "Oh, that's so ridiculously absurd."

At least I laugh with her. "I know, but he said he wasn't aware she was in love with Marlak. Maybe it was just pointless hope blinding him."

"But he forgave you."

"He did. And that was before we got anywhere near having fun together. I don't think he's a bad person."

"Perhaps not." Lidiane looks down, her eyes sad. "And yet his leadership has plunged the lower fae into so much suffering. He needs to be deposed."

"He'll be dead soon. No need to worry." I'm flippant, sarcastic, angry, but not at her.

A shadow crosses her eyes. "What's with the castle? Did he explain it?"

I tell her what he told me, that the castle master needs

magic, that he can't simply appoint someone else, and that he calculated that the castle would end up in the Fiery Gorge and cause a fissure, destroying a city.

She takes a deep breath and shakes her head. "I don't want to be that person, but if Renel hadn't taken Marlak's throne, none of this would be happening."

"You don't say. Do you think it has ever crossed Renel's mind?"

My sarcasm is obvious, and she just rolls her eyes and chuckles.

I don't know how she does that, and ask, "How can you laugh?"

"No matter what happens, I told myself a long time ago that I would never let my spirit break. That's what they do; they try to break your spirit first, and if you let them, they win before even trying."

I'm not sure I see things the way she does. "For me, it's different. My master wanted me to be cheerful, happy, and dutiful, as if being his tool was some stupid honor. My anger is my rebellion."

"I'm angry too, Tarlia, but I can't let the weight of that anger bury me. It's why I find something to laugh at. You might be upset that Renel might die soon, but then Azur will die too. As much as it pains me, he was such a prick that I won't be as sad as I should."

I'm sure that's exactly what Azur wanted; to prevent her from suffering, but I decide not to tell her what I think. Perhaps it's better for her to remain annoyed at her soulmate. I can't imagine the pain she must be feeling.

Mine is a fraction of hers, and it's ripping me from the inside out. And then again, I don't even trust that Renel's in love or that we'd ever have a happy ending, so my pain is inane.

"What now? Where are we going?" I ask.

"To my house. There's a way to do it using the rivers, but I don't know if it will work. If not, we can walk or take a boat."

Her smile is cheeky as she turns to me. "Ready for some walking?"

"It *is* better than running, so I'll look at the bright side."

"There's always a bright side. You can't have shadows without light."

"Well, if you go to a closed room at night, there's no light, and there's still plenty of darkness. Pure darkness."

"Thanks for ruining my metaphor."

She's kidding, but I still want to fix my blunder. "I suppose we only call it dark because we also know light, right? Otherwise it wouldn't have a name and we wouldn't even know what it was. So you still have a point."

"Silence," she mutters. I guess I truly annoyed her.

"I know I sometimes ramble—"

"Sush." She places a finger in front of her lips, her eyes wide, attentive.

I freeze in place and try to hear what she's hearing.

The landscape here has more trees and bushes than on the other side of the river, and the only sounds that reach my ears are some leaves rustling. I don't dare ask her what she hears, afraid to disturb her focus.

I grab my dagger, ready to face whatever threats may come.

Out of nowhere, some ten fae guards appear around us. Lidiane doesn't flinch, and I realize they're her illusions.

Something zips past me. I assume it's an arrow and try to dodge it, but then a large, brown thing falls over us, then trips us. It's a net made of some kind of thick rope. I pull my dagger to cut it, then feel a dart hitting me. I'm not even sure how I didn't see any of that, how we were such easy targets.

I want to keep fighting, break free, but instead, my eyes close and I don't feel anything anymore.

30

ASTRA

If we're up north, we're close to the sanctuary where Marlak was captured, the sanctuary where we confessed our love for the first time. Why is it that thinking about Marlak squeezes my chest?

He just went south to rescue his sister, and his magic is powerful enough that he can deal with most threats. And yet I can't wipe away the presentiment that something awful might be happening to him.

"Where are we?" I ask, perhaps trying to shut down those fearful thoughts.

"These lands are unclaimed," Ferer says. "We'll soon cross the Charmed River, and then…"

"Shadow Lands!" Nelsin waves his arms in a dramatic gesture.

"It's not dangerous during the day, is it?"

Nelsin shakes his head. "Barring giants, not horrible, no."

"Are *giants* dangerous? Didn't they rescue Marlak?"

"Giants don't like us," Ferer says. "I suppose they blame us for the magic keeping them confined to the north. They have fought both against and beside the fae in the past. The thing is, they have their own goals, and they might not align with ours." He looks me straight in the eye then, his expression serious. "The one thing you must never, ever do is fight them. Never. In principle, giants do not kill. They can kidnap you, but they won't kill you—unless you fight them. Then they feel threatened and will certainly kill you. Even if you see one or two small giants, and if you're sure you can defeat them, it's not a good strategy. There are always more of them."

I'm not sure why he's giving me this lecture. "I wasn't planning on fighting giants."

He shrugs. "If something happens, don't react, it's all I'm saying."

"What if they kidnap me?" I ask.

"They'll want something. You'll need to negotiate."

Nelsin snorts. "The problem is that giants are terrible with words. They speak our language, but poorly. Their communication is different."

I never learned much about giants, and was mostly told they weren't intelligent, but Nelsin's words change my mind. "So technically, we're the ones who don't speak *their* language, and they're the ones putting in the effort."

"Sounds right." Nelsin points at me.

Ferer stops and looks at the ground. "This is it."

I come closer and see a tiny brook. "What do you mean by *it*?"

"The Charmed River." Ferer's voice is solemn, grave, contrasting with the minuscule body of water ahead of us.

"River?" I chuckle. "I can jump over it. *This* is keeping the giants in the north?"

"Magic, Astra." Nelsin makes circles in the air with his hands.

"I'd pick something bigger to separate fae and Shadow Lands."

"Further west, it's the Shadow Hills," Ferer says. "Anyway, it's daytime, but we still need to be alert. We'll go north through the plains between the forest and the desert. I know you said the castle is in the forest, but that area is a difficult, unexplored terrain, hard to move through. Once you find the location of the castle, we can go deeper under the trees."

I nod. "Thank you both for being such great guides. I would have no idea what to do without you."

Ferer takes a deep breath. "I've never been to the Shadow Lands. We'll see what happens once we're there."

I jump over the tiny stream, expecting to feel something different, but there's nothing. It's still the same forest, even if there are fewer and fewer trees ahead of us. After a few steps, I feel it, some kind of raw, powerful magic, something dangerous and alluring at the same time. Strangely, the feeling that comes to me is comfort, almost... belonging.

I wonder if they also sense it, and say, "I can feel a difference now."

Nelsin shudders. "Spooky, right?"

"Maybe." I don't dare tell them that I feel at ease here. Is this where Tiurians are from? Does part of me recognize an ancient home? Or is it the proximity to the Amethyst Palace? I don't know.

"Any idea where the castle is?" Ferer asks.

"Deeper north, I think." To be very honest, I have absolutely no idea where the castle is, and as much as I feel it calling me, it's not giving me any direction. Still, my hunch is that it's deeper into the Shadow Lands, and not near the border.

I can see what they mean by plains between the forest and the desert, as the vegetation slowly becomes sparser. To the right, there's even less vegetation, while on our left, it gets thicker and thicker until it ends in what looks like black curtains rimmed in dark green on top. It makes sense that we should not be walking there.

All of a sudden, in my mind's eye, I see Marlak in a flying carriage with Azur, Renel, and two pixies. Then I'm Marlak in the vision, astounded, awestruck, horrified at what I'm seeing. Azur is transcending a carriage.

To transcend a carriage with four people in it—that's something out of legend.

Then I see Marlak stepping out of the carriage and standing in front of a kind of fortification in the desert. And the vision stops.

I turn to Ferer and Nelsin. "The keep where Marlak was taken. Is it near here?"

Ferer narrows his eyes. "Slightly north still, but further east, deeper in the desert. Why?"

"I… just had a vision of him coming here."

Somehow, my heart speeds up, still in that horrifying awe at seeing what Azur was doing. I decide to ask about it.

"Is it unusual to transcend a carriage with people in it?"

"What do you mean?" Ferer asks.

"In the vision, Marlak was surprised that Azur transcended the entire carriage, and brought it straight into the desert."

"You'd need two powerful circles," Ferer says. "And someone with a lot of transcending power. So yes, it *is* unusual."

"It means that Renel's guardian is quite powerful."

Nelsin chuckles. "Hard to believe."

"He's great with air magic too," I say. "Better than Marlak, but Marlak's air is quite weak."

"Weak?" Ferer widens his eyes. "Marlak's one of the fae with the best air wielding I've seen. He's not great at floating, but he's quite precise at using it against enemies."

"Well, once he made me jump out of a super high window, and we almost hit the ground and died, so I don't trust his air magic."

Ferer shrugs. "Nobody's great at their secondary or tertiary element."

"Have you ever seen his fire?" I ask, wondering what it would look like, wondering how powerful he would have been.

"No," Ferer says, his voice dry. "I met him before it all happened, but I didn't see his magic at the time. Then after… he never used it again. I don't blame him. Still, repressing his main element obviously stunts his power. Then again, his water magic is remarkable, so I suppose there's no loss."

"Stop," Nelsin says, his top ears perked. "I hear steps."

I hear nothing, but it's true that I don't have the advantage of four ears. Then I see them; some eight giants circling us, as if appearing from out of nowhere. They're much taller and larger than I expected, like eight or ten times taller than me. I think they don't even fit in the forest and wish we were under the protection of the trees. They look like humans, except that their bodies are broader, and they dress in simple brown tunics.

A giant woman with blond hair crouches in front of us.

"Girlie, girlie, why you here?"

"Taking a walk," I say. I don't want to mention any secret castle, at least not yet.

She points to the ground. "Stop. Something coming." She points at me. "Stop it."

"You want me to stop something that's coming from down under?"

"Yes. Stop."

"What is it?" I ask.

"Under," the giantess says. "Shake, shake, shake. If it keeps shaking, it breaks."

I look at Nelsin and Ferer, hoping they understood her words, but they don't look any more enlightened than me.

The woman giant is terrifying, and I feel I need to give her an answer. "I'll do my best to stop it. I'll do my best." I think about Marlak's promise and how he kept it reasonable.

The giantess smiles. "Good. You stop. We take your friends. When you stop, you get your friends."

Is she suggesting kidnapping my knights? As I'm trying to think how to get out of this, Nelsin steps forward and points at Ferer. "She needs his help to walk in the Shadow Lands. Alone, she will be lost, and won't be able to stop anything. Take *me*."

"No!" Ferer says.

The giantess gets up and grunts to her companions. I suppose they're debating what to do.

"It's the only way," Nelsin whispers. "They're scared and desperate. We need to give them hope, and they'll feel safer if they get some kind of deal."

I approach him and whisper, "I don't know what they're talking about."

"You'll figure it out. You will. Trust yourself. They wouldn't be asking you if you had no power to stop anything."

Ferer shakes his head. "*I* should go."

"No. You're the responsible one, and you'll take good care of Astra."

"I..." Ferer looks at me, then at Nelsin. "Don't trust her like you do."

"Which is great!" Nelsin smiles. "A voice of reason."

The giantess crouches again and points down. "Take him only. But stop. Don't let it break. Stop. And you get your friend."

One of her companions crouches and puts Nelsin on his shoulder. The fae knight smiles and waves, and yet I can see that his hand is shaking. Ferer watches the scene with his fists clenched.

They're taking Nelsin. My friend, my knight. Ferer's beloved. They're taking him, and they'll only give him back when I stop *something* from breaking, and I don't have the slightest clue what that something is.

When they disappear in the distance, I turn to Ferer. "I'm sorry."

His breath is ragged and he swallows. "Not your fault."

I brought them here, so yes, it is my fault, but I'm sure that stating the obvious won't help anything.

He then says, "The castle might be the key, so let's keep moving."

I try to think about something that will cheer him up, and remember his own words. "You said they don't kill their hostages."

"Usually no, but they're uneasy, scared."

Indeed. I try to think. "Perhaps it *is* connected to the Amethyst Palace. I also have this odd feeling that something bad is about to happen if I don't find it. And they're here. They must feel it. Would they know where it is?"

"If it's Tiurian, I'd say no. If they could do something, they would have already done it, instead of coming and asking *you* to do it. It's on you, Astra."

On me.

Besides saving Marlak, now I have to save Nelsin and stop whatever it is from breaking free. I'm sure it's something nasty, and still don't know how I'm supposed to accomplish any of that.

RENEL

I'm myself and not myself, as if a stranger had replaced me and I was looking at the scene through a foggy glass. My worst nightmare is about to come true, and instead of yelling or curling up in a ball, I need to stand strong and try to find a solution in an impossibly short time.

At least Silvan has agreed to see me and should be coming to the castle at any moment. Easily the most scheming and ambitious member of the council, I hope he will serve my purpose.

I stand by my usual seat in the council chamber, Azur beside me. He changed his clothes and has a long-sleeved black shirt on, but hasn't removed his hat. I point at it.

"Perhaps you could—" I mimic removing my nonexistent hat.

He presses his lips together, then shoots me a glare. "I can't." He moves his hand through the hat. "It's a glamour. *She* made it for me. If it's a problem, I can leave."

I shake my head. This was a minor request, and I need Azur here. I don't even know what kind of magic Silvan has, but I'm not willing to take unnecessary risks, even with the Shadow Ring.

The door opens and the fae man walks in, staring at the empty chairs as if only now believing he's alone.

"Your majesty." Silvan bows. "What an honor."

"Take your seat." I wait for him to get to his usual chair, then continue, "You know, for a long time now, I've been thinking we could have a different leadership."

The corner of Silvan's mouth lifts, then he narrows his eyes. "Where's Zorwal?"

"He's not around, and I decided not to wait for him to return. If he returns, he'll be just a member. We need a new leader."

Silvan's eyes sparkle. Of course he wants this.

Even though I'm breaking down inside, I speak with my best king's voice. "I need someone with ambition and wit, who'll consider the well-being of the kingdom, and especially someone who will act as a real leader in the matters of the council."

"I'm assuming you have a candidate in mind?"

"Obviously. And it's the reason I called you here. I'm trying to figure out who could be a good leader. You spend most of your time in the Jewel City, do you not?"

"Sometimes I travel."

"Yes, but you have friends there, family."

He narrows his eyes. "What is your majesty implying?"

I realize that my words might have sounded like a threat, and aim for a softer tone. "You care about that city, and that's important. Now, you'll hear it from me first. One of the best magic scholars in the kingdom has predicted the direction that the castle moves. As much as I try to steer it, it's unfortunately on its own path. Old magic, let's say. In as little as a day and as long as a week or maybe a month, it will reach the Fiery Gorge, and then it will create a crack. That crack will go all the way to the Jewel City, and it will destroy it."

Silvan blinks. "What scholar?"

"That's not something I can reveal, unfortunately." It's me, obviously, but I'll never say it. "The thing is, The Jewel City needs to be evacuated immediately."

The councilor frowns at first, then laughs. "That's... madness. Nobody will agree with it. Where are they supposed to go? You can't just transplant a city somewhere else, and the high fae aren't going to step away from their houses based on what? A prophecy? Now, if you are *certain* that this fate will pass, the best we can do is inform the members of the council and a few select families who'll inform their close ones. It needs to be a secret, or it will create panic."

"A crack through the city will create even more panic, don't you think?"

"Yes, but before that, nobody will believe it. They won't budge, and they'll hate us if we force them."

It's as if he can't understand my point, so I try to explain it some more. "And then, a few days later, they'll be thankful. You'll be a hero who saved many lives, Silvan."

"No. I'll be the villain who didn't stop the city from being destroyed. If it has to come to pass, let it be an accident, a completely unpredictable accident, one that has nothing to do with this castle or with Your Majesty. Warn them, and they'll question *you*, point fingers at *you*. And then it will be *your* mess to clean."

I'll be dead by then, so that's not exactly a problem, but I'm not going to tell him that.

"What I'm gathering is that you don't want to be the council leader, is that it?"

"If the cost is to be the harbinger of doom, of course not. It's suicide. If the city is never destroyed, they'll hate me for causing unnecessary panic. If it *is* destroyed, they'll blame me. I can't, Your Majesty, and if that's the direction your reign is going, I'm afraid you won't be naming council leaders for long."

I definitely won't, so I suppose he is insightful. "What would you suggest, Silvan? Should we let everyone in the city die?"

"I'm sure your council leader will help you come up with a

wise decision. I'm just a member, Your Majesty, and quite an insignificant one." He gets up. "Now, if you'll excuse me, I'll take my leave."

"The council will meet in half an hour."

"My sincerest apologies. I have businesses to attend to."

He simply walks out, his retreating steps echoing in the chamber. I could ask him to stay, even order him, but for what?

Once the door closes behind him, I turn to Azur. "Was I that bad? I thought my argument was good."

"He might not believe you. I mean, you're obviously saying the truth, but consider that *a scholar predicted* doesn't really command trust."

"Should I tell him *I* predicted it?"

"Do you think they'll take your word for it?"

"No." My shoulders sag. "For them, I'm a nobody, just a tavern maid's son."

"It's intriguing, Renel. You spent what, twelve years doing everything they wanted, and they still don't respect you." Azur has a mocking, sardonic edge to his words.

"I pushed back as much as I could, and you know that. It's not easy to keep the council happy."

"It's certainly easier than defying them."

"It's harder. Had I defied them, I would have been assassinated years ago, and then I would no longer be dealing with any of this crap. Being dead is easy." I look at Azur. "What's your suggestion? How do I evacuate the Jewel City?"

"If they don't want to leave, it's their problem, isn't it?"

"If they don't know the risks, how can they even make a decision? And there are enchanted fae there. How are they going to decide to leave?"

Azur chuckles. "Right. How are they going to do anything at all?"

"I don't know why you're laughing."

"I'm not laughing because their lives are funny. Your sudden worry is the strange thing here. Renel, the enchanted fae's lives are doomed regardless. Do you think they want to live any longer? Live through servitude? It makes no difference to them.”

“You don’t know that. And while they live, there’s hope. They could be set free one day. Who knows?”

“Set free by who? If even the acting king can’t do that, who’s going to set them free?”

“Things can change. Regardless, I don’t want to be responsible for their deaths.”

He shrugs. “You could try to talk to the other members.”

“I fear they would try to assassinate me rather than create what they think is unnecessary panic.”

“Didn’t you say you’re going to die anyway when the castle reaches the Fiery Gorge? Why are you suddenly worried about your life?”

I can’t believe he’s even asking that. “Azur, if I can’t evacuate the city while I’m living, do you think I can do anything when I’m dead?”

He takes a deep breath. “You said the Fiery Gorge will cause a crack, right?”

“Yes, it’s what’s been predicted.”

“That part could be wrong. While yes, you have successfully predicted the direction of the castle, you can’t know what will happen once it gets there. And a crack might take a while to reach the Jewel City. They will escape and look for shelter. Now, if evacuation *was* going to be your solution, lots of things could have been done previously, such as having easier escape routes. They could have been forewarned a long time ago about the possibility of a tremor, let’s say. They could have prepared, and yet they didn’t. Now you want to warn them one day or one week before disaster? It won’t work.”

“I thought I would be able to prevent it. I thought I had more time. Zorwal never let me even speak about any of that. He wouldn’t have let me prepare some escape plan. I...” No words come to me, and even if they did, they would be some stupid excuse. “I failed.”

“Sometimes you can’t change fate, Renel. Accept it.”

"Right. So let's cross our arms and let it happen. Also, you look quite cheerful for someone about to die."

He raises an eyebrow. "Should I be upset?"

"That would be a normal reaction, yes."

"It won't change my fate, so there's no point."

"No point. Too late." I point at him. "I haven't forgotten that you never gave me a *single* suggestion on how to deal with this. Maybe some flirting tips when I asked. Other than that, not a single suggestion. Instead, you kept saying that there was something I wasn't seeing, that a castle wouldn't self-destruct. Have you changed your mind yet?"

His face is placid as he looks at me. "First, I'm your guardian, not your advisor. That role, as far as I understand, you gave to your precious and dear Zorwal. Second, the castle has not *yet* reached the Fiery Gorge, and the kingdom has not *yet* been destroyed, so you can't be sure of anything."

"My precious Zorwal. You have to be kidding me. What would you have me do? Appoint *you* as the leader of the council?"

Azur rolls his eyes. "That would make no sense, considering you think I'm an overpowered idiot."

"I don't think that, and you're my friend; I *always* seek your advice."

"For small, personal matters. When it comes to the kingdom, it's what the council and Zorwal want."

I huff. "They'll depose me otherwise."

"You've told me that—quite a few times."

"Then be more understanding. It's hard to be the acting king."

He runs his hand over his hair, crossing the glamour hat. "I'm not debating it. I'm just explaining why I cannot solve your problem."

I exhale. "And I guess I'm explaining why I haven't yet solved it. Or taken any measures."

"I understand. Can I take my leave? I'd like to rest a little.

Call me when you need me. The ring and the guards should protect you for now."

"Go. Rest. I'll be here scouring my mind for a solution. But I'll need you for the council meeting."

"I'll be back."

Azur leaves me in this huge, empty room—empty like me.

Every life is precious, and yet if I can't convince the council to evacuate the Jewel City soon, thousands of them might be lost.

But how?

LIDIANE

My body feels strange, painful, while I notice that the floor beneath me is moving. When I open my eyes, I realize that my wrists are handcuffed and I'm sitting in a large wooden cage transported by a cart. A thick canvas covers us, so that only some dim sunlight comes from the bottom of the cage and through the fabric. Tarlia is curled up, lying beside me, also handcuffed.

I want to wake her up, and yet the first thing I feel is a tug. Tug, tug, tug calling me. Azur is calling me, pulling me. If it goes both ways, he'll sense I'm in danger. Depending on what he's doing, worrying about me might distract or endanger him. And then there's my brother. I don't want either of them to worry about me, so I imagine myself safe in my house, eating a warm, delicious apple pie, feeling protected, then I project that feeling through the bond. No fear, no danger—just safety.

Will that work? I don't know. What I know is that I have to find a way to escape.

I keep that feeling of contentment, joy, safety, and shake Tarlia.

"Tar," I whisper. "Tar."

She opens her eyes, looks around, and sits up. "Someone caught us. Did you see who?"

"No. They might have had some glamour for invisibility or not being noticed. Or else they were fast. I'm sorry."

She frowns. "It's not your fault."

"I should have sensed it."

Tarlia's thoughtful. "Do you know who could be behind this? Do you have any enemies?"

"Marlak's enemies," I mouth, afraid of being overheard. "But almost nobody knows I'm his friend. Only Azur, but he wouldn't..."

"Hurt you? He wouldn't."

The cart then stops.

"Lie down," I whisper and pretend to sleep while keeping my eyes slightly open. Outside the cart, steps retreat. After a few minutes, I sit up again.

"I think they left."

Tarlia checks the bars of the cage. "This is wood. We could break it."

"Fae reinforced wood. You'd need a powerful axe and it would still take a long time. If we try using our daggers, we'll blunt them and have no weapons."

"We already have no weapons." She checks her pockets. "They took them."

"True. How do you expect to break it?"

She looks at the base of the cage. "Not sure. It's not made of one piece, right? So it must have a weak link."

I take a closer look. "The bars are bolted to the base. Hmmm. Maybe. And you, do you have any guess who's behind this?"

She shakes her head. "I was attacked before, but they were after Ziven, and the attackers were all killed. I doubt humans would come this far, and I doubt anyone would bother coming after me. Renel's enemies... How would they find us all the way north, almost in the Shadow Lands? How would they know where we'd come from? Unless women get kidnapped in fae lands. I've heard... stories. Not about fae, but about humans. Monsters, I suppose, but human monsters."

"You can't capture a fae against their will if there's no deal. The exception is when there's a ruling by a court. We could be taken by royal guards, but it would be different. Unless..." Can it be? "It's Zorwal."

She stares at me, a mix of shock and disbelief on her face. "You truly think he survived."

"I'm positive. There was a strange energy, an odd magic, and it kept acting on Azur. It's why he couldn't transcend properly. I felt it." My entire body shudders remembering that council leader.

"What kind of being survives a beheading?"

"Something evil, unnatural."

"No kidding." She huffs. "Now, we heard steps, so it's more than one person. Either he has allies, or it's not even him yet, just his thugs. We need to escape."

It should be my turn to tell her *no kidding*, but instead, I take a deep breath. "Let's think. And find a way out."

31

RENEL

The dark sphere still floats above its pillar as if to mock me. I'm at the castle's heart, its highest room, with large glass walls from where I'll have the best view of my doom.

The council didn't come. I chuckle. They didn't come. Every single one of them sent a silly excuse. This probably means they decided to meet without me and conspire. My only consolation is that if they're in the Jewel City, their plot won't go very far. What an incredible consolation.

Now I'm here, staring at this stupid sphere and wondering if there's any way to bend it to my will. I suppose I should start by not calling it stupid. The Shadow Ring is on my finger, laughing at me and my imbecilic plan to seduce a Tiurian.

"Renel," Azur calls from the other side of the door. "Are you there?"

I open the door, and he enters. "So no council meeting?"

I stare at the sphere. "No."

"Do you have a plan?"

"I'll ask the gods to help me."

"They don't interfere."

"I'm asking for an exception."

"Right." He has one eyebrow raised and gives me an unconvinced look.

"I'm serious. Other than asking, I'll be here, trying to control the castle. Why wouldn't I have any magic? Not even a drop of it? What if a drop is all it takes? What if I can summon it at the last moment?"

Now he's staring at me as if I'm insane. "I suppose you can try."

"I don't know what to make of your carelessness about your own demise."

"What would you expect me to do?"

"Care." I shrug. "At least a little."

Azur looks down. "You don't know how I feel."

"True. And I'm sorry. Sorry for your bond, sorry for my failure." He nods and stares out the window. I look too. "These fields, this region, it reminds me of a time when things were easier, when I was happy."

"What's the next stop? For the castle?" His expression is grim, and I realize it's true that I don't know how he feels.

"North," I say. "Close to Serenade."

His eyes widen.

I add, "Not close enough to damage that village."

"Serenade," he mutters, his voice cracking with emotion.

Apologies won't help, so I keep silent and walk to the window. As I run a finger over the handrail, it trembles. At first, it's a soft, almost imperceptible rumble, and yet I know what's happening.

The sky outside gets dark, and yet it's not the sky, it's the castle moving in the space between spaces, going to its final resting place before doom. When daylight returns, we're near the fae territories and the forests in that area.

Strangely, I feel no fear. I suppose the certainty of my destiny has numbed me.

I turn to Azur. "It's time. The royal guard was told to evacuate the castle and keep only a safety perimeter around it.

Check if they're obeying. The doors of the Royal Terrace are to be permanently closed. Find the castle workers, such as cooks and servants, and make sure they leave."

"Enchanted servants have nowhere to go, Renel. And they can't simply abandon their post. Their enchantment won't let them."

"Give them a task that will make them go outside."

"Then if the castle is destroyed, they'll be looking for it forever. Let them die with the castle, if it comes to it. It's a kinder fate."

"It's a cruel fate, Azur. Let them survive this catastrophe. Who knows, maybe their enchantments will be broken. Maybe there's still hope for them. Get them out of the castle."

"Yes, master."

He's saying this to annoy me, but I decide to ignore it.

Then he adds, "The castle could take days, even months to move. Are you sure you want to go without servants?"

"It could take days, yes, but it won't take months. It's a pattern, Azur. The intervals got shorter and shorter. Either way, I suppose I can go to the kitchen and find myself something to eat if the castle takes more than a few hours. Otherwise, I'll be here. Make sure the castle is empty. You can leave too."

He snorts. "That's not how my bond works, and you know it."

"Maybe I should find something useful for you to do outside the castle."

"Won't save me. If you die, so do I."

"Go say goodbye to your soulmate."

He gives me a murderous glare. "Why would I give her such a wound? Why would I make her miss me?"

I look down and run my hand over the rail. "Sometimes, knowing that you were loved once can get you through hard times. You can miss someone and still treasure your times together as a memory."

My own words make my eyes misty. Is this about my mother, my father? Tarlia? Not her, since we never mentioned any feelings. Perhaps there were none—and it was still worth it, still a cherished memory.

Azur huffs. "Lidiane will find love and joy, and I'll be but a passing, insignificant shadow in her life. When I die, she won't shed a single tear. That's my gift to her. I could have given her my heart, my life, but if all I can give her is freedom from the suffering of this bond, then so be it."

"That's selfless, I suppose."

"Maybe. Anyway, I'll go and evacuate the castle. Anything else, Your Highness?"

"That's all for now."

He leaves me here and I approach the sphere again. Could the castle be sentient?

Can I try to convince it to save itself?

My ideas are getting ridiculous, my mind is getting muddled, but at this point, I have nothing to lose.

TARLIA

I explained *leverage* to Lidiane, and the idea that we could use something as a lever to crack those bars, but the truth is that we have nothing, so my idea was pointless. I tried to hold on to the bars, push my feet against them, then pull, but nothing moved.

"What about your magic?" I ask.

"My element is air, but I'm horrible at it. I would get exhausted and nowhere near cracking anything."

I try to think. "Wouldn't Azur... sense you?"

"I'm trying to block him."

I'm impressed. "You can do that?"

"I'm trying."

I'm also puzzled. "He's very powerful. Why wouldn't you want him to find you?"

"It could be a trap for him. I'd rather escape without his help."

I glance at both our handcuffs. "What are the odds?"

She shushes me, and I pay attention to the sounds around us. Someone's approaching. They throw something into the cage. Two small balls.

Drusils. I tremble.

"What's that?" she asks.

"A candy I like. From human lands—or Krastel, at least. Few people know I like them."

She frowns. "No fae would know."

"Renel does, but he wouldn't tell anyone about it. I mean, even if he were captured and tortured, nobody would ask him about something so meaningless."

I stare at the two little balls. Even though they were thrown in the dirty cage, I'm wondering if I could wipe them and eat them, but that would be quite stupid, since they could be poisoned.

"Then who?" Lidiane asks.

There's only one explanation, even though it doesn't explain much. "It's my master. But I don't know how or why."

Someone pulls part of the canvas covering the cage. Otavio stands there, wearing one of his long robes.

He smiles at me. "Good guess. Finally. I was almost giving up, *Tarlia.*"

I return the smile and pretend to be happy to see him. "Master, you found me! Did you come to rescue us?" I show my handcuffs.

His chuckle is to my ears what pepper would be to my eyes. "Do not pretend to be stupid. You know well I'm the one who captured you."

I frown as if confused. "That makes no sense. I work for you."

He raises an eyebrow. "Do you? Or do you think you can fend for yourself? Do you think you can trick me?" He snorts. "Pretending to be Astra! As if you could come even close to her."

At least Lidiane is quiet, watching him. I wouldn't want her to attract his wrath, and I know he can be dangerous.

"Didn't I do a good job?" I smile again. "I could do better next time. When did you figure it out?"

"Why should I tell you? Now, you're not very smart, are you? Pretending to be Astra, you were caught just like she was." He smirks. "Funny that *your friend* never warned you. Or do you think she's your sister?"

"No such delusions, master."

That said, Astra did tell me that she had been located because of the hair coloring, and I realize that's how he found me. To my defense, I didn't plan on going to the Shadow Lands or leaving the castle, and didn't know he would come after me.

"At least you're finally being useful. You were always by far the prettiest, and yet you squandered all the beauty I worked hard for you to have." He points at one of the drusils on the floor. "Did you really suck a kitchen assistant's cock for one of those?"

It was just a hand job, he was cute, and I was hungry. But I'm not going to confess it. I smirk. "Of course not. I let the assistant and the male cooks all take turns fucking me. It was more delicious than the drusils."

He chuckles. "I'm glad to hear they had some joy before dying."

A bitter taste comes to my mouth. "Dying?"

"What do you think the penalty is for using royal property, Tarlia? What do you think you are?"

Dead? I noticed that I never saw any man in the kitchen again, but I could never have guessed… That's horrific. "They were innocent. And I'm lying. They never touched me."

"We couldn't take the risk. Their deaths are your fault."

"But the guards who came to my room were not killed."

"No. They were doing their job." He sniggers. "You think you're some kind of rebel? You think you were *defying* me? You were not. You were doing exactly what I expected. Those men were doing what they were told would be one of the perks of the position."

A chill runs down my spine.

He chuckles. "You're surprised. How can you be surprised? Still, to be honest, your lack of ambition always disappointed me. Any woman in your place would set her sights higher, would use her body to her advantage. Did you ever think Sayanne got preferential treatment?"

"Not really. Astra did."

"Astra's a different story. Now, between you two worthless humans, didn't you notice Sayanne always got what she wanted? Didn't you wonder how she got it? Ambition, Tarlia. She set her sights higher. First her master, then the princes, and now, look at that, she's going to be the Krastel Queen."

I think I'm going to puke. "You made her... seduce the king?"

His laughter is loud and sounds genuine. "Oh, no. It was her own initiative. Vision, Tarlia. And now she thinks she hates me, just because I left her. And yet she managed to wipe the Krastel royal family from the map. Wipe an entire family, Tarlia. Isn't it beautiful? A family who would have killed and enslaved my kind, mind you. She'll be queen soon, and who knows, I might return and she might forgive me. I might see my child on that throne."

"Aren't you too old for that?" This was part curiosity, part the need to jab him.

"Not really." His smirk is creepy and disconcerting. "With proper care and a healthy lifestyle, people like me can sire children when they're five hundred years old or more. I'm not nearly there."

"What are you?"

"Someone better than you. Stronger. More powerful. But I was talking about Sayanne. Beautiful, smart Sayanne. She has vision, ambition. Did you know it was her idea to kill you and Ziven?"

"I survived." And I hope they think Ziven's dead.

"She thinks she succeeded, and that's enough for my plans.

You were not *my* target, even if you were such a disappointment. You never looked up. Never dreamed higher. You were the greatest beauty in the entire kingdom, and instead of using it, you chose to be a cheap slut."

"Not cheap. I don't recall charging anyone." I smirk. "And disappointing you made it all sweeter."

"Oh, no. It wasn't all bad. I took great pleasure in watching you."

I chill and tremble from head to toe. My stomach is empty and at the same time revolving.

He chuckles. "Oh. Don't tell me you're embarrassed. Worthless sluts don't get the luxury of being prudish. I enjoyed every second of watching your perfect body. I won't deny it, I was disappointed you never invited your master to your bed, but I blamed it on your lack of vision. And yet you finally managed to accomplish something. The Crystal Court King. Well done. Very well done."

"He's not interested in me."

His laughter is cruel and eerie. "Oh, don't be silly! I mean, you do have a valid point. It's not really *you* he wants, it's what he *sees* in you, what he *scents*. Why do you think I spent so long working on your hair? Your skin? You think it was just a beauty treatment? It was not. I was turning you into a being so completely irresistible that you could make any man fall in love despite your vulgarity and poor manners. And it worked. This time, I'll tighten the rope around your neck and make sure you dance to the tune *I* play. If you don't, it's fine as well. You're also valuable as a hostage."

"I always had a vision for surviving, and that hasn't changed. Tell me what to do. I'd rather help you than be a hostage." Of course I don't want to help him, but I need him to free me.

"We'll see. I still need to decide if you're useful to me alive. And you need to help me find Astra. So your survival will depend on your good behavior."

The disgusting words he told me earlier come to mind. As

repulsive as this thought is, it could be the perfect opportunity to kill him.

I run a hand through my hair, ending at the tips, near my breast. "You should have told me you wanted to come to my bed, master." Somehow I manage to make my voice husky, seductive. "Perhaps you were right that I didn't set my sights higher. Perhaps I thought I wasn't worthy of a man like you, and yet I regret all the days you had to watch me all alone, when *you* should be the one in my bed. But it's not too late to remedy that."

His eyes flicker over my body. Disgustingly devouring eyes. Then he laughs. "Tarlia, Tarlia, I'm not *that* stupid. I don't want a dagger in my back. You think you disguise it, but I can sense your hatred. It seeps through your skin, girl. The only reason I kept you alive was because somehow I thought that anger could eventually be useful to me. And I was right. Oh. And I never watched you alone. Either Andrezza, Sayanne, or a maid kept me company. I'm not *that* pathetic."

Sayanne. That's why she kept calling me a slut. And yet I can't even be angry at her. Is it true that it was her *vision* and *ambition*? Or was she more malleable to his manipulations? Perhaps more afraid than us?

"So what now?" I ask.

"You'll remain in this cage until I have the need of your services. Don't try anything funny. I don't truly need the fae." He points at Lidiane. Oddly, I had forgotten she was here—and now I'm worried.

"Oh," he adds. "Also, Astra was never your friend, nor your *sister*. She was always ashamed of you. Don't let any misplaced loyalty make things harder for you."

I want to think it's a lie, but I'm not sure. "Didn't you want me to help you find her? Let me help you."

I'm hoping that perhaps he could free me, get me out of this cage. Once I'm out, I won't hesitate to strangle him. I hesitated too long, and now I'm paying for it.

"Oh, you will. Don't worry. For now, you're exactly where I want."

He places the canvas over the cage and walks away, his steps quiet on the earth. I keep imagining him watching me in bed with my companions, then I wonder if it's a lie, if he's saying it to mess with my mind. And yet I still have a lump in my throat while angry tears gather in my eyes. How dare he humiliate me like that?

Lidiane exhales, then whispers, "I have a plan."

Her confidence is enough to change my mood.

ASTRA

We've been walking north for hours. At this point, both Ferer and I know that there's no turning back, that we'll still be here when night falls. I trust the light that has always guided me, the light that protected me and Nelsin, and I know that I can brave the night here, but I'm not so sure if Ferer trusts me. I can sense his worry, and a lot of it is about Nelsin.

The Amethyst Palace is like a scent the wind sometimes blows in my direction. Sometimes, it's the fragment of a known song. I can feel it's near, can even feel it calling me, and yet I still don't know where it is. I look at the forest and see no hills, even if there were always hills in my dreams.

The sky is getting darker and darker, the sun touching the top of the forest on the left of us.

"Night's falling," Ferer says. "You might want to... Whatever you do for protection. Soulsuckers are deadly."

"Walk closer." I think about light and the Almighty Mother. She is real, even if Tiurians might have given her a different name. I can feel her light and protection enveloping me, enveloping Ferer. It's a real light, casting a visible glow around us, now that the daylight is fading.

"We'll find the palace," I add.

"I know you will. Even the *giants* trust you, why shouldn't I?" He chuckles, but it's a chuckle full of sadness.

"Yes. And they'll release Nelsin. Have you considered forgiving him?"

"Every day. Every hour. Every second. I want to touch his skin, kiss his lips, feel his embrace. And yet he needs to take the first step."

"He's giving you space, waiting for you to be ready to forgive him."

"I suppose the giants just gave me the space I need. I want him back. But we'll figure it out." He stops. "Do you hear that?"

"I don't have fae super hearing."

He points outside the circle. At a distance, I see strange creatures, brown as if made of mud, and yet shaped like humans. I look up and realize the sun is now completely hidden behind the horizon. Chills run up my spine.

"Ghouls," he whispers. "But your light's keeping them at bay."

Indeed it is, and I trust it enough not to let fear overcome me.

I've heard tons of stories about ghouls, but I don't know what's true and what's a lie, so I ask, "What do they do?"

"Bite, mostly. One or two is not a problem. A large group of them *can* be an issue."

"They won't approach us." I can sense the light repelling them. It's a resilient, stable light that doesn't even demand that much effort or focus. "When I was young, I was told they could steal us from our beds at night if we misbehaved, but I was also told that Tiurians commanded them, and that made me quite confused."

"I'm glad most of that confusion is clearing away."

"Yes. I can't deal with any confusion now."

I glance at the ghouls surrounding us.

I can't fail, can't let my light fail, can't fail to find the Amethyst Palace.

32

ZIVEN

We're so screwed.

I know Marlak knows, he knows that I know, and yet neither of us will mention it. Of course leaving this island will be hard—if not impossible.

The upside is that at least I can hope that one day, someday, *someone* will come. Astra, Nelsin, and Ferer know where we are, so that's a good start. The issue is whether any of them would find us, see us, or be able to open that bridge. And then there's whoever has been coming and dropping in supplies. Maybe it's almost time for their visit? I sure want to hope, just because it's better than being depressed.

Other than that, there's the bird-eating monster. No sign of it yet. And no sign of Marlak's sister. He already told me twice that she was solid and real, and I don't want to risk my luck by asking again. He has called her name a few times as well, with no answer. I suppose she must be sleeping really heavily.

We sit outside, eating some of the dried meat we brought. It's our second meal for the day and almost the end of our supplies. Why did we have the moronic idea to travel light?

"Want to know what I'm thinking?" I ask.

"Probably not, but go ahead; I'm sure you're eager to tell."

I should just shut up and leave him curious, but every second of silence just amplifies my anxiety. "I'm hoping next time the monster brings a dead bird, it's not all eaten. We could roast the rest. And have some fresh meat."

"You roast it and let me know so I stay far away."

I almost crack a joke about him being afraid of fire, but then it hits me; that's probably true. Marlak fears or at least dislikes fire. Makes sense, considering what he's been through.

"I'll do that." Then I change the subject. "We'll need a place to sleep soon. I think I'll set up the tent, so I keep watch outside. You can find a bedroom, so you're near your sister. Unless you have another idea—or want to sleep in the tent."

He shakes his head slowly and takes a deep breath. "I need to understand where my sister is. This morning, it *was* her."

"I saw her too, and even hit her with a jet of water, then secured her feet with ice. Perhaps there's a spell that makes her sleep a lot."

His eyes are distant, deep in thought. "Where?"

"We'll figure it out."

He turns to me, his eyebrows contracted. "Are you truly this optimistic? Or is this your coping mechanism?"

"Does it make a difference? Perhaps that's what defines each person; how they cope."

He chuckles. "Not only are you optimistic, you're philosophical. Surprising." He's definitely making fun of me.

"At least I don't hate people for no reason."

Marlak turns to me, his glare cold and hard. "You think I have no reason to hate my brother?"

"I was talking about me."

"Oh, please." He rolls his eyes. "You need to be at least a little significant to deserve to be hated. You're a stranger, that's all."

"Right. Insignificant stranger."

"You implied I hated you, and I don't. What do you want? A friendship bracelet?"

"Of course not. We're not even friends. Well, I'll set up the tent."

Marlak stares at me. "No. We shouldn't split. There's time to make a bedroom mildly decent just for tonight, and we'll bar the doors."

"Oooh, now you're taking the bird-eating monster seriously —and inviting me to sleep with you? How sweet."

He gets up. "You know what? Sleep in the tent."

"I will."

He turns around and heads for the kitchen door. It's the only working door in and out of the tower, and we cleared a lot of the debris—and bodies.

The sky is getting pink around me, and I take the tent. Shit. What if there *is* a monster?

This is going to be the greatest humiliation of my life, but I have no choice.

I run inside the tower. "Marlak!"

As I walk into the broken dining room, I almost collide with him, since he's coming in my direction.

"Ah." He chuckles. "So you came to your senses?"

"I did. It would be wise for us to share a room."

He nods. "Let's find one."

My heart is banging on the walls of my chest, begging me to turn around and run. But run where? Outside? Where a monster might find us? And then again, is the inside of the tower any safer?

There's no way to know.

TARLIA

We've been in this cage for hours, and Lidiane refused to tell me or even give me a hint of her magnificent, mysterious plan. She points around the cart as if to mean she fears someone will hear her.

My stomach is growling, even though I still want to puke. I can't wipe from my mind the image of Otavio watching me. Was he behind a mirror? Was it a peephole? I wonder if anything he told me is true. Sayanne loved to brag. Wouldn't she brag about that? Give an inkling that she had seen me?

My stomach turns to ice. She did. A few times, over breakfast, she'd stare at me and mention something I did. I used to think the guards had big mouths and somehow our activities were getting to her ears, but now I wonder if she was the one who saw me and made the entire elite tower aware of who slept with me and when. Now she's with the Krastel King. He's so much older than her, with folds of skin hanging down his neck —and we look like his daughter. Disgusting.

She has vision.

No. Otavio messed up her mind, that's what he did. When did he even start sleeping with her? Oh, gross, some thoughts are too troubling to be expressed as words.

I truly regret not killing him during all the opportunities I had.

Also, what is it he wants? Other than finding Astra, what else can he want with me? With Renel?

Renel. I remember the kiss and the look he gave me and want to cry. I wonder if he's going to find a solution for his castle, if Zorwal is dead for good, if we'll ever meet again.

Some dreams are too big for me to hold into my thoughts, so I send them to my heart, and then it wants to explode.

And now I wonder if Renel's sweet words were because of Otavio's enchantment or whatever he did to me. Was it all a lie?

It's the explanation that makes the most sense. I don't know how I manage to feel sad about it, when it's so obvious.

Meanwhile, I'm still waiting for Lidiane's big, secret plan. I wonder if she told me that just to give me some useless hope— but she can't lie.

That said, if she has some crazy, pointless hope, I don't think being a fae precludes her from voicing her delusions. And then again, it's not like *I* have a genius plan. I can't even think when my stomach's growling.

And I miss Renel, miss him like I've never missed anyone. I think I'm also missing my brain.

Lidiane taps on my shoulder, then looks at me and places a finger over her mouth. I almost complain that I was silent, but then I realize I can hear soft steps near the front of the cart.

In a second, she changes the way she looks. Instead of the beautiful fae she is, I see the most disgusting man I've ever seen; Otavio.

"Sarin, Sarin!" She yells. Her voice doesn't sound exactly the way Otavio does when he yells, but it's a decent impersonation. I'm surprised she caught this person's name. "Come here!"

Someone lifts part of the canvas, and a green-skinned fae man peers through and frowns.

"What are you looking at?" Lidiane yells. "Come free me. The girl, she tricked me."

I'm assuming she's talking about some other event in the past, so as not to lie.

He blinks. "How did you get there?"

"I was tricked. Now come and open it."

The fae glances at Otavio-looking Lidiane, then at me. "What if *you're* tricking me?"

"What trick? I'm asking for your help. What's the trick in that?"

"But you can lie." He tilts his head, still examining her. That makes no sense. If he thinks that's really Otavio, he should be helping him. The reality is that Lidiane can't lie.

"What do you think I'm doing here? Having fun?" Lidiane sounds furious—and scary.

Her yells finally convince the fae. He pulls a large key from his pocket, inserts it at the base of the cage, then lifts the walls and ceiling all at once, allowing us to walk out.

Sarin takes a smaller key and undoes Lidiane's cuffs, then looks at me. "Her too?"

"Yes. It turns out she's innocent."

I can't believe it when he finally releases my arms and I can move my shoulders back and then rub my wrists together to alleviate the discomfort. Lidiane walks away fast, and I follow her.

"Hey!" the fae man yells. "My payment!"

I'm not sure what she does, but it makes my entire body tingle. The man's yells sound muffled and distant in my ear, and she pulls my hand and runs.

"Can you swim? Hold your breath, at least?" Lidiane asks without reducing her pace.

I remember choking water on a lake's sandy bank, then being told to jump in again, only to inhale water once more. Water terrifies me. But being caught by Otavio again terrifies me even more.

"Is that the only way?" I ask.

"It's the fastest."

"I'll hold my breath."

"Great."

I glimpse an opening in the trees and realize it's a river's edge. Lidiane holds my hand and jumps, and I hold my nose closed with one hand. I guess that is one thing I learned.

We're sinking, sinking, and sinking much deeper than I expected, and I don't even know what we're doing anymore, as the current pushes then revolves us. I thought we were just going to cross the river, and now I feel as if I'm a potion ingredient in one of Otavio's churners. Ugh. The thought makes my stomach spin, my head spin. In fact, my whole body is spinning and I don't understand what's happening.

We're still going down when something pulls me by the hair. I turn to fight it, but then realize I breached the surface. Lidiane is the one pulling me to the shore. No, not shore, it's a tiny island in the middle of a river. I'm not choking any water and I'm feeling proud of myself, but I don't understand why she was pulling me like that.

"Ouch. By the hair?"

"You'd pull me to the bottom otherwise."

"Weren't we already at the bottom? I felt like we went down and down and down, but never up."

"It's how it feels, I know. You'll be safe here until we get rid of your hair color."

I look around. "Won't they find us? They know we came in this direction."

"We're far. It's like transcending through the circles, except that we can also do it in the rivers."

"I didn't know that."

"Almost nobody does. It's a secret, so keep it as such. Renel must never, ever hear anything about it."

"I might never see him again." I feel a pang in my chest, but nothing more. It's like when you're already in pain and something pokes you and feels insignificant.

She shakes her head. "No. We have to warn them. I think your master cut a lock of your hair and maybe even mine. I don't know what he's going to do, but he might threaten to hurt you and demand something from Renel. You need to let him know you're alive and free. I don't think your master will try to do the same to Azur, but I can't risk it either. We have to go to the castle. But before that, we need to do something to your hair."

My fake black hair, over fake red hair. I pull a strand and look at it. "Otavio once said that lemon can remove the color. I don't know if it's true."

"We can try. I'll bring some. Sage and thyme also work on wards. If this is magic..."

"It has to be magic. What kind of chemicals would let him

locate me like that? I mean, if I was close, I could say it was some special scent, but far?"

She nods. "Magic, then. The river will conceal you, I hope. Wait here while I bring the ingredients."

"Can you bring something to eat?" I didn't want to sound whiny, but I suppose I did.

She chuckles. "Yes, I will. If someone comes, lie down and hope the glamour works. I'll be right back."

"Wait. What if he finds you?"

"How? Your master didn't touch us or give us any object that could be traced. He wouldn't know where I live or the places I go. Even then, I'll avoid them, just in case. I'll be right back, then we'll go to the castle."

"Do you even know where it is?"

She nods. "I can find it, yes."

"Are you always this confident and resourceful?"

"I'm confident?" She emits a surprised chuckle. "No. I'm often a mess. That said, I can evade a human captor. Is he even human?"

"Tiurian, but Tiurians are human, I suppose. Unless... Not fae, I don't think, with the amount of lies he utters, not to mention his round ears, of course."

"Marlak is fae and can lie—but it's rare." She smirks. "It might be the ears."

"I've never heard of magic that lets you locate someone."

"There are many types of magic, and many types of Tiurian magic, if that's what he is. Anyway, I'd better go. I'll be back soon."

She jumps in the water and swims across, with no strange spinning or dragging her to the bottom, then she disappears among trees.

I sit here, glad to have escaped Otavio's clutches, and yet wondering how many of those still linger in my mind.

I'll see Renel. My heart is jumping and I don't know if it's fear, joy, or excitement. I don't know how much it will hurt to learn he hasn't found a solution to his castle or how much it will hurt to tell him my master tricked him. I have to tell him.

More than anything, I hope he's alive, and that the man Azur beheaded in his castle didn't survive.

Then, after that, I don't know where to go or what to do. My future is an open road—open, empty, and with no indication of where it's going.

ASTRA

We've been walking for a while now, our way lit by the stars and the glow of my own light, while the ghouls around us multiply and multiply. It's not like they're even trying to breach my defenses or attack me.

Perhaps they're waiting.

I can feel that the Amethyst Palace is close, except that I'm not sure exactly where.

We tried getting into the forest, but without a trail and with such thick vegetation, it's too hard to walk in it. I fear I'll be walking until the morning and still will see no sign of what I came to find.

Would the Nymph Queen and the giants be wrong about me? What is it that they see?

The castle calls me, yes, and yet I can't sense it. It's like a voice whose direction I can't pinpoint.

I can't keep walking aimlessly, and decide to stop.

Ferer doesn't say anything, doesn't ask anything. Of course he's anxious like me, perhaps even more, and yet he's letting me figure it out on my own.

I think back to what Nelsin said about the Almighty Mother, that even if she's from Krastel, it's still something that guides me. And that's what I have to do. Let her guide me.

Almighty Mother, where's the Amethyst Palace?

Trust. Trust. Trust.

I can't complain about the answer I got. If that's the answer, that's the answer. *Trust.*

Let go and trust.

I take a deep breath. My trust in the Almighty Mother is unshakeable.

Please guide me, I ask. *Tell me how to find the Amethyst Palace.*

Trust us.

That's a different voice, not one, but many. Many voices.

Trust them.

A thought comes to me; a memory of Andrezza's words, telling me that darksouls command ghouls.

Darksouls.

What am I?

A cold shiver settles inside me from my stomach to my chest. It's about to move up to my neck—when I tell myself to stop. That's fear.

Fear of myself? Fear of my power? I need to trust, surrender, and if I truly trust, there's no reason to fear.

The creatures have been surrounding us and haven't tried to attack us. The ghouls.

I don't sense any malice or antagonism from them. Don't sense any anger or fear. They're peaceful.

"Ferer." He looks at me, and I say, "Stand close and trust me."

I quench my light while still trusting in the protection of the Almighty Mother. That feeling of belonging overwhelms me, now that I can see the stars above us and look further in the distance, when there's no light to limit my view. Ghouls until the eye can see. Beside me, I hear Ferer's breathing coming in and out in sharp, fast blows.

I look at the creatures. "What do you want?"

The ones in front of me kneel, followed by the ones behind them, and behind and behind, like a wave. They serve me.

A thin, phantom shiver runs down my spine. And yet now I have my answer.

ASTRA

I'm not sure if this is a scene from a dream or a nightmare. Hundreds of ghouls surround me and Ferer, all kneeling.

They want to help me.

I don't know if my idea will work, but I decide to give it a try, and ask, "Can you lead me to the Amethyst Palace?"

My voice sounds firm, certain, and I'm glad I was able to bury my fears. Still, can these creatures know the location of the place of my dreams?

Ahead of me, the ghouls step aside, opening a path. I step onto the path they're opening. Two ghouls step ahead of us, and we follow them until we leave the large group behind. We enter the forest through a path wide enough for a person to walk through. Eventually, after about an hour, they stop and step aside. We're in the midst of the forest, and all I see are vine-covered trees ahead of me.

All I *see*, and yet that's not necessarily true. I take a step, my hand reaching forward, and it touches something cold—some metal like copper or brass. Slowly, a humongous door appears in front of me. Just the door, nothing else. On it, a plaque has a sign with a heart, an eye, and a drop of blood. I hope they're not expecting any royalty here, and that being Tiurian would be enough. It has to be, if I've been seeing this palace, sensing it calling me. I poke the tip of my thumb with my dagger, then rub it onto the drawing of the eye. Ferer observes me in silence.

The ground trembles when the door screeches and moves back to give us passage. Ferer and I enter it, and then the door shuts. He ignites a lightstone and I see that we're in an immense hall. Thankfully, none of the ghouls came in. As helpful as they were, their proximity peeved me. I take a look at the place, and my stomach feels tight and cold.

This is a place from nightmares, not dreams.

The walls might have been white some time ago, but now a thick, black liquid seeps from the impossibly high ceiling, while thick, dark vines cover the ground. Strange vines that almost look like veins of some sort.

"Is this it?" Ferer asks.

My breath falters, wondering if this is a trap, wondering if the ghouls led us to some cursed place, but then I look at the white marble of the floor again. It's the same marble I've stepped on when getting up at night to meet my husband on the balcony. The balcony was much higher though, probably above this floor. Just because I've never been in this hall, it doesn't mean this isn't the right place, and I have to consider that it has been abandoned for a long time.

"I think so," I whisper. It's odd that I fear what could be hiding here. Maybe not odd. I have had dreams about something dangerous lurking in this place. "But stay alert."

"No kidding."

I look around for some stairs, something. We need to reach a higher floor, and yet I don't see any way to get there. If anything, this looks like the interior of a hollow tower.

Ferer points to a wall. "I think there's a door there."

Behind vines, covered with that strange black liquid, indeed there's a door that once must have been white. He goes ahead of me, avoiding the vines, and pushes it just enough for us to walk through, so that we reach another hall. There's no furniture, just vines and vines and that awful liquid. The ceiling here is high, but not as much as in the previous room. On the back, I finally see what looks like a staircase, even if it's so dirty that it's barely recognizable as such.

"We need to go up," I whisper.

"I'll go first." Ferer steps ahead of me.

This is wrong. If this is my castle, from my dreams, I'm the one who needs to lead.

"I'll go." I hold his arm and smile at him. "That way, if I fall, you catch me."

He nods.

The handrail is slimy and disgusting, while the steps are slippery and have those awful vines on them. I'm starting to think there's a high chance I might fall, and yet I keep climbing, even if much slower and more carefully than I'd like, as the urgency to reach this place hasn't faded; it has only grown stronger, and yet whatever it is I have to reach, it's upstairs. We climb and climb, passing by empty, dirty rooms, until the staircase reaches an end.

My heart is fidgety in my restless chest as we move through an open, empty room, the floor covered in dark vines. An open door leads to a room above the entrance hall.

I hold a dagger, just in case, and step carefully. There are no sounds, not even wind from outside, just my steps and my breath, as I can't be silent like Ferer. This new room has a glass floor. In its middle lies a round table with a black thing over it. Beside it, there's a crystal arrangement, somewhat like what I saw on the ceiling of the sanctuary, except that the crystals are black.

"Do you think it's safe?" I ask Ferer and point at the floor.

"Yes, but who knows? I'll make a layer of ice."

Icicles form on the walls, then slowly cover the floor above the vines.

He adds, "Careful because it might be slippery."

I step slowly over the new floor Ferer created, and then realize that thick vines lead to the black thing over the table.

As our light gets closer to it, I realize it looks like a human heart—but black. I feel compelled to touch it, even if the idea seems disgusting to my rational mind. Or should I touch the crystals?

With my eyes closed, I think about the Almighty Mother, about my light.

An idea comes to my mind, sharp and clear; I should touch both. I step between the heart and the crystal arrangement, spread my arms, then place my palms on the heart and the crystals.

The crystals turn red and illuminate the room, while the heart pulses as if returning to life.

And then I'm far away, in a different building, fast asleep on an uncomfortable, dusty bed, while something moves in my direction. Ziven is sitting nearby in an armchair, his eyes almost closing. This is Marlak. Marlak, in danger.

The scene changes, and I'm looking at him asleep on calm, green fields—and yet there's something coming, some creature, some monster.

I touch my husband's face. "Marlak. Wake up."

He holds my hand and smiles at me.

"Wake up, husband, wake up."

The thing is getting closer and closer, and my heart is speeding up. Marlak is still smiling at me, the fool.

Then I scream at the top of my lungs. "Now!"

MARLAK

After all these years, I found my sister—only to lose her again. I called, looked, and found nothing.

Ziven and I picked a room with a functioning lock and an unbroken glass window. Despite the dust, we were able to clear two beds that were decently clean under the covers.

I keep sneezing and almost change my mind and decide to

sleep in the tent, but if there's something out there, we need to be careful.

Of course, we don't look like birds, and we're much bigger than them, so perhaps our fear makes no sense. Still, I can feel something eerie, strange, something lurking, even if we haven't yet seen or heard anything. It's possible we're being paranoid. I truly hope that's the case.

From the window, I can see the cliff and the stars outside. I'm wondering if we could stretch something over the lake, perhaps some sheets or curtains tied together. The issue would be to get it to the other side.

A screech makes me turn.

Ziven raises his hands. "It's me. I was pushing this drawer chest. To block the door."

I pause. What if my sister needs me? What if she wakes up and wants to talk to me? The fear wins.

"Let me help you." I approach him and help him push the piece of furniture, blocking the door. Blocking my sister's way.

"If she calls, we can move it," he says, as if he could sense my thoughts. Then again, I'm sure my feelings are quite obvious.

"Sure."

"Should we take turns keeping watch?"

Should we? I take a deep breath. "The door is locked, the window is closed." Still, I have that feeling... "I don't know."

"Get some rest. I'll wake you up in a few hours."

"Aren't you tired?"

Ziven shakes his head. "A heavy heart is a heavy weight. It can exhaust us. You're more tired than I am. Tomorrow we'll find her sleeping spot. It could be inside a wardrobe or under a bed. We'll do a better search. And we'll figure out a way to leave this place."

I almost make a comment about his unrealistic optimism, but stop myself. I should be glad he's neither moping nor complaining.

Instead of some jab, I say, "Thank you."

"We'll sort it all out. Now rest. We have a long day tomorrow."

No. I have to say something. "When did you get all wise? Did something hit your head?"

He laughs. "Trust me. I'm far from wise. Now sleep. In a few hours, it's going to be my turn, and you'd better be ready to keep watch."

My heart is so tormented that I'm not ready for anything, not even sleep, and yet I understand the wisdom in his words, his suggestion that I'm more tired than he is, that my worry is a weight dragging me down.

I try to remember Mirella as a little girl, the two of us learning magic with her father, sometimes challenging each other. Most of the air magic I know I learned with her. Air used to strike me as a rather feeble, almost useless type of magic, but it's not. Not only can you bring down walls, it's extremely efficient against enemies, as it can disable them quickly. I was so foolish then, felt so powerful with my fire magic.

The memory makes me shiver despite the heat and humidity of this place. But the stupid ten-year-old me thought I was some incredible prodigy with magic more powerful than most adults and fire magic never seen in years and years.

A few rare fae can wield fire, but not like me. I could burn an entire orchard if I wanted. I could set a building on fire, even if its walls weren't flammable. Why that magic brought me pride is something that puzzles me now. Was it because the king treated me as someone so special? Because everything changed when my magic emerged?

These thoughts make me nauseous and I'm glad I'm no longer that person.

Instead of our youth, I remember Mirella this morning, relieved to see me, relieved to know that I cared. I can hold on to that image and picture the three of us leaving this place. We will find a way, and we have friends out there—and Astra, with magic as mysterious as it's powerful.

But I'd rather not get her involved in any of this. I hope she's safe in the island hideout. I miss our home so much. I miss my wife and her kisses, her smiles, even her cutting words.

Rest, Marlak. I imagine her sweet voice in my ear. *We'll meet again soon.*

Of course we will. That is the thought that soothes my heart and carries me through the threshold of sleep.

W e're in our castle, on the balcony overlooking that forest, and I hold Astra as tight as I can, cherishing this moment, delighting in her presence, her scent, her comfort.

Her lovely eyes are worried when she turns to me. "You're in danger, Marlak. You need to wake up."

I kiss her forehead. "No. You won't be there when I wake up. Every second without you is torture, Azalee. Don't make me leave you yet."

"Wake up, husband. Wake up." Her voice is kind, soft, and all it does is make me want to spend forever here, holding her.

"I will. Soon."

She steps away from me. "Now!" Her yell rings in my ear and speeds my heart.

I sit up, startled, and find myself in that dreadful dusty room in the Blue Tower.

Ziven is sitting on a chair. "Want to take watch?" His voice is slurred with tiredness.

There are no strange sounds, no threats. "Is there something wrong?"

"Hmm. Do you want a list?"

At least he makes me laugh. I should be crying, though.

Next time I meet dream Astra, I'm going to have some words with her. How dare she interrupt such a lovely dream?

"How long have I slept?"

"Feels like a couple hours, but I could be wrong."

My heart is still beating fast while my entire body's on alert, startled. I'm even wondering if we're exaggerating by keeping watch, considering the room is locked. If we find out it's safe, tomorrow we can both sleep through the night.

Tomorrow. What a depressing thought. And then, we might have tons of tomorrows. Even more depressing.

I stare out the window, where a waning moon illuminates the landscape. Then, it disappears—too fast to have been clouds. Even though I'm curious to find out what creature is flying toward us, I retreat to the back of the room, away from the window—and not too soon.

A second later, glass and wood shatter everywhere and huge, jagged pieces fly in our direction, but I manage to blow them back.

Through the broken window comes the ugliest animal I've ever seen. It looks like a gigantic, almost featherless raven with a silver, sharp beak, so huge that it could certainly behead either of us, and claws long and sharp like daggers.

It advances in silence, beak wide open, and I manage to use my air magic to throw a pointy shard to its throat.

Except it never reaches it. A burst of water moves the shard, and then ice locks the bird's feet in place.

Ziven stares at me, eyes wide.

I don't understand what he's doing. "Why did you block my strike?"

"You said your brother was a monster, right?"

Is this the right time to bring it up? "Yes, and?"

"Wrong sibling, Marlak."

TARLIA

I sit on the rough ground, leaning back on my elbows, while Lidiane pours river water on my head. We applied lemon, let it sit for half an hour, and then she insisted on applying her herbal mix with thyme and basil. All the while I was nibbling some rock-hard bread, which she claimed was the only thing she found.

"What if it doesn't work?" This is a pessimistic question, for sure, but we need to plan for that. "Maybe we could split up, so if Otavio finds me, it's only me."

"I'm not that confident that you can find your way on fae lands by yourself, Tarlia."

"You could go on your own to the castle." The idea makes sense, and yet it stings. I wanted to see Renel again—and maybe that's why I shouldn't go.

She huffs. "It will be fast, and I'll use a glamour on us so we aren't noticed. It was different when we came from the Shadow Lands. I wasn't alert at the time. Now I am. I'll keep you safe."

"That's very kind. You could have just dumped me."

"No. Being selfish sounds smart, but it's not. We all need friends. Who knows, tomorrow you might help me."

"So far, I haven't helped a single fae."

"You fought well against the ghouls. That's helpful. Maybe that's what made Renel so obsessed."

"I doubt he had never seen a woman fighting before. And if Renel is interested in me, it's probably because of whatever Otavio did." I'm so silly that the idea that he fell for some trick still hurts me.

"I don't think so. I would notice something unnatural on you, and I didn't. Your master was probably lying to make you think you depend on him."

"If his plan was to convince me I needed him, why didn't he open that cage?"

"He gave me the impression of someone still thinking, still calculating, not yet sure what to do. I bet he wasn't expecting Astra to disappear—or to be replaced."

"I'm glad she's far from him. After we leave the castle, are we going to meet her?"

"We can go back to my house and wait for Nelsin or Ferer to come and see us. She's in a secret location."

"Secret even from you?"

"Yes. Rude, right?" She giggles. "No. Fae do that sometimes. It's better to keep some of us in the dark for our safety. We can't lie and sometimes we can be compelled to speak, so sometimes ignorance is the best strategy."

"It makes sense. If Otavio decided to torture me, for example, to give him Astra's location, it wouldn't work." I exhale. "I'm glad he didn't try. And I think you're right. He was still considering his options." I look back and glance at her. "Speaking of options... Aren't you worried about seeing Azur again?"

"I'll let him know I'm safe and that I'll hide, and tell him not to worry about me."

"Will you worry about him?"

"Unfortunately, yes. I keep asking myself why. Why should I be bonded to him?"

"Maybe there's a way to break the bond."

She's dropping more water on my hair, but then pauses. "I don't want to break it."

"I thought you didn't like it."

"I don't *understand* it. It's not that I hate it. Why him? Why now? Is he really going to die soon? And yet, strangely, I still cherish the bond, cherish having something so special with someone, even if our ways have to part."

I turn around to face her. "I'm sorry."

"No sorrow. A glimpse of joy is better than no joy."

"Long-lasting joy is better than a glimpse."

"I choose to appreciate what I have." Her smile is laughter and life, then she gets serious again. "We'd better go. I think we undid whatever your master used to locate you. Ready?"

"Yes."

I'm glad I can lie.

The thought of going to the castle turns my insides into yarn. I imagine Renel seeing me without Otavio's tricks, then rejecting me. If I never saw him again, I could carry on with the sweet illusion that whatever we had was true, that someone, once, liked me enough.

At least the farce will be over, and then Otavio won't be able to manipulate him anymore.

She nods, then adds, "My glamour should protect us even if Zorwal has survived."

"You still think he did?"

"I can't sense anything out of the ordinary happening to Azur, so if he survived, he hasn't shown up yet."

"Perhaps he'll remain hidden—or dead."

"It's what I hope."

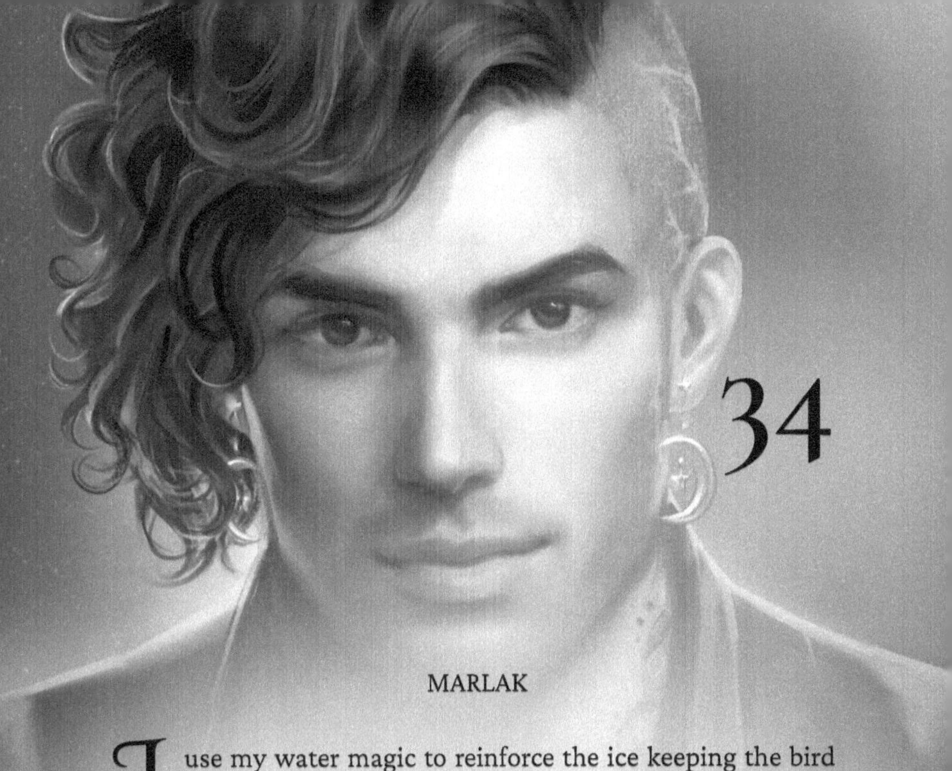

MARLAK

I use my water magic to reinforce the ice keeping the bird monster in place, but I also want to smack Ziven's head. My sister!

"Are you insane?" I ask. "Or did I misunderstand you?"

"I'd pick insane."

"Why would you assume that's my sister?"

"Just look." He points. "Blue eyes. Her face—kind of."

The creature's eyes are blue indeed, but eerie, and nothing like fae eyes. They're small, horrific round balls. And the monster's face is uglier than any bird I've seen, with almost no feathers.

"You're suggesting my sister's ugly."

"I said nothing about ugly, Marlak. I said the monster bird has her face and her eyes. And think! Why did she disappear during the day? Why was she the only one to survive? What do you think she ate all these years, if she has never touched the kitchen or the supplies?"

The bird manages to shatter most of the ice keeping it in place, so I blow it back with a gust of air, then form more ice around its feet. I can't believe I'm having such a ridiculous debate with the human prince—even if he's making some good points.

"Ziven, she's imprisoned on this island. Why would she be able to fly in and out to catch coastal birds?"

"She's still returning, right? So it's a kind of prison. And maybe having to stay on this island only affects her human form. You know it makes sense." In a lower voice, he adds, "And I know it must hurt to see her like this. But she's alive. The rest can be fixed."

I decide to block the monster's air and make it faint. As I'm about to do it, it emits a horrifying scream. And then, when I try to connect with the air around me, it's gone. My connection with the humidity is also gone.

"Marlak, something's happening to my magic. I can't use it."

"Same. Let's run."

At least the ice keeping the monster's feet in place is still there, as we rush to the drawer chest, push it away, then dash through the door.

The interior of the tower is all open, and with so many broken windows and doors everywhere, it's likely that the monster bird will soon reach us.

Still, we descend the stairs in a hurry, as if going down or up could make any difference.

Ziven yells, "We could hide in one of the boxes outside."

"It's wood. The bird shattered the window grids."

"Then what's your idea?"

It's a stupid idea perhaps, but the only thing that crosses my mind. "Rolled sheets, curtains, something. We can trip its feet, wrap around its neck to hold it back."

Without a word, Ziven pushes open the door to a room, pulls a sheet, while I pull another.

He's breathless as he says, "We could even try to tie something on it and climb on its back. Then when it flies away, we can escape."

"Your optimism astounds me."

He pulls a blanket and rolls it fast. "You're the one suggesting we fight that thing with sheets. You think it's any less optimistic?"

"If your ridiculous suggestion that it's my sister is correct, what can we do? We can't use swords."

"So you admit I'm right."

"No. But I'd rather not take the risk."

The monster bird appears at the door, screeching again. The opening is too narrow for us to try to wrap anything around its body—or for it to enter. The monster bangs its head against the door, but it's thick rock, and even though it cracks, it doesn't break. It retreats and leaves, and that's when I realize the window is broken.

"It will come in from outside," I say. "Once it gets here, we leave this room, since it still won't be able to cross the door. I'm wondering if there's a cellar, something more closed downstairs."

"Weren't we going to fight it with sheets?"

"We'd need to surprise it; catch it from behind—or above."

The monster then dashes through the open window. Ziven throws an unfolded blanket on it, managing to cover its head, and we run out of the room, then descend more stairs. When we reach the broken dining room, Ziven stops.

"Shit, Marlak." He puts a hand over his heart. "Can you feel it?"

"Deep anguish? Yes. Now let's run."

He shakes his head while his knees buckle. "I... can't."

"Great. Now I have to carry you."

"Just run and find a place to hide. You'll have a head start while it attacks me. Try to survive, then tell people exaggerated tales of my bravery. I don't want to be forgotten."

"Sush with the drama." I crouch and pull him up, over my shoulder.

Then everything revolves around me. Not only my magic is gone, but my senses are foggy and my breathing is shallow. I can barely breathe. At least I have time to kneel so as not to drop Ziven. I'm about to faint—while there's a monster bird ready to attack us.

I have to fight this magic. I have to. I try to get up, but it's no use; I get dizzy and lose my balance. All I can do is gather all the strength I can to drag Ziven to a corner, then pull the top of the broken table and cover us. How long that will keep us safe, I don't know.

All I know is that my eyes are closing despite my effort, and all my muscles are giving way.

I can't faint. Can't. I have to fight this.

Despite all my will, the world still fades.

I see Astra, so beautiful, so powerful, focused on something in front of her, and send her all my love. This goodbye is heartbreaking, is too soon, but it's not forever. She'll carry on.

ASTRA

The echo of my scream still rings in my ears.

"Something wrong?" Ferer asks.

"Marlak's in danger."

I can see him awake and fighting, running, something bad happening to him, and yet now I don't know what to do. He's not sleeping, so I can't reach him in his dreams.

A voice then comes from the heart. "Please, help me."

It almost sounds like Marlak, but it's different. And the voice is too calm, even if it's pleading.

"Can you hear it?" I ask Ferer.

He nods. I'm more worried about my husband than this heart, though.

"What do you want?" I ask.

"Help me stop this castle," the heart says.

Not the heart. I recognize the voice and frown. "That's Renel. Why am I hearing his voice?"

The crystals get even redder and brighter. I'm annoyed at

that voice. Marlak's in imminent danger, and I don't have time for a Renel-sounding heart.

"It's important." A different voice says, a voice that sounds female and distant.

"Help me save Marlak." I close my eyes again and see him running, fighting some kind of monster. Despite all his magic, all his power, I know he can't stop the creature.

A vision comes to me of his dead body and a fae woman weeping by him. It makes no sense.

"Help me stop the castle," the heart with Renel's voice repeats. "If it gets to the Fiery Gorge, an entire city will be destroyed. They don't deserve to die. Help them, please. Stop this castle."

"Why is he talking to me?" I ask Ferer, even if I fear he might not know the answer either.

"The heart must have a connection with magic and magical objects. He must be talking to some artifact."

I do my best to ignore the heart and say, "Marlak's in danger. There's some kind of monster threatening him. I thought I had to come here to save him, but I don't know how." *I* am desperate.

"The heart should be the answer," Ferer says. "It might be able to control magic outside it. Take a deep breath and trust. Remember: trust."

Trust. It's what Nelsin asked me to do.

Renel's still pleading, and even though his issue sounds serious, my priority now is Marlak. I decide to ask the heart.

"How can I save him?"

"Cut the bonds," a female voice says. "Cut the magical bonds, and you'll save your husband."

"How do I cut it?"

"It's the vine to your right. You'll need the Sundering Dagger."

The dagger I activated in the sanctuary comes to mind, but that's not a solution. "I don't have it."

"Call upon it," the voice says.

I'm starting to think it's the crystal talking to me, or else it's nobody, the castle, or the Almighty Mother. I decide to trust the voice, remove my hands from the heart, and recall the feel of that dagger, recall the moment Marlak showed it to me, explained why he needed an opus stone to activate it, remember his look of awe when he realized the dagger was working. With all that in mind, I imagine the dagger in my hands and close my eyes.

For a second, I feel Marlak behind me, as if he was in this castle with me, his presence giving me strength, amplifying my magic. I use all that magic to focus on the dagger.

When I open my eyes, I see the artifact lying by my feet. I don't have time to be impressed at my accomplishment and bring it up to cut that vine.

"It will break *all* bonds," the voice warns. "You cannot choose. But it might be a good thing."

"Great." I don't hesitate, and move the dagger against that black vine, which strangely feels soft like butter. The problem is that a searing pain reaches my arm, so much pain that I feel I'm being torn into thousands of pieces, being turned upside down. I know it's the heart fighting back.

I pull my dagger back, place a hand on the heart, and whisper, "It will be fast, and it will be good for you. Bonds enslave us." I take a deep breath—and cut.

Blinding pain seizes me. I can't hear or feel anything other than pain, so much pain.

RENEL

"Please help me," I repeat for what must be the thousandth time.

It's night already and I'm glad the castle has not yet moved. I don't know why I still hope, but what else can I do? Then I wonder if it's real hope, if what I'm doing counts, or if it's the excuse I'll give myself once my actions cause the death of thousands.

See? I kept talking to a magical stone until the end. I tried.

Even I want to laugh at my pathetic excuse, but I ran out of options by now, and I'd rather try *something* than nothing.

The door opens, and Azur walks in. "I checked and double-checked. The castle's empty, unless there are still fae hiding really well. Some of them were in cupboards, closets, or under beds. Like I said, many didn't want to leave, but I made them go, like you asked." He adds a hard edge to the last words.

"Thank you. I know you'd rather let these poor souls die, so I'm sorry I forced you to save them."

Azur snorts. "You truly think they'll have a fruitful life after the castle is consumed in fire?"

"They'll have a chance, Azur. Who knows? *Every life matters,* my father used to say."

"The quality of their lives should matter a little, no?"

"Sure. Now let me keep talking to the heart."

Azur stares at me. "You've been doing this for what? Five hours now? What difference do you think it will make?"

"I don't know. I'm trying."

"Do you need help while you beg for some magical intervention? Do you want a drink? Something to eat?"

That doesn't sound like a true offer of help, just Azur being grumpy Azur. Some fresh food would be appreciated, but not if he's going to roll his eyes and whine as if he's being oppressed.

I point to the corner of the room where I have a jug of water, bread, and cheese. "I brought food. You can rest. Leave the castle if you want. Who knows? Maybe you'll survive."

He chuckles, then all of a sudden, his eyes widen. I hear a scream somewhere, or maybe it's my imagination, or perhaps someone outside. It doesn't make much sense. Exhaustion is getting to me after all the running yesterday.

Azur's eyes are still wide as he stares at me, then he laughs and pulls a sword from his scabbard. It's not his sword, the one lost when he beheaded Zorwal, but a new, cheap one he might have taken from a guard.

I feel bad for him and say, "If I survive, I'll make sure you get a new sword."

He laughs. Laughs like a maniac. Exhausted as well, no doubt.

"You can rest," I say.

Azur sneers and steps forward, the tip of his sword close to my belly. I'm not sure what he's trying to show or say, and raise an eyebrow. "Yes, it's crappy. You'll get a new one."

He throws the sword aside. "For goodness sake, Renel, don't be so dim." He's trembling, angry, but then, he's often angry.

"I'm tired. Say what you want to say."

Azur crosses his arms. "Can't you feel it? Let me guess: you can't, since it makes absolutely no difference to you. It hasn't reshaped your life, hasn't enslaved you."

I'm too tired to deal with his tantrums. "Speak clearly."

"The bond is gone. I no longer serve you."

"Truly?" I don't think I've ever had such a relief exhale in my life. "You can leave then. You'll survive!"

"Stop it. Stop pretending you care. Stop making me not want to kill you. I told myself I'd kill you the moment this bond was broken, and now you're here, looking all happy for my life. What's wrong with you?"

"Can't I be happy you're not going to be consumed in fire? Why wouldn't I be happy? Here I am, feeling awful for dragging you into this mess, and now you're telling me you're free. How am I supposed to feel? Upset that I'll have no companion in my painful death? Are you insane? And why would you want to kill me?"

Azur shakes his head and laughs. "You don't get it, do you? You think we're *friends*. You think I never resented being here. You think I love being your personal slave, I suppose."

Why do his words wound me when I've known them to be true for a while? "I know you don't like to be bound to me. I know that."

"No, you don't. Did you ever try to break the bond? Try to research into it?"

"Is there a way to do it?"

"You'll never know, because you don't care. Because it's comfortable to depend on Azur for all your dirty work, it's comfortable to depend on dear, reliable Azur to protect you, isn't it?"

I swallow. "I... didn't know there was a way to break the bond."

He shakes his head. "Never tried to find it. Which is fine. I was your servant, and you don't have to excuse yourself for benefiting from it."

"You are—were—my friend too."

"Friend?" He sneers. "I'm a lower fae, you nitwit. Do you think I don't see all that you've done?"

That makes no sense. "Lower fae? Where? You don't look like one. And I've done my best to protect the lower fae. Before me, any lower fae could be enchanted. I made changes, so that only those who commit a crime—"

"You literally legalized the enslavement of the fae, and your corrupt courts upheld that. Before, it was something still frowned upon. Once it was accepted as a punishment, it became widespread, and then they looked at the enchanted fae as if they deserved it."

"You never told me that, never told me your opinion."

"The bond, Renel, it didn't let me criticize you. Even then, I tried. Oh, I tried. Would you listen to me? Would you? Or would you listen to your dear, beloved Zorwal?"

"He knows how to control the council, Azur. I needed them."

"You did not. You *chose* to govern for them, for the powerful. You *chose* to bend to their demands. And don't tell me it's because you wanted the kingdom to remain peaceful. Oh, no. You did that because you know damn well that you have absolutely no right to pretend to be king, and all you were trying to do was secure your power. Tell me it's not true."

"Who would rule instead of me? They'd never accept my brother. My sister's cursed. Would you want me to let the council pick a new ruler? Do you really think they'd find someone better?"

"It would be the same. The same. Someone to govern for them, someone to help them bleed the lower fae dry, to help this stupid kingdom absorb and erase older, smaller courts. It would be absolutely the same. And you know that. Of course you do. You're not dumb, Renel. You know very well who you govern for, and whose interests you uphold."

"If I cross them, they'll kill me. It's not that simple."

"Exactly. Upholding your own stupid power is all you care for. And that's why I thought I'd kill you. Strangely, I'm looking at you now and all I feel is pity."

There's a knot around my throat. "Why didn't you ever tell me that? Any of that? For me, you were my friend. I loved you, Azur."

"Loved me like a brother, I suppose." His voice is mocking and manages to pierce through my last remains of dignity. "I hear you. Oh, I hear you. It's very easy to love when you make no concessions, when all you do is benefit from the relationship, when you only take. Oh, it's so easy to love."

I disagree—people can suck others dry and still despise them—but I don't say anything.

He laughs. "At least now it will soon be over, won't it? Stop begging, Renel. Have some dignity. Take up a sword. Let's duel. I won't even use my magic."

I roll my eyes. At least his ridiculous proposal makes me laugh and gives a nice excuse for the tears coming to my eyes. "Sword fighting, Azur? No magic? You can't beat me."

"Yes, I can."

I sigh. "Let me try to save the castle, save the Jewel City. If I survive, we can have a duel."

"Stop it. There's nothing to be saved. Where does that dreadful council live? Where? Where does Zorwal have a second residence, where he might be hiding? What's the city with the most enslaved fae? Let it be destroyed. It's appropriate. If it ends the Crystal Court, great."

I can't believe he thinks that. "There are also innocents in that city, Azur, and in the path of the fissure."

"They'll die for a greater good, for a new civilization. Nature does that sometimes. It's the cycle of life. We'll all go one day. For the enchanted fae, it's a favor."

"I disagree. There's always hope."

"What hope? Nobody cares about us. What hope is there?"

"You think I'll fail, and you might be right. Let me try, Azur. Let destiny run its course. Escape the castle now, find your soulmate, and be happy. I enjoyed your company, and I'm sorry you didn't feel the same."

My voice cracks with emotion and I'm definitely convinced I'm pathetic.

He stares at me, likely taking note of my state. Finally, he says, "I'll go. Enjoy your conversation with the castle stone. Maybe *it* can be your friend. You're not worth any more second of my time."

His steps retreat and I feel already dead inside, even if my demise hasn't yet come. I think back to all my moments with Azur, from when I was still almost a child, when I thought I finally had a friend. As my brother got more and more distant from me, as I still mourned my father, I had a friend. I had someone to talk to, someone who listened. I told him my fears, my hopes, my worries. We told each other about our first and second times. I had Zorwal protecting me, giving me guidance, and I had Azur.

Both gone. The truth was that all this time, I was alone—so alone. So silly, so naive, thinking I had a friend. I had nobody. And now I'll die alone.

Tarlia comes to mind, and I wonder if she'd also laugh and tell me she hated every moment we had.

I don't know why I kept living for so long, stubbornly surviving—for nothing. What's the worth of a lonely life?

My eyes close while my heart weeps. I take a deep breath and approach the stone again.

"Help the kingdom. Please."

I'll still try to save the castle.

I might fail, but I tried.

Tried—that's all I've ever done. Never accomplished anything, never did anything to improve the kingdom. What Azur said was true, as much as it hurt. Perhaps it hurt *because* it was true. I was a coward.

In the end, there was nothing but failure.

35

MARLAK

My eyes open as I sit in silence beside an unconscious Ziven, hoping the bird monster won't find us, won't sense us here. A slanted tabletop is the only barrier between us and the creature, hardly enough to keep us safe. I still don't think the strange, gigantic bird is my sister. Perhaps it's just that I refuse to accept the truth despite all the evidence.

Beside me, Ziven stirs and opens his eyes. I put a finger over my lips, and he nods.

My magic is still dormant, but at least I'm alert, and so is Ziven. We have a fighting chance. A slim chance—except that if we're awake and capable, being cornered here might not be the best idea. I look at him and gesture as if to push the table, then mouth, "Should we?"

A screech and a bang on the table are the replies I get. Perhaps we should have left this corner earlier. Another bang, and the wood cracks, catching the bird's talons.

I push the tabletop, jump over it, and pull my dagger. Sister or not, at least if I wound this creature, it won't kill us.

As I aim for the belly of the beast, the bird disappears.

Vanishes.

I look at the ground and realize the monster hasn't vanished —it transformed. My sister's there, lying down, wearing the same dress as this morning, the same tiara.

Ziven raises his eyebrows as if saying *I told you.*

I crouch by my sister and whisper, "Mirella."

She opens her eyes and sits up, her body trembling, then looks around. "What's happening?" Her eyes settle on me. "Marlak?"

"I'm here," I say. "I never stopped trying to rescue you."

She frowns. "What was I doing? Was I..."

I swallow, unsure how to tell her the truth, shaken by seeing her so lost, so vulnerable. "You're fine now."

Her breathing is heavy, labored. Then she notices Ziven. "Who's the human?"

"A friend," I say. "He also came to save you."

"Save me?" She seems confused, lost, then looks at her hands. "How long... how long has it been?"

"A few years." I don't want to shock her. At the same time, I'm wondering if she'll become a monster bird again. "Do you know when you transform? What causes it?"

"Transform?"

Ziven steps forward. "Do you dream about flying sometimes? You sleep most of the time, right? Do you know what makes you sleep or awake?"

"Sunrise wakes me." She glances at the broken window. "It's night? I haven't seen the night in forever." She turns to me. "Were those dreams real? Was I flying? Flying all the way to the ocean, trying desperately to escape, then being pulled back to this cursed island. I was free when flying. I could feel the breeze on my face. I could hunt. Then I woke up in this hell. Who put me here?"

Renel, and I hate him for that. Still, for some reason, I don't want to say that. "I'm not sure."

She shakes her head, her eyes wet with tears. "It was like a hazy dream, nightmare, I don't know. My father, didn't he try to save me?"

I sigh and look down. "He's... no longer living in this world."

My sister sniffs and dries her tears with the back of her hand. "Who's sitting on the Crystal Court throne?"

I can't see how it makes a difference now. "We need to find a way out of this island, need to—"

"Who's on the throne?" she insists.

"Renel's the acting king."

"I knew it. I knew it." Her laughter is bitter and pained. "I have to go back."

"How?" I ask.

"It's open. Can't you feel it? Something... opened it. There's a passage." She exhales. "And my magic is back."

A gust of air hits my face.

"What opened?" I ask. "Passage where?"

"The castle! I have to go back. Immediately." She gets up and dashes out the front door.

I run after her. "Mirella! Don't! It will be dangerous!"

Ziven's right after me, running down the front steps.

She runs around the castle until near the old orchard where we buried the bodies. I can see now a faint trace of an old faerie circle, likely no longer active. I reach her and pull her hand. "No. It's too dangerous!"

"Then stay." She blows so much air that pushes me back, even though it doesn't hurt me, then steps into the circle.

Shit, she's going right to the Crystal Castle or who knows where. I have a half second to act, and right after she disappears, I jump into the circle, hoping her transcending magic will still be active to drag me with her. Everything turns dark.

When light hits my eyes again, it comes from lightstones on the wall of a place I know well, a place where I spent a good part of my childhood—the Crystal Court Castle.

I'm on the ground floor, in front of the main stairs. We're incredibly lucky there are no guards here.

Mirella uses her air magic to go up the stairs quickly, and I follow her by running up the steps. The only reason I don't call her name is to avoid unwanted attention from guards. She's not in a decent mental state, sure, but to run like this into Renel's castle is absolute lunacy.

I see her exiting the stairs on the sixth floor and keep running up. I'm almost there when I hear someone climbing down, wearing a hat. I barely have time to register who it is, when a gust of air pushes me away from the stairs, making me fall through the middle gap.

With no time to try to get my air magic to work, I summon some water from the humid air surrounding me and push it upward below my body, so that it slows my fall enough for me to land on my feet.

In front of me, someone descends gracefully using air magic. I throw a jet of water at him, but he pushes it away with his air.

Meanwhile, Mirella's upstairs—alone.

"Marlak, what a joyous day." Azur glares at me. "I'm no longer bound. Do you know what that means? I can finally kill you."

"You're welcome to try. But make it fast. I'm in a hurry."

He points a finger at me. "I'm not insignificant. I'm not a toy for you to play, mock, and mutilate."

"Great, since I wasn't planning on doing any of that."

He laughs, then pushes the front door open with his air magic. "Outside. Let's settle this once and for all. People still claim you're the most powerful fae alive, and it's not true, is it?"

What's he getting at? "Why? You think it's you? I can give you a badge if you want. *Azur: the most powerful fae in the Crystal Court.*" He frowns, and I continue, "A trophy, maybe? From the real king. You can display it in your home and show it to anyone. Does it solve your problem?"

Azur sneers. "Oh, you think you can mock me. Go on, mock me. Pretend you forgot what you've done. Well, I didn't forget."

He's not making any sense. "What did I ever do to you, Azur?" As I say this, I focus on the air around and inside me, ready to block his magic.

"Perhaps there were so many lower fae you tormented that you forgot. Was I that insignificant?"

He's gaga, that's the only explanation. "Since when are you lower fae? Since when did I torment anyone?"

"You think you're so hilarious. Don't you remember ignoring your brother while currying favor with your brutal stepfather or his demonic daughter?"

"You're taking my brother's pains now? I thought you said you were free. Now to your question: *he* was the one who turned his back to us."

Azur rolls his eyes. "And you never wondered why."

I sigh. "Azur, we can talk later if you want—"

"No, we'll duel to death!" he roars. "Air magic only."

"Suits a coward, your first element against my third."

He disappears, then I hear his voice behind me. "Air is *not* my first magic."

"You're an incredible transcender. Amazing. I'll be glad to name you the most powerful fae in the world. Badge or trophy?"

I feel the air in my throat being pulled, but counter it with my own magic and throw an ice stake at him, just to distract him. He counters it, as predicted.

"Fight me," he yells. "Don't ignore me. If you don't fight me, I'll kill you with no honor, just like you deserve."

I'm honestly flabbergasted at his hatred for me. I *can* fight him. I don't know if I can beat him with air only, but with water and air, there's no doubt I can win. I'm considering what to say, when I hear another voice.

"You will do no such thing!" It's Lidiane, standing at the door, furious.

I'm relieved to see that she's safe, and yet her anger is not fair.

"It's not my fault!" I say.

At the same time, Azur looks relieved and smiles. "Lidiane!" He seems like a completely different person, his posture relaxed, most of his fury gone from his face.

I'm extremely confused.

"Stop it!" she yells at Azur. At Azur? "Leave him alone."

Azur points at me. "You want to protect *him*? *Him?* Do you know who mutilated me?"

"Mutilate?" I ask. "You look perfe—" My stomach turns cold. I've never seen him undressed. That's horrific.

He sees my face and scowls. "My horns, you idiot. Don't you remember?"

My confusion increases. "Why would you have horns?"

Lidiane holds Azur's hands. "Leave. Him. Alone."

"Why would you protect him?" Azur asks her. "What's he to you?"

"My friend." She's now holding his wrists.

"And yet you chose *him* over me?" Azur's eyes are gleaming with a dangerous mania.

Now *I'm* the one getting furious.

"Let her go!" I yell. "Whatever you have against me, deal with me, not her."

Lidiane sighs and looks down. It's true that she's the one holding him.

Azur glares at me, and she holds his face. "Talk to me. Forget him."

I need to find my sister, but I'm also worried about Lidiane, and this is too weird, like some strange dream where nothing makes sense.

He looks at her. "What's he to you?"

"A friend!" she yells. "A friend who's happily married and in love with his wife. He's like a *brother* to me. *Brother*."

Is he *jealous* of her? But why would she even look at him?

Azur's anger quiets down and his stare softens as he looks at Lidiane.

She turns to me and mutters, "Leave us. I'm fine."

Is she fine? Or is the world upside down? She's still holding Azur's face, and I take a lot of offense in that. I saved her life, helped her brother raise her, for that? Of all men, Azur?

But she's fine. And she's grown up. What if she has awful

taste? I suppose it's not up to me to decide. I need to find my sister, so I dash up the stairs again. I glance back and see Lidiane and Azur staring at each other, now holding hands. Strange world.

ASTRA

My back touches the ice above the floor as I stare at the dirty marble ceiling that must have been white once.

Ferer crouches beside me. "What's happening?"

"Pain. Just pain. But it's gone now."

He extends a hand to me, and I get up. I'm afraid of touching the crystals but do it anyway—and see Marlak, relieved, alive. I no longer sense any danger around him, and can finally breathe after all the excruciating fear and agony of the last hours. He's not in danger.

"I saved him."

More images come to me. Pixies look around them, blinking as if waking from a long sleep. Enchanted servants escape houses, farms, and shops where they were enslaved.

"You broke them all," that strange female voice says.

I turn to Ferer, astonished at what just happened. "Whatever I did broke all the enchantment bonds."

"Really? That's a lot of fae."

I feel more and more relief, joy, but also some anger, strife. "I don't think it will be easy, but I think it's good."

He smiles. "Change is always hard."

"Help me, please," Renel's voice comes from the heart again.

I have no intention of helping Marlak's cruel brother, and yet something about the despair in his voice, the earnestness in it, makes it hard to ignore his plea.

The crystal is the one that lets me see things, so I touch it and think about the Crystal Castle, trying to figure out what's happening to it.

I'm back at that dinner table and see the castle being engulfed in angry, hot flames, then I see a crack appearing on the earth like a splinter on a wood board, but spreading faster and faster. People fall into it. Horrible screams reach my ear.

Down under the earth, in a cave, the earth parts, a glass ball breaks, and a strange man looks up. He has long, dark hair, and wears a crown with a black stone. It's not his appearance that's strange—it's the fact that I know who he is.

I open my eyes and gasp.

"The Witch King."

"What?" Ferer frowns.

"That's what the giants fear. He's here, in the Shadow Lands, but underground, in a sphere made of something that looks like glass, like a strange type of prison. The castle is moving somewhere it shouldn't, where there will be fire. When the castle gets there, not only will it cause vast destruction, it will free him."

"Can't Renel just not put the castle there? No, wait. That's a stupid question. He wouldn't be asking for help if he could, right? Do you think you can do something with the heart?"

I touch the crystal again, hoping for an answer, but all it does is show me that man leaving his hiding place, then reaching the desert close to where I walked not long ago. I think about the Almighty Mother, asking for an answer, some guidance.

All that comes to mind is my vision of Marlak getting to the Shadow Lands, observing Azur and his strange power.

To transcend a carriage with four people in it—that's something out of legend.

I have an answer.

"Ferer, what's the fastest way for us to get back to the Crystal Court? We might have to do some running, then figure out where the castle is."

"You want to go to the castle?"

"Immediately. I don't know how long we have."

He looks around. "We might not have to run. Every castle has a faerie circle. There should be one here. It's a matter of finding one, then getting close to the Crystal Court castle."

"But we don't know where it is."

"See it, then describe it to me. The Crystal Court is not that big that its castle will be in an unknown place. We'll find it."

I nod and touch the crystal again, trying to focus on the voice I heard coming from the heart, trying to remember what I saw in my vision, trying to see the castle.

If this doesn't work, we're all doomed.

RENEL

"**H**elp me, please."

Why do I still have some stupid hope? Why do I have any hope at all?

Azur's words echo in my mind. Out of everything he said, why do I have to focus on the least important parts? *Enjoy your conversation with the castle stone. Maybe* it *can be your friend.*

I run my hand over the castle stone. "Hey there, pal. It's me and you in the end. Nobody else."

At least it won't turn around and tell me I'm a horrible, selfish fae and a terrible leader. At least I hope not.

I imagine it growing a little mouth, then saying, "Renel, of course you're horrible. So useless. So friendless. Such a sad little fae."

There's no doubt that I'm sad.

I hear steps at the door and my heart races. I suppose Azur hasn't said all he had to say—or else he decided to kill me at once rather than leave it for chance.

I never tried to break his bond.

True, but I made sure he was happy, that he had some free-dom. I'm glad I didn't tell him any of that. It's like saying I gave him a long, comfortable chain. The sad thing is that I never saw it as a chain, perhaps never considered that he wasn't my friend, that he was just magically bonded to me.

Perhaps a fast death won't be so bad after all. I've tried what I could for the castle.

But the person who steps in is not Azur—it's my brother. My heart has no more room for shock, surprise, or even fear. All I feel is resignation.

His eyes look so cold, so full of hatred. I know what he's here for.

"Ready to kill me?" I ask.

I had a deal with him so that we couldn't kill each other. It was a deal to protect me, not him, considering he's the one with more than enough magic to kill me ten times. But if Azur's bond was broken, there's a chance that our deal might have been broken as well.

He doesn't reply. Instead, he advances toward me.

I feel the cold sting of a blade in my stomach, piercing it, then moving up. He stabbed me.

Strangely, up until now, as much as I feared him, part of me didn't think him capable of doing that. And yet he stabbed me.

He smirks, turns around, and leaves. No words for me.

I kneel, then fall back on the floor, thick blood pooling around me. My only consolation is that nobody will miss me. Nobody will mourn me. Tarlia, maybe? But I don't want her to be sad.

This is how I die; lonely and forgotten, having failed to stop a rogue castle. My own fault.

MARLAK

I rush up the stairs, still astonished that the castle is completely empty. Not even a single guard or servant in sight. I don't know what's happening, but I feel I need to go up to the highest floor, to the heart of the castle.

The door's wide open, and the room is empty. Not empty. My brother's lying on the floor, bleeding.

I thought I hated him. Perhaps part of me still does. A few times, I wished I could kill him. Still, all I see now is my brother, the brother who grew up with me, who peeled sleepberries for me, who read me bedtime stories. That's the brother I see on the floor, not the one who imprisoned my sister and made me run away from home when I was still a child.

I kneel by him. "What happened?"

He frowns. "Before or after you stabbed me?"

He must be delirious or something. "*I* stabbed you?"

"You just did."

"My hands would be bloody, would they not?" I show him my clean palms. "My clothes would have some blood."

"I saw you."

I shake my head. "It was someone else. You're confused. Let me see your wound. I want to help you."

I open his shirt, but when I get to his abdomen, my breath falters. Whoever did this butchered him.

"I'm dying, right?" he asks.

"We'll find a healer. We'll do something. Hang on, Renel." I hold his hands.

"It must be nice to be able to lie like that. Why are you sad? I thought you wanted this."

I shake my head and hold his hand tighter. "Not this, no. I wish things were different. I wish... Mirella. Do you even know what hell she's been through?"

His eyes close and he speaks with difficulty. "It's the curse. There was nothing I could do."

"Who cursed her?"

"I can't say. Still can't say. It wasn't me." He makes a sound similar to a chuckle. "Obviously wasn't me."

"You were my big brother and I trusted you. You hurt me, Renel, when you cast me out. I know… I know it was my fault. I know I killed our parents. I still didn't want it to end this way."

"Our *mother*. That despicable fae was never our father. But it wasn't your fault, Marlak. Not your fault. I tried my best, but it seems I did everything wrong."

I press my lips together, unsure what to say. Perhaps I should start with the truth. "You're dying."

"I'm ready to go, frankly. You can all have a party and celebrate my demise."

"I'm not going to celebrate it."

I sense a shadow behind me and turn. It's Zorwal, a healer my stepfather hired to try to bring out the magic in Renel, who ended up becoming the council leader thanks to my brother.

He glances at Renel. "Fatal wounds, yes. Yet I can heal him." He steps into the room and stands beside us.

Renel turns to him. "Long time no see. Nice neck scar you got."

It's true. The old man has a horizontal, fresh scar around his entire neck. I raise an eyebrow. "Were you beheaded by any chance?"

Zorwal smirks. "Small things. Nothing a good healer can't fix."

He can't be serious. I turn to Renel, who nods softly. Zorwal survived a *beheading*? How? And I thought I was making a snide comment.

The man continues, "Renel, I can heal you. All I ask in return is a life bond. Not too much, since I'll be giving your life back."

"No chance," Renel spits.

"So you'd rather die?" Zorwal asks.

"Yes, yes, yes," Renel says. "I choose death over serving you."

The healer turns to me. "What about you? Did you know *you* owe me your life?"

"He owes you nothing," Renel says. "Nothing." He turns to me. "Don't listen to him."

"As I was saying," Zorwal continues, looking at me, his voice full of malice. "I saved you. Do you think anyone can survive having half their body burned? I tried to fix the scars, but there wasn't much I could do. Still, I saved your face, even reconstructed your ear. Do you know who asked me to save you?"

It can't be. "Renel?"

My brother shakes his head. "Ignore him."

Zorwal laughs. "That's how you survived, Marlak."

I frown. "Then I was cast out and hunted like a dangerous animal. That doesn't make any sense."

"You survived, young king," Zorwal says. "And now you're here and can return the favor. Would you bond your life to mine?"

Renel grabs my wrist. "Absolutely not."

It would be madness. After all my brother did...

And yet he's bleeding and bleeding.

Zorwal smirks. "Time's running out."

LIDIANE

I'm holding Azur's hands, and yet I want to punch his face.

"I'm sorry," he says, his voice so soft, his tone so apologetic...

I pull my hands. "Why are you sometimes so... horrible?"

He looks down, then back at me. "Can't I be upset? Can't I have enemies? Why would he be more important than me?"

"Because Marlak's my friend! I've known him for over thirteen years, since I was a child! You, I have no idea who you are."

Azur takes a deep breath. "He's done... horrible things."

"When?"

"A long time ago. It was him and some of his friends who almost killed me, then cut my horns."

"I don't believe it, but even then, he was a child! And we can clear up this story later."

"Fair. Let's ignore him. Can we talk outside?" He presses his hands together. "Five minutes, please."

"Sure."

We walk out the front door, descend the front steps, then stand in front of the castle.

He kneels and takes my hand. "I ... " He looks like he's grinding his teeth. "Promise to respect your friends, family, and everyone else you ask me to respect. I'm free of my bond now, and I want to ask you if I can court you."

He's free? I'm happy, relieved, but at the same time, still annoyed, and I don't know what to say. "You kneel like that and it's all weird and awkward."

He gets up and snorts. "I don't know how to do this. Obviously. But I'm free now. All that I did in the Shadow Lands... was because I didn't want you to suffer, didn't want you to miss me, considering I was so sure of my impending death. But I'm free now, and can start over. I realize it's hard to start over when I ruined what little we had, and the worst is that I ruined it on purpose."

"You hurt me in the Shadow Lands. And you're still hurting me now. *What is he to you?* Friend. I said friend, and you wouldn't listen. But I know that deep down, you have a good heart. A little too deep."

Azur chuckles, and it's such a lovely, happy chuckle that I want to forgive him right then, tell him I'd love him to kiss me. I'm too soft, too forgiving.

"I'll try to bring out my heart more. What else?"

People approach running. My brother! And Astra! She's glowing like some goddess, with incredible purple hair.

"Let go of her!" Ferer yells.

Oh, no. This is going to be so, so awkward.

I say, "He's a friend."

"Friend?" the three of them ask at the same time.

Astra's shocked. My brother's horrified. Azur is offended.

"Yes, friend." I glare at him, then whisper, "For now at least."

Astra approaches us, her steps fast, her face full of determination.

I gesture to the castle. "Marlak's in there."

She points at Azur. "I want to talk to him."

Azur blinks. "Me?"

"He didn't hurt Marlak," I say quickly.

Astra frowns. "Obviously."

She says it as if doubting Azur would be capable of hurting Marlak, and I fear he'll take offense.

Instead, Azur asks, "What do you want?" His tone is surprisingly polite.

"The castle, it's headed to the Fiery Gorge," Astra says. "It might get there at any moment."

Azur crosses his arms and raises an eyebrow. "I'm aware."

"Right. But we can stop it."

He narrows his eyes. "Why would I care to stop it?"

"Fae will die," she says.

Azur tilts his head, still looking unimpressed. "Enchanted fae, living a horrific life of servitude, and their masters, who won't be any loss."

He's so cold. I can't believe this creature is my soulmate.

"No." Astra shakes her head. "I freed them. Cut all the bonds. There are no more enchanted fae."

Azur's eyes widen and his arms drop to his sides. "What?"

"Really?" I also ask.

"Yes," she says to me, then turns back to Azur. "Except that many of these free fae will die. But that's not the only problem. If the castle gets there, the Witch King will be freed."

Witch King? Still alive?

Azur grimaces. "Freed from where?"

"From an underground cave in the Shadow Lands. Somehow, it all connects, but we can stop it."

"We?" Azur looks confused.

I'm not sure what she wants to do either.

"You have an incredible transcending power. Legendary, I'd say." Does she expect him to transcend the castle? The entire castle?

"No, no." Azur chuckles. "A whole castle? I can't. Even if I wanted, I'd die and I would still not manage—"

"I'll help you," Astra sounds confident. I don't think she'd want to send him to his death.

Azur looks unconvinced. "If you broke all the bonds, if you're so powerful, why don't you do it on your own?"

"I can't transcend, and the heart of the forest can't stop the Crystal Castle. We'll need to *physically* put the castle somewhere else."

Azur looks at her, eyes narrowed. "How?"

"I'm Tiurian," Astra says. "If I drink your blood, I'll have access to your magic. Both our magics combined could move the castle."

He stares at her. "I think you're insane. You're in love with Marlak, right? You *are* insane."

MARLAK

I can save my brother's life, and yet it's the wrong thing to do. If I bond myself to Zorwal, what will become of me? Of Astra? With all my power, what would he have me do? And yet it breaks my heart to see Renel bleeding like that.

"Time's running out, young king," Zorwal says. "At any second, he'll die."

I want to chuckle at his use of the word king, as if flattering me would change my mind. And yet if I save my brother, we could maybe figure out all these things later.

"Don't, Marlak," Renel says.

I hear soft steps and see Astra's friend entering the room. She stares at Zorwal wide-eyed, then kneels by Renel and takes his hand.

"Tarlia," he mutters.

"Whatever you feel, it's not real," she tells Renel. "My master put an enchantment on me or something. So don't worry."

"No," Renel mutters, then holds her hand tighter. The look he gives her…

He's in love. And it hurts to see him dying.

"Time's almost up," Zorwal says, then turns to Renel. "Do you want to die and leave her?"

"We'll all die," Tarlia whispers, then turns to the healer. "What about me? Would you take my bond to you?"

It's a sweet offer, and I'm sure it will warm Renel's heart, but Zorwal won't accept it.

"No, no, no," Renel mutters with difficulty.

The healer looks at her.

She continues, "But you need to promise not to hurt me as long as I obey you, and not to hurt them."

The corner of Zorwal's mouth lifts. "I won't hurt you as long as you obey me, and won't hurt them *today*, as long as they don't hurt me *today* either. Deal?"

"And you save him," she says.

Zorwal has an amused expression. "Obviously."

She nods. "Deal."

"No!" Renel yells.

I should have said *no*, should have warned her, but I could never imagine that Zorwal would accept her offer.

"I'll be fine." She smiles, then gets up.

Renel closes his eyes, then his organs mend back in place, and slowly, his skin does the same.

"He'll still need to rest," Zorwal says, then gestures to Tarlia. "Come."

"No," Renel grunts.

"It's fine." She smiles again.

"A deal is a deal," Zorwal warns us, then walks out the door with Astra's friend—Renel's love.

And I let this happen.

"I'm sorry," I mutter, even if words can do so little to fix the damage.

Renel gets up with difficulty and roars, "Get out!"

I understand he's upset, but I have an important question to ask. "Is it true you asked him to heal me?"

"Makes no difference. Out! This castle's doomed. Do you want to die?"

"Doomed?"

36

ASTRA

I never liked Azur, from the moment I heard him suggesting disgusting things to Marlak at that corona-tion, but he might have saved me from falling. Now, looking at his impassive face, I wonder if he's indeed a monster.

"Azur," Lidiane says his name with so much sweetness. "I know you have a good heart. And your magic is extremely powerful. If you two could double it…"

He glances at Lidiane, then at me. "We might die."

"I think we can do it. I feel it." I don't know if that will be enough to convince him.

Azur turns to Lidiane. "I'll do this for you, and for all the lower fae. If I die…" He takes a deep breath.

Lidiane takes his hands. "You'll do fine. I trust you."

He smiles at her. I glance at Ferer, standing at a distance, and watching his sister with wide eyes. She and Azur can't be romantically involved, can they? She's too sweet, too pretty, too nice for him. He's good-looking, sure, but that's where it ends.

Azur turns to me. "How much blood?"

"A drop. Just a little cut on your finger or something."

He raises an eyebrow, then punctures the tip of his little

finger. This part is quite gross, actually. I didn't think this through. Still, I take his hand and lick his finger quickly, just enough to feel the metallic tang on my tongue.

And yet I feel nothing. Nothing—then everything.

The air around me comes alive, as if it was clay for me to mold. I can sense the air in everyone's lungs, everyone's bodies. I can see far and close, as if I was here and elsewhere at the same time. The power feels strange, foreign, something my body wants to expel.

Marlak's magic feels like my own, harmonizes with mine. This is like eating food my body can't take, dressing in too-small clothes, but multiplied by a thousand.

Uncomfortable, eerie, strange.

I should have considered that I have no compatibility whatsoever with Azur and his magic—and now I want to vomit, except that magic cannot be vomited.

I'm trembling as I look at Lidiane, Azur, and Ferer.

"Are you all right?" Ferer asks.

"It's strange, that's all." I turn to Azur. "How do you transcend?"

"I need to visualize the destination."

"That's all?"

He looks up, thinking. "I imagine myself moving whatever I need to move as well, as if... For people, we hold hands, but I can imagine my energy permeating through them, like a magical handhold. If it's an object, it has no hands, obviously, but it's similar. I hold it, then move it."

"Right. So we need to imagine a destination. Can it be where the castle was when I was brought to it? By that hill? I don't know much of the Crystal Court."

"It can be there, sure. We'll need to go inside." He turns to Lidiane. "Stay here. If something goes wrong..."

She nods. "Good luck."

He gives her one last look, then climbs the steps to the castle and we enter a large atrium. I still want to puke all that strange magic coursing through me. Powerful magic, though.

Azur swallows, then says, "Hold my hands and imagine the castle moving there. You don't *need* to close your eyes, but it helps. That said, if you feel something strange, sense enemies, for example, don't hesitate to open your eyes and look."

"Won't it interfere with the transcending?"

"Obviously. But it should be fast." He raises an eyebrow. "Unless we fail and die. Our bodies could end up split between the two locations, or maybe lost in the space where things don't exist."

I don't even want to picture any of that, fearing I could make it true. "Let's not fail, then."

He extends his hands and I hold them. Cold hands, and I wonder if that's because he's afraid. Still, I have to trust that we won't fail, trust that I saw him taking Marlak to the Shadow Lands for a reason.

"Now imagine it," he says.

I close my eyes and remember the moment when I got to the castle, merely a few days ago. Then I see it in that place. No, that's just a memory and not doing anything. I see the castle now, surrounding me, see myself in it, then imagine it reappearing in that same place where I saw it before. It feels like moving a box from one place to the other—a heavy box.

And yet there's someone pushing it with me. I see Azur, except that he's all made of light against a black background, the space of nothingness. I see the castle and everything and everyone in it as balls of light, and see them crossing through space and time, ripping the fabrics of reality. We're ripping those fabrics.

Except that there's something else pulling the castle—a stronger force.

I see a fiery mountain calling us, pulling the castle as if using an invisible cord, then I feel Azur's hands again, holding mine, as if I was returning from that magical space. No, I need to go back. I ignore the mountain, ignore the calling, and see the castle by that hill, in the place it needs to go—and yet it refuses to go there and shakes.

"Keep it up," Azur whispers.

I picture the castle by that hill and surround it with the brilliant, protective light I've always known. I imagine that light breaking the cord pulling it, imagine myself cutting it with the special dagger.

The castle trembles, still resisting. I imagine myself putting it by the hill, as if it was a toy castle or as if I was bigger than a giant.

The cord pulling it to the Fiery Gorge splits—I feel it. And yet breaking it used such a surge of magic that all my strength left me. My muscles don't obey me anymore, my hands let go of Azur's, and I feel my body being dragged where it shouldn't be.

Cold hands grab my wrists like vices. "Keep seeing it," Azur says, his voice shaky. "I got you."

I picture the castle, picture it peacefully standing by that hill, just like when I first arrived at it—and yet there's something wrong.

The castle feels distant, while something's still pulling us.

And I feel numb—all my senses dead.

TARLIA

I don't regret giving my life to this strange man who survived a beheading. I don't regret it.

As much as I hate a lot of what I learned in the Elite Tower and despise my master, there's something he told me once that got stuck in my mind ever since: *survive first, fix things later*.

I'm still alive. Renel's alive. We'll find a solution—or at least I hope so. That is, if the castle doesn't end up engulfed in flames, taking Renel with it, making my sacrifice pointless. And yet I still don't regret it.

And now I'm following Zorwal through a small spiral staircase, I suppose to escape the castle. He opens a hidden door leading to a narrow ledge, right as the castle trembles. I grab onto the opening of the door. All of a sudden, Zorwal turns, and a young woman with black hair yells and doubles over.

Zorwal takes a step toward her. "Do not try to choke me, Mirella. I'll use your magic against you."

"You lied to me." She's so desperate, so angry. I see myself, see my own anger reflected in her.

Zorwal smiles. "We'll talk. I'm glad to see you here."

"No, you're not!" Her eyes are filled with tears. "You sent me to that dreadful, horrific island. You cursed me!"

"I did not *curse* you," Zorwal says, sounding perplexed. "You did it to yourself."

"Liar!" she screams. "Liar. You tricked me. You wanted to get rid of me, didn't you?"

The look he gives her is full of pity. "No. And I'm still half fae and can't lie. You killed the king. I never told you to do that. Never. You should have been crowned queen, like I promised you, but you ruined my plans."

"You told me to anger Renel, to cause a fight. It's all I did."

"Not true," Zorwal says. "Your air magic killed your father, your stepmother, and almost killed Marlak."

"I would *never* kill them. Never hurt them!" she roars.

"And yet you did. Trying to blow the fire was foolish, and you killed your father. There was no way I could undo a royal curse. You ruined all my plans, girl. But come with me. There's still time to fix them."

A flying carriage slowly approaches us, lifted by four strange creatures that look like moths from here.

The young woman is weeping and trembling. "I lost my youth, spent years trapped in a strange nightmare. It was horrible!"

"I wasn't able to help you." His tone is gentle. "I don't know how you were freed and had the path out of the island reopened, but I'm glad you're here. I'm your best chance to get that crown, to take control of the kingdom."

"How?" Most of her desperation is gone.

"There are infinite ways to do it. But I have a plan. You'll need to come with me."

She looks back. "Marlak…"

"Won't help you. He's the crown prince, and has been calling himself king ever since your father died."

She frowns. "That can't be true."

"I'm not lying, Mirella, and I can help you. Marlak wants the crown for himself. I would much rather see you as the queen."

"How can I trust you?" Her voice is sad.

"Trust is silly, when we can make alliances, deals, and only then help each other."

The carriage stops by us, still floating. Zorwal gestures for us to enter it. My heart jumps at the prospect of stepping into a floating object, but it's not like I can disagree with this horrible man, so I do what he says. My new master. Can't believe I got myself back into chains, even if I don't regret it.

I glance back at the castle and realize it's shaking again. Is it about to move? On a window above us, I see a face I recognize. Ziven! He's all right. Unless the castle ends up in a pit of fire. I wish I could gesture to him, warn him, but the best I can do is pretend I haven't seen him.

"If you want the throne, follow me," Zorwal tells Mirella as he enters the carriage.

She hesitates, but enters after him and looks down. "I never wanted to hurt them."

"I know." There's something about his voice. I'd say a gentleness, but it's not only that. His words are strangely soothing, calming. He continues, "Your suffering is over, and great things lie ahead of you. A new beginning. Different, perhaps, than what we planned originally, but a new beginning nonetheless. The kingdom's in chaos, and we can make something out of chaos. And there are others. Like me."

Like him… Could that be Otavio?

Zorwal turns to me. "What do you know?"

I find myself unable to even come up with any excuse and blurt, "My former master; Otavio. He's a great beautician and might have some magical abilities. He claims he's very old, and that he's not fae. There's something similar between him and you." They're both creepy, and I'm glad I was able to keep that detail for myself.

"Beautician. Hmmm. You'll tell me about this Otavio."

Mirella looks at me as if seeing me for the first time, then turns to Zorwal. "Who's she?"

"Just a human. The key to control Renel, though."

She frowns. "Renel? Why do you want anything with Renel? Even if he's alive, he doesn't have any magic."

Zorwal gives her a pitiful smile, as if her words were quite idiotic and he knew a lot more than her.

"Does he have magic?" she asks.

He keeps that smug smile. "We'll see."

I turn back for one last look at the castle, but it's no longer there. There's nothing behind me, and I don't know where we're heading.

I guess I'll see.

MARLAK

The floor beneath me trembles. I'm still not sure how to process having seen my brother almost dying, now seeing him alive and well.

"Out!" Renel yells. "Or I'll throw you out the window."

A bold thing to say to someone with much more magic than him. I know he's wearing the Shadow Ring, but I can't feel it blocking my magic this time.

"Out!" He repeats. "The castle's headed to the Fiery Gorge! I can't control it." His voice is urgent, desperate.

The floor shakes again, and I say, "If that's the case, I don't want to be falling or walking outside while the castle moves."

Renel sighs. "You want to die with me?"

"Dramatic much? Once we get there, I can lift us away with air magic."

"Your air?" He looks horrified. "Over a pit of fire? That's certain death."

"My air magic has improved, Renel." The castle then shakes so much that I hear windows breaking. "It didn't use to do that."

"No. Something's different. As to your kind offer, I'd be pulled back to the castle when it self-destructs."

"You don't know that."

He exhales. "I studied, researched. I know it."

"Is it true you asked Zorwal to save my life?" I insist.

He stares at the window. "It makes no difference."

The shaking is so loud now that I feel the castle's about to break in half. "Makes all the difference and you know it."

"Did you really not stab me? Just now?"

"I told you my hands had no blood."

He grimaces. "That's literally what a guilty fae would say; point to a small and true detail and use it as an excuse."

"You know I can lie, so what's the point in saying I didn't?" I shrug. "I don't know why you think it was me."

"First, because it looked like you. Second, you've said many times that you wanted to kill me."

He has a point, but some of what he's saying makes no sense. "What do you mean, looked like me?"

The stars outside disappear as the sky turns dark. The castle is dashing through space. And the sky remains dark.

Renel stares at the window, his eyes wide, then turns to me. "Your face, your hair. You."

Everything's still black around us. It never took this long.

"It could be someone wearing a glamour," I suggest, perhaps because I don't want to mention the fact that we're hanging in the space between spaces.

"A glamour to pretend to be someone else? That's impossible."

"I know someone who can do it." Lidiane comes to mind. "But it wasn't her."

"Why would they do that?"

Everything's still pitch black around us and I'm losing my patience. "Why would I gut you then kneel by you and feel sad?"

"Guilty conscience."

"I can kill you with air magic. Fast, easy. No blood."

He lifts his hand with the Shadow Ring. "I have this."

I take a better look at the artifact—and understand why I'm not feeling anything. "It's a replica, Renel."

"Oh." He stares at his hand. "Oh. But the real ring can't be stolen."

"Who gave it to you? Under what deal?"

"Otavio. He lent it to me. I had to provide protection and shelter to him and his pupil; Astra."

"So he took it back." I snort. "And you just reminded me that I have a good reason to kill you. You kidnapped my wife."

"First, she came willingly, no idea why. Second, he told me *you* had kidnapped her. Third, when I asked you, you assured me you felt nothing, absolutely nothing for her. I'm not the villain here."

"I wanted to protect her! I feared you'd torture her."

He shakes his head. "When did you decide I'm capable of something like that? When?"

"When you cast me out! I was a kid, my parents had just died, and you were my brother. I trusted you!"

"I also lost my mother that day, Marlak. I almost lost my brother. I was alone, I was still almost a child, and I had to fix everything."

"Did you really ask him to heal me?"

"I'm not supposed to talk about it."

I guess that means *yes*, and yet his subsequent actions make no sense.

The castle trembles again, and this time I fear part of it is indeed going to collapse. And then it stops. There's a hill by us and the outline of a starry sky above. No Fiery Gorge.

"See?" I chuckle. To be honest, I'm relieved. "You were wrong."

"No. Something happened." His voice trembles. "Something happened. Truce, Marlak, please."

"You think I'm going to *murder* you?"

"I don't know. If the castle's disaster has been averted, I need to gather allies urgently. The castle guards are sworn to me, but the city guards are not, and yet my guards were left behind."

He sounds so calculating, so cold.

"Aren't you even worried about the girl who saved your life?"

He glares at me. "How do you think I'll get her back? By *begging*? It's why I need a truce. I can't fight the council, Zorwal, and you at the same time."

"Then don't sit on the throne that should be mine."

"Let me get Tarlia, then the throne is all yours. You can finally put your crown on your head and tell the entire court who's the legitimate king. But we'll need to do this right, so you'll have the support you need."

I can't believe he's giving up his power so easily. It must be because he almost died, or maybe because of Astra's friend. Still, as late as it might be, it's the right thing for him to do. "Sounds like a deal to me."

"Then you have your deal, brother." His voice is pure acid, as if hating me for even mentioning my proper title.

"Marlak!" Lidiane's at the door, Ferer beside her.

Ferer. What's he doing here? My stomach contracts and my skin turns cold. "Where's Astra?"

"She saved us," Lidiane says. "She steered the castle away from the Fiery Gorge."

"She also broke all the bonds," Ferer adds. "Servitude bonds. All the enchanted fae have been freed."

I don't want to hear another word. "Where is she?"

Lidiane and her brother hesitate.

I feel as if something is slicing me in two. "Where is she?" My cry is desperate, loud, and a ball of ice hurls out of my hands toward the window, shattering it. Ice is forming on the floor.

My magic is about to go berserk.

I'm trembling as I look at the siblings and try to control my voice. "What happened to her?"

Lidiane raises two hands, as if to calm me down. "She and Azur were transcending the castle."

Nothing makes sense and a loud buzz fills my head. "Azur?"

"Because he can transcend like nobody else can," she says. "And Astra can use other people's magic. She tasted a drop of his blood, then they combined their transcending magic and put the castle elsewhere, not the Fiery Gorge, as you can see. They succeeded, but..."

"But what?" I'm dreading what comes next.

"They disappeared," Ferer says.

My vision is blurry, my thoughts confused, and my heart, my heart feels like a hollow void. "How?"

"Marlak, they're alive. I can feel it," Lidiane says. "I know they're fine. I bet you can sense it too."

When I try to see Astra, all I get is darkness. "No. Something's wrong." I'm crying. I failed. Failed. "Why? Why didn't she wait for me?"

"She saved you, Marlak," Ferer says. "She broke the bonds to save you. You'd be dead if she had waited for you."

"But she'd be alive!"

"She's *still* alive," Lidiane says. "And she's powerful. We'll meet her again, I'm sure we will."

I'm trying to make sense of everything. "What do you mean she broke the bonds? *She* was the one who broke Mirella's curse?"

Ferer takes a deep breath. "Probably. She did something to save you, and whatever she did saved all the enchanted fae. Then we came here to save the castle. Not just the castle. She saw that if the castle reached the Fiery Gorge, the Witch King would be freed. She wanted to stop it. In fact, she *was told* to stop it. Both the…" He glances at Renel, and I realize he was about to mention something my brother is not supposed to know. "She was told to do that. The giants took Nelsin and told us they'd return her once she stops something from coming from the underground."

I close my eyes, trying to take it all in, then turn to Lidiane. "You can sense her, you said? Where do you think they are?"

"I can sense Azur."

"Azur?"

She rolls her eyes. "Yes. I don't want to explain why right now. But they're fine. They're somewhere… Underground. He still has some of my magic, a silly glamour hat I gave him. I can feel it. We'll find them."

I'm so angry, so upset that I'm shaking. "She's with Azur. Azur. That maniac. He wanted to kill me."

Lidiane narrows her eyes. "You look quite alive, Marlak. I doubt he even tried to hurt you. Azur's grumpy, yes, but he won't hurt Astra. I'm sure they'll help each other, and they're both powerful. They'll be back."

Renel approaches us. "The enchanted fae were freed, you say?"

"Yes," Ferer replies, his tone stiff.

My brother paces back and forth. "The Jewel City must be pure chaos right now, and some other places too. We need to act quickly to avoid—"

"Let the lower fae be free," I say, horrified at my brother and his calculating ways.

Renel huffs. "Prevent them from being massacred, you dimwit. They're disorganized, even if they're more numerous. I need to take control of the royal army before Zorwal and the council do. Or *you* take control. I don't care. But we need to act."

Ferer glares at my brother. "You're going to pretend you care for the lower fae now?"

"I always did," Renel says. "I always tried. Tried doesn't

help, I know, but I tried. Great excuse, you're going to say. Regardless, this is urgent."

"Finding Astra's urgent too." I look around. "And where's Mirella?"

"Mirella?" Renel's eyes widen.

"Yes, Mirella, who survived years of horrors, and escaped not thanks to you."

He opens his mouth to say something, then closes it, and looks at the door. I turn, expecting to see my sister, but Ziven's the one standing there.

"You made it." I exhale, relieved to see that the human prince didn't stay behind.

Ziven nods. "I jumped in the circle after you—not that you even bothered to look, but I understand. You were worried about your sister." He takes a deep breath. "I know where she is."

I don't know if my heart can take any more bad news. "Where?"

"She left with an older man, thick scar on his neck. Tarlia was with him as well, I'm not sure why."

"Zorwal," Renel says.

"If he's the fae with the neck scar, then that's him. Mirella's his ally."

I'm sure he's exaggerating. "She must have sought him for advice."

"True. Advice on how to take the throne," Ziven says. "Apparently, he promised her she'd be queen."

That makes no sense. "When would he have promised her that? When she was *thirteen*?"

Ziven shrugs. "It seems they had some deal, but things went wrong." He stares at me. "You told us you killed your mother, Marlak."

That familiar coldness fills my chest. "I did."

Ziven shakes his head. "It was Mirella. Her air magic pushed your fire. To be fair, I don't think it was intentional. Still, it's why she was cursed. She doesn't like Renel, but she says she would never hurt you. Still, she wants to be the queen of the Crystal Court. I'm just telling you the conversation I heard. Then they entered a flying carriage and left."

Ferer frowns. "There should be no more pixies moving carriages."

"There were not pixies, but something else," Ziven says, a clear trace of fear in his voice. "Something dark, with wings. I couldn't see well."

Everything I'm hearing is too much, and doesn't make me feel better. "Even if her air caused their deaths, it was still my fire. *My fire*, and she was the one in that horrific prison." I turn to Renel. "You never told me."

"I couldn't. Zorwal warned me it would make you sad."

I can't believe him. "Sad? And yet you had no qualms telling me to run away and not threaten your throne or you'd hurt my sister."

There's an odd emptiness in Renel's eyes. "At that point, you were already convinced I was a monster, and two heirs would result in one of us getting killed. At least that was the advice I got. It sounded wise at the time. You lived, I lived, and as to Mirella, it was her own doing and I could do nothing about it."

"I saw you choking her." I point at him.

"Yes," Renel says, not a hint of remorse in his tone. "My hands around her throat blocking her windpipe. True. And what do you think *she* was doing to me? What do you think she did tons and tons of times with her air magic?"

"She was a child."

"A poisoned child, I suppose. What about me? Was I an adult? I studied the king killer's curse, Marlak, and intention matters. Had she been blameless, she would never have been cursed. *You* were not cursed."

I touch the scarred side of my head. "I thought... this was the mark. King killer's mark. The curse."

"Those are *scars*, Marlak," my brother says. "Your body was half burned. Sometimes we survive but still bear marks. Hate me if you want, for casting you out. In retrospect... I don't know.

For now, I need a truce, or else Zorwal will take control of the kingdom."

"I agreed with your truce already," I say.

Lidiane puts a hand on my shoulder. "We'll get Astra back."

I realize then why she can sense Azur, why she was the one telling him to leave me alone, and why he was listening to her. It was so obvious. She's suffering too. I place a hand on hers. "Azur too. But he needs better manners."

Her chuckle is sad but relieved.

I glance at Ferer. "Nelsin too. We'll get him back."

"I know." He nods.

"And Tarlia," Renel and Ziven say at the same time, then stare at each other.

Ziven then adds, "And your sister."

I take a deep breath. "We'll fix this."

ASTRA

"Wake up. Wake up. This is not the time for magic fatigue. Not the time."

The voice calling me is grating and unpleasant, and I don't want to listen to it.

"Wake up."

I open my eyes just to make that voice stop, and see stalactites hanging from a cave's ceiling. Then I realize someone's carrying me in his arms like a baby. Azur.

"I can walk," I say.

He exhales and whispers, "Oh, finally. But not yet. I need to talk to you."

I glance around and realize we're walking towards a humongous throne made of stone, hundreds of ghouls on either side of us parting the way for us to approach it. Two of them are behind us, and I suppose they'd push us if he stopped.

Something about them is different. I don't feel that I can control them, even if I don't think they're going to attack me.

It's embarrassing to be carried like that, but it makes sense that it's the only way we can talk.

"What of the castle?" I whisper.

"You fainted, but I finished the job. Something pulled me here, though, and I decided you didn't want to remain back there in the middle of nothingness, so I pulled you with me. My magic's not working. None of it."

"Fatigue?"

"Something else. I've had it before. I think we're in the Shadow Lands."

I glance at the ghouls around us and raise an eyebrow. "Think?"

"I'm pretty sure. Look, I have no beef with you. We'll need to stick together if we want to survive. You'll need to trust me— and vice versa. Trust me, please."

"I don't think we have a choice."

"Of course we do. We could backstab each other or decide to care only for ourselves, but that won't help us. I pulled you with me, and I didn't have to do it. Maybe I could have escaped if I hadn't used my last magic to bring you here. The least you can do is trust me."

Trust the fae who told Marlak he wanted a taste of me? I still remember his words in the Court of Bees, when he didn't know I was listening.

Even if he was testing him, it was gross. But it's true that our chances are better together.

"I'll trust you."

We stop in front of the throne. He nods and finally puts me down.

Entirely made of some rugged stone, that throne gives me the creeps. More than that, it clouds my mind and even my body with a horrific presentiment.

A man comes out from behind the throne, a man with long, black hair and fae ears, wearing a crown with a black stone, his face pale, and his eyes black.

I suck in a breath. The Witch King.

Above the throne, I see the crystal ball that had been enclosing him—broken.

Shit. We didn't prevent him from escaping. While we might have saved the Jewel City, I couldn't prevent everything.

"Welcome, visitors," the Witch King says. "And thank you for freeing me from my inner prison. Are you friends? Or enemies?"

"Friends," I say.

Beside me, Azur kneels, and I do the same. I realize why he needed me to wake up so desperately; he can't lie.

"Now, are you useless, or have you come to free me from this cave?"

I smile at him. "We're at your service. And came to free you."

He descends from the dais and stares at Azur.

"Why do you look familiar?"

Azur bows, then says, "My great-grandfather fought beside you; King Faliel. My name's Azur Sestin, king of the Nether Court. I was raised to seek revenge upon the Crystal Court. And now I'm here."

His words stun me and make me shiver. King? Revenge? None of that sounds good.

Azur then adds, "And I'm committed to protecting her."

I think he wants to remind me that he's still on my side, that we need to work together—despite everything. At least for now.

The Witch King smiles, then stands in front of me, placing a long-nailed hand under my chin.

"I know you." I try to keep my face calm as he stares at me with his dark eyes. "No, not you. Your mother." He sighs. "I still miss her dearly."

Could this creature have ever loved? Could he have known my family?

He tilts his head. "Or grandmother? Great grandmother? It's been so long. And yet I'm glad to see my blood alive—and here to help me."

His blood. I feel cold inside, then glance at him again. His hair is not truly black, but dark purple. It takes a lot of effort to control myself to keep from trembling, to keep my voice steady.

"Family, right? We stick together." I sound so dumb, but my head is buzzing and that's the best I can do.

"Look at that," he says. "The Tiurian heir herself, and the most powerful fae alive. We'll be invincible."

Azur looks at me. "Of course we will."

Me and him. If we work together.

We'll survive this.

And I'll meet Marlak again. If we manage to escape and not unleash this evil upon the world.

ACKNOWLEDGMENTS

I want to thank all the Kickstarter supporters who have supported book 1 or other books before that. You made all the difference! 1000 times thank you!

Thanks to my beta readers Andra Prewett, Susan Macfarlane, and Donna Daigle. Super thanks to my sprinting partners T.F. Burke and Lusine Torossian for some brainstorming help.

Finally, thanks so much to my amazing PAs Rozanne Visagie and Meghan Macphail.

ABOUT THE AUTHOR

Day Leitao loves to write books with lots of romance, magic, and banter.

Sign up for her newsletter for special bonus material, news, freebies, updates, and more at **dayleitao.com**